Sins of

Sadie Gordon Richmond

All characters and events in this publication, other than those clearly in the public domain, are fictitious and any resemblance to real persons, living or dead, is purely coincidental.

Also by this author:

Front Page News
Sticks and Stones
Shadow Lines
One in a Million

For Chris

Rugby is a beastly game played by gentlemen;
soccer is a gentleman's game played by beasts;
football is a beastly game played by beasts.

– Henry Blaha

'Could you do that?'

Francis turned. 'Huh?'

Scott repeated the question, nodding towards the laptop screen.

'Yes.'

Scott's eyebrows rose in excitement. 'Really?'

Francis nodded, returning his attention to the DVD.

*There was a pause before Scott asked, '*Would *you?'*

Francis frowned. 'No.'

'Not even if –'

'I said no,' Francis snapped.

Several seconds passed before Scott asked, 'Why not?'

It was the sort of thoughtless response Francis had come to expect from Scott. The lack of awareness no longer surprised, but the brazen insensitivity still irked.

'Because I have a grasp of the implications. I don't live in a fallout-free TV drama.'

'Chicken,' Scott goaded.

Francis gave him a cold look. 'I meant the moral implications.'

Scott smirked. 'Like you're in a position to take the moral high ground.'

'I'm sorry?'

Scott responded wordlessly, miming several actions before raising his eyebrows expressively.

'You're confusing what's right with what's acceptable. Rules and ethics aren't one and the same.'

'You can't call abuse of trust ethical.'

'I'm not. I don't believe that's what it is.'

'I doubt his parents would see it like that.'

Francis shrugged. 'I don't have to live with his parents. I only have to live with myself.'

'If you're going to take a relativistic moral standpoint –'

'Bircham!'

Francis jumped, looking up from the blank notebook that lay on the bench in front of him. He had no recollection of the nineteen minutes that had passed since he had sat down, and precious little memory of the classes he had sat through that morning. The day had passed in a haze of anticipation, thoughts and ideas falling over one another, and adrenaline had left him short of breath. Of all the emotions he might have expected to feel, impatience and excitement were far from top of the list.

Three weeks earlier, the idea had seemed abhorrent. Especially in light of what had happened to Simon. Scott had argued that had been Simon's choice; to Francis that presupposed possession of the kind of free will he wasn't at all sure Simon had had any grasp of towards the end. But then Scott never had been any good at seeing things from anyone else's perspective. And his black-and-white world view left no room for shades of grey.

'Sorry sir. I didn't –'

'Spare me the predictable excuses,' Dr Latimer interrupted. 'Sometimes I wonder why you bother coming to my classes at all! Now answer the question!'

Francis looked at the blackboard, hoping for some clue to what that might have been. Ten compounds were listed, the first six accompanied by an assortment of numbers, pluses and minuses. The seventh was oxygen difluoride. Guessing his teacher was after the redox states of its two constituent elements, he said, 'Minus one, plus two.'

'Thank you,' Dr Latimer responded, with heavy sarcasm, moving to chalk the numbers up. Francis followed the movements before his eyes strayed left over the fume cupboard, his thoughts returning to the events of Wednesday evening. To the moment Scott's idea had segued and mutated into his own.

His plan relied on the knowledge that Scott had considerably more regard for the future than he did; should Scott call his bluff, Francis knew he would have no difficulty standing his ground. He also knew Scott would expect him to fold. Scott thought he was spineless, he'd said so often enough. But then Scott didn't understand the difference between stiff upper lip and backbone, and was too selfish to comprehend the lengths some people might be prepared to go to on another's behalf.

Francis wasn't afraid of being dead. He didn't believe in God, heaven or hell, so to his mind death was merely a state of matter.

What did concern him – what had, in fact, long been a subject of considerable preoccupation – was the means by which his death might occur. And that was precisely why the twelve hours that lay ahead should have left him paralysed with fear.

'Now, Mr Wilkinson,' Dr Latimer continued. 'Would you like to tell me why in this instance oxygen doesn't have its usual oxidation state of minus two?'

Beside him, Curt hesitated. Francis guessed he was having even more trouble focusing, if that was possible. He glanced at his friend. Curt looked just as Francis suspected he himself ought to feel: terrified. His face was white and he was clutching his inhaler.

'I – um –' he managed.

Francis drew breath to answer the question on Curt's behalf, but Dr Latimer apparently anticipated this and cut him off with, 'Thank you, Francis, I didn't ask you. Perhaps you might work on answering the questions directed to you in a more timely manner before you start on those I put to everyone else?'

Curt coughed, raising a hand to his chest. He looked panicked.

Dr Latimer's impatience gave way to concern. 'Curt, are you feeling all right?'

Curt shook his head.

'Do you want to go to the san?'

He shook his head again.

'Are you sure?'

Curt nodded. 'Yes sir,' he whispered.

Dr Latimer looked uneasy but didn't push the matter, moving on to the next student at the bench.

Curt scribbled something down, folded the page over and passed it to Francis. Francis didn't immediately open it, waiting for his teacher's attention to be focused further afield. He already knew what the note was going to say. As Dr Latimer turned to write on the blackboard, he unfolded the piece of paper in his hand and looked down.

I'm sorry, I can't. I'm sorry.

Francis absorbed it at a glance. It didn't matter. Curt's decision changed nothing. Going it alone might be logistically challenging, but it wouldn't be unmanageable. When it came down to it, he didn't have much choice. Reaching for a pen, he added his reply beneath Curt's neat, cursive hand. He kept it brief. There wasn't really much to say.

I'll sort it.

One

'Are you going to eat that?'

Curt shook his head, pushing his plate in Scott's direction. Scott helped himself to his friend's fish, asking, more out of politeness than because he was particularly interested, 'You ok?'

'Tired.'

Scott grunted in acknowledgement, reaching for the Ketchup. Curt was always tired, these days. Although usually he had more to say for himself than he did this evening, he'd barely raised his eyes from his plate in the five minutes they'd been at the table. Scott felt a twinge of apprehension. Perhaps Curt *knew*. Perhaps Francis had told him. Perhaps ... he shook his head, dismissing the idea. If Curt had known the truth, he'd have challenged him. Scott certainly would have done, in Curt's position. And he certainly wouldn't have sat opposite his friend, eating fish and chips, pretending it was just another Friday night.

'We've some beers stashed for later if you want to join?' Scott offered, hoping to draw more response.

Curt sighed, meeting Scott's eyes for the first time since they'd sat down. 'I've a chemistry paper due in the morning.'

'Bummer.'

Curt nodded, reaching for a slice of iceberg lettuce.

'What about tomorrow afternoon?'

Curt shrugged, picking increments of lettuce off the main body of the slice and dropping them onto his plate.

'That Churchill film is on at the Odeon.'

'Awww. Taking your girlfriend to the movies?' A voice interjected. Scott glanced up as Sid dropped into the chair next to his own.

'Don't be a dick.'

'Maybe you could go to see *The Wizard of Oz*.'

Scott elbowed Sid in the ribs. 'Enough already!'

Sid smirked, looking over at Curt. Curt met his gaze and Sid averted his eyes. Francis had once asked Sid whether he was insecure, in the closet or just an arsehole; his acetic humour was one of the few things Scott liked about him. Curt and Sid tolerated one another; Francis had no time for such niceties. He might be pathetic, but two-faced he was not.

'I'm collecting ideas for Sunday's obstacle course,' Sid said, as he drowned his chips in malt vinegar. 'We've the usual cargo nets, tyre runs and commando crawls, but it'd be good to have something a bit quirky to throw the guys from St John's.'

'River run?' Scott suggested.

'In February?'

'Gate vaults?'

'Hardly novel.'

'Electric fence, perhaps?' Curt put in, with only a hint of the sarcasm Francis would have applied. Scott laughed. Sid looked less amused, and Scott suspected he wasn't entirely sure Curt was joking.

'I said assault *course*, not plain assault,' he replied, irritably.

'Well that makes a change,' Curt returned, evenly, taking another slice of lettuce from his plate. Scott regarded him in surprise. Curt might not be afraid to voice an opinion – he was one of Scott's favourite debating partners, particularly on matters political and philosophical – but he wasn't normally one for snide remarks. That was Francis's department. Clearly something was up.

'Do you want to repeat that, Wilkinson?' Sid demanded, leaning forwards across the table.

Curt met Sid's eyes and did as bid, enunciating his words clearly and with disarming calm. Given that Sid was considerably broader and stronger than Curt, Scott felt a combination of unease and grudging admiration.

'I thought your room mate was the suicidal one?' Sid bit back, dangerously.

'Handbags, please, ladies,' Scott said, lightly, in an effort to diffuse the situation.

Sid turned on him. 'Don't you fucking dare insinuate that I –'

'Woah!' Scott held his hands up in surrender. 'Take a joke, mate!'

'Jokes are supposed to be funny!'

'Says who?' Curt submitted. 'You're not.'

Scott stared at him. What was he *playing* at? Sid's fists clenched around his knife and fork, and for a moment Scott thought he might go for Curt with canteen cutlery. Seconds ticked by, the tension rising. Then Sid rose abruptly from the table, the legs of his chair grating over the ridges in the wooden floor. 'You are fucking *dead*!' he spat at Curt, before snatching up his tray and walking away.

Scott watched him go before looking back to Curt. 'What the hell was all that about?'

Curt shook his head slightly, tossing the piece of lettuce between his fingers onto his plate. 'Like you don't know,' he answered, coolly. He moved to stand. 'The two of you are playing the wrong game.'

'Eh?'

'A game played by gentlemen, et cetera.'

Scott frowned. He still didn't get the reference.

'Never mind,' Curt added, reaching for his tray.

'But I don't get it. Why wind him up like that?'

Curt shrugged. 'Maybe I've just had enough of sinning by silence.'

Scott frowned. 'Do you want to stop talking in riddles?'

'You're the American, you should know that one,' Curt responded, lifting the tray from the table and turning to go. 'Lincoln. Abraham. Look it up.'

Leighton Campbell hadn't ever expected to feel grateful to his mother for turning down his repeated offers to buy her a dishwasher. In the three years since she had been diagnosed with rheumatoid arthritis, he'd also offered several times to pay for a cleaner, but Lorna Campbell was having none of that, either, and they'd had more than one heated conversation on the subject. Given that in the past she'd been perfectly happy for him to provide a new fridge freezer and a widescreen television, the reason for her obstinacy clearly wasn't financial, and he suspected it was rooted in the pride she took in her role as housekeeper. Between ironing everything from socks to bath towels and carefully lining up cleaning products, tins of food and drink mats, her unrelenting tidiness wasn't far off obsessive, and Leighton sometimes got the feeling that if she could, she'd have tidied him away, too. Then again, if he'd spent forty years living with his father, he'd probably have been equally desperate to find some way to occupy himself. As it was, just one day at home had been enough for him to offer to do the washing up.

The morning had passed relatively pleasantly. Leighton had driven his mother up to Wakefield to make their monthly visit to his elder brother, Tom. His father had, as usual, declined to come, and had already started drinking by the time Leighton and Lorna returned for lunch. He was currently somewhere between belligerent and verbally abusive – also known as about five pints of Diamond White down – and the washing up had afforded Leighton a brief respite from the familiar building tension. Until he'd left home, he'd had no idea how much energy constantly walking on eggshells could consume. For years, gauging his father's mood and degree of intoxication – and, by extension, whether he needed to keep out of the way – had been second nature. He wasn't sure at what age he'd registered that his *normal* was nothing of the sort.

He felt his mobile vibrate before it began to ring, and quickly dried his hands before retrieving it from the back pocket of his jeans. Surprisingly, the name on the screen was that of a Scotland Yard detective with whom he regularly worked, and he wondered whether someone had mixed up the on-call schedule. It wouldn't be the first time.

''Allo 'allo 'allo!' He greeted, jovially.

'Hello Leighton. Sorry to bother you on a Sunday afternoon. Am I interrupting anything?'

'Absolutely. I'm in a meeting with some Fairy liquid and a plate. I'm not sure I can squeeze you in,' Leighton replied, adding, when his colleague hesitated, 'Oh go on, then. What can I do for you?'

'A boy's been stabbed to death at his school – I'm just on my way to pick up Becky to drive over there. I know you're not on call, but Roddy said you were up in Yorkshire, and that's where we're headed, so he suggested –'

'No problem,' Leighton interrupted. 'Where are we going?'

'The school's called Treelore Grammar – it's a boarding school. Fantastic reputation, extortionate fees –'

'Yeah, I know it.'

'No doubt they're worried about their image. I expect that's one of the reasons they want us there. We're supposed to be getting the details at a meeting at eight o'clock this evening, and we'll head down to the school first thing tomorrow. I'll text you the address of the local station.'

'Ok, I'll see you there.'

'Great. Thanks Leighton, I appreciate it.'

'You and me both,' Leighton muttered to himself as he hung up. Returning the phone to his pocket, he worked backwards to calculate how long it had been since he had last set foot in a school. It didn't feel like nearly two decades. If his father had had his way, it would have been longer. Glenn Campbell thought education was a waste of time, and had fully expected his son to get a job when he turned sixteen, despite not having held one himself since shortly after Leighton's first birthday. Leighton had been so desperate to leave home that he'd been more than happy to oblige, and had reconsidered only after Lorna involved two of his teachers and his grandmother, who agreed he could move in with her for the three months that remained before the GCSE exams.

His gran had been the one to encourage him to go to college and study for his A-levels, although even she had thought he was joking when he told her he was going to medical school. When he'd shown her the acceptance letter, she'd been genuinely speechless. Lorna had cried. Tom had been unmoved by the news, but then he had always had less respect for Leighton's academic achievements than the fact he could hotwire a car in under a minute. That Leighton had wound up pursuing a career allied with law enforcement was an irony that was not lost on him. And another decision his father hadn't approved of. One son banged up; the other working for the filth. Leighton sometimes wondered which of them Glenn viewed as the bigger disappointment.

'You're three minutes late,' Rebecca Palmer announced, climbing into the passenger seat of her superior's silver Honda shortly after four.

Lawrence Forrester held out his hands. 'Don't blame me – have you seen the traffic around here on Sundays?'

'Pathetic excuse,' Rebecca replied, pulling on her seat belt.

'That's what you get for living in a trendy place like Highgate,' Lawrence responded, cheerfully, reaching into his inside jacket pocket and pulling out his mobile phone while flicking the car's indicator on and checking his blind spot. 'Would you mind forwarding the first text message in my inbox to Leighton?'

'Leighton?' Rebecca echoed, taking the phone.

Lawrence pulled out from the kerb and jammed his foot on the accelerator. 'He's meeting us there.'

'But he's not working this weekend.'

'I know, but when I spoke to Roddy he suggested giving him a shout. Apparently he's up in Yorkshire already.'

'Roddy's a git,' Rebecca replied. 'You do know it's Leighton's birthday today, don't you?'

'No,' Lawrence sighed. 'I didn't.'

'He's in Yorkshire because he's visiting his family. I swear Roddy's on some kind of mission to wind him up.'

'That could take a while. I don't think I've ever worked with anyone so impervious to provocation. He certainly didn't seem to mind.'

Rebecca wondered whether that were true. She was distinctly peeved at having her weekend cut short, not least because her fiancé, Elliot, was heading off on a three-week tour with his band, Astatine, the following morning. Well aware that Lawrence's nine-year-old daughter, Elise, hated Lawrence working away from home, Rebecca asked, 'How did your departure go down with the little miss?'

'Interestingly, actually.'

'Oh?'

'She burst into tears and said *Daddy Daddy you can't go – what if you aren't back in time for your surprise party?*' Lawrence laughed.

'Ah. Not so surprise any more.'

'No.' Lawrence raised his eyebrows. 'Katie was furious.'

'I can imagine.'

'And you were in on the secret.'

'I deny all knowledge.'

'I'm afraid I don't believe you. Jimmy knows you've been invited, because he wanted to know if Elliot was coming. And might I just add that if I have to hear *Locked Away Forever* one more time, I think I may strangle somebody, so please, don't put it on today.'

Rebecca smiled. Jimmy was Lawrence's thirteen-year-old son, and had recently adopted Elliot as his latest hero. *Locked Away Forever* was Astatine's current single, and Rebecca guessed Lawrence had been subjected to nothing else since its release two weeks previously. Conversely, she didn't think she'd heard it more than a handful of times, as Elliot didn't like listening to his own compositions, and tended to switch radio stations whenever they came on air.

'Where are all the traffic jams you were muttering about?' Rebecca asked, as they sped past East Finchley tube station.

'Evaporated, it would appear,' Lawrence replied, accelerating through the lights as they turned to amber. 'Amazing how that happens, isn't it?'

'I think you imagined it. That'll be old age.' Rebecca leaned back in her seat. The no-longer-surprise party had been planned to celebrate Lawrence's fortieth birthday, which was just a few weeks away, and Rebecca – aged only thirty-two – and several other colleagues had been teasing him mercilessly. Lawrence had taken it all in very good humour, posting up a list of preferred birthday presents on the office wall, including hair dye, and finishing with the comment *all pension contributions will be gratefully received*. A tall, muscular man, his short dark hair was sparsely flecked with grey, and, as he was fond of pointing out, considerably thicker than that of many of his peers. Clean shaven, with hazel eyes, a well defined nose and a strong jaw, he certainly didn't look older than his years, which might, Rebecca supposed, explain why he had been so tolerant of all the jokes. On this occasion, he came back with one of his own.

'Ah, I wouldn't expect a country girl like yourself to understand city traffic.'

'I'm going to kill Leighton for starting that one,' Rebecca replied. 'You know, people have been taking the piss for so long that when Elliot went to Norwich on tour last year he was shocked to find more than a couple of barns and a field of cows.'

Lawrence laughed. 'His geography can't be that bad.'

'No. But it was a lot bigger than he expected.'

'Where's he from?'

'Newcastle, apparently.'

'Newcastle?' Lawrence exclaimed. 'Really?'

'Yup.'

'How come he doesn't have an accent?'

'I think he's managed to lose it along with his natural hair colour and his family.'

'Are you still no closer to finding out why he doesn't see them?'

'No. Whenever I ask, he just says he doesn't *have* a family. Presumably whatever happened is at least partly to blame for his depression, but I've given up asking, because it only upsets him.'

'So what made him tell you where he comes from?'

'We were up there – for a gig – and we'd gone to the pub. When we walked in some guy made a snide comment about *fucking southerners* and Elliot informed him, in no uncertain terms and an impressive Geordie accent, that he wasn't a fucking southerner and demanded an apology. I thought he'd just done it for effect – and the look on the guy's face, which was priceless – and I jokingly asked what was wrong with being a southerner. He said *nothing, but I'm not.* After which I managed to drag that it was his home town out of him before he clammed up again.'

'Do none of his friends have any idea about his past?'

'I don't know. Alec's known him for about ten years, and I suspect he has a fairly good idea, but he just says it's up to Elliot to tell me. Which is true, I suppose – it's a question of whether Elliot ever will.'

'You could always try doing a little detective work.'

'I've been tempted, but if Elliot found out I don't know that he'd ever forgive me, and I don't think it's worth the risk. I guess for now I'll just have to be patient.' Rebecca sighed, her eyes tracing the rows of houses whizzing past the window. Patience, she was the first to admit, was not a virtue with which she had been overendowed, although it might have been easier to bear with the situation had the year since she had moved in with Elliot not been a crash-course in living with mental illness. His initial response to the downward spiral had been to shut her out of his present as well as his past, and Rebecca couldn't help thinking she might be better placed to support him if she had some idea of his background. But, if she were honest with herself, she wanted the details to Elliot's family history for more reasons than concern for him and to satisfy her own curiosity. The fact that, after nearly three years together, he was still keeping so much from her was really beginning to hurt.

Leighton was waiting in the police station car park when Rebecca and Lawrence arrived, leaning against the bonnet of his slate grey Aston Martin. Lawrence had always fancied the same car in racing green, and was more than a little envious. Unusually,

Leighton's long, thick dark hair was loose over his shoulders, presumably owing to the fact he was technically off-duty, and he was dressed casually in bleached jeans, a leather jacket and a blue-and-white-striped scarf. A stout figure of five foot nine, he looked younger than his thirty-four years, and Lawrence suspected the breadth of his experience had, on occasion, been called into question as a result.

Lawrence himself had never had any reason to doubt Leighton's competence in the year since he had joined London's Gresham Pathology Unit – his attention to detail, exacting methodology and scientific knowledge were all exceptional. If Lawrence had a complaint, it was that the young man's focus tended to lapse rather too frequently into coffee breaks, chit-chat and extended lunch breaks in the pub. More frustrating still was the relaxed attitude of Leighton's boss, professor William Maxwell – Max to his friends – to the situation. During a recent conversation with Lawrence, Max had admitted that the calibre of Leighton's work was such that he wasn't particularly concerned about his erratic working practices, especially given that, when it really mattered, Leighton was more than willing to go the extra mile, making no complaint about working around the clock or in all weathers. Or, Lawrence grudgingly acknowledged, being asked to step in on the birthday weekend he'd planned to spend with family.

'Sorry to drag you over here,' he began, climbing from the car.

'Not a problem.'

'Becky tells me it's your birthday,' Lawrence added, noticing Leighton's left eyebrow was suffused with congealed blood.

Leighton waved a hand carelessly. 'Ah, I've been having birthdays for years, truth be told I'm getting a bit sick of them.'

'What happened to your head?'

'Smacked it on the lid of the boot,' Leighton replied, with an expressive roll of his eyes.

'Ouch.'

'Not quite the language I used. How was your journey up?'

'Long,' Rebecca complained. 'Someone got us lost.'

'We didn't get lost,' Lawrence objected.

Leighton looked surprised. 'Do you not have Sat Nav?'

'Broken,' Lawrence sighed. 'I had a route planned on my phone, but the A1 was closed so we had to take a detour.'

'There's an app that'll find one for you,' Leighton replied. 'It's really handy. It'll also warn you about bad traffic, hazards on the road, the whereabouts of the fuzz, the –'

'You can get an app that tells you where the police are?' Lawrence exclaimed.

Leighton nodded.

'How the hell is that legal?'

'Well I don't think they hack into the radio waves, people just report in when they see a squad car or a speed trap.'

No doubt using their phones while driving, Lawrence thought to himself, shaking his head.

'Yeah, I know, it's shocking,' Leighton concurred, seemingly seriously. 'Kids today and their smartphones, eh? They've taken all the fun out of joyriding.' He turned towards the building at the end of the car park. 'In my day, you actually ran the risk of getting caught!'

The head of the local constabulary, Superintendent Robert Younger, received Rebecca, Lawrence and Leighton in his office and dispatched a colleague to fetch hot drinks before outlining the details he had so far. A heavy-set man of about fifty, he looked completely at home behind his desk, and relaxed back in his chair with a mug of tea as they talked. The colour of his hair had faded considerably more than that of his eyebrows and moustache, which were a sandy brown, and he had an unusually deep cleft in his chin. Lawrence guessed it made shaving difficult.

Handing Lawrence a school photograph of a boy in his late teens, Robert said, 'This is him – Scott Ribet.'

Lawrence studied it carefully. Although it was difficult to ascertain the boy's relative size from the picture, his shoulders looked fairly broad and Lawrence guessed he had probably been above average height for his age. He had square jaw, wide-set blue eyes and short blonde hair, which was brushed neatly back from his face. He appeared very self-assured, looking directly into the camera with a confident smile, his hands clasped loosely in his lap.

'Good looking lad, wasn't he?' Rebecca remarked, as Lawrence passed the photograph to her.

'Fantastic rugby player too, apparently,' Robert added. 'His body was found by a couple of pupils taking a short cut through the woods late on Saturday afternoon – he'd been stabbed five times.'

'Poor kid,' Rebecca murmured.

'He was attacked from behind, and there were no signs of a struggle, so it's likely he had no idea it was coming. Had he been aware of what was happening I think he would have put up quite a fight. He was certainly strong enough.' Slipping a hand into a brown envelope, Robert produced the crime scene photographs and passed them across the desk. Lawrence had a quick flick through them before handing them on to Leighton.

'Is there any evidence to suggest the attack was connected with the school?'

'Not directly. Time of death was somewhere between one and six in the morning – I don't think he'd have been out in the woods at that time without a definite purpose. Presumably he was either there with somebody, or to meet someone. Whether that links it to the school as such I don't know, but I suspect Scott knew the person responsible, whoever it was.'

Lawrence nodded.

'The headmaster is understandably very worried because it happened on school grounds – he's obviously concerned about both the other pupils and the school's reputation.'

'I can imagine,' Lawrence responded, guessing that was precisely why one of the governors had called to request assistance from his cousin, Lawrence's ultimate boss, early that afternoon. 'Did Scott have anything on him at the time that might give us some clue as to why he was out in the middle of the night?'

'Nothing whatsoever, just the usual schoolboy junk in his pockets. Loose change, biro lid, headphones –' Robert shrugged.

'Does the school not have any kind of security after hours?' Rebecca asked.

'There's a night porter. He doesn't seem to have noticed anything amiss, but it sounds as if his remit is limited to the area housing the main school buildings. The body was found a good half mile from the nearest of those.'

'What's the school like?'

'Old, traditional, private – exceptional academic record, but I think that's as much to do with the boys they take as the school itself. They have hundreds of applicants and they pick the best of the lot – there are about fifty boys in a year. The sports facilities are pretty impressive too, although academia takes priority.'

'I suppose it has to, the way league tables are compiled,' Lawrence observed.

'Quite,' Robert agreed. 'I met with the head earlier today, and he's expecting you tomorrow morning. I provisionally agreed nine, but if that's not convenient I can change it.'

'No, that sounds fine.'

'Splendid. Have you made any arrangements as far as accommodation goes?'

'We haven't had time yet.'

'Well, if it's of any help, my sister-in-law runs a small boarding house five minutes up the road – I could give her a call for you.'

'That would be very helpful,' Lawrence nodded, turning to Leighton. 'Are you staying as well?'

Leighton shook his head. 'I said I'd head back later.'

'Just two of us, then,' Lawrence concluded, as he looked back to Robert.

'Right, I'll sort that out now – I expect you'll be wanting to get over there for dinner. If I give you all the notes so far, you can go over them at some stage this evening and give me a call if you have any questions. How does that sound?'

'Great. Thank you,' Lawrence nodded, the mention of dinner reminding him that he hadn't eaten since midday. Elise had insisted on making him sandwiches for the car, but he still hadn't had the heart to tell her that hundreds and thousands with chocolate sauce wasn't his choice of filling, and that the sauce had the additional drawback of reducing the bread to a state not dissimilar to that of wet cardboard. He could only hope she would grow out of that particular favourite soon. Thinking about it, Lawrence couldn't help smiling. He'd been waiting for her to grow out of it for almost two years.

Two

'Wow. How much are the fees here?' Rebecca asked, as Lawrence drove slowly into the main turning circle outside Treelore Grammar and they came face to face with the main entrance. A vast structure of red brick, with pillars two storeys high flanking the front door and neat, symmetrical rows of sash windows on either side, the building looked all the more impressive for the setting in which it lay. An enormous expanse of immaculately maintained gardens surrounded the front of the school, the turning circle and the long, rhododendron-lined drive along which they had just travelled. Above the huge oak doors, a few words of Latin were carved into the stonework. Rebecca had never studied the language, but guessed it was probably the school's motto, and raised her eyes further, to where a substantial bell tower stood majestically atop the dark slate roof, the clock reading eight forty-three. They were early. Then again, Lawrence almost invariably was.

'Too much,' Lawrence answered her question, coming to a stop to the left of the entrance. Securing the hand break and switching off the ignition, he climbed from the car and stood looking around himself. Rebecca joined him just as he turned towards the building, and followed him in the direction of the imposing entrance. Lawrence glanced up at the inscription over the doors, raising his eyebrows. 'No pressure, then,' he murmured.

'What does it say?'

Lawrence looked around in surprise, having evidently not intended the comment for her. 'Pardon?'

'I don't know what it means,' Rebecca prompted.

'Dear me, classical education is sadly lacking in the younger generation,' Lawrence teased.

'Well at least I can cook,' Rebecca retaliated, well aware that Lawrence's culinary abilities extended little further than the microwave. 'Anyway, what does it say that's so interesting?'

'The race for excellence has no finishing line,' Lawrence revealed, climbing the front steps as Rebecca gave the words another look. By the time she had finished, Lawrence had disappeared inside, and she hurried after him.

Rebecca hadn't expected to find a modern reception area inside such an old building, and guessed it had been recently renovated. A middle-aged receptionist wearing a dated pink blouse and a black cardigan surveyed their warrant cards with a mild disinterest from behind her computer screen, saying that they would have to wait for the headmaster, who was in the chapel for assembly. Rebecca and Lawrence sat on the easy chairs over to one side, surveying their limited surroundings. The furniture, carpet and paintwork all appeared to be new, and Rebecca couldn't help thinking the plants on the front desk and in the corner behind it looked rather too healthy to be real. She certainly felt more at home in this environment, and wondered whether the school's exterior had been misleading. She hoped so.

After ten minutes spent talking quietly and rather self-consciously, Rebecca and Lawrence were joined by a man in his late fifties who entered the room from a doorway opposite the main entrance. He approached with a polite smile, looking quite relaxed, as if he were accustomed to visits from Scotland Yard.

'Good morning,' he greeted them. 'Sorry you've had to wait.'

'We were early,' Lawrence replied, amiably, getting to his feet and offering a hand. 'I'm DCI Forrester, and this is DS Palmer.'

'Donald Chadwick,' the head introduced himself, shaking Lawrence's hand before turning to shake Rebecca's. Tall but fairly slight, with thin, greying hair, a small moustache and a gentle smile, he lacked the authoritarian air she had expected of a man at the helm of one of the country's most exclusive and respected private schools. In her mind, the word *headmaster* walked hand-in-hand with others like *austere* and *aloof*. Perhaps he came across differently to the pupils. And, much as he might not have the presence she had expected, he was certainly dressed the part, clad in a beautifully cut navy three-piece suit and a plain tie.

'Can I get you anything?' He offered. 'Coffee, tea?'

'Not just now, thank you – we'd prefer to make a start as soon as possible.'

'Of course,' Donald nodded. 'Would you like me to show you around the school quickly so you've more idea of the surroundings?'

'That would be helpful,' Lawrence agreed.

'Right – it probably makes sense if we start with the main quad. I've asked my secretary to print out some maps, which I'll give you later – that way you'll run less risk of getting lost.' He turned back towards the door through which he had entered moments earlier, and Rebecca and Lawrence followed.

Inside the building, Rebecca had hoped she might find something a little more reminiscent of the comprehensive she had attended in her teens, but the school's interior was as grand and traditional as its magnificent facade. The main corridor into which they stepped first was long and wide, with a high ceiling and polished wooden floor. Cabinets lined one wall, stacked with trophies, cups and ribbons, boasting the school's sporting prowess. The other wall was hung with school photographs, the colourful central ones clearly the most recent, those at either end in shades of sepia, fading slowly into obscurity. Doors opened off the corridor at regular intervals, and looking in through the glass panels as she passed, Rebecca could see rows of pupils opening their files and preparing for their first lesson of the week. As she and her companions turned the corner into another corridor, two boys of about sixteen almost ran into them, and hastily slowed to a trot.

'If I catch you running late again, you'll be reporting to my office on Saturday morning, Johnson. Is that clear?' Donald demanded of the boy on the right.

'Yessir,' the boy nodded, anxiously, hurrying past.

'It's always the same ones,' Donald sighed, continuing on down the corridor to a set of double doors. Opening one, he stepped out into the central quadrangle, holding the door for Lawrence and Rebecca. The grounds within the building's perimeter were as immaculately maintained as those inside the gates, and, despite having considerable misgivings about private education, Rebecca felt impressed.

'This is the original building.' Donald indicated the four walls that surrounded them. 'It contains the classrooms, laboratories, the dining room, the library, the great hall – it's where the boys spend their day, unless they're in the sixth form and they have a free period. The boarding houses, chapel and sports block form separate buildings – they're situated between here and the woods, and you can get to them through there –' He indicated an archway at the centre of the rear quadrangle wall, starting to walk towards it. 'This has all been a dreadful shock for everyone –

I spent most of yesterday fielding questions from worried parents, and the boys have all been very subdued. You'll doubtless be wanting to speak with Edward Quast – he was Scott's housemaster – I'm afraid he's away today, but he'll be back early this evening.'

'Where is he?'

'He's giving a presentation to a panel up in London and it wasn't something he felt he could cancel. I've put another member of staff in charge of the Windsor boys for today.'

'Windsor boys?' Lawrence queried, his eyebrows rising.

'Oh – I'm sorry – that's the name of the house. There are four boarding houses – they're named after the original founders of the school. Windsor, Bailey, Fawcett and Pirie. Scott was in Windsor –' he paused. 'I suppose you'll have spoken to the local police already?'

'Last night. We've had some of the details – but I'm curious about one thing. I gather Scott died in the early hours of the morning – what on earth was he doing out at that time?'

'That I don't know. He ought to have been in bed – and he certainly shouldn't have been half a mile from Windsor.'

'Do the boys have freedom to wander about at night?'

'No, they don't, but we can only enforce that so far – they have to be able to get out in the event of a fire. I know boys have occasionally been caught climbing out of windows and onto fire escapes – all I can do is punish those few severely and hope it acts as a suitable deterrent for the others.'

'So they can't just walk in and out the main door?'

'Not without us knowing about it. The door can be opened easily enough from inside, but all the external doors are alarmed at night. There is a code to disable that, but obviously only a few members of staff know what it is.'

'Is it possible the alarm could have been tampered with?'

'No. I've already had the caretaker look at it,' Donald replied, leading them through the archway and out of the quadrangle. Behind the main school building, the grounds sprawled in all directions, peppered with red brick buildings in the same style as that which they had just left. Pointing to these, the head continued, 'Those are the boarding houses – straight ahead. The block to the right is mainly staff accommodation, and behind there we have a new sports centre – you can't see that from here. The woods are out beyond that – there's a track through them which leads to the sports fields, and there's also an observatory. The chapel –' he turned to his left, 'Is behind those trees.'

Rebecca looked in the direction he indicated. Not far from where they stood, she could just make out the spire above a dense crowd of poplars.

'Do all staff live on site?' Lawrence asked.

Donald shook his head. 'No, only about two-thirds. We can't accommodate families, and some people prefer to put a bit more distance between their home lives and their work. The housemasters are obviously required to live on site, but the rest of the staff can make their own arrangements if they wish.' Heading for a door in the side of the archway, he glanced around. 'I'll show you over the place quickly, and then I'll fetch those maps. You'll want to talk to Scott's form tutor, as well – he should be able to give you an idea of which of the boys to chat to first.'

Lawrence nodded, accompanying him to the door. Rebecca stayed where she was for a moment, still taking in the extent of the grounds and wondering what the pupils would be like. She hadn't ever imagined a school could give her such a culture shock.

From his tan, John Richardson looked as if he belonged in sunnier climes, and as it was only a week since half term Rebecca guessed he'd recently been away on holiday. A small, slight man approaching his sixties, he had grey hair that was beginning to thin, an aquiline nose and deep crows' feet. He wore a burgundy v-necked jumper embroidered with a small crest – not, Rebecca noted, that of the school – over his shirt and tie, and was also wearing a wedding ring. Assuming he wasn't a widower, she wondered whether he shared his first-floor apartment or whether he divided his time between the staff quarters and a second home elsewhere.

'Mr Richardson?'

'That's right,' he confirmed. 'Would I be correct in assuming you're from Scotland Yard?'

'Yes. I'm Detective Sergeant Palmer. I understand you were Scott Ribet's form tutor.'

'I was indeed,' John confirmed, stepping back from the door. 'Come on in.'

Rebecca thanked him, following him down a rather dark hallway and into to a large, high-ceilinged living room painted in flawless magnolia, which led Rebecca to suspect the apartments might be decorated – and perhaps also outfitted – by the school, rather than by the staff members themselves. The space was sparsely furnished with a couple of low oak tables and a matching bookcase, and a three-piece suite upholstered in airforce blue. Sitting on the sofa was a slender teenager in school uniform, his mousy, shoulder-length hair tucked neatly behind his ears. Liquid blue eyes and long eyelashes lent a prettiness to his appearance, while the dark shadows beneath his eyes hinted that he hadn't had much sleep in recent days. Rebecca wondered whether he was simply one of John's pupils or whether he might be a relation, and how much mixing there was between staff and pupils at Treelore. She supposed that at a boarding school they would see considerably more of one another than she ever had of her teachers.

'Sorry – I didn't mean to interrupt –' she began, turning back towards John.

'No, no, not at all,' John replied, looking to the youth on the sofa. 'We were just about done, I think?'

The boy nodded mutely, moving to stand.

'Ok,' John continued. 'If there's anything more I can do, let me know. Otherwise I'll see you in history tomorrow afternoon.'

The lad nodded again, making for the door. John gestured for Rebecca to take a seat, reaching to clear the two empty mugs from the coffee table. Straightening up, he turned as if suddenly remembering something. 'Oh, Curt?'

The boy stopped halfway out of the front door. 'Yes?'

'Would you mind asking Dominic to stop by my office before dinner?'

'Not at all.'

'Thanks.'

The door closed and John looked back to Rebecca. 'Can I get you a drink?'

'No, thanks, I've just had one with lunch.'

'Ah, did you brave the canteen?' John asked, abandoning the mugs on top of the bookcase and sitting opposite her.

'We did. And the food was a lot better than I remember my school meals being.'

'They don't do a bad job,' John acknowledged. 'But I am thankful we have our own kitchen.' He rested an elbow on the chair's armrest. 'Anyway, I imagine you're after some information about Scott?'

'Yes. Did you have much contact with him?'

'He was in my form and I taught him history – I saw quite a lot of him, yes.'

'I imagine you knew him well, then.'

'Reasonably so, I suppose.'

'Could you tell me a bit about him?'

John raised his eyebrows. 'Where to start,' he remarked, pausing to consider his answer. 'Rugby and debating are the first two words that spring to mind. He was a member of the first fifteen and he was one half of the team that won the regional debating championships last term. A lot of his time and attention were devoted to those two activities. Academically he was fairly average – by our standards – although he didn't exactly exert himself when it came to his studies. Could do better, to coin a phrase,' he paused again. 'He certainly seemed to enjoy school life – he was a member of several clubs and he didn't want for friends. Oh, and he was prefect to a fourth-form class.'

'Did you like him?'

'He wasn't my favourite pupil,' John admitted. 'He was very cocky and he didn't show much regard for other people's feelings. Last year one of the younger boys reported him for bullying, and although I'm pretty sure there was something to that, we weren't able to substantiate it.'

'Did you take it seriously?'

'It hardly something we can fail to take seriously, is it?' John replied. 'Bullying is a problem in all schools – we do everything we can to minimise it, but it's quite a difficult task. Especially when it's just one boy's word against another's.'

Rebecca nodded. 'Are you aware of any arguments or incidents that might have a bearing on what happened to Scott?'

'I'm afraid nothing springs to mind. Hopefully you might get more of an idea from some of the boys, although I suspect many of them will be reluctant to squeal on their mates. You probably want to have a chat to some of those he wasn't friends with to get a balanced picture.'

'I'm sure we'll talk to as many of the boys as we can. Where do you recommend we start? Who were his close friends?'

'Curt, for one,' John tipped his head in the direction of the front door through which the boy had disappeared moments earlier.

'Not a friendship I'd ever have predicted, but they obviously clicked one way or another. And Curt's room mate, Francis, was friendly with Scott as well. Some of the time, anyway. Then there's Scott's room mate, Dominic. Don't take any nonsense from him,' he paused. 'Aside from those three, you probably want to catch up with the rugby coterie – in particular, Sid Watson and Oliver Grant.' He sat back in his chair. 'And if any of them give you any lip, please do let me know. I will be only too happy to set them a punitive essay on the history of the Metropolitan Police force.'

A small notice Blu-tacked to the door of room 318 announced it as 'Scott and Nicky's Room: The Brewery'. It had been beautifully illustrated with beer bottles, tins and pint glasses, evidently drawn by someone with considerable artistic talent. Lawrence felt astonished the housemaster had allowed it to remain on view. When a knock on the door elicited no response, he tried the handle. Looking in, he was surprised to find the room relatively tidy, and wondered whether the school imposed rules about order. His own bedroom in his late teens had been little short of chaotic, and he didn't remember many of his friends being much tidier.

Had he not known from the sign on the door and the two beds inside, Lawrence could have guessed the room had two occupants from its contrasting decor. On one side, the walls were busy with posters for several rock bands – including Vicious Circle, one of Jimmy's favourites – and an eclectic selection of art prints. The other half of the room was plastered with a combination of pull-outs from sports magazines, depicting various well-known rugby teams and players, and official school sports photographs – the rugby first fifteen, the sixth form fencing team, Windsor House Boat Club. From the picture Robert Younger had supplied the previous evening, Lawrence identified Scott as a member of each.

Turning from the photographs, he took a closer look at the rest of the room. A large, and Lawrence suspected expensive, docking station sat atop the shelf that ran above the two beds, currently minus any mp3 player or phone. The room had two sash windows, with a desk positioned in front of each. The first was peppered with Post-it notes – *hand in English – money for Alex – call Suzanne – card for Nan – collect washing – music for*

Fray. A filing tray in the right-hand corner held several files, and the yellow cardboard cover of the top one, labelled *Nicky Greenwood*, was covered in cartoons and quotations. Lawrence guessed the sign on the door had been decorated by the owner of the folder, and moved towards the other desk.

Around its periphery were a pencil pot, a digital alarm clock, a photograph frame holding a picture of a pretty teenage girl with long red hair, a letter rack overflowing with newspaper cuttings and a handful of letters, and a stress toy in the form of a half pint of Guinness. Other than these, the only item on the desk was a large map of Great Britain, illuminated in different colours – mainly red, blue and yellow – and labelled, 'Political Britain'. Pulling a letter from the rack, Lawrence confirmed that the desk had belonged to Scott, then sat down and emptied the contents of the rack onto the desk top.

Given Scott's age and the ubiquity of email, Lawrence wouldn't have expected him to have received much post at all, and wasn't surprised to discover that more than half of the nine items of correspondence were from his mother. Over and above those, there were two letters from Camille, who wrote in French, one from a girl called Gemma and a card from Michelle, whom Lawrence guessed might have been a girlfriend from the fact she had signed off *hugs and kisses, love you loads*. Most of the newspaper cuttings related to recent political events, and were neatly dated in blue biro in what looked like Scott's mother's hand.

Setting the letters and cuttings aside for the time being, Lawrence opened the top drawer of the desk, where tidiness and order came to an abrupt end. The drawer held a jumble of pens, pencils, notepads, elastic bands, flyers, bus tickets, sweets, batteries, badges, paper clips and numerous other odds and ends. Lawrence closed the drawer, deciding to tackle it later, and looked into the lower one. This was tidier, stacked with notebooks, bank statements and paying-in slips.

Glancing at the first statement he came to, Lawrence was surprised by the size of the figures in the columns. The account held close to twenty thousand pounds, and there were regular credit entries. The statement was dated from early January to early February, and anywhere between one hundred and five hundred pounds had been paid in on a weekly basis. Lawrence arranged the handful of statements into chronological order to find they covered the period corresponding to the academic year. Over Scott's first five months in the upper sixth, the balance of his bank account had risen by more than seven thousand pounds. Running through the transactions on the statements, it became apparent that most had been cash deposits, presumably made by Scott himself. Aside from these and a monthly sum of two hundred pounds, which appeared to be a standing order, the only other entries were sporadic withdrawals.

Placing the statements on the desk top, Lawrence searched the rest of the drawer methodically. Having found nothing else of interest, he carefully lifted it off its runners and pulled it out. He laid it on the bed behind him, then peered into the space below the first drawer, and was intrigued to find a DVD case wedged against the base of the cavity. He wondered whether the boys were forbidden from watching television in their rooms, or whether the sole reason for the DVD's confinement was its 18 certification.

Placing the DVD case on the desk, Lawrence replaced the drawer and turned to open the cupboard on the other side of the desk's footwell. A selection of files were stacked inside, the school's name and crest printed on the spines, and as Lawrence reached for the leftmost file the bedroom door opened. Looking up, Lawrence met the eyes of a striking teenage boy. He was tall, with jet black hair and fair skin, green eyes and mousy eyebrows that betrayed the fact his hair was dyed. Fully dressed in school uniform – sky blue shirt, grey trousers and navy and royal-blue striped tie and blazer – he was clearly surprised to find someone else in the room.

'Hello. I'm DCI Forrester,' Lawrence introduced himself, shutting the cupboard door and moving to stand.

'Hi.'

'Is this your room?'

'Yuh. I'm Nicky.'

'Did no one tell you I might be here?'

'No,' Nicky replied, before nervously running the tip of his tongue along his upper lip.

'Oh,' Lawrence frowned, thinking the boy ought to have been warned. 'Well, I'm sorry nobody mentioned it – I'd like to have a chat with you, if you've got a few minutes?'

'Will it get me excused from rugby?'

'Is that where you're supposed to be now?'

Nicky nodded. 'I'm not really in the mood.' He dropped down onto the bed nearest the door, running a hand through his hair. Lawrence sat on the parallel bed.

'How long have you shared a room with Scott?'

'Uh – eighteen months with just the two of us – but we were in the same dorm for three years before that.'

'Did you get on well?'

'Yeah – Scott was a laugh. We had a lot of fun. We made beer last term.'

'In here?'

Nicky nodded. 'In the wardrobe.'

Lawrence guessed that was what the sign on the door referred to. 'Did you have many classes together?'

'No. I do English, maths, art and music. Scott did history, politics, French and German.'

'That sounds like hard work.'

'He wanted to be a politician.'

'And you?'

Nicky shrugged. 'I don't know. Something with art or music, I guess. I play in a band.'

'What sort of band?'

'We call it retro punk.'

Lawrence was none the wiser. 'Is that at school?'

'Yes. With three of my friends.'

'Was Scott involved in that?'

'Kind of. He didn't play in it – but he appointed himself as our manager.'

'Who are the other members?'

'Fray Bircham – he's the songwriter – Alex Jefferies and Marty Coleman.'

Lawrence went to scribble the names in his notebook, then paused momentarily, wondering how Fray was spelt.

'F-R-A-Y,' Nicky offered, helpfully, obviously guessing his thoughts.

'Is that his real name?'

'No. Francis. He hates it.'

Lawrence nodded, noting this detail before returning his attention to Nicky. 'And what did Scott do as your manager?'

'Nothing. We haven't done much yet – Fray's still writing material. At the moment we've got five songs.' Nicky bent to pick a crumpled Post-it from the carpet by the bed.

'You seem to have a lot of those around,' Lawrence remarked.

'Yeah, I have a terrible memory. I remember totally useless things, but I forget to do anything important.'

'Do you remember what you were doing on Friday night?'

'I wasn't here.'

'Where were you?'

'Edinburgh.'

'Did you not have lessons on Saturday morning?'

'Well, theoretically, yes, but I wanted to take my girlfriend away for the weekend, so I told my art teacher I wanted to visit an exhibition, and he signed a form to excuse me from class so I could get exeat a day early.'

'What was the exhibition?'

'Oh – some modern rubbish – I didn't actually go, I have some postcards from it that my nan sent me when she went, so I'll just take those to my next class and lie.'

Lawrence felt surprised Nicky had no qualms about admitting to this, and asked for the name of the girl who would be able to confirm his whereabouts.

'Suzanne,' Nicky answered, obligingly. 'Plus I signed into the hotel at about ten-thirty on Friday night, and we had breakfast in bed the next morning.'

'Did your parents know about your weekend away?'

Nicky shook his head with a grin.

Lawrence thought it strange the school would grant a pupil leave without parental consent, and made a mental note to ask one of the staff about exeat procedures. 'When did you get back?'

'I had to be here for chapel at seven, since I didn't go to the morning service. We have to go to at least one service every Sunday. Although I never actually made it this weekend, what with everything that had happened.'

Lawrence nodded. 'On that note, did Scott have any enemies here?'

'I don't think so. Not everybody liked him – he could be very opinionated – but I don't think anybody hated him.'

'He didn't fall out with anyone recently, or do anything to upset anyone?'

'No. Not that I know about.'

'And do you have any idea what his plans might have been for Friday night?'

'No. He probably told me at some point, but like I said, I have a terrible memory. Besides, I wasn't very interested in what everyone else was doing.'

'Can you think of any reason why he might have been out in the woods in the early hours of Saturday morning?'

Nicky seemed to think this over before saying, 'No, no idea. Sorry.'

'Did he ever leave the room at night when you were here?'

Nicky shrugged. 'He might have done, but I wouldn't have known. I sleep pretty deeply, and even if I had woken up and noticed he wasn't here, I'd have assumed he was in the bathroom.'

Lawrence doubted anyone would be able to sleep through someone clambering out of a window just a few feet from their bed, but didn't say as much, instead moving on to another topic.

'Do you know anything about Scott's financial affairs?'

'Why would I?'

'Well, you must know a fair amount about him after sharing a room for so long.'

'His parents are loaded. Most people's are, here. That's how they afford the fees.'

'Does that include yours?'

'No – my dad was killed in a climbing accident seven years ago. My grandparents are the ones paying for my existence here.'

'That's good of them.'

'Not really,' Nicky replied. 'I'm here because they want to keep me out of trouble, and because they couldn't face the shame of having their only grandson scraping a living playing the guitar in some ghastly pub in Manchester.' His voice was heavy with sarcasm, and Lawrence guessed Nicky intended to do exactly that as soon as he possibly could.

'Do you have any idea what sort of allowance Scott received from his parents?'

Nicky shook his head. 'Scott was always funny about how much money he did or didn't have – I don't think you'll find anyone who knew much about that.'

'And how about his family? Did he talk much about them?'

'A bit. He had a sister. She's ten or eleven, I think. She worshipped him. And his parents seem ok.'

'Did you ever visit him in the holidays?'

'Loads.'

'Do you think his home life was happy?'

'Yeah, I reckon so. It always seemed really relaxed round there.' Nicky paused, then added, with surprising insight, 'And if your biggest complaints after exeat are that your dad won't eat Chinese food and it was too wet to play tennis on the lawn, I figure you must have it pretty good.'

'Hang on a minute,' a voice responded to Rebecca's knock at the door of room 319. Shortly, the door opened and Curt appeared, still in the uniform shirt and trousers he had been wearing in John Richardson's apartment, although now minus his tie and with the top button of his shirt undone. 'Hi,' he greeted, rather awkwardly.

'Hello again. Do you have five minutes?'

'Um – I guess,' Curt nodded, stepping back from the door. Entering the room, Rebecca realised he wasn't alone. A clean-cut young man dressed in a smart suit was sitting on one of the beds, a book in his hands. He glanced up as she appeared.

'Could we finish up later?' Curt asked.

'Sure,' his companion smiled, getting to his feet. 'How about you have another look at those stats papers and then come and see me with any questions?'

'Yes. Thanks.'

'Ok. See you later.' The young man turned to go, giving Rebecca a smile as he left the room.

'One of your friends?' Rebecca asked, when she and Curt were alone.

'No – he's one of my teachers. He was running through some work I didn't understand.'

Her eyes alighting on the book the teacher had been holding moments earlier, Rebecca felt sceptical. The guitar score for Vicious Circle's *Beautiful Strangers* album hardly seemed relevant to A-level studies, and casually, she mentioned this.

'It's Fray's,' Curt replied. 'Mr Markham was just flicking through it while I was trying to answer some stats problems.'

'Fray?'

'My room mate.' Curt coughed.

'Will he not mind people going through his belongings?'

'Hardly going through,' Curt objected. 'Fray leaves things lying around – he's not exactly tidy.'

'Does that bother you?'

'Sometimes. It makes it harder to keep the room clean, and I'm allergic to dust.'

Looking around herself, Rebecca noticed one half of the room was indeed a good deal tidier than the other. There was nothing else particularly remarkable about it, and she guessed it was similar to most others occupied by sixth-form boys. There were a number of posters on the walls, a stereo, a bookcase stacked with a variety of texts, two desks littered with paper, books, pencil pots and, in one case, a laptop, two beds, wardrobes and chests of drawers. An electric guitar leaned against one of the wardrobes and Rebecca supposed it belonged to Fray, given that he owned the book which had caught her attention.

Curt perched on one of the beds, coughing badly. Rebecca sat on the other, pulling out her notebook.

'I understand you were close friends with Scott Ribet,' she began, when Curt managed to stop coughing.

He nodded. 'We were in the same room our first three years here.'

'Through choice?'

'No – we didn't get to choose until last year – we used to have six to a room, and desks in a separate study room.'

'And now you work in here?'

'Yes. They let us decide who we want to share with – I suppose –' Curt coughed again. 'I suppose because you spend so much more time together.'

'Did Fray know Scott well?'

'Yes. They did history and politics together.'

'Were they friends?'

'To a point.'

'Meaning what?'

'Fray's very reserved. He lost his brother when he was younger, and I think he's scared of letting anyone get too close in case something happens to them.'

Rebecca nodded. 'When did you last see Scott?'

'Dinner. On Friday night.'

'Could you run me through what you did after that?'

'I walked back here with Scott – his room's next door.' Curt clasped his hands and Rebecca noticed his knuckles and fingers were red and flaky with eczema. 'I went to the library to do a chemistry assignment –'

'I thought you said you worked in here?'

'I do unless I need books.'

'Do you usually work on Friday nights?' Rebecca asked, thinking that must take some dedication: she didn't recall ever settling to her homework on a Friday evening.

'We have lessons on Saturday mornings. I had work to hand in.'

'And what did you do after you left the library?'

'I went to see matron because I wasn't feeling well.'

'How long did that take?'

'I stayed the night there.' There was a momentary pause before he added, 'You can check that with her if you want to.'

'You stayed where?'

'The san. Sanatorium.'

'Oh, I see. What time was that?'

'From about nine, I think.'

Rebecca noted this down. 'Do you think Scott was happy here?'

'He seemed to be.'

'What was he like?'

'He was good fun. Always had something to say. He wanted to be a politician.'

'Do you know if he had any plans for the weekend?'

'He was talking about going into town on Saturday afternoon, because over dinner he asked if I wanted to go with him.'

'Are you allowed to do that?'

Curt nodded. 'Sixth form get two trips a week into town – Wednesday and Saturday afternoons. We get a bus that goes past the end of the drive. Scott could never go on Wednesdays, because he always had rugby matches.'

'What sort of things do you do in town?'

'Go to the shops, the bank, the cinema – and the pub, sometimes.'

'Is that within the rules?'

'Not really,' Curt blushed. 'But lots of us do it,' he added, as if to justify the activity. 'We're not in uniform after lessons, so it's pretty safe. You just have to hope you don't run into any teachers.'

'Did Scott mention any plans for Friday night?'

'No, I don't think so – he was more interested in some film that was showing at the cinema.'

'He didn't mention Friday night at all?'

'He might have – I don't remember.'

'Do you have any idea why he might have been out in the woods in the middle of the night?'

Curt hesitated. 'Sometimes he went out there to smoke,' he said, eventually, looking distinctly uneasy.

'He went all that way to smoke?'

Several seconds passed before Curt revealed, 'It wasn't cigarettes.'

'Were you ever party to that?'

Rebecca hadn't expected him to admit to it even if he had been, but in denying it he did at least provide her with a believable answer. 'No. I'm asthmatic.'

'Do you know who else did participate?'

Curt shifted position uncomfortably. 'I don't want to get anyone into trouble.'

'Curt, I'm not interested in what they were or weren't smoking, I just want to know who Scott might have been in the woods with that night.'

Curt said nothing, eyes on his knees.

'Please, Curt, this is important.'

'Nicky.'

'Nicky?'

'His room mate.'

'Was there anyone else involved?'

'I don't know – there might have been. No one ever told me.'

'Aside from smoking, can you think of any reason why Scott might have been in the woods on Friday night?'

Curt shook his head. 'No. Sorry.'

'Was there anyone who disliked him enough that they might have wanted him dead?'

Eyes on the floor, he shook his head again.

'Are you sure about that?'

Curt nodded. He didn't look up.

'Do you know whether he fell out with anyone recently?'

'No,' he answered, his voice wavering slightly.

'Ok,' Rebecca concluded, deciding to leave it there for the time being. 'I think that's all for now,' she smiled, closing her notebook. 'Thank you for your help, I realise this must be hard for you. I'll let you get on with your work.' She got to her feet. 'If anything else comes to mind, please let us know.'

'Sure,' Curt replied, forcing a weak smile. He looked incredibly anxious, and Rebecca suspected he knew a lot more than he was letting on. She would question him again when she had more idea of which buttons to press. At this stage, whether he was trying to protect himself or somebody else was anybody's guess.

A cautious, 'Hello?' greeted Lawrence's knock on the door of room 325. Only one of the room's two occupants turned out to be in, and he was seated at his desk, fully dressed in uniform. Small and slight, he had turned in his seat to see whom he had just invited into his room, his expression wary. Lawrence wondered whether perhaps he didn't have permission to be missing the rugby session Nicky had mentioned. With dark hair and eyes and olive skin, he looked to be of Mediterranean or Middle Eastern extraction; glancing at the list Donald Chadwick had provided, Lawrence guessed the latter.

'Tariq?'

The boy nodded.

'I'm DCI Forrester. I'd like a quick chat, if you've time.'

'Uh – I have loads to do – will it take long?'

'It shouldn't do.'

'Oh – ok,' Tariq nodded. Lawrence perched on one of the beds and Tariq turned a little further in his chair.

'Would I be correct in assuming you knew Scott Ribet reasonably well?'

'He lived in my corridor – that doesn't mean we were friends.'

'No, but I imagine you must have seen him in passing fairly regularly. You've been in the same boarding house for over four years.'

'I guess.'

'I'm getting the impression the two of you didn't get along.'

'No.'

'Would you mind telling me why not?'

'Scott was of the sports-team-arsehole-lad mentality. Part of the group who think you're a hard man if you're in the rugby first fifteen, have the ability to drink a yard of ale, and can piss a long way out of third floor windows. You know the type – think they're better than everybody else and continually pick on other people, but only when they've got the security of their mates about them.'

'I think I'm getting the picture. Were you one of the individuals getting picked on?'

'I still am. Scott was hardly the only one doing it.'

'Doing what, exactly?'

'Calling me names, making fun of me – nothing overtly physical, and nothing I can really pinpoint – they wouldn't dare do anything that might actually get them into trouble. Whispered comments, knocking into me accidentally on purpose –' he trailed off with a shrug.

'How did you handle the situation with Scott?'

'Mostly I ignored him. I didn't want to challenge him in case it made things worse.'

'So how did you feel when you heard about his death?'

'I wasn't sorry, if that's what you're asking. Obviously it was a shock – it's hardly the sort of thing you expect to happen at your school, is it?'

'No, I realise that,' Lawrence acknowledged. 'Could you run through exactly where you were on Friday night, and what you were doing?'

'I was in here all night, working. I had masses of work due in on Saturday morning. At quarter to eleven I was in bed – lights out is at eleven. I think I fell asleep soon after that, and next thing I knew it was morning.'

'Can anybody account for that?'

'My room mate, Lindsay – he was in here from about half-past nine, and as far as I know he didn't go anywhere after that.'

'Do you know whether Scott fell out with anybody recently?'

Tariq hesitated before replying, 'Well, last week he had a massive fight with Fray, and Fray yelled something like *you tell anybody and I'll kill you*, but I expect he said that more in the heat of the moment than anything else.'

'So you don't think he meant it?'

Tariq shrugged. 'I don't know. If I was Fray the idea would probably have at least crossed my mind.'

'Why?'

'Scott could be pretty unpleasant, but he was really vicious with Fray. And Fray was supposed to be his friend. Scott never made any pretense of being my friend. He was nice to Fray when it suited him, and the rest of the time he treated him like dirt.'

'Is Fray a friend of yours?'

'No. I suppose you might call him an acquaintance. If we pass in the corridor we'll say hello. He comes out with some very cutting remarks, but generally they're well deserved.'

'Is there anybody else you can think of who might have been responsible?'

'I think Scott had a fist fight with Sid Watson a week or so ago – but that's more of a rumour – you might want to check it out with someone else. That's all I can think of right now – if I think of something more how do I contact you? Should I just see Dr Quast?'

'That sounds like a good idea,' Lawrence nodded. 'Although you're likely to see me around the school and the grounds quite a bit during the next few days.'

'Is that it for now, then?' Tariq asked, awkwardly.

'You seem anxious to get rid of me.'

'I have to hand in four physics papers before dinner and I've only done two of them,' Tariq admitted.

'Ah, I wondered why you were in here rather than playing rugby,' Lawrence smiled.

Tariq shifted position uncomfortably. 'I'm bunking rugby. You won't tell anyone, will you?'

'I don't think anyone's likely to ask me where you are. I'll leave you to it. Thank you for your time.'

'It's ok.'

'Good luck.'

'Thanks,' Tariq muttered, as Lawrence headed for the door. 'I need it.'

The school map didn't appear to include the sanatorium, and Rebecca had to ask directions from a fifth-form prefect who was walking back from the main school building to, she presumed, his boarding house. Having been told it formed the ground floor of Bailey House, she made her way there, only to find herself no better off, since having entered the house she could find no sign of the sanatorium, nor any directions to it. She spent several minutes going around in circles within the maze that made up Bailey House before giving up and knocking on the housemaster's door to ask his assistance. A surprisingly mousy man, he directed her back out of the front door and around to the side of the building, where she finally found the door to the sanatorium. This was well labelled, but Rebecca couldn't help thinking signposting the door was rather futile considering how difficult it was to find in the first place.

Immediately inside the door was a small office, and an attractive woman in her early forties looked up from her desk as Rebecca entered. A slight figure, she had a long, thin face, and auburn hair that had been scraped back off her face and fastened with a banana clip. She gave Rebecca a polite smile in greeting, her expression expectant.

'Sorry to interrupt,' Rebecca began, politely.

'It's not a problem. How can I help?'

'DS Palmer,' Rebecca displayed her warrant card.

'Ah, this is about Scott, is it?'

'That's right.'

'I'm Vivien Thompson, the school matron. Was it me you were looking for?'

'Yes. I was hoping to check something with you.'

'Oh, right. What's that?'

'Did you see Curt Wilkinson on Friday evening?'

'Surely you don't think he had anything to do with what happened to Scott?'

'It's my job to suspect everyone at this stage.'

'Curt wouldn't hurt a fly. And I doubt he'd have had the strength to tackle Scott. He can't even play sport at the moment.'

'Why not?'

'He's asthmatic, and in recent months it's proved very difficult to manage. He's not been at all well this term.'

'Did you see him on Friday?'

'Yes.'

'What time did he arrive here?'

Vivien reached for a book on the counter behind her and flicked back a page. 'Ten past nine.'

'And what did he say?'

'He didn't say much at all. He could barely breathe, never mind speak.'

'Is it possible to fake an asthma attack?'

Vivien frowned. 'Asthma can be very dangerous. It isn't just some easy excuse to get out of P.E.'

'So that would be no?'

'Absolutely.'

'Can you be sure he was here all night?'

Vivien sighed. 'I really don't think –'

'I understand your reservations,' Rebecca pre-empted. 'But I have to ask. Please just let me get through this.'

There was a pause before Vivien nodded. 'Ok. Well, I was with him for the first hour or so – after that I left him to rest.'

'When was that?'

'About ten, I think.'

'Did anyone see him after that?'

Vivien considered the question for a moment before saying, 'Yes – Guy Markham dropped in to see him not long after that.'

'Is he a friend of Curt's?'

'He's a biology teacher.'

'Teacher?' Rebecca exclaimed. 'Do teachers usually visit pupils at that time of night?'

'Not usually, no – he said something about an assignment and giving Curt an extension since he wasn't well – I didn't pay much attention, to be honest.'

'And how long did he stay?'

'I've no idea. I'm here to look after the boys, not to chase up members of staff. Curt wasn't the only kid I had in here on Friday evening.'

'Do you check on the boys during the night?'

'Not unless I'm particularly concerned about one of them, no. But I seriously doubt Curt went anywhere. He woke me shortly after four to ask for painkillers and he was running a temperature. I thought he was coming down with something.'

'How was he in the morning?'

'He said he was feeling better, although he didn't really look it. But he seemed to be breathing relatively freely and his temperature was back to normal, so I let him go to class.'

'Do you know him well?'

Vivien nodded. 'I've seen a lot of him this year. He's a lovely boy. Very kind.'

'Do you hear much gossip from the boys?'

'Not really – as in all schools there's very much an us and them divide between the pupils and the staff, and as far as the boys are concerned I fall firmly into the *them* category.'

'Is there anything you're aware of that might have a bearing on Scott's death?'

'To be honest, Scott was little more than a name, a face and a reputation to me,' Vivien admitted. 'I don't think I've had him in the san since he was a fourth year. I've heard talk about him – not all of it favourable – but that's it, really.'

'What have you heard?'

'I got the impression he was a bit of a bully. Picked on people and got away with it because he was a big rugby player and so were several of his friends.'

'Is there much bullying here, do you think?'

Vivien sighed. 'It's very hard to say – on a physical basis, probably not much, but I think on an emotional level there's probably quite a lot. That's much more difficult to control, because it's often tricky to know where friendly teasing stops and taunting begins.'

'I think that's a problem throughout life,' Rebecca observed.

'Yes, I'm afraid it is.'

'There's nothing else that comes to mind?'

'Not at the moment. If I think of anything, I'll let you know.'

'Great. Thanks.'

'I just hope you can get to the bottom of the matter quickly,' Vivien reached for a folder on the shelf above her desk. 'At the moment I think everyone's looking over their shoulders.'

On meeting Francis Bircham, the first thought to cross Lawrence's mind was that the boy looked as if he was on drugs. Painfully thin, his cheekbones were unnaturally sharp, and his uniform grey jumper looked to be several sizes too big. His dark hair was surprisingly untidy, and Lawrence guessed Francis had engineered it to be so. He was sitting in a corner of the library, a large text book open in front of him, scribbling notes in a rather frenzied manner in a hardback A4 book. He didn't notice Lawrence approaching, and when Lawrence spoke his name glanced up with a frown, making no attempt to conceal his irritation at the interruption.

'What?'

Lawrence introduced himself, joining the boy at the table. 'I need to ask you a few questions about Scott. I'm sorry if it's difficult.'

He was more than a little taken aback when Francis blinked and said, shortly, 'I'm busy.'

'Well I'm sorry to interrupt, but I'm afraid this is important.'

'Like what I'm doing isn't?' Francis retorted in a strong northern accent, slamming his notebook shut. Lawrence took this to be tacit submission and posed his first question.

'Can you tell me when you last saw Scott?'

‘Friday afternoon. In history.’ The boy raised his right hand to his mouth and bit into the torn skin that bordered fingernails already bitten down to the quick.

‘You didn’t see him at dinner?’

‘I don’t eat dinner.’

Lawrence could well believe it. ‘Why not?’

‘I don’t see how that information has any bearing on your investigation,’ Francis returned, bluntly.

‘What did you do after your history lesson, then?’

‘Chemistry. After that, I was in my room.’

‘Were you alone?’

‘Yes. Curt – my room mate – was at dinner.’

‘What were you doing?’

‘What does that matter?’ Francis demanded. ‘Scott was at dinner, so I don’t see how what I was doing is relevant.’

Lawrence raised his eyebrows. ‘How do you know he was at dinner if you weren’t there?’

‘He walked back with Curt. I heard them talking,’ Francis replied, linking and unlinking his fingers repeatedly. Given his apparent inability to keep them still and his impatient manner, Lawrence suspected he was on some sort of stimulant, although his pupils lacked the wide dilation that normally accompanied cocaine or amphetamine use.

‘What happened after that?’

‘Curt went to the library to do some work – I stayed in my room ’til nine, then I had a band practice.’

‘Was Scott not present at that?’

‘Why should he have been?’

‘I understood from Nicky that he was the band’s manager. Is that not true?’

‘So?’ Francis twisted his fingers together. ‘He was hardly going to be much use at rehearsals, seeing as how he wasn’t involved in playing anything.’

‘Was he not interested in what you were doing?’

‘Interested? Scott didn’t even like it.’

‘Why on earth did he want to be your manager if he didn’t like the music?’

‘Money,’ Francis replied, as if it should have been obvious. ‘Scott didn’t do things unless he was going to benefit from them, preferably financially. I think he figured that if we ever got anywhere, he could make a good deal of money out of having done very little.'

Thinking back to the bank statements he'd leafed through earlier that afternoon, Lawrence asked whether Francis knew much about Scott's personal finances.

'No. He was evasive about anything to do with money.'

'Why was that?'

'I don't know. Some people are, aren't they?'

Lawrence nodded, returning to his original line of questioning.

'How long did your band practice last?'

'We finished up at about ten-fifteen. We had to get back to our houses and ready for bed in time for lights out at eleven.'

'Did you go straight to bed?'

'Yes.' Francis picked at the ravaged skin of his right forefinger with the first finger and thumb of his left hand. In several places his skin looked raw.

'And did you leave your room after that?'

'Not until morning.'

'Can anybody account for that?'

'Dr Quast normally checks on us now and then. I assume he did so, although I can't say for sure because I was asleep.'

'Was your room mate not there?'

'No.'

Where was he?'

'Sanatorium. He had an asthma attack.'

'So no one can confirm where you were or what you were doing between eleven on Friday night and and your classes at nine on Saturday morning?'

'No,' Francis replied, sounding bored.

'Were you and Scott close?'

'Sometimes.'

'Did you ever fall out?'

'Occasionally.'

'How about last week?'

The boy's eyes narrowed slightly. 'I assume you've heard we had an argument and you're fishing for more information. Why don't you just come straight out and ask me?'

Lawrence found Francis's attitude disconcerting. He was no stranger to challenges to his authority, but he hadn't expected to be questioned quite so rudely by a seventeen-year-old public schoolboy. He had trouble keeping his tone reasonable as he said, 'All right. One of the boys on your corridor told me you threatened to kill Scott during an argument last week. What was that about?'

'I was angry. I didn't mean it.'

'What was the argument about?'

'That's none of your business.'

'Well I'm sorry, but I disagree. Answer the question.'

'No.'

'No?'

'You provide me with a single bit of evidence I had anything to do with what happened to Scott, and I'll tell you. Until then, you've no right to pry into my personal affairs.'

'Francis, I'm not here to be told what is or isn't relevant to this investigation. If you won't cooperate, you may find yourself in a great deal of trouble.'

Francis entangled the fingers of his left hand with those of his right, saying nothing.

'What was the fight about?' Lawrence pressed.

'It's personal.'

'Well I'm sorry about that, but –'

Francis looked at his watch. 'I'm supposed to be in class now.'

Lawrence sighed. He had no way of knowing whether the boy was telling the truth, and, making a mental note to find out, dismissed him. As Francis gathered up his belongings and stood to go, Lawrence leaned back in his chair, wondering how he would have dealt with losing a friend at age seventeen in such terrible circumstances. Glancing across the table, his eyes alighted on the book which Francis had been studying prior to the interview.

The chapter was headed 'An A to Z of Poisons and Forensic Detection', and Lawrence reached to close the tome, expecting it to be a chemistry text. It wasn't. *Toxicology and Forensic Science.* He wondered what that was doing in a school library, and cast his eyes around for the librarian who had first pointed Francis out to him. She had disappeared, and, curious, Lawrence noted down the book's title and author. Having done so, he got to his feet, wondering whether he would have much luck locating any other pupils in the middle of a Monday afternoon. He decided to return to Windsor House: were none of the other sixth formers about, he would devote some time to a study of the building. Had Scott left the house after the main door was locked, Lawrence would need to establish how he had done so – and whether all pupils could exit by the same route.

When Guy Markham opened his front door to Rebecca, she immediately placed him as the young man who had been in Curt's bedroom earlier that afternoon. On this occasion, he was in his dressing gown and looked flustered. 'Hello?'

'Hello. I'm Detective Sergeant Palmer – I'd like to ask you a few questions.'

'Can't it wait? I'm about to have a shower.'

'It won't take long.'

'Oh – uh – well, I suppose you'd better come in a minute, then.' He stood back from the door to allow her to enter his small living room. It was attractively decorated, but so meticulously clean and tidy that Rebecca felt immediately uncomfortable. Guy held out a hand towards the sofa. 'Please – sit down.'

Rebecca did as bid. 'Mr Markham, I'd –'

'Guy, please,' he put in, sitting in an armchair that was set at an angle to the sofa.

'I'd like to start with what you were doing on Friday night,' Rebecca finished, ignoring the interruption.

'Nothing much. I had a couple of drinks with a colleague after dinner, then I came back here. I read for a while, then went to bed.'

Rebecca raised her eyebrows. 'Vivien Thompson said you dropped into the sanatorium to visit Curt shortly after ten.'

Guy's cheeks flushed. 'Ah. Yes. I dropped in to see her, really. Curt was my excuse for doing so.'

'Oh, I see. Are you and she involved?'

'No. Not for want of trying,' he smiled ruefully.

Rebecca couldn't help thinking Vivien seemed a bit old for him. Guy didn't look much over twenty-five, although she guessed he was probably nearer thirty. Then again, if their ages had been reversed, she probably wouldn't have thought twice about the difference. She wondered what that said about her own prejudices.

'How long were you there?'

'Not long – maybe ten minutes? Viv seemed to have her hands full, so I left her to it.'

'What did you do afterwards?'

'I headed back here.'

'Did you see anything suspicious?'

Guy shook his head. 'It was all very quiet. I think most of the boys were in bed by that time. And if they weren't they probably should have been.'

Rebecca nodded. 'Did you know Scott Ribet?'

'Not really.'

'Have you never taught him?'

'I've only been here since last April. Scott didn't study A-level biology. I knew who he was, but not much more.'

'But you do know his next-door neighbour. Curt.'

'Yes. He's in my upper-sixth biology class.'

'Do you know him well?'

'As well as I know any pupil here, I suppose. He's a nice boy. Very polite.'

'You were in his bedroom earlier today.'

'I've been going over some statistics with him. He's not been well and he's missed several classes.'

'Are you getting paid for that?'

'The amount people pay to send their kids here, I think they expect any extra tuition that might be required to be free of charge.'

'So you aren't getting paid.'

'No, I most certainly am not.'

'What did you and Curt talk about on Friday night?'

'Not much, really – he wasn't feeling well and he was very tired. I looked in to see how he was, chatted for a bit – that's all.'

'You must have talked about something for ten minutes.'

Guy sighed. 'Curt was worried about Fray. That's his room mate.'

'Why was he worried?'

'Fray's rather unstable. Erratic. Sharing a room with him can't be easy.'

'Do you know him well?'

'No, but I've heard quite a bit about him – he's a concern to the staff as well.'

'I see.'

'That's more or less all I remember us discussing – other than how Curt was. After that I left him in peace.'

'Ok,' Rebecca pushed herself up off the sofa. 'I'll let you get that shower. Thanks for your time.'

Guy stood to see her out. 'Sorry I couldn't help more. I hope you're able to clear things up quickly. It's all very unsettling for the boys, as you can imagine,' he reached for the door handle. 'And for the rest of us, if I'm honest,' he admitted, after a moment. 'It's been a tough twenty-four hours. I don't think any of us really knows how to approach the situation.' He paused. 'It's hardly something they prepare you for when you do your PGCE.'

Three

The porter's lodge was at the end of the drive, just inside the school's main gates. Its red bricks and sash windows matched those of the school's other buildings, and the garden would have benefited from the ministrations of the school's groundsmen. The night porter himself – who introduced himself as Jack Radcliffe – was around Lawrence's own age. For some reason, Lawrence had expected him to be older. Tall and athletic, with thinning dark hair and a Freddie Mercury moustache, he wore a rather flamboyant orange Hawaiian-style shirt and black trousers. Lawrence presumed it wasn't his work attire.

The front door of the cottage opened directly onto the living room, and the bulk of the small space was occupied by two expansive navy armchairs and a coffee table that was heavy in both colour and size. Beyond the table, a German shepherd lay curled up on the hearth. It opened one eye as Lawrence entered, looked him over and, apparently finding him of little interest, returned to its slumber. The mantlepiece above the unlit fire was cluttered with ethnic souvenirs from far-flung destinations – a carved wooden elephant, a painted boomerang, a miniature totem pole – and the tribal theme continued on the terracotta walls, which were hung with wooden masks, spears and the like, and in the animal-skin drums clustered in the corners of the room. Lawrence felt surprised the school hadn't had something to say about the weapons among the collection. Perhaps the staff and governors didn't have any cause to visit the lodge.

'Interesting collection,' he observed, sitting in one of the armchairs.

'My grandfather's,' Jack replied, perching on the other chair and leaning to scratch the dog's head. 'He was an anthropologist. Had a lot of stories to tell.'

'I bet.'

'I imagine you have a few, as well.'

'One or two. Although right now I'm more interested in what you might be able to tell me.'

'I'm not sure I can be much help,' Jack admitted. 'I didn't really notice anything amiss on Friday night.'

'What time do you start work?'

'Ten. I make regular patrols through 'til six.'

'How regular?'

'I do a circuit that takes in the quad – inside and out – the chapel, the boarding houses and the staff quarters at least once an hour.'

'Are your movements regular enough that someone might be able to predict when and where you might be?'

Jack seemed to considered the question before saying, 'To a point, perhaps. I don't always walk the same route, but obviously I can't be everywhere at once and I do take breaks.'

'Presumably you take the dog with you?'

'Yes. Although she wasn't with me on Friday night.'

'Why not?'

'She was at the vet Thursday through 'til Sunday. Managed to get her paws on some chocolate.'

'Where did she get that from?'

'I don't know. At a guess she scavenged it in the woods when I let her off for a run after we finished work on Thursday morning. The boys drop all sorts out there. I should have been more careful.'

'You don't think someone might have poisoned her intentionally?'

'It did cross my mind,' Jack admitted. 'After Friday night, that is. But I thought maybe I was being paranoid.'

'When did you first realise something was wrong?'

'I woke up to her vomiting – about two p.m., I think.'

Lawrence made a mental note to check how long chocolate poisoning took to take effect. 'Had you been with her all day?'

'Give or take. I popped out at about seven to pick up a few things from the farm shop because they're only open 'til noon – then came home and went to bed.'

'Is that – the trip to the farm – something you do regularly?'

'Every week.'

'Who else has a key to this place?'

'Only the caretaker, as far as I know. Although there's probably another copy somewhere in the school. I'm not sure you'd need one, though – Heidi has free run of the garden several times a day, so all it would take would be for someone to lob something over the fence.'

Lawrence nodded. 'Going back to Friday night, did you see anyone at all during your shift?'

'I saw a lot of boys around the boarding houses in the first hour – lights out isn't until eleven for the sixth form. After that I saw a few members of staff, but nobody else.'

'Which members of staff?'

'Um – Ted Latimer, Diane Richardson, Charles Nicholls and Davide Awde.' Jack counted them off on his fingers.

'Can you give me some idea of what each of them was doing and what time you saw them?'

'Smoking, mostly. Apart from Davide. He'd been out somewhere, I saw him come through the gates at about half twelve. He gave me a wave as he drove past.'

'And where do the staff smoke?'

'In the garden around the back of the staff quarters.'

'What was the latest you saw anyone out there?'

'Ted was out just before one. He asked where Heidi was and we chatted for a few minutes. The next time I passed, all the lights were out.'

'Did you see any lights on after that?'

'Not until quarter to six. And there are usually a few lights on by that time.'

'Did you hear anything?'

'I hear a lot most nights. The countryside isn't nearly as quiet as a lot of people seem to think.'

'Anything unusual,' Lawrence clarified.

'No. Well – not at the time,' Jack responded, his tone such that Lawrence guessed he hadn't finished. After a moment he added, 'Things always seem different with hindsight.'

'What did you hear?'

'I assumed it was a badger. I hear them quite often.'

'What did you hear?' Lawrence persisted.

'Well animals make all sorts of noises, but –' Jack paused. 'Badgers sometimes –' he hesitated. 'Sometimes they scream.'

Rebecca knocked on the doors of rooms 320 and 325, getting no response on either occasion. When she tried 326, a voice called, 'Come in.'

'Hello,' she greeted the broad, athletic teenager sprawled on one of the beds, a book in his hands. 'I'm Detective Sergeant Palmer. You are?'

'Sid Watson.' The boy sat up, closing the book.

'I'd like to ask you a few questions, if you don't have to get to dinner.'

'Dinner's not until six – I've a few minutes. Sit down if you like.'

Rebecca sat on a chair that stood in the centre of the room, looking around herself and wondering whether the housemaster was aware of the state the room was in. Clothes were strewn across the floor, interspersed with paper and books, and the air smelled of mud and unwashed sports clothing.

'To begin with, there's a rumour going around that you and Scott Ribet had a fight last week. Is that true?'

'Who told you that?'

'I don't think that matters. Is it true?'

'No. Just a Chinese whisper.'

'Based on what?'

'A group of us were out in town on the last afternoon of half term, and Scott and I got into a ruck with a couple of local chaps. I think there were a few mutterings about a fight, and since Scott and I were both looking a bit worse for wear people jumped to conclusions.'

'What was the fight about?'

'Oh – I don't know, really. Just one of those situations where ragging gets a bit out of hand and you want to save face. You know.'

'Where were you?'

'A pub in town. With some other members of the rugby team.'

'Did you see a lot of Scott off the rugby pitch?'

'A fair bit, yeah.'

'When did you see him last?'

'Friday evening.'

'What time?'

'About half ten. When everyone was getting ready for bed.'

'Did he say anything to indicate he might have been planning to leave the house that night?'

Sid shook his head.

'Do you know why he might have been out at that hour?'

'No. Usually if he'd been planning something he'd have told me.'

Rebecca nodded. 'Do you know whether he fell out with anyone recently?'

'He had a fight with Fray last week.'

'Do you know what it was about?'

'No, but –' Sid stopped as if he had been on the verge of revealing something he shouldn't.

'But what?'

He sighed. 'I'm not trying to make trouble for anyone.'

'If you know anything that could be relevant, you need to tell me.'

There was a pause before Sid replied. 'I don't know what he was referring to, but Fray yelled –' he hesitated. '*You do that and I'll fucking kill you.*'

'Are you sure you heard that correctly?' Rebecca asked, wondering whether that was what Curt had been so on edge about.

Sid nodded.

'Do you have any idea what they were arguing about?'

'No.'

'Do you think Fray was capable of following through with that threat?'

'I don't know. Maybe. Scott said last week he was so far out of his tree he was running loose in the park.'

Rebecca's eyebrows went up. 'That's rather harsh,' she observed. 'Did Fray know what Scott was saying about him?'

'Scott wasn't one to talk behind people's backs. He generally said what he thought to your face.'

'You mean he said that to Fray?'

Sid nodded.

'I was under the impression Scott and Fray were friends.'

'Some of the time they were. Usually when Scott wanted something.'

'Like what?'

'Help with work, mostly.'

'And Fray gave it to him? After what Scott had said?'

'Oh yes.'

'You're inferring that Scott used him,' Rebecca observed.

'All the time.'

'And you consider Scott to have been your friend?'

'Uh-huh.'

'Despite the fact he treated people so badly?'

'He wasn't like that with everybody. Just Fray. But that was his own fault. He should have stood up for himself more.'

'It's not always that simple, though, is it?'

'He's quite capable of doing it when it suits him.'

'I'm getting the impression he's not a friend of yours.'

'No. He's a miserable fuck-up,' Sid replied. Then, realising his language had perhaps been inappropriate, he blushed. 'Excuse my French.'

'Is there anyone else you can think of who might have wanted some harm to come to Scott?'

Sid considered the matter for a moment before shaking his head. 'No.'

'He hadn't done anything to upset anyone recently?'

'Not particularly.' Sid's eyes flickered uneasily to the clock on his desk.

'Are you wanting to get to dinner?'

'I've got a prefects' meeting at half six, and Mrs Richardson has a thing about punctuality,' he replied, awkwardly.

Rebecca could certainly empathise with that particular pressure, and excused the boy. Few things riled her superior more than lateness. Leighton's relaxed timekeeping was a constant source of irritation, as was his apparent immunity to any effort to nudge his work ethic into line with Lawrence's own. Rebecca had once observed that if Lawrence wanted someone who turned up on the dot and followed procedure to the letter, he ought to ask for Roddy: Lawrence had replied that working with an inveterate jobsworth didn't offer a solution, just a different problem, and that he'd rather get first-rate assistance late than not at all. Rebecca suspected he was far from the only one who felt that way; no doubt that was what lay at the root of Roddy's animosity towards Leighton. Sooner or later, she imagined that situation would come to a head. She wasn't at all sure she wanted to be there when it did.

Lawrence's first thought on seeing the IN/OUT slide on the housemaster's study door was what a nuisance it must be having to change it every time you left the room for five minutes. His second thought, when his knock at the door went unanswered, was that if the sign wasn't going to be used properly it ought not to be used at all. He sighed, then, out of irritation, knocked again.

'All right, all right, one minute!' A voice snapped. Moments later, the door was jerked open by a portly man in his fifties who regarded Lawrence crossly over narrow spectacles. His greying hair was brushed across his forehead in an effort to disguise his receding hairline, and his face was flushed in a manner that led Lawrence to suspect he was a heavy drinker. The lack of hair on his head was compensated for by an ample beard, which could have done with a trim. On coming face to face with Lawrence, he attempted to temper his glare.

'Good evening,' he greeted, gruffly.

'Evening. I'm DCI Forrester. Do you have five minutes?'

'Certainly,' the man forced a smile. 'I'm Dr Quast, Edward Quast. Come in.' He stood back from the door to allow Lawrence to enter his study. Bookshelves heavy with old, hardback tomes lined the walls, and Lawrence suspected the dark wooden furniture was antique. The desk was huge, and Edward made his way to the seat behind it, waving Lawrence to one on the near side as if he were a pupil.

'What can I do to help?'

'If you could run me through what you did and who you saw on Friday night, that would be a good start.'

Edward nodded. 'From what time?'

'Tenish.'

'Oh – from then until about one I was either chasing pupils into bed, or else checking they were still there. After that I went to bed myself.'

'Did you notice anything out of the ordinary?'

Edward looked thoughtful. 'No, not that I can think of. Scott was certainly in bed when I went up to do my last check at one.'

'Are you sure about that?'

'Yes. I had to tell him and Dominic off – they were talking. Arguing, I think.'

'Dominic?'

'Scott's room mate. Dominic Greenwood.'

'He told me he wasn't here on Friday night. Said he had early exeat to go to an art exhibition.'

Edward raised his eyebrows, pursing his lips. 'I'm sure he would have liked that, but we don't grant exeats early. Especially not to Dominic.'

'Oh?'

'He's a compulsive liar, Chief Inspector. I'm sorry if he's been wasting your time, someone ought to have warned you. He wouldn't know the truth if he fell over it.'

'Do you know why he tells so many lies?'

'I've no idea. I've really had it up to my back teeth – I've been his housemaster for over four years, and it's beyond infuriating.'

'He also mentioned that his father died in a climbing accident, is that true?'

'Did he?' The housemaster gave a self-satisfied smile. 'This is exactly what I'm talking about. Marcus Greenwood is a personal friend of Donald's and he sits on the board of governors, which is fortunate for Dominic because otherwise it's unlikely he would still be a pupil here.'

'So Nicky was here on Friday night.'

'Yes. In bed at eleven, same as everybody else.'

'And Scott and Nicky were definitely both in their room at one?'

'Yes.'

'Do you know what they were arguing about?'

'No. I can't even say for sure that they were arguing. I didn't hang about to eavesdrop, I just warned them that there would be trouble if they didn't shut up and go to sleep.'

'Was that the last time you saw Scott?'

'Yes. I was told what had happened shortly before dinner on Saturday – I had to break the news to the boys on Scott's corridor.'

'How did Nicky take it?'

'He seemed shell-shocked. I think most of the boys were, to be honest.'

'Would that include Francis Bircham?'

'Francis? Who knows. He's a law unto himself, that one.'

From his tone, Lawrence gathered Edward disliked the boy.

'Not one of your favourite pupils, I take it.'

'Problem kids are never my favourite pupils. They take up an inordinate amount of my time.'

'What is the problem with Francis, exactly?'

'Who knows. He flatly refuses to eat, and there isn't a lot I can do about it. If he won't eat nobody can make him.'

'Do you have any idea why he doesn't eat?'

'None at all. I've just about run out of patience with him. He's recently taken to skipping classes and failing to hand in work –

and he gets away with it because apparently he's depressed and we're expected to be sympathetic.' There was contempt in his voice, and Lawrence guessed he didn't believe depression existed.

'Is he having treatment for that?'

'He's been prescribed antidepressants, but he won't take them.'

'Why not?'

'God only knows. I've long since given up trying to force them on him. If he won't help himself I don't see why I should.'

Lawrence nodded.

'Have you spoken to him yet?'

'I had a brief chat with him earlier, but I didn't get much out of him.'

'That figures. Francis is exceptionally intelligent, as well as devious and manipulative. I expect he probably cried and looked lost, and you ended up feeling very sorry for him. Would that be correct?'

'No, actually,' Lawrence replied, thinking the description didn't much fit the boy he had met earlier in the afternoon. 'He was quite abrupt. Hostile, even.'

'Really?' Edward responded, clearly surprised.

'From what I've gathered, he and Scott had a rather strained friendship – if that's what you can call it – can you tell me much about that?'

'In all honesty, I don't know an awful lot about relations between the boys,' Edward admitted. 'Although he and Scott did have a very heated argument last week. They were screaming at one another. I told them off in no uncertain terms.'

'Can you remember when that was?'

'Wednesday evening. Around seven-thirty.'

'Do you know what it was about?'

'No. I wasn't interested in explanations or excuses – I simply issued them each with a disciplinary slip. Neither of them turned up to see me on Saturday morning when they ought to have received punishment – Scott for obvious reasons. I never got the chance to tackle Francis about it, because by the time I caught up with him, the news about Scott was out, and I had more important things to worry about.'

'I can appreciate that,' Lawrence replied. 'Could you give me some idea of what Scott was like?'

'A fairly typical high-spirited sixth-form pupil, really. He didn't work especially hard, but he generally got work in for deadlines and turned up to his classes. He was a keen sportsman, very outgoing – a bit rowdy at times, and he had his fair share of tickings off – but never for anything particularly outrageous.'

'Did you like him?'

'I didn't dislike him.'

'Have you ever caught him out of the house at night?'

'No, but that doesn't mean he's never been out. I can't stay up all night policing the boys – I have to get to bed myself.'

'How about other pupils?'

'There have been a few occasions when I've caught boys sneaking in or out, yes.'

'What punishment did you impose?'

'Punishments depend on the circumstances. I was once forced to suspend three fifth-form boys for a week, but that was because I not only caught them out of the building, but drinking and smoking behind the chapel. Quite why Scott was out in the woods on Friday night I would dearly love to know.'

'Do you have any idea how he might have left the building?'

Edward sighed. 'From some of the bedrooms it's possible to climb onto the fire escape from the window, and there's only so much we can do to ensure the boys aren't able to do that. It's something of a catch twenty-two, because if we were to put bars on the windows and there was a fire, it's possible they would be trapped. A number of years ago there was a serious fire in Bailey House and several pupils did have to escape through a window – all I can do is impose spot checks in the early hours of the morning to put them off.'

'How regularly do you do that?'

'Every week or two. Last year I caught several boys out by checking on two consecutive nights, and I think that made the rest of them think twice. But, to be perfectly honest, there are always going to be boys who break the rules, and there are always going to be a few who don't get caught. Perhaps Scott's death will bring home to them that we don't lock them in to spite them, we do it for their own safety. Even so, I doubt it will have a lasting effect.'

Lawrence suspected he was right. As with every danger in life, most people tended to adopt the attitude *it won't happen to me*, and he didn't imagine this would be any different.

*****

Leighton was waiting in the front room of the guest house when Rebecca and Lawrence returned shortly after seven, working his way through the cryptic crossword in *The Times*. He had, Lawrence noticed, already completed all three Sudoku squares. Above the cut that ran through his eyebrow, a large bruise now extended up his forehead.

'Bloody hell,' Lawrence remarked, as he sat in an armchair across the coffee table from the one Leighton had claimed. 'What did you do? Headbutt the boot?'

Leighton grinned. 'I know. I really should make up some story about how the other guy came off. Boost my street cred.' He tossed the newspaper onto the table and tucked his pen behind his ear. 'Then again, you lot would probably have me up for GBH.'

'Do you not fancy prison food?' Lawrence joked.

'Well I'm not fussy, but I promised Mum I'd be back for tea and she'll have me shot if I spoil my appetite.' He glanced at his watch. 'And on that note, I need to get a wriggle on. Although I don't imagine this'll take long, I've toss all that wasn't in the original pathologist's preliminary report.'

'So you concur on cause of death.'

'Yep. Massive haemorrhaging from a tear in the aorta, inflicted with a six-inch blade. There are four other wounds, but that's the one that would have killed him. And pretty quickly at that.'

'How quickly?'

'Probably within a few minutes.'

'Would he have been able to make much noise?'

'Initially, perhaps. Did anyone hear anything?'

'The night porter said he heard what sounded like screams – he thinks some time between two and three – but says he assumed it was a badger.'

'Well, to be fair, given the location that's statistically a lot more likely than someone being stabbed to death,' Leighton observed.

'But is it plausible? Do badgers' screams sound anything like those of humans?'

'They can do. Creepily so,' Leighton raised his eyebrows for emphasis. 'Could put you off camping for life. As if sleeping in a tent wasn't enough to do that.'

Lawrence nodded. He wasn't a fan of camping, either. 'While we're on the subject of animals, do you know much about dogs? Or, more specifically, dogs and chocolate poisoning?'

'You do realise I'm a doctor, not a vet, don't you?' Leighton joked.

'If you don't know it would be quicker if you could just say so,' Lawrence returned, his tone sharper than he had intended. It hadn't taken long to forget Leighton was doing them a favour. Fortunately he didn't seem to take offence, instead opting to answer the original question.

'It's caused by an alkaloid called theobromine. In high concentrations it's also toxic to humans, but you'd have to eat a hell of a lot of chocolate for it to kill you. Whereas in dogs, a small amount of good quality dark chocolate can be fatal.'

'How long does it take to set in?'

'Usually you'd see symptoms within a few hours, but it can take longer.'

'Does it often happen accidentally?'

'All the time. Dogs will eat anything. It's really common at Christmas, when people tend to have a lot of chocolate lying around. Why?'

'The night porter has a German shepherd he usually takes out on patrol, but she was at the vet on Friday night being treated for chocolate poisoning. He wasn't sure whether she'd found something discarded by one of the boys or whether it was malicious. If it was the latter, it would mean the attack on Scott was premeditated.'

'Either is possible. And I suspect you're never going to know.'

'You're probably right,' Lawrence sighed. 'How about the knife used to kill Scott, is there any sign of that?'

'Nope.'

'How strong do you think his assailant would have needed to be?' Rebecca asked.

'Not particularly so. He was attacked from behind, and there are no defensive wounds indicating any kind of struggle, so I suspect he didn't have a chance to put up a fight. I don't think you're going to be able to narrow things down much on that basis, if that's the question.'

'It was a specific case I was thinking of, actually. I spoke to Vivien – the matron – to try to corroborate what one of the boys told me, and she said she didn't think he'd be strong enough because he's severely asthmatic.'

Leighton shrugged. 'So was I as a teenager, but if it was bad enough that I couldn't walk half a mile and shove a knife in an unsuspecting victim, then no way was I well enough to be at school either.'

'Did you make a habit of that?' Rebecca teased.

'I tried, but stabbing people in the back didn't really do it for me. Probably why I didn't go into politics.'

'Did you have a chance to look over the crime scene?' Lawrence enquired.

'What was left of it. After more than forty-eight hours and yesterday's rain there wasn't a lot to see. Lovely grounds, though. Looks more like a five-star hotel than a school.'

'Probably costs about as much per night, too,' Rebecca observed. 'The parents must have pretty deep pockets.'

'Unlike our murder victim,' Lawrence replied. 'He doesn't seem to have spent much at all.'

'Perhaps he didn't have a lot of money.'

'According to his bank statements, he had an awful lot. He's been paying in substantial sums every week since at least the end of September. Two of his friends mentioned he was cagey about his finances – I wouldn't be at all surprised if he was blackmailing somebody.'

'How about drug dealing?'

'Possible, I suppose, but I'm not sure he'd make this much money in a school – we're talking as much as five hundred a week.'

'If he was dealing pot, maybe,' Rebecca replied. 'But something like coke would be a higher price range.'

Lawrence nodded, thinking back to his interview with Francis. He felt certain the boy was on something, and if Scott had been supplying it that might have formed the basis of the argument they'd had the week before.

'Let's face it, those kids can probably afford it,' Rebecca added.

'True enough.'

'Would you like me to go over the kid's bedroom?' Leighton asked. 'That might shed some light on the matter.'

'Can't hurt,' Lawrence nodded. 'Although we'll need to clear that with the school and Nicky – the room mate. I also need to find somebody who can trawl Scott's computer.'

'I can have a look if you like,' Leighton offered.

'Are you qualified to do that?'

'I can manage data recovery and I can read. Unless you think the kid's the next Gary McKinnon that's probably sufficient.'

'All right,' Lawrence agreed. 'Thank you.' He looked to Rebecca. 'There are a number of boys I still want to interview, and a couple I'd like to talk to for a second time. But I think the first thing we ought to do in the morning is pay a visit to Scott's parents.'

'Whereabouts do they live?'

'Totteridge, North London.'

'Fifteen minutes from my flat by tube. Good of them to let us know before dragging us all the way up here,' Rebecca grumbled.

'I know, I know,' Lawrence acknowledged. 'It's not ideal.'

'Aw, cheer up, it could be worse,' Leighton put in. 'There's a little pub just down the road from here that's just crying out for a visit.' He moved to stand. 'Sadly, I have to get off. But someone really ought to check they're not watering down the gin or serving past time, or anything like that.'

'I'm surprised you haven't yet managed to find the time,' Lawrence observed, drily.

'Oh come on,' Leighton returned. 'You can't expect me to do all the work. Do you have any idea how many pubs there are in Yorkshire?' He broke into a grin, reaching for the leather jacket that hung over the back of the armchair he had just vacated and fishing his car keys from his jeans pocket with his other hand. 'Even Father Christmas couldn't get round *all* of them in one night.'

Four

The beautifully manicured gardens surrounding the drive that swept up to Scott's family home reminded Lawrence of those at the school. The house, a large, attractive early-twentieth-century building set back from the road, was similarly grand, and Lawrence wondered what Scott's parents did for a living. A black Daimler was parked towards the end of the drive, and to the left of the building he could see a tennis court. He half expected to be received by a housekeeper or a butler. As it was, the door was opened rather hesitantly by a tired-looking man in his fifties, dressed in old navy trousers and a casual short-sleeved shirt. He regarded Lawrence and Rebecca with a suspicious frown.

'Yes?'

'Mr Ribet?' Lawrence enquired.

'Yes.'

'I'm DCI Forrester and –'

Before he had the chance to introduce Rebecca, the man interrupted with, 'Oh – I'm sorry – we've had rather a lot of visits from the media. Please, come in.'

The front door led onto an enormous foyer, with a wide central staircase and a stunning chandelier hanging from the ceiling. Julian Ribet led Rebecca and Lawrence through a doorway to the right and into a light, airy drawing room, tastefully decorated in pastel blue and white. The mantelpiece held a collection of photographs, mostly of Scott and a pretty pre-teen girl, whom Lawrence guessed was his sister, and the sideboard was scattered with silver trophies.

'Please – have a seat. Can I get you anything?'

'No, thank you,' Lawrence sat on the sofa. 'I'm sorry to have to put you through this now, but we'd like to ask a few questions about Scott.'

Julian nodded, perching in an armchair. 'You don't need to speak to my wife as well, do you?' He asked, anxiously. 'She's sleeping – the doctor gave her some pills –'

'I'm sure you can tell us everything we need to know,' Lawrence assured him.

'Let's make a start, then.'

'Was Scott happy at school?'

'Loved it. Couldn't wait to get back at the start of each term – I sometimes found it slightly insulting that he didn't want to come home.'

'Did he see many of his friends over the holidays?'

'Oh yes. A couple of them live in London, so he was out with them a good deal of the time – and he had friends to stay, visited others –'

'So you'd be able to name his close friends for us, I imagine.'

Julian nodded. 'He had several pals from rugby – Oli, Sid, Damon – and then there was his room mate, Nicky. He's trouble, that one.'

'Oh?' Lawrence raised his eyebrows.

'Not in a bad way – I meant he's always up to mischief. Scott thought he was great, because he could always be relied upon to do something wild.'

'Any other names you can think of?'

'There was Mark, and –' Julian paused. 'Actually, I don't think Mark's still at Treelore. I think he was in the year above Scott.'

'How about Curt?' Rebecca asked.

'Oh, yes, of course. He's visited us quite a few times – very well-read lad. Particularly when it came to philosophy. He and Scott would have sat up half the night debating different aspects of one tenet or another given half the chance.'

'And Fray?'

'Who?'

'Fray,' Rebecca repeated.

Julian looked blank. 'That's an odd name. I don't think I've heard it before.'

'It's a nickname. His full name is Francis,' Lawrence explained.

'That doesn't ring any bells either – but then I suppose Scott probably had a lot of friends who didn't get mentioned so often. We mostly saw Sid, Nicky, Curt and Mark.' He paused, then added, 'We had organised a dinner party for his eighteenth birthday – that would have been over Easter. I could give you the list of those he invited, if that would be of any use?'

Lawrence confirmed that it would, and Julian stood and hurried from the room, obviously anxious to help.

'He doesn't seem too cut up about it, does he?' Rebecca remarked, quietly.

'I expect it hasn't fully hit him yet,' Lawrence replied.

'Perhaps not.'

'You sound doubtful.'

Rebecca shrugged.

Lawrence turned to look out of the window, 'I do like this bit of London. Plenty of green space.'

'You're not thinking of moving, are you?'

'In my imagination, maybe. If the kids weren't settled at school and stamp duty wasn't daylight robbery.'

Rebecca nodded.

'I don't –'

'Here you go,' Julian said, as he re-entered the room, a slip of paper in his hand. 'I've crossed out some of the names, because they were friends of Scott's from his prep school in London. None of them is at Treelore, as far as I know. There were eight boys he invited from there.' Julian handed Lawrence the list. Scanning it, he noticed with interest that Francis's name didn't appear.

'Had Scott invited them yet?'

'Yes – a couple of weeks ago. He was getting quite excited.'

Lawrence nodded, folding the list and pocketing it before moving on to a different subject. 'Would you mind telling me how much money you gave Scott by way of an allowance?'

'Two hundred pounds a month. He regularly complained it wasn't enough, but –' Julian sighed heavily. 'I don't think it's right to give kids a vast amount of money just because you have the means to do so. Otherwise you're providing them with a standard of living they may never be able to replicate, and you're not teaching them anything about the value of money.' He paused, then went on, 'I think parents have some responsibility to do that. Especially since I am very aware of what it's like to live on a tight budget. Until Scott was seven, I was earning very little, and we didn't buy anything we didn't need. I was of the opinion fifty pounds a week was sufficient, Scott disagreed, but I wasn't giving him more just because Nicky's father handed out bank notes like Smarties.'

'Do you think money is something of a status symbol at the school?'

'To a point I think it is everywhere, but I suppose when you're at a school like Treelore it must be, because you've got to be well off to afford the fees. I don't want you to get the impression we were mean with Scott – if he wanted more money for something in particular I wasn't opposed to giving it to him. I paid for him to go on tour with the rugby team last year, and for a trip to New York with Nicky over the summer.' Rubbing his forehead with the fingers of his right hand, Julian continued, 'I think Nicky was the problem, to be honest. I don't think his father has any time for him, so he just gives him anything he wants to keep him quiet. Last time Nicky came to visit he was asking me what he ought to invest in, and I remember Scott's ears pricking up at that.'

'Do you think that was genuine?' Lawrence asked, feeling sceptical.

'I didn't think to question it. It wasn't as if it seemed unlikely. The kid lives on the Bishops Avenue, and his father has apartments in Paris, New York, Rome – you name it. I'm well off, but I'm not a billionaire. Marcus Greenwood is.'

'Do you know him?'

'Not well, but I've met him on a couple of occasions when I've dropped Scott at Nicky's home in Hampstead.'

'Do you have any idea what the other boys were given as pocket money?'

Julian shook his head. 'Nicky was Scott's room mate, and probably his closest friend as well, so I think what Nicky had was what really mattered. I'm sure there are others in the year who had more than Scott, but I'm sure there are also a lot who didn't.'

'Aside from money, was there anything at school that Scott was worried about?'

'Not that I know of. He always seemed to be having a good time whenever we spoke to him.'

'Have you any idea why he might have been in the woods in the middle of the night?'

'No, but I can appreciate there's always an element of fun to breaking the rules when you're away at boarding school. Last year he and Nicky made beer in their room, and Scott was very pleased with himself because they didn't get caught.' Julian lowered his eyes, adding sadly, 'Scott admired Nicky because he had the nerve to do just about anything, and I got the feeling he wanted to impress him. I don't know if that has anything to do with it, but it's only explanation I can come up with for what Scott might have been doing out.'

'Do you think it's possible he was taking drugs?'

'No I do not,' Julian snapped, defensively. 'What sort of delinquent do you think my son was? He may have flouted the odd school rule, but he certainly wouldn't have broken the law!'

'I'm sorry, I didn't mean to suggest he would, it's just a question we have to ask.'

'I never had any reports from his teachers about him misbehaving. Although I know Nicky did. Frankly, I think he just wanted some attention, and he was willing to do just about anything to get it.'

'Because he wasn't getting it at home, you mean.'

'Exactly. I think his father sent him away to school to get him out of the way, and as a result, he plays up. He's a nice enough boy, but I think he was probably a bad influence on Scott, and I suspect he's broken just about every rule that school has.'

Lawrence nodded, remembering what Dr Quast had said about Nicky's still being a pupil because his father was a friend of the headmaster's. That certainly inferred he was a troublemaker, a suggestion backed up by the string of blatant lies he had fed Lawrence the day before. Lawrence wondered what information Donald Chadwick would be able – or willing – to provide about the boy. He was certainly keen to know what lengths Nicky might go to for attention.

Curt tracked the circular path of his alarm clock's second hand, watching it whittle away his lunch break one increment at a time. He felt faint, whether through lack of sleep or lack of food he wasn't sure. He had lain awake all night, hearing the same seventeen words again and again, and hadn't been able to face breakfast or lunch. How he was going to make it through the afternoon, he couldn't imagine. Lights out seemed a lifetime away.

The door opened and Francis appeared. 'Hey,' he greeted, tossing his blazer over his desk before looking in Curt's direction and frowning in concern. 'Are you ok?'

Curt shook his head.

'Do you want me to get someone? Dr Quast, or matron, or –'

'No,' Curt answered, quickly. He couldn't run the risk of getting sent home. Not now.

'Are you sure?' Francis perched on the bed opposite him. 'You look awful. What's wrong?'

Curt reached into the inside pocket of his blazer and drew out the slip of paper he'd come across the night before. He handed it to Francis and watched his friend's face as he read the single sentence written in the centre of the page. His expression barely changed. Several seconds after Curt knew he had finished reading, Francis raised his eyes. He looked uneasy, but there was no sign of the shock Curt had expected – or perhaps hoped – to see.

'Did you *know*?' Curt managed, at length, his voice unsteady.

There was a pause before Francis nodded.

Curt swallowed. 'How long?'

'What does that matter?'

'*How long?*'

Francis sighed. 'Only since Wednesday.'

'And you didn't –' Curt stopped as two and two suddenly made four. His heart jumped. 'Is that why –' he broke off again, raising a hand to his mouth. He felt sick.

Francis nodded.

'And you let me wash my hands of it when –'

'No,' Francis interrupted, firmly. 'That was my bargain, not yours. You're not responsible for my choices.'

'Why didn't you tell me?'

'I didn't want you to feel obligated. Like I said, it was –'

A knock at the door stopped him short. Curt willed him not to answer. Seemingly picking up on this, Francis raised his eyebrows expectantly. Curt shook his head. Francis gave a single, perfunctory nod, standing and going to the door. He pulled it open and leaned against it. 'Hi.'

A familiar voice returned the greeting before asking, 'Is Curt here?'

Curt held his breath.

'No,' Francis returned, shortly.

'Who were you talking to just now?'

'I was on the phone.'

'Do you know where Curt is?'

Francis shrugged. 'Lunch?'

'Tried that, no go. Any other ideas?'

'I'm not his keeper. Call his mobile.'

'It's switched off. I'm really concerned about him – in class this morning he looked dreadful.'

'Well then maybe he's gone to the san.'

'Maybe, yes. Look, if you see him, could you please ask him to call me?'

'Sure.'

'Thanks.'

Francis closed the door and stood motionless behind it, his fingers on the handle. He met Curt's eyes, saying nothing. Some seconds later, he eased the door open six inches and peered out. Closing it for a second time, he observed, matter-of-factly, 'You're going to have to speak to him sooner or later.'

'I know,' Curt nodded, drawing a deep breath, which immediately set him off coughing. 'I know,' he repeated, when he managed to stop, reaching for the inhaler that lay on the shelf by the bed. He didn't need Francis to tell him he couldn't run away from the truth forever, but at present he hadn't a clue how to tackle the situation. How could he even begin to voice his thoughts when he had no clear idea of what they were? He wasn't accustomed to feeling out of control, and the experience was terrifying. Thus far, he had veered between a sense of unreality and blind panic, and hadn't come close to reaching the decision he knew he would be forced to make before long. And, in what seemed like a modern twist on *Macbeth*, as he struggled to hold himself together Francis appeared to have been infused with an unexpected sense of purpose. For the first time in a long while, Curt envied him.

There had been a serious accident on the A1, and Rebecca and Lawrence spent some time sitting in traffic jams during their return to Yorkshire, so it was almost five o'clock by the time they finally arrived back at Treelore Grammar. Donald Chadwick looked as if he'd had a similarly trying afternoon, and didn't seem pleased to have it extended by Lawrence's visit. Putting what he was doing aside rather reluctantly, he asked, 'How can I help?'

'I'd like to talk to you about Dominic Greenwood.'

'Oh?'

'Edward Quast mentioned that his father is a friend of yours.'

'That's right. We were at Oxford together.'

'He also said something along the lines of Nicky's still being here resulting directly from that.'

Donald's eyebrows rose. 'I suppose you could say that, yes.'

'I'd like to know why.'

'Nicky's caused a good deal of trouble during his time at this school. I don't think academia interests him in the slightest, and he can think of a good many things he'd rather be doing than studying here. The reason we've kept him on is that his father is well aware of this, and doesn't want Nicky to get his own way simply because he's engineered his expulsion from school. I'm inclined to agree.'

'Did Nicky get his place here on account of his father?'

Donald's eyes narrowed fractionally. 'If that's a veiled enquiry into our selection procedure, the answer would be no. Marcus put Nicky's name down, but Nicky had to go through the entrance exams and interviews the same as anyone else. He's a very bright boy, which makes it all the more frustrating when he refuses to apply himself.'

'How exactly has he caused trouble?'

'He tells no end of lies – although whether he does it for kicks or whether it's actually a pathological problem is as yet unresolved. He also shows a blatant disregard for school rules, which is the main problem.'

'For example?'

'He skips classes, he goes into town when he's not supposed to, he gets drunk in school – the crunch came last year when he was caught smoking cannabis in his room. I had him suspended for two weeks, and I don't know exactly what went on between him and his father, but he's been somewhat better behaved since.'

'Is he afraid of his father?'

'I don't know,' Donald admitted. 'He does something he shouldn't, gets sent to see me, doesn't seem to care in the least that he's in trouble, then I threaten to call his father and he gets upset and begs me not to. I'm inclined to think he does it to get out of whatever it is as much as anything, but it's hard to know for sure. I obviously don't know what goes on behind closed doors at home, and I can see that somewhere along the line Nicky has a problem – it's just hard to determine exactly what that is.'

'Have you asked him about it?'

'You can ask Nicky about a lot of things, but there's no way of knowing whether what he tells you is the truth.'

'Do you think he does it for attention?'

'I don't doubt he does.'

'How far do you think he'd go for that?'

Donald drew breath to answer, then stopped, his expression changing. 'Are you asking whether I think he would go as far as murdering his room mate?'

'Yes.'

Several seconds passed while he apparently considered this question. 'I couldn't say for sure, but Nicky doesn't tend to go out of his way to disguise his activities – he's generally quite happy to admit to them,' he answered, at length. 'He causes a lot of trouble, but he doesn't really do anyone any harm. I've never heard reports of him bullying other boys, or pressuring anyone to do something they didn't want to do – and he's never blamed anyone else for his misdemeanors. He's more of a nuisance to myself and the staff than anything.'

'A couple of members of staff have mentioned that Francis Bircham is a problem, as well.'

'Francis is more of a worry than a problem. He doesn't cause much trouble, but he's barely eating, and that's beginning to be a serious concern, because if he continues not to eat he's going to make himself ill.'

'Guy Markham referred to him as unbalanced. Would you agree with that?'

Donald's eyebrows contracted into a frown. 'What does he know about it? He's barely been here a year, and he's never taught the boy!'

'Francis isn't a general topic of conversation among the staff, then?'

'No, he most certainly is not. I strongly discourage gossip amongst the staff because I'm well aware fact has a habit of changing into fiction as different people hear and misinterpret different bits of information, and I think it's unfair on the boys if staff misunderstand a situation. I've discussed it only with Edward Quast and Francis's form and subject teachers – I don't see that it's relevant to anybody else.'

'Where do you think Guy got that impression from?'

'I don't know. I'd certainly like to.'

'Well, however he came by it, would you agree with him?'

'Not exactly, no. Francis isn't unbalanced so much as unhappy. I'm not really sure why, although I've tried talking to him. Edward would know a lot more about it.'

Lawrence nodded, already well aware of Edward Quast's opinion of the boy. He was more interested in Guy's opinion, or, more to the point, how – or why – he had formed it.

If Rebecca hadn't known from her map where the music rooms were, she would have been able to find them simply by following the music, which she could hear from the floor below. The song drifting down the corridor sounded vaguely familiar, and on arrival at the door she stopped to listen, knowing better than to interrupt. She had once, and only once, made the mistake of interrupting Astatine, and Elliot had been furious. Leaning against the wall, she tried to make out the lyrics, but the echo in the corridor made it impossible.

She didn't have to wait long, and in under a minute everything went quiet. Four pairs of eyes turned her way as she opened the door.

'Sorry – I'm looking for Francis Bircham,' she said, awkwardly. 'Would that be one of you?'

Looking irritated, a tall, thin boy with an electric guitar slung over his shoulder replied, offhandedly, 'Yeah. What d'you want?'

'I'm Detective Sergeant Palmer. I'd like a word with you.'

'*Now?*'

'Yes.'

'For fuck's sake,' he muttered.

'Could you give us five more minutes?' One of his companions asked, hesitantly. 'We've only one more song before we're done, and then we can get to dinner.'

Hoping it might improve Francis's humour, Rebecca nodded. 'All right. Mind if I stay and listen?'

'Can't you listen from outside?' The bass player enquired, timidly.

'Marty, if you can't play to one person how the hell are we going to play gigs?' Francis demanded, lifting his guitar strap over his head and putting the guitar down. Glancing at Rebecca, he said, shortly, 'Stay if you like.'

'Thanks.'

'Wake up, this is supposed to be acoustic,' Francis snapped, impatiently, looking back to his band mates, who hurriedly exchanged their electric guitars for steel string acoustic ones. Francis adjusted his microphone towards an electronic keyboard, hit a few keys to test the volume, and turned to see that the rest of the band were ready. It seemed they were. 'Ok, let's go.'

Rebecca wondered what Elliot would have made of the song. It had a mournful tone – presumably, from the little she had learned about music during the course of their relationship, it was in a minor key – and the lyrics were similarly sad. Rebecca guessed from their content that the song was about the brother Francis had lost. She was impressed that four seventeen and eighteen-year-olds could produce such a polished performance, although she didn't get a chance to congratulate them, because the moment they finished Francis turned his back to her and attacked the bassist once again. 'Every time we play that, you come in late! How many times do I have to tell you?'

'Sorry,' the unfortunate boy muttered, dropping his eyes to the floor.

'Stop apologising and get it right! And tune the fucking E string while you're at it!'

'Yeah, ok.'

Francis looked around at Rebecca. 'What do you lot want to know this time?'

'How about we go next door while the others pack up?'

Francis shrugged his consent, striding from the room. Rebecca sensed he wasn't going to be particularly cooperative, and followed him into the small room at the end of the corridor. Francis leaned against the front desk, and Rebecca sat on a stool opposite him.

'That was very good.'

'Don't take the piss,' Francis snapped, jiggling his legs backwards and forwards. Rebecca wondered whether he needed the toilet.

'I'm not.'

'What would you know about it anyway?' He retorted, scathingly.

'Quite a lot. My fiancé plays in a band.'

This revelation provoked both surprise and interest. 'Really? What's it called?'

'Astatine.'

'That's a chemical element,' Francis remarked, pushing himself away from the desk, then dropping back against it.

'That's right. Now –'

'It forms from radioactive decay but then decays itself, so it's inherently unstable,' he continued, as if she hadn't spoken, tracing shapes in the air with his left forefinger as he spoke, his words almost tripping over one another. 'That's where the name comes from. The Greek. Astatos. Which is also –'

'I'm not here for a chemistry lesson,' Rebecca interrupted, firmly. 'I need to talk to you about Scott.'

'I don't want to talk about Scott. He used me and I let him. I shouldn't have done. End of.' He pushed off from the desk again.

'Francis –'

'Fray,' he corrected.

'Ok,' Rebecca acknowledged. 'Do you know what Scott might have been doing in the woods on –'

'Taking drugs, probably. That's what he usually did out there.'

'Did you ever partake in that?' Rebecca asked, thinking the boy's impatient, restless manner more or less answered the question: thanks to a few of Elliot's friends she was all too familiar with the effects of a cocaine high.

'I'm not fucking stupid!' Francis retorted. 'Scott said addiction was an affliction of the weak and that if people couldn't use drugs sensibly they deserved to die, but everyone thinks they can handle taking stuff other people can't until it's taking them and it's not just them either, is it, Simon used to say we were going to –'

'Who's Simon?'

'My brother. He died of a heroin OD when I was eight. Simon always used to –'

'Fray, please,' Rebecca stopped him. 'I'm sorry to hear about your bother, but can we please focus on Scott? I understand you and he had an argument last Wednesday – what was that about?'

'I already told your colleague I don't want to talk about that! Why does nobody ever listen to me?'

'I'm afraid it's not optional. For one thing, you threatened to kill him, that's–'

'That doesn't mean I *did*!' Francis returned, sounding incredulous. 'I was just angry and I didn't want him to say anything! It's not even as if he took it seriously, so I don't know why anyone else would, I mean –'

'Say anything about what?'

'What?' Francis frowned, seemingly disorientated by the interruption.

'What did you not want Scott to say?'

'That's none of your business! And it's totally irrelevant, because I didn't do anything!'

'I'm afraid it isn't irrelevant. What was the argument about?'

'I don't have time for this!' Francis threw back, making for the door. Rebecca leapt up and stepped backwards against it to block his exit.

'You're going nowhere until I get an answer.'

Francis looked exasperated. His eyes flickered back and forth between Rebecca's face and the doorhandle several times before he said, 'Fine! Scott was blackmailing me, ok? Can I go now?'

'Why was he blackmailing you?'

'What does it matter?'

'How long had he been blackmailing you for?'

'Since October.'

'And how much money was involved?'

'Five hundred quid a week.'

'Did you argue about it before?'

'He said he wanted more. I already gave him all my savings and I have no way of getting any more money. Ok? Are we done?'

'Did Scott threaten to report you when you said you couldn't pay?'

Francis nodded vigorously. 'I told him I'd kill him if he did. I didn't mean it! I just didn't want him to say anything! *Now* can I go?'

'Why was Scott blackmailing you?'

'You can't keep me trapped in here!' Francis exclaimed, turning and heading for one of the windows. Guessing he wouldn't hesitate to climb out, despite the fact they were on the first floor, Rebecca stepped away from the door. Francis shot past her, yanked the door open and disappeared out into the corridor, leaving Rebecca wondering where he was heading and what he was in such a hurry to do. If, indeed, it wasn't just to avoid answering any further questions.

Lawrence was about to give up waiting for Nicky when the boy returned to his room, guitar case in his hand. On seeing Lawrence, he immediately said, 'I'm on my way to dinner.'

'Well, you can go as soon as I've finished with you.'

'But –'

'And this time I'd like the truth, please.'

'About what?'

'The night Scott died. I know you weren't in Scotland.'

Nicky didn't appear at all concerned that he had been caught out. In fact, he looked amused. 'No – I would have liked to have been, though. I'm planning to go up for the Fringe in summer.' He set the guitar down and sat on his bed.

'This isn't funny, Nicky. This is a murder investigation, not a practical joke. What were you doing on Friday night?'

'I can't remember,' Nicky replied, casually.

'Don't push your luck.'

'I told you before, I have an appalling memory.'

Infuriated, Lawrence had to fight the urge to seize the boy and give him a good shake. Drawing a deep breath, he tried again. 'Nicky, please just tell me what you were doing on Friday night. I don't want to have to arrest you, but if you continue to treat this so flippantly, I'll have no choice.'

'I didn't really do anything,' Nicky responded, after a brief pause. 'I went to band practice after dinner, I came back here, I went to bed, I fell asleep, I woke up in the morning, I went to breakfast. Can I go to dinner now?'

'No. I'd like a few more details before you go anywhere. What time did –' Lawrence broke off as he was interrupted by a piercing siren.

Nicky grinned. 'Fire alarm. We have to clear the building,' he said, standing and making for the door. Lawrence had no choice but to follow him from the room and descend the stairs with the other boys who had not yet left the house for dinner. Realising he was due to meet Rebecca in five minutes, he decided to finish questioning Nicky the following day, and left him waiting in the yard behind Windsor House while the register was taken. He was anxious to confirm exactly what Guy Markham had said about Francis.

Oliver Grant glanced up from tying his shoelace in response to someone shouting his name. Turning his head towards the boarding houses, he saw his room mate bounding across the lawn towards him.

'You headed for dinner?' Sid asked, breathlessly, drawing level with Oliver as he straightened up.

'Yep.'

'The rozzers are back. Have you spoken to them yet?'

Oliver shook his head.

'That little sergeant is delicious. Almost worth committing a crime for.'

'Well I'm sure she'd be very interested to hear where you were last Friday night.'

Sid frowned. 'What?'

'I woke up at quarter to two and you weren't in bed. Where were you?'

'I expect I'd gone for a slash.'

Oliver raised his eyebrows. 'And how long does that take?'

'Oh come on, Oli, you don't think –'

'I don't know what I think.'

'I didn't touch him. I swear.'

'I'm not lying for you,' Oliver replied, turning to continue on his way towards the quad. Sid hurried after him.

'I'm not asking you to! Just say you were asleep all night. That's virtually true anyway.'

'And that's not asking me to lie?'

Sid shrugged. 'Not really.'

'You know you can do time for giving someone a false alibi, don't you?'

'Saying you were asleep isn't giving anyone any kind of alibi. It's just a statement of – I don't know –'

'Fiction?' Oliver finished for him.

'No! Jesus! I can't believe you even think I had anything to do with it!'

'*Where were you?*'

'Nowhere!' Sid insisted. Clearly seeing the look on Oliver's face, he sighed. 'Ok, ok, so I was pissing about in the John. That's hardly a crime.'

'Who with?'

There was a long pause. 'Scott,' Sid admitted, at length.

'Oh perfect,' Oliver muttered, making for the archway that led onto the quad.

'He was fine when I last saw him!' Sid protested, a note of hysteria in his voice. 'I swear to God!'

'I am not getting involved.'

'You don't have to get involved! That's the whole fucking point!' Sid exclaimed, as they rounded the corner into the archway, almost colliding with Francis as they did so. His expression looked oddly intense.

'You all right, mate?' Oliver asked, thankful to have an excuse to change the subject.

'Oh he's just queer,' Sid put in, before Francis had a chance to respond.

'Don't you fucking wish,' Francis spat, as he skirted past them. Sid hauled him back and slammed him against the wall of the archway.

'You take that back!'

'What, like that'll stop it being true?'

'I'm warning you!'

'You're warning me *what*?' Francis retorted, contemptuously, pushing Sid away. Sid shoved back, harder, and Oliver stepped in to intervene.

'Mate, let him go.'

'He's going nowhere 'til I get an apology!' Sid snarled, his hand on Francis's chest, inches from his throat.

'Well then we're going to be here an awfully long time,' Francis replied, icily.

'Sid, seriously,' Oliver took his friend's arm. 'Let him go.'

Sid held Francis where he was for another couple of seconds before releasing him, pushing him roughly to the side as he did so. 'Off you go then!' He jeered. 'But don't for one moment think we're done!'

'Oh, we're not,' Francis returned, with a smirk. He turned to go, then paused, looking back. 'And you have no idea what I'm capable of.'

When Lawrence returned to his car, Rebecca was leaning against the passenger door, twisting her engagement ring back and forth around her finger. She smiled as he approached. 'Hurry up and unlock the car, I'm freezing.'

'I'd like to pay Guy Markham a quick visit before we go.'

'Oh?'

'What exactly did he say to you about Fray?'

'Um –' Rebecca pulled her notebook from her bag and flicked through a number of pages. 'Unstable and erratic.'

'And you said he got that impression from the staff?'

'I wasn't sure how much was from Curt and how much the staff, but yes.'

'Donald Chadwick told me he discourages the staff from discussing the boys on a general level – I'd like to find out exactly where Guy got that information.'

'Ok,' Rebecca nodded, returning the book to her bag and starting back towards the school.

'Did you manage to find Fray?' Lawrence asked, as they walked.

'Yes. Although talking to him was hard going. He seemed wired. Hyper. And agitated. If I had to guess, I'd say he was on coke.'

'Yes, I wondered about that too,' Lawrence admitted. 'He certainly looks the part. I found him borderline aggressive. Yet neither agitated nor aggressive are words anyone else has used to describe him. Edward Quast implied he's apt to cry over anything and everything, and when I asked Donald just now he said he wouldn't refer to Fray as unbalanced, just unhappy. It's almost as if we're hearing about one person and meeting another.' He paused. 'Did you manage to get anything out of him about the argument with Scott?'

'I did. You were right, the money in Scott's bank account was derived from blackmail.'

'Who was he blackmailing? Fray?'

'Apparently so.'

'Why?'

'That I don't know. But he did admit the argument arose because Scott wanted more money, and he couldn't pay.'

'If he is on coke, that would be an obvious thing for Scott to have used as blackmail material. And given the cost of a coke habit, if Fray was running short of money that gives us two motives in one.'

Rebecca nodded. 'He told me he'd run out of savings to give to Scott.'

'Julian Ribet's attempt to teach Scott the value of money didn't work quite as he intended, then,' Lawrence observed.

'No. Although I can't say I'm surprised, anyone sending their kid to a place like this clearly has more money than sense.'

'Ouch,' Lawrence replied. 'Do I sense someone disapproves of private education?'

'What, do you think this is a healthy environment?'

'No,' Lawrence agreed. 'That it isn't is becoming increasingly apparent.' He entered the five-number code and opened the door to the staff accommodation block. 'You'd better lead the way, since you know exactly where we're going.'

'Just down here,' Rebecca indicated, walking towards the door of a ground floor apartment. She knocked sharply. Lawrence joined her as the door opened, and a young man of twenty-something appeared. Guy Markham, Lawrence guessed, correctly.

'Good evening Mr Markham,' Rebecca began. 'This is a colleague of mine, DCI Forrester. Could we have a minute, please?'

'I've got guests,' Guy objected, irritably. 'Can it wait?'

'No,' Lawrence put in, bluntly.

Guy stepped out into the corridor, pulling the door to behind himself. 'What is it?'

'You told my colleague you thought Francis Bircham was unstable and erratic. How did you come to that conclusion?' Lawrence asked.

'Mainly from what I've heard.'

'From whom? Is it general knowledge amongst the staff?'

'Fray's room mate, primarily,' Guy answered, after a moment's hesitation. Lawrence didn't miss the fact that he was the first member of staff not to call the boy by his full name.

'Why did he discuss it with you? Surely it's more relevant to his housemaster?'

'I didn't ask. If one of my pupils is worried about something, I'm quite happy for him to talk to me about it.'

'So you don't actually know Fray.'

'Not really, no.'

'But you know him well enough to call him by his nickname.'

'That's what –' Guy stopped. Lawrence mentally concluded the sentence. *What Curt calls him.* Guy finished with, 'That's what he prefers to be called.'

'What did Curt expect you to do to help?'

'I don't think he expected me to *do* anything.'

'Were you surprised he came to you about it rather than another member of staff he's known longer?'

'Not really. I assumed he found me easy to talk to. I suppose maybe it's easier for the boys to relate to someone who isn't so far off their own age.'

'Has he come to you with any other concerns?'

Guy frowned. 'I don't see what the problem is here.'

'There isn't necessarily a problem at all.'

'Then why are you quizzing me so aggressively?'

'Why are you being so defensive?' Lawrence countered.

'Because I don't like being interrogated over having tried to do a good job. I have a responsibility to the boys I teach, and Curt happens to be one of them.'

'It just strikes me that you've seen rather a lot of him in the last week. You've visited him in the sanatorium, you were in his bedroom yesterday –'

'I was going over some work he he'd missed.'

'In his bedroom? Is that normal procedure?'

'In case you've not noticed, Curt isn't in the best of health. If he'd rather work in his room, I'm quite prepared to help him there,' Guy snapped, crossly.

'I see,' Lawrence nodded. 'Well, thank you for your time. I'll let you get back to your guests. Perhaps we could discuss this further when you've calmed down.'

'I'm perfectly calm. I just object to your inferring that I've acted inappropriately. Teaching doesn't begin and end with school work, you know. We do have a duty of care.'

'I don't recall inferring anything,' Lawrence replied, pleasantly. 'It would seem you've assumed that, which is very interesting. Good evening.' He turned and strode back down the corridor. Rebecca hurried after him, leaving Guy standing at his door, glaring after them.

It was coming up to half-past eleven when Rebecca climbed into bed. Guessing Astatine's set would by now be finished, she dialled Elliot's number. He answered on the third ring.

'Hi Becca.'

'Hey. Is this a good time?'

'Yeah, we're done,' he answered, rather flatly. Rebecca wondered what had gone wrong, because usually after coming off stage Elliot was on something of a high.

'Are you ok?'

'Not really. I have wicked stomach pains.'

'When did that start?'

'I've felt like crap all day. Ed keeps throwing ibuprofen at me and telling me to quit moaning. How are you?'

'Fine thanks.'

'How are you finding being back at school?'

'Quite a culture shock. It's really posh. And it feels so –' Rebecca struggled to put her thoughts into words. 'Regimented, I guess. Makes my school look like a free-for-all.'

'At my school they were just pleased if people bothered to turn up.'

Rebecca smiled. 'Did you?'

'Mostly. I quite liked school.'

'I never dared bunk off,' Rebecca admitted.

'Bunking off was overrated,' Elliot replied. 'If you'd no money there wasn't a whole lot to do, and you just ended up hanging around some park or shopping centre all day. At least at school you got lunch.' His words sounded slightly slurred and Rebecca guessed he'd been availing himself of the free drinks backstage.

'My mum always –' Rebecca broke off as the background noise suddenly surged.

'Hang on,' Elliot put in. There was some muffled scuffling and a couple of thuds before she heard what sounded like a door being closed and the ambient noise dropped as abruptly as it had risen.

'Sorry,' Elliot apologised.

'Are you guys having a party?'

'Kind of. Damian's mum and sister came down. And a load of his mates.' He sighed. 'His sister's so proud of him. She's had a t-shirt made with photos and single covers and stuff all over it. Got us to sign it in permanent marker.' He sounded despondent, and Rebecca guessed the presence of Damian's relations had served to emphasise his own family situation.

'That's a nice idea.'

'Yeah, it was really sweet.' He paused. 'I wish I could have that. I wish –' he paused again. 'I wish I could be a half-decent friend and be happy for him and join in the party.' His voice wavered. 'But I just want to shut myself in the dark, close my eyes and wait for everything to end.'

Rebecca didn't know what to say. It had been some time since Elliot had sounded quite so down. The previous summer, having stopped taking medication Rebecca hadn't even known he was on, he had become so depressed that for a couple of months he had struggled to even get out of bed. On the occasions he had managed to do so, it had usually been only to visit the off licence. Rebecca had eventually managed to persuade him to take the drugs his doctor had prescribed, and although in the six months since he had seemed more stable, he still wasn't himself. At least, not the Elliot she remembered. Sometimes she wondered whether he had just kept the more melancholy side of his personality hidden before they had moved in together, but it seemed unlikely: by all accounts she wasn't the only one who was aware all was still not right. Ian, the band's bass player, had attributed it to the change in Elliot's medication. And she suspected the combination of feeling unwell, being surrounded by Damian's family and having consumed a probably not inconsiderable volume of alcohol had conspired to make things worse. She wished she could be there with him.

'I don't deserve to have friends,' Elliot continued. 'I don't deserve to have you. All I ever do is let people down, and I'm sick of hating myself for it.'

'Oh love, that's not true.'

'I wasn't there for Ian when his dad died, and all I've done since is make his life harder. And now I'm ruining Damian's night. And yours.'

Rebecca sighed. 'Elliot, I'm sure Damian has more than enough people to occupy him this evening. If you're not feeling well he's not going to mind your heading back to the hotel.'

Elliot didn't immediately reply. At length he said, 'I'm sorry. You don't need this.'

'It's ok.'

'It's not.'

'You're allowed to have a bad day. You don't have to apologise.'

'I miss you. I wish you were here.'

He wasn't the only one. Rebecca couldn't imagine being able to sleep in the knowledge he was so miserable, especially when she had no way of knowing whether anyone was keeping an eye on him. Damian clearly wouldn't be, and she was well aware relations between Ian and Elliot had been strained in recent months, most likely for the reasons Elliot had just articulated. Ian had lost his father and Elliot had been too depressed – and much of the time too drunk – to even acknowledge what his friend was going through. Ian didn't blame him for his illness, but he had been less than forgiving about Elliot's decision to stop taking his medication, not least because it apparently wasn't the first – or even second – time it had happened. Rebecca could empathise with Ian, but it wasn't making her life any easier. She suspected she was going to be on the phone a long time.

Five

'Morning,' Rebecca interrupted Lawrence's perusal of the local paper.

'Ah, at last,' Lawrence teased, folding the paper and setting it aside.

'Everything all right?' Rebecca asked, joining him at the table.

'No, not really. I've just had a call from Donald Chadwick. Fray tried to kill himself last night.'

'Oh God – poor kid. What happened? Is he all right?'

'Apparently he slit his wrists – I don't know the details. He's in hospital.'

'Alive?'

'Presumably, but what state he's in I don't know. I said we'd get to the school as soon as we could, so you'd best make it a quick breakfast.'

'I can take some toast in the car, if you want to go now.'

'No, there's no point in us getting there before assembly's over, because we'll have to wait around. We'll leave in about ten minutes.'

'Plenty of time,' Rebecca replied. 'When I was at school, I used to get up fifteen minutes before I was due in, shower, throw my clothes on and leg it down the road.'

'One of my friends at university was like that. Rolled out of bed at five to nine every morning. Personally, I need at least half an hour to adjust to being awake before I can interact with other people.'

'So long as I get my caffeine hit, I'm fine.' Rebecca reached for the cafetière in the centre of the table.

'I don't know – relying on drugs to start the day,' Lawrence shook his head laughingly. 'I suppose that's what comes of living with a rock star.'

'Rock star? Minor underground celebrity maybe, but rock star, no. Well, not yet, anyway.'

'How's Elliot's ego shaping up to it all?'

'It's rather fragile, I think,' Rebecca poured a cup of coffee. 'Or rather, he's rather fragile. Some days I think he finds it all a bit much.' The night before that had certainly been true. Although by the time they had said goodbye, shortly before one, he had seemed to be in a better frame of mind. She could only hope the same would be true this morning.

'Where is he today?'

'Um – they were playing in Wolverhampton last night – I think it's Glasgow tonight, so they'll be driving up there this morning, because they'll need to get there in time to soundcheck this afternoon.' Rebecca spread butter on a slice of toast.

'When did you last hear from him?'

'Late last night. He wasn't feeling well, so he was quite subdued.'

'Hangover?'

'I don't know. He said he had stomach ache so I imagine it's more likely to be whatever junk they eat on tour.' She paused. Not wanting to discuss her concerns about Elliot's mental health with her superior, she changed the subject with, 'How are Katie and the kids?'

'Fine. Aside from Elise playing up because I'm not there.'

'Why does she get so agitated when you're away?'

'She's seen too many TV dramas, and she's convinced the police get shot at all the time. We try to control what she's watching, but it's difficult when kids need computers for schoolwork – you can limit what they access online, but they still effectively have their own private DVD player and TV. And I suspect Jimmy's shown her things he shouldn't have.'

'I've been using my laptop to watch TV for months,' Rebecca replied. 'Our TV hasn't worked since last year. Elliot promised me he'd have a look at it, but so far he hasn't.'

'Is he any good with them?'

'He's generally very adept with electrical equipment – he's always taking amps and equalisers apart in the middle of the living room floor, and he says he knows what to do with the television – he just hasn't bothered yet.'

'Has he had time?'

'He hasn't *made* time. When it comes down to it, Elliot doesn't like televisions, and therefore isn't particularly keen to fix ours, because while it doesn't work I can't watch anything.'

'And he gets more attention, I suppose.'

'I don't know. I suspect he comes from a home where he was told *quiet, I'm watching this* rather too frequently, but since I know next to nothing about his home life I can't be sure.'

'Perhaps he might have a word with Elise,' Lawrence suggested with a wry smile. 'And while he's there, maybe he could fix our stereo.'

'What's wrong with it?'

'The amp keeps cutting out. Oddly enough, it never seems to do it to Jimmy, he manages to play that damn Astatine single on a loop for hours at a time. I think I could sing it backwards in my sleep.'

'Does he still want a guitar?'

'Yes. I'm running out of arguments. It's all very well saying no he can't have a hot air balloon, or no he can't have a formula one racing car – but I can't exactly say we've nowhere to keep a guitar, can I? I wouldn't mind so much if he wanted an acoustic one, but the thought of Jimmy having access to volume control –' Lawrence shook his head.

'You could forbid him from playing it when you're in.'

'Yes,' Lawrence acknowledged, slowly, 'But I have the feeling that might put me on a fast track to the divorce courts.' He paused. 'And even Jimmy on a guitar can't be *that* bad.'

Donald Chadwick looked up as his secretary showed Lawrence and Rebecca into his office. 'Good morning. Have a seat, please.'

The two sat opposite the head, who leaned back in his chair.

'Is there any news on Francis?' Lawrence enquired.

'I've just spoken to someone at the hospital, and thankfully he's all right. Well, he's alive – I don't know that *all right* is quite the correct way of putting it.'

'What exactly happened?'

'Curt found him – at about nine-thirty. He ran straight downstairs to fetch Edward Quast and an ambulance was called – I was told soon afterwards. I had to inform his parents.'

'Has the room been tidied up?' Rebecca asked.

'No – we thought you might want a look around – just in case it wasn't as black and white as it appeared. Edward locked it as soon as the paramedics were done. Curt didn't spend the night at Windsor either – finding Francis like that was obviously a terrible shock, he was very upset – Vivien Thompson's been looking after him. I'll visit him later.'

'Did Francis leave a note of any kind?'

'Yes, I've got it here.' Donald opened a drawer and fished out a crumpled piece of A4 paper. The fact it had been torn down one side indicated that it had been ripped out of a notebook. 'Eloquent kid, isn't he?' Donald observed, passing the suicide note to Rebecca. She read it quickly.

The confusion, the blackness, the brightness of life
The coldness of steel, the sharp of the knife
The pent-up frustration, the need for release
This violent attack in hope of some peace.

Slice with the razor and tension flows freely,
Along with the blood I'm in control really
Extinguish the cigarette, flesh burns away
The moment is brief, the scars are to stay.

This distorted relief, afforded by pain
Is used 'just the once', then again and again
The heat of the moment, is there expiation
For deliberate pain and self mutilation.

Under this, scrawled in red pen, were the words, *I'm sorry, I'm sorry, forgive me.*

'Forgive me?' Rebecca frowned, passing the note to Lawrence. 'Do you think that refers to what happened to Scott, or to the suicide attempt?'

'I don't know,' Donald shook his head. 'But you might find your answer in something one of the groundsmen brought to me this morning.' He stood and went to the cupboard under the window. Opening it, he took a plastic bag from a shelf and placed it on his desk.

Rebecca reached for the bag and peered in at the contents: a long-sleeved blue shirt, heavily stained with blood. 'Where did this come from?'

'It was partially hidden under a pile of vegetation earmarked for a bonfire. Over towards the sports fields. The sleeve is soaked in blood – my guess is that it has something to do with Scott's death.'

'Any idea who it belongs to?' Rebecca asked, not wanting to touch it before Leighton had had a chance to examine it.

'It has a name tag sewn into it.'

'And?'

'Francis Bircham.'

Rebecca's eyebrows rose.

'I don't know quite how you plan to proceed – it all looks fairly cut and dried to me.'

'Things aren't always as simple as they seem,' Lawrence replied, as Rebecca twisted the top of the bag to seal it. 'We'll go up to the hospital and see whether we can visit Francis. Hopefully we can get to the bottom of the matter today.'

'Right,' the head nodded. 'You will let me know when you have more information, won't you?'

'Of course.' Lawrence moved to stand, and Rebecca followed suit. 'Thank you for your time.'

'Hello,' Lawrence began, arriving in the doorway of the small hospital room to which he and Rebecca had been directed. A tall, slender man of fifty-odd who had been standing by the bed turned and walked in their direction.

'Mr Bircham?' Lawrence guessed.

'Yes.'

'I'm DCI Forrester. I'm sorry to intrude, I appreciate this is a very difficult time, but I do need a word with your son.' He wondered whether Francis's parents called him by his full name.

'Is that really necessary?'

'We wouldn't trouble him if it wasn't.'

With a sigh, Mr Bircham stepped back, allowing Lawrence and Rebecca into the room. Francis was lying in bed, very pale, his wrists neatly bandaged and a drip running into his left arm. His dark eyes were bloodshot. Sensing the presence behind him, Lawrence turned. 'Do you think we might have a few minutes alone with Francis?'

Mr Bircham's eyebrows contracted in concern. 'I'd rather not leave him –'

'Five minutes.'

Reluctantly, the man nodded, making for the door. Lawrence returned his attention to Francis.

'Right. What's all this about?'

'I dunno,' Francis replied, weakly.

'You don't know?' Lawrence exclaimed.

'I can't remember.'

'What do you mean, you can't remember?'

'I don't know what happened. I was tired, so I went to bed early. After that all I remember is being in an ambulance.'

Not sure what to make of this response, Lawrence presented him with the poem provided by Donald Chadwick. 'Is this your handwriting?'

'Where'd you get that?' Francis frowned, reaching to take it.

'It's your suicide note.'

Confusion clouded the boy's face. 'But that's not about suicide.' He raised his eyes, his expression anxious. 'I don't understand. Why don't I remember?'

'Did you write this?'

'Yes.'

'When?'

'Oh – I don't know. Ages ago. It was in my poetry book.'

'Your poetry book?'

'It's just a book I keep them in. It's been ripped out – you can see the paper's torn down this side.' He frowned. 'That's not my writing,' he observed, pointing to the red scrawl at the bottom of the page. 'I don't feel well. Can't I talk about it later?'

'No, I'm afraid not. I'm also after an explanation for this.' Lawrence produced the bag containing the bloodstained shirt. 'It has your name sewn into it, and blood all down one sleeve. Anything you'd like to tell me?'

Francis stared at the shirt, swallowing hard.

'What happened?'

'I didn't hurt Scott. I never touched him!'

'What happened?' Lawrence persisted.

'I didn't do it,' Francis shook his head. 'I didn't!' He looked to Rebecca rather desperately. 'Why does everyone always pick on me?'

Rebecca tried a gentler approach, saying, 'Fray, we're not trying to victimise you, but right now, everything seems to point right at you! You have no one to substantiate where you were on Friday night, two days before Scott's death you had an argument in which you threatened to kill him, and you've admitted Scott was blackmailing you and that you couldn't afford to pay him any longer. Now we find your shirt like this –'

'It's not Scott's blood!'

'Well then whose is it?' Lawrence pressed.

'I didn't hurt anyone!'

Lawrence felt impatient. 'Fray, we're going to have forensic tests run on the shirt, so you might as well tell us the truth. The sooner you do that, the easier this will be for you.'

'But I haven't done anything wrong!' Francis exclaimed, tears coming to his eyes.

'If you've done nothing wrong, why did you hide the shirt in a bonfire?'

'What?'

'This shirt was found by one of the groundsmen this morning, on a bonfire in the woods.'

The boy's expression appeared to be one of genuine confusion. 'But it was at the bottom of my wardrobe. I was going to wash it.'

'Are you sure about that?'

'Yes,' Francis nodded, raising a shaking hand to his brow. 'Please can I have a break? My head is splitting.'

'What do you remember about last night?'

'Nothing. There were voices – but they were a long way away. I couldn't understand them.' He rubbed his eyes. 'I don't remember anything. My head aches – I can't think straight.'

'All right, we'll go over it again later on,' Lawrence agreed, turning to go. 'Perhaps you might try to remember something by then,' he added, pointedly.

Francis didn't reply, and Lawrence strode towards the door. Pausing to allow Rebecca to go ahead of him, he glanced back. Francis met his eyes. Through the pain and the tears, Lawrence sensed something odd about him. He looked almost defiant.

Nicky seemed rather subdued when Lawrence looked into his bedroom early on Wednesday afternoon. He glanced up as the door opened, and, seeing Lawrence, cast his eyes down again.

'Hello,' Lawrence began.

'Hi.'

Lawrence sat on the bed that had previously belonged to Scott. 'Were you here last night when Curt found Fray?'

Nicky shook his head. 'No.'

As Lawrence drew breath to ask another question, Nicky posed one of his own.

'It's something to do with what happened to Scott, isn't it?'

'I don't know. Possibly.'

'Do you think Fray killed Scott?'

'Do you?'

Nicky shook his head again. 'I know he didn't.'

'How?'

There was a long pause before Nicky revealed, 'Because I was with him.'

'With who?'

'Fray. On Friday night.'

'Were you with him all night?'

'Until about six.'

'What were you doing?'

'That's not your business.'

Lawrence took a moment to consider his answer before asking, 'Are you and Fray more than friends?'

'No! I'm not a poof! I like girls! The fact I like music and painting doesn't make me gay any more than Darwin's theory of evolution makes people straight!'

'Well then what were you doing?'

Nicky said nothing, his eyes fixed at a point on the opposite wall.

'Nicky, I need to know what went on that night.'

'I'll get in masses of trouble. So will Fray. We'll both get expelled, and my dad will kill me. I can't tell you, but it has nothing to do with Scott.'

'I'm afraid I'm going to need more than that.'

Nicky shook his head.

'Can you at least tell me where you were?'

Nicky opened his mouth to speak, then thought better of it, and closed it.

'Were you in the woods?'

'No.'

'Did you leave this building?'

There was a pause before Nicky nodded.

'And where did you go?'

'I can't tell you that. But when we headed off – about one-fifteen – Scott was asleep. At least, I think he was. And I never saw him again after that.'

'And what time did you get back?'

'Just before six.'

'Didn't you think it odd when you returned to your room at six in the morning and found Scott not in bed?'

'Not really. Scott used to get up early all the time – he often went rowing before breakfast. I just thought he'd gone down to the river.'

'I wonder where he thought you'd gone,' Lawrence mused, aloud. 'Do you suppose he followed you?'

Nicky shrugged.

'Do you have any idea where he might have gone?'

'No. Maybe if I'd been here he'd've said. But I wasn't.'

'And where were you?'

Nicky didn't answer, and Lawrence added, 'Come on, Nicky, this is important. I'll try not to drop you in it with the school. Nobody else needs to know where you were.'

Nicky sighed. 'We were –' he broke off. After some seconds had passed, he finally gave in. 'We were in the lab.'

'In the middle of the night?'

'Uh-huh.'

'And what were you and Fray doing in the lab at that hour?'

Nicky shook his head. 'I can't tell you any more,' he said, his voice sounding strained.

'Was it something illegal?'

'No,' he snapped, defensively.

'So why can't you tell me?'

'I just can't. But I was with Fray. All night.'

'And how do I know I'm getting the truth on this occasion?'

Nicky shrugged. 'I guess you don't,' he said, at length. 'But then again, you don't know whether what everyone else has told you is the truth either. Honesty is only ever a good policy if you can't get away with lying.'

'Hello,' Rebecca greeted Vivien, as she stepped into the matron's office.

Vivien looked up with a smile. 'Morning. How can I help?'

'I was hoping to have a chat with Curt. How is he?'

'I'm quite concerned about him,' Vivien replied. 'He was in a terrible state last night – at one point I thought we might need to get him to hospital. His breathing seems to have settled down now, but he's clearly very anxious and I don't think he's had much sleep. Poor kid's had a tough week.'

'Do you think he's up to talking to me?'

'I think that's probably for him to say.'

'Where can I find him?'

'Down that corridor, third door on the left,' Vivien indicated.

'Thanks.'

Curt was lying propped up in bed, staring blankly at the book in his hand, his face colourless and his eyes half shut. He hadn't made it past the first page yet. He didn't respond to Rebecca's arrival in the doorway and she had to say his name twice before she got a reaction.

'Oh. Hi.'

'Hello. How are you feeling?'

'Sick.'

'Do you feel up to talking about last night?'

Curt drew a deep breath, which was far more audible than it ought to have been. 'Not really, but I guess I should.'

'I'm sorry to put you through this, but with everything that's happened we can't take any chances.'

Curt nodded. 'I understand that.' He struggled to pull himself up into a sitting position, coughing as he did so.

Rebecca perched on a chair near the bed. 'What time yesterday did you last see Fray? Before you found him, I mean.'

'He came back to the room around dinner time.'

'Was that before or after you went to dinner?'

Curt coughed. 'I didn't go.'

'Why not?'

'I wasn't feeling well.'

'But you were well enough to go out later on in the evening?'

'Not really – but Mr Markham organised some talks for us with outside speakers. Famous geneticists. I didn't want to miss them.'

'So what was Fray doing when you left him?'

'He said he was going to bed early.'

'Does he often do that?'

'No, but he's not really been sleeping, so I figured he was tired.'

'What do you mean, he's not been sleeping?'

Curt shrugged. 'Just that. He's been up writing songs at all hours.'

'Did that start before or after Scott's death?'

'He didn't hurt Scott,' Curt replied. 'The only person Fray's capable of hurting is himself.'

'That's not what I asked.'

Curt sighed. 'He's been doing it since half term,' he answered. 'Or at least, that's when I first noticed.'

'Have you noticed anything else different about him in that time?'

'I thought he seemed a bit better. He's been really withdrawn and miserable for months, but in the last ten days he's seemed to have a lot more energy and more – I don't know – direction. I figured maybe he was coming out the other side of it.' Curt swallowed. 'But since last night I just keep wondering whether maybe he'd already decided to –' he trailed off with a shrug.

'How was he when you left him?'

'He seemed on good form. He was really chatty. It took me ages just to get out the door because there was so much he wanted to tell me.'

'When I saw him shortly before six he seemed high. Do you think he might have been taking drugs?'

'No way. He's really anti them. His brother died of an overdose. He won't even take prescription meds.'

'And where did you go after you left the bedroom?'

'The Great Hall. I was meant to be there 'til ten, but I really didn't feel up to it, so I left about nine.'

'Did you go straight back to your room?'

'I was going to come here, but I ended up having to sit down in the quad for a while because I felt really dizzy and I thought I was going to pass out. After that I started out to come here, but it's further than to Windsor, and by the time I got that far it seemed like another five miles, so I just went to my room.' He swallowed. 'I don't even want to think about what might have happened if I hadn't.' He coughed before adding, as an afterthought, 'I guess he wasn't all right. I shouldn't have left him alone.'

'Don't blame yourself, Curt, it's not your fault.'

'I've often wondered if this would ever happen,' he admitted.

'So you weren't surprised.'

'No. I was shocked – and upset – but it wasn't the sort of situation where I couldn't believe it had happened.' He coughed again, leaning his head against the wall that ran parallel to the bed. 'I guess I just always figured if he failed I'd feel relieved, more than anything. But now –' he shrugged weakly. 'I don't know. I don't even have the words.'

Miss Greene, the school librarian, was a severe-looking woman in her fifties who reminded Lawrence of a teacher from his own school days. Her spectacles were held on a chain about her neck, her greying hair short in length and on style. She glanced up from covering a text book to view Lawrence's warrant card, regarding it as one might an undesirable insect that has just crawled into view.

'Yes?' She said, with a frown.

'I've a few questions, if you don't mind.'

'What about?'

'The books in this library.'

This clearly took her by surprise. 'What about them?'

'On Monday one of the pupils was reading a book on forensic science and toxicology – it didn't strike me as the sort of book one would expect to find in a school library.'

'That would be Francis Bircham, I should imagine,' Miss Greene replied, putting what she was doing aside.

'That's right.'

'Yes. He regularly orders books on that sort of subject – medical texts as well – we can get anything he wants on inter-library loans.'

'Is that normal practise?'

'No, but Francis isn't a normal pupil. He's very bright, and Donald is keen to encourage him.'

'Any particular reason why?'

'Francis did twelve GCSEs and came out with the top mark for the board for five of them and the top in the country for two. He's probably equally capable of doing so at A-level, and in these days of league tables that looks very good for the school.'

'So if he asks for a book, you get it for him.'

'Yes.'

'Could you possibly provide me with a list of all the books he's asked for in this academic year?'

The look Miss Greene gave him told Lawrence in no uncertain terms that it would be a major inconvenience for her to do so. 'If it were absolutely necessary,' she said, coolly.

'I'd like a list, then, please.'

Turning to the computer that sat on the right-hand side of her desk, she tapped a few keys, then clicked on the mouse. Moments later, the printer behind her buzzed, squeaked a few times and began to print. After filling almost two A4 pages, it stopped, and Miss Greene retrieved the resulting sheets and handed them to Lawrence.

'Thank you,' he smiled, turning towards a nearby table. Setting the pages down, he reached for a chair.

'Excuse me?' A timid voice spoke behind him as he sat down. He turned to find an anxious-looking boy in his early teens hovering behind him. He was short and rather overweight, wearing a blazer that was a little too tight. His blonde hair looked as if it had been washed and then slept on whilst wet, and he ran a nervous hand through it as he said, 'Um – our teacher said we had to tell you if we knew anything about the other night.'

'Oh, right,' Lawrence nodded, wondering which night the boy was referring to. He pulled the adjacent chair out from the table, saying, 'Come and sit down for a minute.'

The boy shuffled closer and perched on the edge of the chair.

'I'm DCI Forrester. You are?'

'Adey. Seth Adey.'

'And what was it you wanted to tell me?'

'On Friday night – I saw one of the sixth formers outside.'

'Do you remember what time that was?'

'About half-past one.'

'And do you know who it was?'

'I don't know his name. I've only been here a term and a half. He's got dark hair. And he's very thin.'

'Which house is he in?'

'Windsor. That's where I live.'

'Where did you see him?'

'He was walking towards the quad.'

'Can you tell me anything else about him?'

'I know he does chemistry, because the sixth form sometimes wander in and out of the lab during our lessons. And he's friends with our class prefect.'

'Who's the prefect?'

'Greenwood.'

'Nicky Greenwood?'

'Yes.'

'What were you doing up at one-thirty in the morning?'

There was an uncomfortable silence before Seth replied. 'I couldn't sleep.'

'Is there anything else you can tell me about this boy, or the night you saw him?'

Seth shook his head. 'That's all. Can I go? I'm supposed to be in class.'

'Of course. Thank you for telling me.'

'Ok,' Seth nodded, getting up and hurrying towards the door. Lawrence remained where he was, thinking over what he had learned so far that day before returning his attention to the book list he had obtained prior to Seth's arrival.

Considering that they were only halfway through the academic year, the list was extensive. Titles ranged through pathology, forensic medicine, poisons, toxicology, organic and inorganic chemistry, biochemistry, microbiology, neuroscience, neuropathology, psychology and, curiously, botany. Also listed were a few politics and history books that Lawrence imagined were relevant to Francis's A-level courses. As to what use Francis had had for the other books, Lawrence could only speculate. It seemed it was time to pay the boy another visit.

Six

Entering room 320, Rebecca recognised the boy at the desk, and for a moment was unable to place him. He was short and slight, with dark hair and olive skin, and a nose that turned up slightly at the end. He was dressed in an old pair of jeans and a school rugby shirt, and was seated at his desk, sorting through a vast selection of photographs. Realising he was the drummer in Francis's band, Rebecca smiled, saying, 'Hello again.'

'Hi,' he smiled nervously in return.

'Is it Alex?'

He nodded.

'I'd like to ask you a few questions if you have a few minutes.'

'Oh. Ok.'

She sat on one of the beds, and was about to make a start when Alex asked, hesitantly, 'Have you seen Fray today?'

'We visited him this morning.'

'Is he all right?'

'He was a bit upset.'

'But he's ok?'

'On a physical basis, at least.'

Alex looked reassured.

'Were you here last night?'

He nodded. 'I didn't bother him, because he said he was really tired. I thought he must have gone to bed, because it was very quiet next door.'

'Is that unusual?'

Alex scrunched up his eyes and nose. 'It varies. Usually I can hear his stereo if he's in. The walls aren't all that soundproof.'

'Can you hear conversations?'

'Only if people are talking loudly. Mostly you can just hear the bass line of the music. It can get a bit annoying when you're trying to work.'

'I've heard Scott and Fray had quite a set-to last Wednesday. Since you said you can hear raised voices through the wall, did you overhear any of what was said?'

'You can't hear everything – the walls aren't made of paper, you know,' Alex countered, clearly flustered.

'I didn't ask if you heard everything, I asked if you heard any of it.'

Reluctantly, Alex replied, 'I heard a few bits towards the end when they started yelling. After that, Dr Quast interrupted them and it all went quiet.'

'What did you hear?'

'Uh – I remember Fray calling Scott a moral dead zone – and something about him being devoid of empathy and conscience – Scott replied that it was better than having no backbone.' Alex paused for a moment's thought. 'Then Fray said something obscure I didn't get. Although from Scott's response I'm not sure he got it either.'

'I've been told that at one point Fray said *you do that and I'll kill you*. Did you hear that?'

Alex nodded, looking down at his hands.

'Do you know what he didn't want Scott to do?'

'I think Scott threatened to report someone.'

'Do you think Fray would have been capable of going through with that threat?'

Alex shrugged. 'He's my friend. I can't imagine any of my friends being capable of murder, but I guess most people must think that. You're hardly going to make friends with someone if you think they're a psycho, are you?'

'So you think it's possible?'

'Anything's possible.'

'Do you know what sort of state Fray was in after the row?'

Alex shook his head. 'I would have gone to see if he was ok, but Scott was still in there, so I left well alone.'

'How did Fray seem on Thursday and Friday?'

'I didn't see a whole lot of him. He doesn't do any of my subjects, and he doesn't go to dinner.'

'Did you not have a band practice on Friday evening? How was he then?'

'A bit uptight, I guess. But Fray's a perfectionist. He expects things to be done right. That doesn't always make for fun rehearsals.'

'So the way he behaved last night wasn't unusual?'

Alex lowered his eyes. 'I'm not sure I'd call it usual,' he admitted, at length.

'What was different?'

'Since half term he's seemed really – impatient. Like nothing is happening fast enough.'

'So he hasn't been himself.'

'I guess not,' Alex conceded.

'Has anything else happened that seemed out of the ordinary?'

Alex bit his lip. There was a pause before he nodded. 'At dinner on Friday night.'

'What happened?'

'Scott and Sid were sitting further up the table from us, and Sid suddenly got up and said *you are* –' his cheeks coloured, and he hesitated before saying '*fucking dead*'.

Rebecca's eyebrows rose. 'Sid said that?'

'Yes.'

'Do you know what that was in reference to?'

'No. I didn't hear any of what they were saying before. But Sid sounded pretty mad.'

'Did he say anything else?'

'No, he just stormed off.'

Rebecca made a note of this, then returned her attention to Alex. 'Would you mind running me through where you were between one and six on Saturday morning?'

Alex looked put out that she had asked, so she added, 'It's a routine question we have to ask everybody.'

'Oh. I was here. Asleep. I woke up about half two because Mike – that's my room mate – was snoring. I threw a pillow at him and went back to sleep.'

'Did that wake him up?'

'I don't know. He swore at me.' Alex managed a smile. 'But then he usually does.'

'Where is he at the moment?'

'Rugby match. Away game. Leeds.'

'I assume he was on the same team as Scott.'

'Yeah, but they hated each other.'

'Oh?' Rebecca raised her eyebrows.

'I don't know why – it goes back a long way – since before I really knew Mike. You'd have to ask him about it.' Alex glanced at his watch. 'I'm late for my photography workshop – can I finish this later?'

'I think that'll do for now. Thanks.'

'Oh.' Alex nodded. 'Ok.' He stood up, gathered up the photographs on his desk, and hurried out of the door without even waiting for Rebecca to leave.

'I'm busy,' Francis snapped, without looking up at Lawrence. He was sitting up in bed, a notebook in his lap, obviously feeling better. Lawrence noted with interest that the boy wrote with his left hand.

'Doing what?'

'Writing.'

'Writing what?'

'None of your business.'

Lawrence sat on the chair at the side of the bed. 'What are you intending to do next year?' He enquired, conversationally.

Francis shrugged. 'No idea.'

'You haven't applied to university?'

'No.'

'Do you intend to?'

'Not especially.'

'That seems an awful waste.'

Francis raised his gaze for the first time. 'Does it?' He stated, coldly.

'Yes. From what I gather, you're clearly very bright.'

'I have a good memory, and I'm capable of repeating what I'm taught. That's hardly difficult.'

'I've heard that you're an exceptional student. Your headmaster thinks you could get a first at Oxford or Cambridge – do you not think you should put your talents to some good use?'

'You assume a degree is the only way to do that.'

'Not necessarily, but it's a good start.'

'I don't like studying. Why would I volunteer for another three years of it?'

'For someone who dislikes studying you've spent an awful lot of your sixth form in the library.'

'Just because I don't like it doesn't mean I don't do it,' Francis returned, coolly.

'The librarian tells me you take a great interest in forensics and toxicology.'

'Is that a crime?'

'Not at all. It just seems rather an odd interest, especially for someone your age.'

'Well, I find it rather odd that people collect stamps and put them in albums, but people still do it.'

'If forensics interests you so much, why not study it properly?'

'I can study perfectly well by myself.'

'But if you were to do it at degree level, you'd probably be able to get a job in the field. You're obviously academically capable, you have a fantastic memory, and, from what I've seen, a very agile mind. If I were considering employing you, I'd be suitably impressed,' Lawrence observed, hoping flattery might encourage the boy to give away information that gave some clue to his recent activities. It was a tactic that often worked, and for a moment Lawrence thought he might be getting somewhere, because Francis smiled and replied, 'It's very nice of you to say so.' Tipping his head to one side, he added, 'But I'm curious. Why all this praise? What are you hoping I'll say?'

'What makes you think I'm hoping you'll say anything?'

Francis's eyes narrowed. 'By appealing to my ego, you're expecting me to respond by providing you with information that proves I'm as clever and knowledgeable as you say I am. I can only assume you have some motive in that, because I can't see any other reason why you'd be pursuing a conversation with me about my future when you're supposed to be investigating a crime.'

Lawrence felt irritated, more with himself than Francis, who clearly wasn't easily fooled.

'What were you doing wandering the school grounds at half-past one on Saturday morning?'

'I wasn't.'

'I have a witness who says you were. Were you on your way to meet Scott, or were you off to the lab?'

'The lab?'

'There's no need to repeat it, Fray, just answer the question.'

'Why would I have been going to the lab at half-past one in the morning?'

'Nicky told me all about your little project.'

'Nicky makes stuff up all the time,' Francis returned, contemptuously. 'I would have thought *that* would have come to your attention by now.'

'Why do you suppose he told me you were with him, then? Was he just trying to get you into trouble?'

'How should I know?' Francis demanded. 'I don't know why Nicky makes stuff up! But I wasn't with him on Friday night and I wasn't in the lab!'

Lawrence sighed, feeling incensed. He had actually thought Nicky might be telling the truth – or at least something approaching it – on this occasion, and wondered whether, in fact, he had been trying to provide Francis with an alibi.

'So once again you have no one to substantiate your activities on Friday night.'

'What do you think I'm going to do, make something up to give you an alibi? What sort of daft logic is that? You'd only disprove it and then have something on me because I'd lied.'

'Logic?' Lawrence echoed. 'If you want to talk about logic, let's try attaching some logic to your behaviour, shall we? One of your friends is dead, I'm trying to ascertain what happened in order to dispense justice, and you're being about as unhelpful as possible. What does that suggest to you?'

'I'm not being unhelpful, Chief Inspector, I'm simply not providing the answers you want because you're on completely the wrong track. I'm telling you the truth, and it's not my fault you don't believe me.'

'Fray, I intend to get to the bottom of this, however long it might take.'

Francis smirked, regarding Lawrence with some contempt. 'Even if I had done something, you'd have to prove it. When people break the law they usually get caught only because they're either too stupid to get away with it or too arrogant to keep it to themselves.'

Stunned that Francis had the audacity to talk to him in such a way, Lawrence struggled to think of an immediate reply. 'You're suggesting you're neither,' he managed.

Francis lifted one eyebrow slightly. 'If I said yes I think I'd be disproving my point, don't you?'

'So you think you won't get caught,' Lawrence concluded.

'I said *if* I'd done something,' Francis replied, his dark eyes unmoving. 'As it is, I haven't.'

'I don't believe that for a second.'

'Well that's not my problem.'

Lawrence sighed. He was clearly getting nowhere, and was finding Francis's attitude increasingly infuriating. Getting to his feet, he said, 'You'll be seeing me again. I suggest you give this situation a little more thought.' He paused for a moment before adding, 'Perhaps you might also give some thought to Scott's parents, and the little sister who is now minus a brother.'

The look on the boy's face told Lawrence he had hit a nerve, and he felt a degree of satisfaction. Perhaps now Francis would stop playing games.

Sid wasn't in his bedroom when Rebecca knocked on the door, and the well-built eighteen-year-old sitting on the floor against the end of one of the beds introduced himself as Oli before turning his attention back to what he had been doing prior to Rebecca's arrival, which appeared to be cutting pages from magazines. He had short sandy hair and almost no neck, and wore a skin-tight t-shirt which emphasised his muscular physique. Rebecca guessed he was a rugby player, and was pleased to learn she was right.

'I'm supposed to be playing in Leeds this afternoon, but I've done my knee in,' he revealed, when she asked.

'What are you doing instead?' She enquired, perching on the bed that ran alongside where he was sitting.

'I'm making a collage. It's part of a modern art project.'

'Would you mind running me through your movements on Friday night while you do that?'

'That won't take long. I had a German essay in on Saturday morning, so I was doing that.'

'What time did you finish?'

'Ten past twelve.'

'Is that not after lights out?'

'Yeah. After eleven I had to use a torch.'

'And after that?'

'I went to sleep.'

'Did you hear anybody moving about?'

'Leaving the building, you mean?'

'Yes.'

'No, I wouldn't have been likely to. If you want to get out of here then you climb out the window in room three-one-eight or nine. I'm on the wrong side of the building.'

'So you can't get out from here.'

Oli shook his head.

'Have you ever left the building after lights out?'

'Sure, I think most of us have done.'

'And how did you do that?'

'I went out Scott's window. With Scott.'

'So he was a friend of yours.'

'Yeah.'

'Why did you do it?'

'For a laugh. You get dared to do silly pranks – like tying girls' underwear to the front of the headmaster's car.'

'Did you not worry about getting caught?'

'That's half the fun. Besides, if you're not doing anything that breaks other rules and you've not been caught before, you'll probably just get a talking to and have to write an essay on *why I must not.*' He shrugged. 'Rules are made to be broken.'

'While we're on the subject of rule-breaking, your room mate told us he and Scott went to a pub in town the weekend before last. Were you there?'

'Yes.'

'I hear Scott and Sid were involved in a fight.'

'Yeah – this local kid kept calling them girls, so they laid into him outside the pub. The guy's mate got involved too. It was quite amusing.'

Amusing wasn't a word Rebecca could imagine ever applying to a fight, but she didn't say so, instead asking, 'Did you see a lot of Scott?'

'Yes. We played rugby and took German together. And I do two subjects with Nicky, as well, so I used to be in their room all the time.'

'What about Curt and Fray? Do you see much of them?'

'They live virtually opposite me – I'd be hard pressed to miss them.'

'Are they friends of yours?'

'Not really. Curt's a decent guy, but we don't have a whole lot in common. Fray keeps himself to himself, unless you provoke him. And I don't feel the need to do that.'

'Unlike your room mate.'

Oli sighed. 'Yeah, I think he has trouble dealing with people who show emotion. He's big on the idea of men being men, and Nicky and I get ragged all the time for taking art.'

'Does that bother you?'

'Nah. It's kind of to be expected. I just laugh when I get called a pansy.'

'Sid called you that because you study art?'

Oli nodded. 'Nicky gets more teasing because he does music as well, but he doesn't really care, because just about everyone's met his girlfriend.'

'Has anyone else come in for those sorts of comments from Sid?'

'At some point. He thinks it's funny.'

'I can guess he wouldn't if they were directed at him.'

'No, that's true enough. He called Fray queer yesterday, and Fray replied with *don't you effing wish*. I thought Sid was going to clout him, I really did.'

'Why did he say it in the first place?'

'We were on our way to dinner and Fray was walking the other way. He looked a bit – I don't know – strange – so I asked if he was all right. Sid said *he's just queer* before Fray had a chance to reply.'

'How is homosexuality viewed here?'

'It kind of depends who you are and who you hang around with. Sid thinks it's disgusting, and he spent the whole of dinner last night ranting about what Fray had said. But I'm not all that bothered,' he paused. 'Then again, I've heard people say the most homophobic people are the ones who actually are that way inclined,' he remarked, reaching for the scissors. 'It's as much a way of denying it to yourself as anything.'

'Right, I've had just about enough!' Lawrence announced on entry to Nicky's bedroom. 'This is your last chance, and if I don't get the truth this time, I'll have you charged with wasting police time!'

'What?' Nicky frowned, looking up from the book in his lap.

'Your latest fabrication about your trip to the lab with Fray. He says he knows nothing about it!'

'Wouldn't you?'

'I want the truth. Now.'

'I told you,' Nicky protested. 'It's not my fault if you believe Fray and not me.'

'Well, if you were in my position, what would you be inclined to think? You've already told me more lies than truths, and almost everyone I've spoken to has referred to you as a compulsive liar!'

'And doesn't that make it easy for Fray?' Nicky replied, rather bitterly.

'If you had told the truth from the start, you wouldn't be in this situation!'

'No, I'd probably have been expelled.'

'Well perhaps if you tell me what you were doing in the lab I might believe you!'

There was a tense pause as Nicky apparently weighed up his decision. At length, he said, 'Photos.'

'Photos?' Lawrence frowned.

'We were in the dark room.'

'You and Fray were developing photographs in the middle of the night?'

Nicky nodded.

'Why? Couldn't you get permission to do it during the day? Or simply take them to a shop?'

'They weren't – regular photos,' Nicky replied, awkwardly.

'Oh?'

The boy didn't respond, his eyes lowered.

'Could you please elucidate what was irregular about them?'

Several seconds passed before Nicky responded. 'They were kind of pornographic.'

'And how did you come to be developing pornographic photographs?'

'They were for my girlfriend.'

'Your girlfriend?'

Nicky raised his gaze. 'She wants to – model – for –' he stopped. 'She wants to be a glamour model. She needed some shots. She got me to take them when I went home for half term, and I brought them back here to develop them for her.'

'Why didn't you just use a digital camera and print them out?'

'Suz wanted real photos.'

Lawrence felt unconvinced. 'And what was Fray's involvement in the venture?'

'He does photography. On Wednesday afternoons. I asked him to help me because I didn't know what to do.'

'How did you get into the lab?'

'Through the window.'

'On the first floor?'

'There's a drainpipe, running up the outside of the building. It's behind the trees, so you can't see it from any of the boarding houses.'

'And how did you get in the window? They don't open more than two inches.'

'Yeah, when the security screws are in. Fray unscrewed them.'

'From the drainpipe?' Lawrence asked, disbelievingly.

'He's not an octopus,' Nicky retorted. Then, clearly seeing Lawrence's expression darken, he added, 'From the lab. Sometime on Friday.'

'So the window now opens how far?'

'Two inches. Fray fixed it back on Saturday morning before class.'

'All right, how far did it open when the two of you climbed in?'

'I don't know. Far enough. At least a foot.'

'And once you were in there, what did you do?'

'We developed the photos.'

'How?'

'I don't have a clue. I just did what Fray told me to do, because he was the one who knew what he was doing.'

'Do you have any copies of these photographs?'

'I've got a few.'

'I'd like to see them.'

Nicky climbed off the bed and went to his desk. Opening the second drawer, he pulled an envelope out from beneath a handful of files. Turning back towards the bed, he tipped the contents of the envelope onto the duvet.

Whether or not the pictures were of Nicky's girlfriend, Lawrence could see that the girl in the photographs had the attributes a glamour model would require. She was a slim, pretty strawberry blonde, with pert breasts, a narrow waist and long, slender legs. The five pictures Nicky possessed showed her in a variety of poses, wearing a basque in three, scanty underwear in another, and, in the final one, topless. The photographs themselves had obviously been taken with a good camera, and looked extremely professional.

'This is your girlfriend, is it?'

'Suzanne.'

'And how do I know you didn't just buy these pictures from someone?'

After a brief pause, Nicky reached for a photograph frame on the shelf by his bed. The picture was of the same girl, this time dressed in jeans and a tight top, arms around Nicky, who stood beside her.

'Does Fray have any of these pictures?'

Nicky frowned. 'Why would he?'

'For the same reason glamour models have jobs, Nicky. Men like looking at them.'

'Yeah, well Suzanne's my girlfriend, not Fray's.'

Lawrence didn't point out that, Nicky's girlfriend or not, were she to make a career of glamour modelling, there would doubtless be many men gazing at Suzanne's pictures in the future. Instead, he said, 'I'd like an address for her, please.'

'She lives in Ealing. In a flat.' Nicky returned to the desk and reached for a pen. Moments later, he handed Lawrence a Post-it note with a name and address scribbled on it.

'This is the correct address, I suppose?'

'Yes,' Nicky returned, indignantly.

'Right, thank you. I'll no doubt see you again soon – and you can have these back when I've finished with them.' Lawrence gathered up the pictures and replaced them in the envelope. Nicky drew breath to speak, probably, Lawrence guessed, to protest at the loss of his photographs, then thought better of it and said nothing.

'Good evening,' Lawrence finished pleasantly, opening the bedroom door.

'Bye,' Nicky snapped, crossly. Lawrence suspected his ill-humour had more to do with the idea of someone else having the opportunity to drool over his girlfriend than the actual loss of the photographs, although replacements might be hard to come by. He wondered what had become of the negatives.

Sid was still in rugby kit when Rebecca caught up with him, a patchwork of dried mud covering his clothes and skin. He was in good spirits, having apparently scored a try, and looked pleased with himself as he heaved himself up onto the wall that ran around the front of the boarding house. His eyes hovered over Rebecca's breasts, and she crossed her arms, raising her eyebrows pointedly. 'When you're ready.'

Sid blushed, looking up.

'I'd like to have a chat about Friday evening.'

'Uh-huh?'

'I understand you ate dinner with Scott.'

'Not exactly. I joined him for a minute, but not long.'

'Long enough to have an argument, from what I've heard. Apparently you said – and I quote – *you are fucking dead*. Would you like to tell me what that was about?'

Sid lowered his eyes. 'I wasn't talking to Scott when I said that.'

'So you did say it.'

Sid nodded. He didn't look up.

'Who were you talking to?'

Sid sighed. Several seconds passed before he replied. When he did, the answer took Rebecca by surprise. 'Curt.'

'What did he do to deserve that kind of response?'

'He was being a jerk.'

'What did he do?' Rebecca pressed.

'What does it matter? I didn't mean I was going to kill him!'

'Just give him a good kicking, I suppose,' Rebecca surmised, from what she had learned of Sid and Scott's modus operandi.

Sid shrugged.

'It wouldn't have been a very fair fight, would it?' Rebecca remarked, hoping to incite further comment.

'Curt's not as sweet and innocent as I'm sure he'd have you believe,' Sid sneered.

'Meaning what?'

'Just because he comes across as if butter wouldn't melt doesn't mean he has nothing to hide. He just knows how to play the game, and he's very, very good at it.'

'Do you think you could be more specific?'

Sid didn't reply.

'You don't actually have any examples, do you?' Rebecca goaded. 'You're just trying to deflect attention from the fact you're no more than an overgrown playground bully.'

'I'm not a snitch.'

'This is a murder investigation, Sid. If you know something that might have any bearing on that then you need to tell me. Otherwise you could find yourself in a lot of trouble.'

There was a long pause. At length, Sid said, 'Ask him about the observatory.'

'The observatory? What happened at the observatory?'

Sid held her gaze. 'I'll leave Curt to tell you about his little rendezvous under the stars. He'll do a much better job than I.' He smirked slightly. 'He's always been good at telling stories.'

Lawrence looked into the physics laboratory to find a young man in his mid-thirties with dark skin and hair dismantling a complex piece of apparatus, presumably from his afternoon class. He glanced up as Lawrence entered. 'Hello, can I help?'

'I don't know – I'm looking for Dr Awde.'

'You've found him. I'm Davide Awde.'

'If you've time, I'd like to ask you a few questions.'

'Certainly,' Davide left his clamp stands and weights and perched on a nearby stool.

Lawrence joined him at the bench.

'Do you carry out any form of research in these labs out of hours?'

Davide laughed. 'Hardly. The apparatus isn't up to much – I've been trying to squeeze money out of the head for new equipment since I arrived.'

'What times of day are you in here?'

'Oh – any time from eight in the morning until – I don't know – maybe six? Occasionally six-thirty.'

'So if anyone wanted to use the lab, could they do so after that without being disturbed?'

'No. I lock up when I've finished for the day.'

'Who else has a key?'

'The technician, the caretaker – I suppose the cleaning staff must have one – or at least access to someone who does.'

'So there are a number of keys.'

'Yes, I suppose so. Why?'

'One of the pupils claims he and a friend were working in the dark room on the night of Scott Ribet's death. I'm just trying to establish whether they would have been able to.'

Davide frowned. 'Little blighters. I'll have them shot if I find out they've damaged my equipment. Who was it?'

Lawrence ignored the question. 'Do you think the boys might have been able to get hold of a key?'

'Even if they had done, the main corridor's alarmed. There's no way of getting in here at night without disabling that, and only a few people know the code.'

'Do you?'

'No. If I ever wanted access, I'd have to ask Charles Nicholls to let me in. He's the caretaker.'

'Is the lab itself alarmed?'

'Not to my knowledge – but you might want to check that with Charles.'

'Could anyone climb in the window?'

'Not unless they were two inches thick. There are security bolts on all the windows, and there's no way you could take those off from outside – we're on the first floor, after all.'

'What time did you leave on Friday night?'

'I'm not sure,' Davide admitted. 'One day tends to blend into another in this place.' His eyebrows contracted as he apparently gave the matter some thought. 'I have the third form on a Friday afternoon – oh, yes, that was the day we were looking at hydraulics, I remember Fray commenting on it at lunch time.'

It struck Lawrence that Davide was the first staff member, other than Guy Markham, to use that form of the boy's name. 'What was Fray doing in the lab?'

'He dropped by with Curt, who wanted to borrow a couple of books.'

'What books did he want?'

'I didn't ask. He doesn't need my permission to borrow text books for the odd day or two, sixth form can just help themselves.'

'So why were you with them?'

'I wasn't. I came in with the apparatus for the third years – I was setting up some demonstrations for the afternoon. Curt was going through the books on the shelf and Fray was gazing out of the window. When I entered he came over to see what I was doing.'

'Do you remember how long they were there for?'

'A few minutes, perhaps? I left them looking at books and went to fetch the rest of the equipment. When I returned, they'd disappeared.'

'You didn't find it odd that Fray came with Curt when he doesn't study physics?'

'I would have found it more odd had he not come – those two are like Siamese twins.'

'Do you know either of them well?'

'Not really. I teach Curt, but further than that he's a nice kid and a very good student I couldn't tell you much about him. I taught Fray at GCSE level – he's exceptionally bright – he's not looked all that well this term, but I didn't realise there was much amiss until I heard about last night.'

'You haven't heard anything about him through other members of staff?'

Davide shook his head. 'No. Donald makes it very clear that if your nose isn't invited into a situation, you keep it well out. And if you know what's good for you, you do exactly that.'

'Fray seems to be a name used more by his friends than the staff – is that how you know him?'

Davide smiled slightly. 'Certain members of staff are rather old school. But I don't find it necessary to adopt a strict disciplinarian attitude to maintain the teacher–pupil relationship – I find the boys are often more receptive if you grant them the odd small concession. So I tend to use whatever name a boy prefers to be known by.'

'Do any of the boys you teach bring problems to you?'

'Other than with physics, you mean?'

'Yes.'

'Not often. That's not my job – it's the housemaster's responsibility.'

'What if a boy didn't get on with his housemaster, or didn't feel able to discuss the problem with him?'

'In that case, he'd probably go to his form tutor. Housemasters don't have responsibilities to a specific class for that reason. I've seen a few boys in that respect, but Curt and Fray have never been in my form. Generally the boys don't discuss their concerns of a non-academic basis with the staff – that's what their friends are for.'

Lawrence nodded. 'Going back to last Friday, did you check all the windows before leaving?'

'I always make sure they're shut. At this time of year they almost invariably are.'

'Is there any way of knowing whether the security bolts were still on?'

'It's not something I usually check, if I'm honest. I'd only notice if they weren't and the window opened further than it should.'

'Supposing they weren't. Do you think it would be possible to force the window open and climb in?'

'Very possible. That's one of the reasons they're there in the first place – sash windows are hardly the most secure, are they?'

'What other reason is there?'

'It stops the boys opening the windows and leaning out to talk to people outside. Or, in the ground floor rooms, from climbing out,' Davide raised his eyebrows expressively. 'According to one of my pupils, the use of doors to enter and leave a building, and windows for ventilation is but one interpretation of their utility.'

'Perhaps he ought to study philosophy,' Lawrence replied.

The young man grinned. 'That's exactly what I said.'

Curt was picking at a bowl of pasta when Rebecca returned to the sanatorium shortly after six, and managed a weak smile in response to her arrival. 'Hi.'

'Hello. Are you feeling any better?'

'Some, thanks.'

'Would you rather I came back after you've eaten?'

'It's ok. I'm not really hungry,' he set his fork down.

Rebecca sat beside the bed. 'I gather you had something of a run-in with Sid Watson at dinner last Friday.'

Curt shrugged.

'Would you like to tell me what that was about?'

'It wasn't a big deal.'

'I've heard he ended the exchange with words along the lines of *you're dead*. That doesn't sound like no big deal to me.'

Curt retrieved his fork and prodded a piece of fusilli, saying nothing.

'What happened?'

Curt sighed. 'Sid and Scott were talking about ideas for an assault course for a tournament on Sunday. Sid wanted to surprise the team from St John's. I made a joke about using electric fences and Sid replied that he'd said assault course, not just assault.'

'And?' Rebecca prompted, when Curt didn't continue.

Curt shifted position uncomfortably. 'I said that would make a change.'

Rebecca felt her eyebrows jump. 'What was that in reference to?'

'Sid's a bully. He picks on people.'

'Did he pick on you?'

Curt coughed. 'Not really. But that's hardly the point.'

'From what I've heard Scott was just as bad. Yet he was your friend.'

'Yeah, well I had a few things to say to him, as well.'

'On Friday night?'

He nodded.

'Why then?'

Curt appeared puzzled by the question.

'One of the younger boys reported Scott for bullying last year,' Rebecca observed. 'Clearly it wasn't anything new. Why did it suddenly bother you enough to mention it on Friday?'

'I think I just reached breaking point with it. I don't know. It seemed like a good idea at the time.'

'So it had nothing to do with the blackmail, then?'

Curt looked alarmed. 'What?'

Rebecca repeated herself.

Curt cast his eyes down. 'I don't know anything about that.'

'I don't believe you.'

No reply.

'Fray already told me.'

Curt swallowed, reaching for the inhaler that lay on the bedside cabinet. He still didn't speak.

'Do you know why Scott was blackmailing him?'

Curt's eyebrows moved halfway into a frown before relaxing back. He shook his head. 'He said it was best I didn't.'

'Was Sid involved in that?'

'I really have no idea.'

Guessing she wasn't going to get anything further out of him on that subject, Rebecca moved on. 'Sid suggested I ask you about the observatory.'

Curt blinked. 'What about it?'

'Apparently you met up with someone there.'

'I'm not sure how I'm meant to have done that when it's kept locked.'

'Interesting that you automatically assumed I meant inside it.'

Surprisingly, this observation didn't seem to unsettle Curt. 'What would you go all the way there for if you weren't going to go inside?' He asked, his blue eyes unmoving.

'Have you ever been inside?'

'I'm not sure if anyone has. I don't think there's even a telescope in there.'

'Scott's body was found not far from the observatory. Do you suppose he was meeting someone there?'

Curt shrugged. The movement set him off coughing, and he used his inhaler.

'If you've not been up there recently, why do you suppose Sid suggested otherwise?'

Curt used the inhaler again, whether because he needed to or simply to delay answering, Rebecca wasn't sure. Setting it back down on the cabinet, he said, 'I expect he wanted to teach me a lesson. He's not used to people talking back to him. I may have pushed him a bit far on Friday night.'

'Given his reputation were you not afraid of what he might do?'

'Not really, no. Although I probably should have been.' He paused. 'People always say you should stand up to bullies, don't they?' He rubbed the side of his face. 'I wouldn't mind betting those people have never had to.'

'Did you learn any more about what happened to Fray last night?' Rebecca asked, as Lawrence drove them back to the boarding house.

Her superior shook his head. 'No. There's something very odd about that boy. Wherever Guy Markham got the idea from, he was right when he called Fray erratic. This morning he was in pretty much the state I'd expect of someone who'd just attempted suicide – but by this afternoon he was totally unruffled. And he seemed a lot more collected than when I spoke to him on Monday, as well. Nothing I asked seemed to faze him, he challenged half my questions – it was all very calculated.'

'He's an intelligent boy, he's not likely to say anything stupid, is he?'

'It was more than that. He seemed – I don't know – cold. It was almost like he was playing some sort of absurd game with me. I honestly think he's of the opinion that he's clever enough to beat us.'

'That would be rather arrogant when one considers the value of forensics.'

'Arrogant is just the word. Although I suspect he's done his research. The librarian told me he's fascinated with forensics and toxicology, so he's probably well aware that forensic science is a lot less reliable than they make it look on TV.' Lawrence sighed. 'He basically said that unless people are unlucky, stupid or arrogant, they can get away with just about anything, and I think to a point that's true.'

Rebecca nodded. 'Did you get any more sense out of Nicky?'

'I really don't know,' Lawrence admitted. 'Today's story was that he and Fray were in the physics lab on Friday night. Developing photographs for Nicky's girlfriend. It seemed a bit far-fetched when they could have just printed them out using a computer, but I suppose it's possible.'

'Why would they have been doing that?'

'These photographs are supposedly of Nicky's girlfriend, wearing – well, not wearing much, which was the problem with developing them at some other time.'

'Ah,' Rebecca acknowledged, with a lift of her eyebrows. 'And what did Fray have to say about that?'

'Denied all knowledge.'

'I'm surprised he didn't take the opportunity of an alibi.'

'So was I, but he said it would be daft to lie about it because if we disproved it he'd be in a worse position.'

'He certainly seems to think things through.'

'Generally, yes. The suicide attempt seems to be something of an exception.'

'He didn't think Curt would be back for another hour.'

'Oh?'

'Curt went to some lectures organised by Guy Markham. He left early because he wasn't feeling well, went back to the room and found Fray.'

'So it seems Fray was serious about what he was doing.'

'That doesn't necessarily mean he's guilty of anything.'

'He may not be, but I'm sure he's up to something.'

'Curt didn't seem surprised Fray had attempted suicide. Perhaps we shouldn't assume the two events are related.'

'Rather a coincidence if they weren't,' Lawrence observed.

'And Nicky says Fray was with him when Scott died.'

'Today he does, but who knows what tomorrow's version of events might be.'

'What was Fray's involvement in Nicky's story?'

'Fray does photography on Wednesday afternoons, so he knows his way around the dark room. Nicky certainly has some photographs of this girl – whether that's where he got them from is another matter. I'm assuming Leighton can tell us how they were developed, at least. I've left a message asking if he can pop by to pick them up – presumably that'll be in the morning now.'

'Yeah, he said something about going to see some owls this evening.'

Lawrence frowned. 'He said what?'

Rebecca shrugged. 'I dunno, it was a text message. Maybe it was a typo.'

Lawrence's frown suddenly lifted. 'Did he say some or the?'

'What difference does it make?'

'If he said *the* Owls, he probably meant he was going to the football.'

'Oh,' Rebecca realised aloud. 'Yeah, that would make more sense.'

Lawrence looked amused.

'On that subject, have you been up to the school sports fields?'

'No, not yet. Why?'

'I wondered whether you'd seen the observatory. I heard about an argument Sid and Curt had last Friday, and when I spoke to Sid he had a few things to say about Curt that took me by surprise – not least the implication he had something to hide that involved meeting someone at the observatory.'

'Was that all he said?'

'I had a job getting that much out of him. Although whether it's true I don't know, if it is Curt certainly isn't giving anything away. I might have another go at Sid tomorrow.'

'If memory serves, the observatory isn't far from where Scott's body was found.'

'I know.'

'Maybe we could take a look at it in the morning.'

Rebecca nodded.

'If that doesn't throw something up I'm not sure what to try next,' Lawrence admitted. 'I just hope Leighton comes up with something useful. I'm starting to get the feeling I'm going round in ever-increasing circles.'

Katie had left Lawrence two messages within the space of half an hour, and in the second one she sounded more than a little impatient. She had no doubt just returned from Elise's school parents' evening – which Lawrence had also been due to attend –

and, leaving Rebecca to order dinner, he headed for his room to return the calls, hoping Katie's irritation was borne of his absence and not whatever Elise's teacher had had to say. The previous month's event had yielded less than glowing reports about Jimmy, who was apparently disinclined to apply himself to anything beyond the playing field. Noticing as he sat in the chair that overlooked the street that the lights were still on in the pharmacy opposite the guest house, he dialled his home number.

'Hello?'

'Kate, hi.'

'Finally,' Katie snapped. 'You know that bit in *Pretty Woman* when Richard Gere's girlfriend says she speaks to his secretary more than she speaks to him? That's how I'm starting to feel about your voicemail.'

'I'm sorry, I've only just finished work. How are you?'

'Tired,' Katie answered. 'It's been a long day.'

'What did Elise's teacher have to say?'

'She said Elise certainly knows why she's there,' Katie replied. 'And that although she's rather too easily distracted by gossip, she's doing very well, particularly at English and history.'

'Well that's good to hear.'

'Yes, she was very complimentary. She said it was a shame my husband couldn't be there to hear about his daughter's achievements.'

'Kate –'

'Elise also has some news she wants to tell you herself,' Katie continued. 'I'll let her do that in a minute. But first I need to talk to you about Jim.'

'Right,' Lawrence acknowledged, guessing from Katie's tone that he wasn't going to like whatever was coming.

Katie drew a deep breath. 'I had a call from the school this afternoon to tell me he's being put on detention every night next week for swearing at one of his teachers.'

Lawrence sighed, suspecting from the severity of the punishment that the infraction had involved more than a throwaway remark. In his own school days the first-line response to pupils' use of swear words had generally been a sharp 'language, please' and he didn't suppose the rules had changed markedly since. 'What happened?'

'I'm not really sure, to be honest,' Katie admitted. 'When I tried to talk to Jim about it he just shrugged and said *Mr Faulkes is a twat*. But from what I gathered from the headmaster, whatever disagreement they had culminated in Jimmy telling the man to go –' Katie hesitated, leaving the offending word to Lawrence's imagination and finishing, 'Himself.'

'Marvellous,' Lawrence muttered, sarcastically.

'And if he pushes his luck any further he'll be suspended.'

'Is he there now?'

'Yes. Do you want a word with him?'

'Yes, I most certainly do.'

'I'll get him. In the meantime, there's someone here who's itching to talk to you.'

There was a momentary pause before Elise's excited voice said, 'Daddy?'

'Hello pumpkin. Mummy tells me –'

'I got my level two gym award!' Elise interrupted.

'That's fantastic, well done,' Lawrence responded, trying to muster the appropriate degree of enthusiasm in the wake of the news about Jimmy. 'And I gather you're doing very well at school, as well. I –'

'My gym teacher said I should try trampolining,' Elise put in. 'Can I? Please?'

Lawrence found himself smiling. As far as Elise was concerned, a gymnastics badge clearly trumped a good school report. 'I don't see why not.'

'Yes!' Elise exclaimed. 'Sherri says it's really fun!'

'I'll look into it for you tomorrow.'

'When will you be back?'

'I'm afraid I don't know that yet.'

'It's not the same when you're not here.'

'I know.'

'Do you miss me?'

'Of course I do. I miss all of you.'

'Mummy said you're working at a boarding school.'

'That's right.'

There was a brief pause before Elise said, hesitantly, 'You won't ever send me away, will you?'

'No, pumpkin, of course not,' Lawrence reassured her. He wouldn't have been able to afford the fees even if he'd wanted to, but the question recalled to mind one he'd already asked himself a number of times that week: what motivated people to pack their sons or daughters off to boarding school? When Julian Ribet had said he thought it likely Nicky's father had sent his son to Treelore to get him out the way, Lawrence had wanted to ask why Julian had enrolled Scott. Some children, raised on a diet of *Harry Potter* and *St Trinians*, no doubt pushed for the chance to board themselves, but Lawrence suspected many weren't given a choice.

Boarding was an obvious solution for those who lived – or travelled frequently – abroad, but if the boys Lawrence had met that week were a representative sample, that accounted for only a fraction of cases. In others, no doubt, it was an upbringing the parents had themselves known; they were presumably of the mind that the experience hadn't done them any harm. Meanwhile, the opportunity to outsource the management of difficult teenage years was certainly an appealing prospect, Lawrence thought, wondering how a school like Treelore would deal with Jimmy's recent outburst, and whether handing over responsibility for discipline so completely for eight months a year diminished the capacity for familial conflict or simply condensed it. His relationship with his parents had certainly improved after he moved out, but by then he had been an adult himself, and the duration of his return visits had been limited by the pressures of work and geography to a few days at a time. Had he returned for weeks on end, he suspected the results would have been less than harmonious.

However, having travelled for the best part of an hour at both ends of the day for much of his school career, he could see how a paucity of good schools in the local area might well prove a motivating factor. So, indeed, might the desire to remove a child from that area altogether. He wondered whether the loss of one son to drug addiction had prompted Francis's parents to consign the other to a seemingly safe, controlled environment – realising, almost as he thought it, that it was equally possible Francis's elder sibling had himself been a boarder. Or perhaps not. If they'd wittingly set Francis on the same course as his brother, Lawrence couldn't even begin to imagine how the Birchams would be able to sleep at night.

Seven

John Richardson had just finished teaching a class when Rebecca tracked him down on Thursday morning, and as the boys filed past her, he shouted after them, 'If that essay isn't on my desk by half nine tomorrow morning, God help you!' Turning back to the front desk, he removed his spectacles and carefully slid them into their case. Once the sea of fourteen-year-olds had dispersed, Rebecca entered the classroom. 'Mr Richardson?'

'John, please.'

'Do you have another class now?'

'Not right now, no. If you've more than a couple of questions, could we go over them in my office? This classroom's in use for the next period.'

'Certainly.'

Gathering up his books, he started towards the door. Rebecca followed him from the room and along several corridors until he stopped outside a door headed with his name. Fishing a bunch of keys from his pocket, he unlocked it and pushed it open. Planting his load on the desk by the window, he offered Rebecca a seat with a flick of his wrist before dropping into his own. Rebecca sat, looking about herself. The room was small and tidy, and lined with bookshelves. The effect would have been very smart, were it not for the lopsided blind at the window.

'How can I help?'

'I'm interested to know how prefects are chosen,' Rebecca began. 'Because the ones we've come across so far seem like rather odd choices. Besides Scott, there's Sid Watson – who appears to entertain himself by picking on people, much as Scott seems to have done – and Nicky Greenwood, who more than one person has described as a compulsive liar.'

John sighed. 'I understand where you're coming from,' he acknowledged. 'As far as Sid's concerned, the decision on house prefects lies with the housemaster. And between you and me, I rarely agree with Edward's choices. In Nicky's case, it was hoped some responsibility might be good for him. That, I have to admit, was a gamble that doesn't seem to have paid off.' John leaned back in his chair, loosely crossing his legs. 'There are always a few boys who stand out as good prefect material, and it's usually not hard to select the head boy and his deputy, but there are always some difficult decisions to make, as well.'

'Who is the head boy?' Rebecca asked, realising she'd not even been aware the school had one.

'A lad called James Robinson. He's in Bailey House.'

'And the deputy?'

'Curt Wilkinson. Although, to be honest, this term he's barely been well enough to manage his school work, never mind any extra duties. It's a shame. He's a nice lad, and he's a very good public speaker – which I know you'd never guess from talking to him – but in the past six months or so his health has deteriorated quite badly.'

'I don't imagine it helps that he's worrying about his room mate on top of that.'

'No,' John raised his eyebrows. 'And God only knows what it must have been like for him finding Francis on Tuesday evening.' He shook his head. 'Francis has been a real concern, not least because we have no idea what the problem is. Curt thinks he has an eating disorder, but I don't know that he's right. I've seen a couple of boys with that sort of problem before, but they were inclined to eat very little and do ridiculous amounts of exercise. I don't think I've ever seen Francis so much as put a tracksuit on without being ordered to do so.'

'Did Curt say anything else on the subject?'

'No, not really. Only that he was worried and didn't know what the problem was. I asked him because I couldn't get a word out of Francis.'

'So he didn't come to see you of his own volition.'

'Neither of them did. The whole point of having housemasters and form tutors is to keep an eye on the boys. If we think there's a problem, we don't hesitate to ask.'

'Perhaps they might get to the bottom of it now he's in hospital.'

'I sincerely hope so. I'll be going down there later today to see how he is.'

'How does that procedure work?' Rebecca asked.

'What procedure?'

'Visiting boys. In hospital, or in the san. Is that a regular staff practice?'

'No, not for all staff, but obviously form tutors and housemasters have a greater responsibility to the boys. If one of the boys in my class is unwell for more than a day or two I usually make a point of looking in on him.'

'Would you be surprised if other members of staff did the same?'

'I suppose it would depend on the circumstances.'

'How about Curt?'

'That wouldn't really surprise me, no. He's spent about as much time in the san as he has in class this term. His mother didn't even want him coming back after the Christmas holidays. She's concerned he feels under pressure from his father to keep up with his studies. I'm inclined to agree that he's not really well enough to be here, but when I've talked to him about it he's been adamant he wants to stay, so –' John held his hands out rather helplessly.

A thought occurred to Rebecca. 'If the boys required extra tuition, where would that be given?'

'That would depend. Probably in a classroom, or possibly in a teacher's office. It would really hinge on the number of boys involved.'

'So not in a boy's bedroom.'

'Definitely not. That wouldn't be appropriate.'

'How about a teacher's apartment?'

'Ditto, I think.'

'You met with Curt in your apartment earlier this week.'

'That's true, but that wasn't about work and it wasn't a scheduled meeting. If they come knocking on my door I don't turn them away.'

'Why did he want to see you?'

'That's between me and him.'

Rebecca nodded. She was about to change the subject when a knock came at the door.

'Come in!' John called, shooting Rebecca an apologetic look.

A boy in his mid-teens peered around the door.

'Ah, Mr Hitchcock,' John sat up in his chair. 'I presume you've come to explain the absence of yet another essay?'

The boy squirmed uncomfortably. 'Yes, sir.'

'And what totally implausible excuse would you like to offer this week?' John enquired, drily. 'Perhaps Communist Russian hard-liners have stolen it?'

Rebecca had to suppress a smile.

'Uh – no, sir.'

'You do surprise me. Green activists, was it?'

'I did start writing it – but then I got upset and couldn't concentrate.'

'I see. What was it that upset you?'

'Bircham, sir. He lives in my house – and –' the boy broke off, dropping his eyes to the floor.

'Would you like to explain how that upset you to the point where you were unable to write an essay, considering Francis isn't in your year, nor, as far as I am aware, is he a friend of yours?'

'I'm scared, sir.'

'You're scared?' John echoed, looking puzzled.

The boy raised his gaze anxiously. 'Someone's already tried to kill two people in my house – what if they try to kill me, too?'

'And where did you get the impression that in this instance anybody other than Francis was involved?'

'Greenwood, sir.'

'Oh for goodness' sake, surely you don't give any credence to Dominic's nonsense? You must know him well enough by now.'

'Hang on,' Rebecca interjected. 'What exactly did he say?'

'He said he couldn't see why anyone would want to kill him when he seemed to be doing such a good job of it himself.'

'Meaning what?'

'I don't really know. I thought it was supposed to be suicide, but when I said that, Greenwood –' he stopped again.

'What did Nicky do?'

The boy swallowed. 'He – he said *but that's what you're supposed to think. Clever, eh?* It didn't seem like he was joking.'

Rebecca nodded, digesting this information. After a moment, John dismissed the boy, saying, 'All right, Hitchcock, I'll let you off this time, but I want that essay tomorrow, first thing. Clear?'

'Yes sir,' the boy nodded, turning and scurrying away before his teacher had a chance to change his mind.

'That's an interesting story,' Rebecca observed.

'Dominic tells an awful lot of interesting stories. He gave his third year class a fantastically vivid account of his childhood in Nepal. The boy grew up in Hampstead. He likes being the centre of attention, and if saying something peculiar achieves that, you can almost guarantee he'll say it. I wouldn't read too much into it.'

Rebecca didn't reply, wondering why the idea hadn't occurred to her before. Thanking John Richardson for his time, she rose to leave. Perhaps it was time she met the boy she had heard so much about.

Rebecca had barely drawn breath to update Lawrence on her meeting with John Richardson when his mobile rang. He glanced at the screen before answering it.

'Hello, I wasn't expecting to hear from you yet.' Several seconds passed before he said, 'Now? Ok, we'll be right there.' He hung up. 'Leighton,' he offered, by way of explanation, as he looked to Rebecca. 'Apparently he's waiting for us in the drive.' He turned for the double doors onto reception.

'Why didn't he just come in?'

'I've no idea. Maybe he wants to torment me some more with that car of his.'

Rebecca smiled. 'You do know he didn't buy it new, don't you?'

'Yes. Although even so, how he can take it to Gleadless Valley and sleep at night, I have no idea.'

'What?'

'That's where his parents live.'

'How do you know where his parents live?'

'I asked him,' Lawrence replied, simply. 'And given the estate's reputation, I'm amazed his car has any windows left.'

'Maybe the reputation is exaggerated.'

'I don't know. I asked Leighton and he just flashed that cheeky grin of his and said nobody would dare mess with it, which I have to say left me a little nonplussed, given that he's one of the least threatening people I've ever met.'

Rebecca imagined the remark had related not to Leighton's character but to that of his elder brother. But, guessing her friend might not appreciate her telling his colleagues about Tom's fairly lengthy rap sheet, she said, 'Maybe he has a garage.'

Lawrence laughed. 'I never thought of that.'

As predicted, Leighton was leaning against the bonnet of his car, which looked to be in perfect nick, his long hair roughly fastened in a pony tail. He was clad in jeans, a leather jacket and a grey t-shirt proclaiming *Religion is stupid*, which Rebecca suspected answered the question of why he'd not come into the school building.

'Nice shirt,' Lawrence remarked, sarcastically.

'Some of us didn't get to pack for the week,' Leighton replied, pleasantly. 'I had to raid Tom's wardrobe.'

'Does Tom wear that kind of thing to work?'

'The words *Tom* and *work* are about as familiar with one another as vegetarians are with foie gras,' Leighton returned. 'Between obscene cartoons and offensive jokes about Tourette's, this was the best I could do. And at least I don't disagree with the sentiment.'

Lawrence raised his eyebrows but didn't comment further, saying, 'Did you have a chance to pick up the photographs?'

'Yep. And they're not digital. I can't tell you where or when they were developed – at least, not at a glance – but they were produced the old-fashioned way.'

'And did your sweep of room three-one-nine throw up anything interesting?'

Leighton shook his head slightly. 'I'm not sure. Something doesn't quite add up and it's bugging me.'

'Well what have you got?'

'First up, there are traces of chloroethane on Fray's sheets. I'm not sure whether that's relevant or simply an artefact of the fact he studies chemistry, because other traces included iodine, potassium permanganate and red phosphorus.'

Lawrence blinked in surprise. 'Are the lab technicians up here on steroids?'

'Nah. I prevailed upon a mate who works in the chemistry department at Leeds Uni.'

Lawrence frowned. 'Much as I appreciate the quick turnaround, you should not be outsourcing police work without authorisation! You do realise that –'

'Relax,' Leighton interrupted, sounding mildly exasperated. 'I didn't outsource anything, I just borrowed his lab and mass spectrometer.'

'Since when did you know how to do that?'

'It's hardly rocket science,' he remarked, before adding, with a grin, 'Mind you, I've never been convinced that's particularly complicated either. Stick a mass of fuel under a payload, strike a match, *voilà*.'

'Ok,' Lawrence acknowledged with a nod. 'So what makes the chloro – whatever it was – interesting?'

'Chloroethane. It's an anaesthetic. It's not used medically as such any more – at least, not in the UK – but you can use it to knock people out.'

Lawrence's eyebrows rose.

'Second, the blood on his shirt. I can't tell you whose it is yet, but there's no sign of the kind of spatter pattern you'd expect from proximity to wounds like those inflicted on Scott. It looks more like it's been soaked in blood. The stain is also on the right sleeve, and –'

'Fray is left-handed,' Lawrence put in.

'Yes.'

'So we may not be looking at attempted suicide at all,' Lawrence observed. 'It could be attempted murder. Someone else may have put him out and cut his wrists, implicating him for Scott's murder with the shirt – presumably soaked in his own blood – and the poem.'

'That would explain why Fray claims to remember nothing about it,' Rebecca put in.

Lawrence nodded.

'I know it makes for a nice neat theory,' Leighton acknowledged. 'But I also found a scalpel blade under the bed, and the only prints on it belong to Fray.'

'Could someone not have orchestrated that?' Lawrence asked.

'It's possible, but there's blood residue along the blade, and that looks undisturbed. It seems unlikely someone could have wiped the rest of it clean without interfering with that.'

'But if he did do it himself, how did his shirt turn up half a mile away and covered in blood the following morning when he'd been in hospital all night?'

Leighton held out his hands. 'This is what's bugging me. Something doesn't make sense.

'Fray didn't say he knew nothing about the shirt,' Rebecca observed. 'He said it wasn't Scott's blood and that he had been going to wash it.'

'You're suggesting someone found the shirt already like that?' Lawrence asked.

'Maybe,' Rebecca replied. 'Whether or not he attempted suicide, he did write that poem. He said it wasn't about suicide.

Perhaps it was about self harm. That would also explain how he came to have a scalpel blade with his fingerprints on.'

'You think he cuts himself?'

'It's possible.'

Lawrence shook his head. 'I don't understand what possesses people to do that.'

'It's a coping mechanism. It helps people to dissociate themselves from emotional pain.'

Lawrence regarded her quizzically. Rebecca felt uncomfortable. She didn't want to reveal the source of that information – Elliot – and wished she'd kept her mouth shut. To her relief, Leighton deflected her superior's attention, saying, 'Well if that is it, clearly at least one other person knows about it.'

'Curt,' Lawrence guessed. 'Although I doubt he's the only one, in a place like this I should imagine it would be pretty difficult keeping something like that to yourself.'

'Not necessarily,' Leighton countered. 'Most people are a lot less observant than you give them credit for. Plenty of people knock their kids about for years without anyone ever noticing.'

'Yes, I know,' Lawrence conceded. 'Something else I find totally incomprehensible.'

'Speaking of incomprehensible, I've just heard about a rather interesting comment of Nicky's, pertaining to the question of what happened to Fray,' Rebecca revealed.

'Oh?'

'He apparently gave one of the younger boys the impression that what happened to Fray was attempted murder. When the boy said he thought it had been suicide, Nicky replied *that's what you're supposed to think*.'

'Did he now. Well then I think we want to find out what he was doing on Tuesday evening.'

'Perhaps we ought to see what Fray has to say about his shirt before we go any further,' Rebecca suggested.

'That's probably a good idea. Do you want to do that while Leighton and I take a look at the observatory? After last night I think I've had just about all I can take from that boy.'

'Sure.'

'I'm beginning to hope he wasn't involved. It would make life immeasurably easier.'

*****

The observatory comprised a small, octagonal red-brick building that stood to the west of the sports fields, its domed roof ice green with the patina of copper carbonate. A low hedge ran around its perimeter, coming to a neat halt either side of the heavy oak door. The school's crest appeared above the entrance, the date 1905 carved into the shield, and the lintel bore a one-line inscription in Latin, attributed to Copernicus. Leighton's knowledge of the language was largely confined to medical terms and species names, but he managed to make out the words *highest, all* and *stars*.

Surprisingly, the aged lock turned silently, although the rusty iron door handle let out a low groan as Lawrence twisted it clockwise. He stepped inside, holding the door for Leighton, and flicked on the light. A bare bulb screwed into a socket fixed directly to the wall, this provided illumination that could barely be described as adequate, and revealed that the observatory's interior had been lined almost exclusively with wood. The beams that made up the wall – Leighton presumed it wouldn't take the plural, given that it was a single circular structure – were arranged vertically, while those of the tapering panels within the dome had been stacked horizontally, not unlike those inside the cap of the Suffolk windmill he had visited the previous summer. The cords rigged up to operate the shutters were grey and fraying, and he guessed they would no longer be up to the job. Given that the room was bereft of a telescope, it seemed they were, in any case, redundant.

'How come this isn't in use?'

'I'm not sure,' Lawrence admitted. 'The head said it was decommissioned about twenty years ago, but he didn't say why. Maybe it's not relevant to the syllabus. Or maybe it's just easier to use pictures from NASA's website.'

'Maybe,' Leighton echoed. 'But surely seeing it for yourself is more inspiring than looking at images from Hubble and Spitzer?'

'I suppose it's a matter of time and resources.'

Leighton grunted in acknowledgement, crouching down and running a finger across the floorboards. 'Do you know how often this place is cleaned?' He asked, looking up into the dome.

'No. But I don't imagine it's done often.'

'Maybe not, but it's been cleaned recently. There's no dust on the floor. And I can't see a single cobweb.'

Lawrence looked around himself before nodding. Leighton returned his eyes to the floor. At first glance he drew a blank. On the second sweep, a fleck of light towards one side stopped him short, and he shuffled forwards to take a closer look. The source of the light – a reflection of that cast by the lone bulb – was wedged between two floorboards, and he reached into his inside jacket pocket for his Swiss Army Knife.

'Do you always carry that?' Lawrence asked, as Leighton coaxed the tweezers from their nook at the end of the tool.

'Pretty much,' he glanced up. 'Why, you going to charge me with possessing an offensive weapon?'

'If you were stopped and had one of those on you, technically you could be.'

'Yeah, yeah, I know,' Leighton replied, returning the knife to his pocket. 'It's absurd. Or should I say arbitrary. There's no law against carrying pencils or guitar strings, but I've seen people killed using both.'

'With a *pencil*?'

'Uh-huh. Straight through the eye into the brain.'

Lawrence winced at the thought and Leighton adjusted his grip on the tweezers before guiding the tips between the floorboards. A couple of seconds later, he drew out a thin strip of foil that looked as if someone had taken pinking shears to the ends.

'What's that?'

'At a guess, a strip off a condom wrapper,' he turned it around and noticed several minuscule characters running parallel to the straight edge. 'And given that it's dated two years hence, I'm guessing it's been here weeks or months rather than years.'

Lawrence raised his eyebrows. 'That is interesting.'

Leighton searched his pockets with his free hand and, failing to locate an evidence bag, carefully wrapped the sliver of foil in a paper napkin from Pret a Manger. Pocketing it, he cast his eyes around the room again. 'Do you know how many keys there are to this place? There's clearly no other way in or out.'

'A handful, by all accounts.'

'And do you think Scott was heading here the night he died?'

'It's possible. He wasn't all that far away.'

Leighton nodded, straightening up and turning to open the door in the hope of getting better light. The door handle felt loose as he opened it. 'This could do with tightening,' he observed, plying it back and forth. 'It's got a –' he broke off as something caught his attention, bending to take a closer look.

'What?' Lawrence asked.

Leighton indicated the points at which the screws fixed the handle to the door, pulling it first one way, then the other. In the millimetre or so surrounding the screws, the rust that blanketed the handle had completely rubbed away. 'Rust doesn't just disappear,' he observed. 'Either this door has seen a lot of use recently or someone's been having a hell of a go at it.'

'You mean –'

'Someone's been shut in here and trying to get out.'

'Morning,' Rebecca greeted Mr Bircham, who was hovering outside Francis's room at the hospital. 'Is Fray with the doctor?' She asked, noticing that the door was shut.

'Psychiatrist,' Mr Bircham replied. 'And don't think I'm going to let you upset him again once he's finished.'

'I'm sorry?'

'What did your colleague say to him yesterday? Fray was all right when he arrived – afterwards he was inconsolable for almost two hours!'

'Fray's not been particularly cooperative. I'm sorry if DCI Forrester upset him, but I think he was trying to bring home to Fray that this isn't a game.'

'What do you mean, he's not been cooperative?'

'He won't answer a good number of our questions.'

'Why should he? What's he done wrong?'

'That's a very good question.'

There was a moment's shocked silence before Mr Bircham replied. 'You're not suggesting he had anything to do with what happened to Scott, are you?'

'We can't rule anyone out at the moment.'

'How dare you?' He demanded, furiously. 'For God's sake, my son has just tried to kill himself and you're in here accusing him of murdering one of his friends!'

'I'm sorry, I understand that –'

'You understand nothing! And you will not speak to Francis again without the doctor's say so! He's in a bad enough way without any help from you!'

Rebecca sighed. 'Perhaps you might be able to help on this occasion.'

'Me? How?'

'Do you know whether Fray cuts himself?'

There was a long pause before Mr Bircham nodded. 'Yes. Yes, he does. Why do you ask?'

'We found a shirt that was heavily stained with blood – we wondered how it came to be like that.'

'Fray doesn't like people to know. He doesn't want anyone thinking he does it for attention.'

'Do you suppose any of his school friends know?'

'I've no idea. I doubt Fray's told anybody, but then he didn't tell us either.'

'How did you find out?'

'Adam – that's our other son – told us. I don't know how he knew.'

'Fray told me his brother died of a heroin overdose.'

'Simon didn't overdose. He committed suicide.'

'Oh – I'm sorry – I must have misunderstood –'

Mr Bircham shook his head. 'Fray tells a lot of people that. Sometimes I think he believes it himself. But he had two brothers – Adam's the eldest. He and Fray don't really get on, especially since Adam told us about –' Mr Bircham stopped awkwardly. 'Fray was furious.'

Rebecca nodded. 'Well, thank you for your help. I realise this must be a very difficult time for you.'

'I'd rather you talk to me than Fray. He's fragile enough as it is.'

'I'm aware of that,' Rebecca replied. 'My fiance suffers from severe depression, so I do have some idea of what Fray's going through, and I don't want to add to that, but so far he's been extremely unhelpful.'

'He can be rather uncommunicative,' Mr Bircham acknowledged.

That, Rebecca thought, was an understatement. The boy hadn't just been uncommunicative, he had almost gone out of his way to hinder the investigation. That he was still hiding something, she had little doubt.

* * * * *

'Come!' An unfamiliar voice answered Lawrence's knock on the door of room 318. It seemed Nicky was not alone. Lawrence opened the door to find an immaculately dressed man in his fifties standing beside the desk, stopped as if he had been pacing. Tall and lean, he wore a beautifully fitting grey suit that Lawrence suspected was bespoke, a sky blue shirt and a dark tie with a small, repeating red motif. A white handkerchief was folded neatly into his breast pocket. His hair – which looked unnaturally dark for his age – was carefully groomed, his narrow rimmed spectacles positioned halfway down his pointed nose. From the similarity of their builds, Lawrence guessed the man was Nicky's father.

'Yes?' He said, with a frown.

'I'm DCI Forrester, this is DS Palmer – we'd like a word with Nicky.'

'Lord alive, Dominic, what have you done now?' The man exclaimed. Turning to Lawrence, he offered a hand, saying, 'Marcus Greenwood.'

Lawrence shook his hand, pleased to have the chance to see Nicky and his father together.

'What's he been up to this time?'

'I don't know that he's been up to anything. I'd just like to ask a few questions in relation to recent events at the school.'

Marcus nodded, taking a seat at Nicky's desk. 'Go ahead.'

Lawrence turned towards Nicky, who was sitting on his bed, head bowed and eyes on the floor.

'We've been told you don't think Fray attempted suicide at all, Nicky. To quote what we've heard, you said *that's what you're supposed to think*. Would you like to tell me what made you say that?'

Nicky didn't immediately reply, and Marcus snapped, 'You heard the question, Dominic, answer the man.'

When he did, Nicky's demeanour in the presence of his father was so subdued that Lawrence was left in little doubt the boy was terrified of him. 'I dunno,' Nicky muttered, not looking up.

'Don't be ridiculous, Dominic. You don't make a statement like that for no reason. Explain yourself.'

Nicky shrugged. 'It seemed funny at the time.'

'Funny?' Lawrence echoed. 'One of your friends was in hospital and it seemed funny?'

Nicky murmured something inaudible.

'Speak up, Dominic! And look at people when you're talking to them!'

Nicky raised his head, very pale. 'I don't know. I didn't really think about it.'

'I see. What would you say if I told you we're treating what happened to Fray as attempted murder?'

The look on Nicky's face was of complete and utter shock. Lawrence wondered whether that was at the revelation itself, or the fact someone had worked it out.

'What?' He whispered.

'We think someone tried to kill Fray and make it look like suicide. Do you have anything to say about that?'

Nicky swallowed hard, his face discolouring.

'What exactly are you suggesting?' Marcus asked, coldly.

'I'd like to know why the idea occurred to him. It certainly didn't occur to me until I received the results of some forensic tests. Nicky doesn't have access to forensics, as far as I'm aware.'

'Is that a subtle way of saying you think he's been trying to murder his friends?' Marcus demanded, looking incensed.

'Not necessarily, no. I'd just like to know whether he knows anything that led him to form that idea.'

'You think he's involved somehow? That's ludicrous!'

'Is it?' Lawrence returned his attention to Nicky. He hadn't moved, and had his hands clasped tightly. His knuckles were white.

'My son's no angel, I'm well aware of that – it doesn't make him a killer!'

'I'd like an answer from Nicky.'

Nicky went to speak, but didn't manage to form any words. There was a long pause before he struggled to his feet. 'I feel sick,' he said, his voice choked.

'Sit down and answer my question.'

Closing his eyes, Nicky sank back onto his bed. 'I didn't mean anything by it,' he said, weakly. 'I just say stupid things sometimes. I don't know why.'

'I'm afraid I don't believe you,' Lawrence replied.

'I don't know why,' Nicky repeated.

'Chief Inspector, he talks nonsense most of the time. It doesn't mean anything,' Marcus defended him. Turning to his son, he added, 'I told you all those lies were going to land you in trouble one day, didn't I? How many times have I warned you?'

'What were you doing on Tuesday evening, Nicky?' Lawrence asked.

'I was in the art department.'

'Doing what?'

'Some sketching. Preparing for Wednesday's class.'

'Until what time?'

'I don't know. I spend so many evenings there. I like art.'

'I'm running out of patience, Nicky.'

Nicky met Lawrence's eyes. 'I honestly can't remember. I have a really bad memory. I forget things all the time. I get lost in art, or music – and everything else just fades into nothing.'

'This bad memory of yours has been rather convenient, hasn't it?'

'He's telling the truth,' Marcus put in. 'He has an appalling memory. How he passes exams I have no idea.'

'Were you in the house when Curt found Fray?'

'No.'

'Are you sure?'

'Why would I hurt Fray?' Nicky ran a shaking hand through his hair. 'What's he ever done to me?'

'It seems someone wanted to implicate him for Scott's murder.'

'I told you. I was with Fray that night. He never did anything!'

'But Fray denies being with you on Friday night.'

Nicky shook his head. 'Well he's wrong.'

'Do you have any proof he's been involved in any of what's happened this week?' Marcus enquired, icily.

'I'm not accusing Nicky of anything at this stage.'

'From where I'm standing it sounds exactly as if you're accusing him, and if you're going to pursue this any further, I shall be forced to call my solicitor. My son's not answering another question on the subject without legal advice.'

'We –'

'No. I've said no more questions, and I mean it. That's your lot.'

Lawrence looked to Nicky. The boy had rested his elbows on his knees and buried his face in his hands. Marcus had moved so that he stood protectively in front of his son, between Nicky and Lawrence.

'All right,' Lawrence agreed. 'We'll leave you to it. No doubt we'll be seeing you again.'

Marcus made no reply. He looked furious. Lawrence wondered how much of that fury was likely to be taken out on Nicky.

'He wasn't exactly what I expected,' Rebecca remarked, as she and Lawrence descended the stairs of Windsor House. There was a pause before she added, 'I can see he perhaps had opportunity, but thus far we're pretty short on motive.'

'I know. But the housemaster seemed to think Scott and Nicky were arguing in the hours before Scott died, so who knows what may have gone on between them. It undoubtedly doesn't help that at least half of what Nicky has told me has been total fabrication. I'll see if I can have another chat with him later, when his father isn't around.' Lawrence drew his mobile from his pocket and glanced at the screen. 'Right now, I want to speak to Curt.'

'Why?'

'Whoever cut Fray's wrists must have known where to find the poem, and quite possibly the shirt. Curt knows Fray better than most, and he shares a room with him.'

'But he was the one who found Fray.'

'Perhaps he lost his nerve, or changed his mind. Where was Curt before it happened?'

'At a lecture in the Great Hall.'

'That's right. Do you know where he went from there?'

'He said he sat in the quad for a while, then went back to the room.'

'In the quad? I don't suppose anyone can account for that, can they?'

'Sir, he really isn't well. I don't think he'd have had the strength.'

'How much strength does it take to anaesthetise a sleeping person? On top of which, Curt studies biology and chemistry – I should think he'd have a fair idea of how to go about it all. Since you've spoken to him before, you'd best come with me. How do we get to the san?'

Vivien Thompson glanced up from filing her nails as Rebecca and Lawrence entered her office.

'Hello. Are you looking for Curt again?'

'Yes,' Rebecca confirmed. 'Is he any better?'

'No, not really. He fell asleep yesterday evening, then had a nightmare and woke up screaming. I gave him some sleeping pills in the end, but he just screamed in his sleep instead of waking up. I don't think it's done him any good, to be honest.'

'Can we go through?'

Vivien hesitated before nodding. 'Ok. But be gentle with him. He's been quite tearful today. I think everything's starting to catch up with him.'

Curt was lying in bed, a blue Ventolin inhaler in the slack fingers of his right hand. He looked desperately tired and his face was pasty. He glanced up as Rebecca and Lawrence entered the room and Rebecca bid him hello before introducing her superior.

'How are you feeling?'

'Pretty rough.'

'I'm sorry to have to ask you more questions.'

Curt closed his eyes momentarily. 'Do I have to do it now?'

'It won't take long.'

He nodded resignedly.

Rebecca sat down. 'Do you know a lot about Fray?'

'As much as anyone knows about him, I suppose.'

'Yesterday you told me the only person Fray was capable of hurting was himself. What did you mean by that?'

'After what happened on Tuesday night, I should have thought that was obvious,' Curt replied, coughing and struggling to sit up.

'Is that all you meant?'

'Why?'

'Do you know whether he cuts himself?'

Curt cast his eyes down, nodding. 'Yeah.'

'Does anyone else know about that?'

He shrugged, then began coughing again.

'How about his poetry?'

'What about it?'

'Do many people know about it?'

'Probably. He writes poems all the time.'

'Does he let you read them?'

'Only the ones that form song lyrics.'

'Have you ever had a look when he wasn't around?'

'Do you think I have no respect for his privacy?' Curt returned, clearly upset by the implication.

'Do you know whether anyone else has read any of them?'

'I don't know.'

'Can you take us through your exact movements on the night you found Fray, please?' Lawrence asked.

Curt's eyes flickered towards the doorway, his expression growing still more anxious. Rebecca turned to see Guy Markham standing in the corridor, looking rather shocked to find himself face to face with Rebecca.

'Hello,' she greeted him.

'Hi. I'm looking for Vivien. Do you know where she is?'

'No.' Rebecca looked to Curt. 'You?'

Curt shook his head, his respirations quickening.

'Ok. Thanks.' Guy flashed a smile and disappeared. Curt ran a shaking hand through his hair.

Lawrence repeated his question.

'I don't feel well. Please can I do this later?'

'It won't take long. When you've been through Tuesday evening we'll be done.'

Tears filled Curt's eyes. 'I can't,' he whispered. 'I can't do it now.'

'All right,' Rebecca agreed, mindful of what Vivien had said. 'Maybe you could try writing us an account when you're feeling a bit better.'

Curt raised a hand to dry his eyes, which promptly filled up again. He drew a rather unsteady breath before starting to cough and reaching to rub his chest.

Reluctant to leave the boy alone, Rebecca looked to Lawrence. 'Maybe you should find Vivien.'

Lawrence nodded, making for the door. Rebecca turned back to Curt, who was clearly struggling to maintain some degree of composure.

'I'm sorry, I know this must be very painful for you,' she offered.

'I just –' he pursed his lips, blinking rapidly. 'I can't – I –' he shrugged, raising a fist to his mouth.

'It's all right.'

'I'm scared,' he whispered, roughly wiping his eyes again.

Rebecca frowned. 'What of?'

He bit his lip. 'What's going to happen t–' he stopped himself.

'What's going to happen to who?'

He shook his head.

'Please tell me what's worrying you.'

There was a long pause before Curt drew breath to answer. As he did so, Vivien appeared in the doorway.

'It's all right, my love,' she soothed, perching on the bed and reaching to hold Curt. 'You're ok.' Looking to Rebecca, she said, 'Do you think you could give him some space?'

'Of course,' Rebecca agreed, moving to stand. 'I'm sorry we upset him.'

Vivien nodded, giving her a cursory smile, and Rebecca joined Lawrence in the corridor outside the room, pulling the door to as she left. The two of them walked slowly in the direction of the exit.

'Well, something freaked him out,' Lawrence observed, as they left the building.

Rebecca nodded. 'He said he was scared about what's going to happen.'

'To him? Or at the school?'

'I don't know, Vivien came in before I got that far.'

'Do you think it had something to do with what happened on Tuesday evening? He clearly didn't want to talk about that.'

'I'm not sure whether that was what upset him, or whether it had something to do with Guy Markham. Whatever the case, it can't be much fun for him being reminded of what happened.'

'Guy didn't look too thrilled to see us either,' Lawrence observed.

'No, he didn't.'

'I'd like to know what he was doing on Tuesday evening. There's something about him that bothers me. He seems –' Lawrence paused, searching for the word he wanted. 'Edgy,' he concluded. 'I think, perhaps, we might pay him a visit.'

'You off, son?' Glenn Campbell called from the living room as Leighton carried his bag down the stairs.

'In a minute.'

'Your mam left a book out for you, on the side in the kitchen.'

'Thanks.' Leighton set his holdall down in the hallway before looking into the living room. His father was sitting in his chair by the door, a mug of tea on the table beside him and a copy of *The*

Mirror open in his lap. He was in the process of trying to roll a cigarette, his hands shaking badly. Sensing Leighton's presence behind him, he turned, holding it out. 'Can you do this for us?'

Leighton wordlessly took the folded cigarette paper, tapped it a few times to even out the tobacco's distribution, then carefully rolled the paper into a neat cylinder.

'What happened to your face?' Glenn asked.

Leighton met his father's eyes. The whites were yellow with liver disease, but the irides were the same steel blue as his own – one of many features they shared. The fear of turning out like his father was never far from his thoughts. Returning his attention to the rollie in his hands, he replied, coolly, 'You weren't that drunk.' He licked the edge of the cigarette paper before sealing it and handing it back to Glenn.

'Cheers,' Glenn reached for the lighter on the table.

'Has Mum turned the heating down again?' Leighton asked, noticing the heavy condensation on the windows. He'd dropped in unannounced early in January to find her wearing gloves and a scarf indoors, the thermostat set to thirteen degrees, and had promptly put fifty pounds on the gas meter. Perhaps he needed to repeat the exercise.

'Nah,' Glenn replied as he lit up. 'The radiator's playing up.'

'It probably just needs bleeding.'

'Probably,' Glenn concurred. 'I'll have a look at it in a bit.'

Leighton sighed. Where his father was concerned, *in a bit* could mean anything from hours to weeks. 'I'll do it,' he offered, turning back towards the hallway. A large cardboard box stamped with the logo of the convenience store where his mother worked was obscuring the door to the cupboard beneath the stairs, and he moved it aside, surprised she had allowed it to remain there. The asymmetric cupboard door had been warped for as long as he could remember, and he pressed down on the doorknob as he tugged it towards himself to free it from the frame.

The paraphernalia stored out of sight beyond the door had been as exactingly arranged as everything else in the house, and Leighton half expected the contents of Glenn's tool box to be similarly ordered. They weren't, and it took him the best part of a minute to locate a radiator key among the assorted screwdrivers, nails, hacksaw blades – most of them rusty – rawl plugs, fuses, wire cutters and wrenches. He flicked the heating off and grabbed a tea towel from the kitchen before returning to the living room.

'So,' Glenn said, conversationally, as Leighton crouched between the sofa and the sideboard. 'When are we going to meet your new woman?'

'Eh?' Leighton looked around with a frown.

'Your mam's been on about some girl called Pandora.'

'Pandora's a cat, Dad.'

'A cat?' Glenn exclaimed. 'What the hell have you gone and got one of them for?'

Leighton sighed. He hadn't *planned* on taking in a furry lodger. The little black and white creature had simply turned up in his garden one day, half starved. He'd called an animal-welfare charity on her behalf; their advice had been to stop feeding her and she'd go away. When he'd objected that he couldn't ignore the animal's plight and asked whether the charity couldn't do something for her, the response had been that if she wasn't microchipped they would put her to sleep. So Pandora had stayed put, and in the weeks that followed had graduated from eating outside the back door to dining in the kitchen, and from sleeping under the decking to snoozing on the sofa. Guessing Glenn's response to this story would be to endorse the charity's proposed course of action – if not worse – he said, 'She keeps the rats away from the cookie jar.'

'I'd be surprised if the rats could get a look-in,' Glenn returned. 'When did you ever leave cookies in the jar?'

Leighton ignored the jibe, fitting the key into the radiator and nudging it anticlockwise. After a moment, Glenn continued in his original vein. 'Have you seen Millie recently?'

'Yes, Dad. I took Dylan to the match last night, remember?'

'Is that why you didn't come home?'

Leighton felt irritated. 'I wasn't aware I was under curfew.'

'So that's a yes,' Glenn assumed. 'You know, I never understood why you didn't marry that girl.'

Leighton resisted the temptation to make a flippant remark about how one in three marriages ends. In truth, he had been more concerned about how a few of the remaining two-thirds end: the statistics on intergenerational violence had seemed far more pertinent than those on divorce. At one stage, a couple of years earlier, he had considered proposing to Millie. He'd even gone as far as looking at rings. A few days later, Tom had put his wife in hospital with a skull fracture. After that, Leighton had been consumed by the fear that he might hurt Millie, or Dylan, her young son from a previous relationship. The idea that he might be capable of subjecting Dylan to the kind of childhood he had endured had been more than he could cope with, and within a matter of weeks the relationship had fallen apart. He and Millie had remained in touch only because of Dylan, who had been too young to remember a time when Leighton hadn't been there. Despite the fact they'd never lied to him about his parentage, the boy, now aged nine, still called Leighton *Dad*.

'Ok, that should do it,' he said, the radiator offering a welcome means of changing the subject. 'If it doesn't you might want to give that another go before you call the council.'

'Thanks Lee.'

'And remember to turn the system off first.'

'Will do.'

Leighton took hold of the sofa's armrest to pull himself up from the floor. As he straightened up, he caught one of the picture frames on the sideboard with his elbow, knocking it over. Reaching to right it, he glanced at the contents: a photograph of him in the kitchen, aged about ten, carrying out an experiment he'd bought during a school trip to a science museum. It had involved growing some sort of crystal, and to his impatience the long, tapering projections had taken the best part of three weeks to form. These days he could probably cook some up in the lab within a couple of hours.

Almost as the thought crossed his mind, he wondered why the idea hadn't occurred to him before. He felt almost certain it had already occurred to someone else.

It took Rebecca and Lawrence some time to find Guy Markham, but they eventually tracked him down to the biology laboratory, where he was cleaning out a large tank of stick insects. He glanced up as they entered the room.

'Hello. You looking for me?'

'Yes,' Lawrence confirmed. 'We'd like to know where you were between eight and nine-thirty on Tuesday evening.'

'I was in the Great Hall.'

'All that time?'

'Yes. I'd organised two lectures on genetics for my sixth-form classes, and those were scheduled from eight until ten. After that we had half an hour for the boys to ask questions before they had to get back to their houses. I was there for the duration, since I'd asked two of my university lecturers to come along to give the talks.'

'Who can confirm that for us?'

'I should think any of the lower- or upper-sixth biology pupils.'

'How about Curt Wilkinson?'

'Oh – no – he wouldn't be able to, actually, because he left after the first talk. He said he wasn't feeling well, so I excused him.'

'He didn't seem too well when we spoke to him this afternoon either. He was very upset.'

'Poor kid. Tuesday night must've been hell for him.'

'What do you know about that?'

'Chief Inspector, when something like that happens, the entire school knows in a matter of hours. It's hardly something Donald can keep quiet, is it?'

'I didn't ask what everybody else knew, I asked what you knew.'

'What I've heard is that Fray attempted suicide and that Curt arrived back at the room earlier than expected, found him and alerted his housemaster. Donald informed all the staff first thing on Wednesday morning so that we were fully aware of what had happened before classes.'

'I'd like a list of all the boys who were at the talks.'

'Certainly,' Guy smiled pleasantly, leaving his stick insects and walking in the direction of the office that adjoined the laboratory. Lawrence and Rebecca followed. Rebecca's first thought on entering the narrow room was how untidy it was compared with Guy's apartment in the staff quarters. There were stacks of papers and books on most available surfaces, plants overflowing from the windowsill and, in one corner, a cage holding two gerbils, which scurried through tunnels and down chutes. As she watched, one of the pair stood up on its hind legs and regarded her quizzically from alert black eyes. It took her back to her childhood. She had owned gerbils: two girls that had turned out not to be two girls. Rebecca smiled as she remembered her mother's horror on realising that overnight they had become a nine-gerbil family. That had been before Nathan was born. She had cried for days after her mother gave away the pets that left her baby brother rubbing his eyes raw. She started. Allergies. Gerbils. Dust. *Curt.*

Rebecca turned to Lawrence as soon as she was confident they were out of earshot of the biology laboratory. 'I don't think Guy was looking for Vivien earlier at all. I think he and Curt are involved in some sort of relationship. In fact, I think I'd put money on it.'

'What makes you so sure?'

'Within the past week, Guy's been in Curt's bedroom and to visit him in the san, neither of which, according to Curt's form teacher, are regular staff practices. Curt also appears to have told him an awful lot about Fray that he doesn't seem to have told anybody else. On top of that, Curt's been determined to stay on at school, despite the fact neither his mother nor his form teacher think he's well enough. And then there's Guy's office. It's a mess, and his apartment is immaculate.'

'So?'

'Curt's allergic to dust. He told me so himself. Guy's apartment looks as though someone hoovers it every hour. His office probably hasn't seen so much as a duster since term began.'

Lawrence nodded slowly. 'You could well be right,' he agreed. 'There's something odd going on, and that's quite possibly what it is.' He paused before adding, 'And if Scott knew anything about it, what's the betting he would have tried blackmailing one or both of them?'

'I think he did know. I suspect that's what Sid was alluding to.'

'And Nicky,' Lawrence realised, aloud. 'He made a rather strange comment yesterday. At the time I didn't think much of it, but now –' he paused. 'When he told me he'd spent last Friday night with Fray, I asked what they were doing, and whether the two of them were more than friends. Nicky replied that his liking art and music didn't make him gay any more than Darwin's theory of evolution made people straight. A curious example, considering Guy is Curt's biology teacher.'

'Supposing Scott did know and was blackmailing one or both of them. Guy is the one who has the most to lose. If the school found out a staff member was involved with a pupil, I would think they'd see the pupil as a victim. They probably would have been fairly sympathetic towards Curt.'

'Yes. Guy, on the other hand, would have found himself out of a job and with his career in a mess – and he's done very well so far, considering he can't be more than about thirty. I think what we need to do now is talk to some of the boys on this list, and see whether Guy really was in the Great Hall throughout Tuesday evening's lectures. If not, I think we've got him.'

Between them, Lawrence and Rebecca spoke to seven sixth-form biology pupils, and while none of them could guarantee that Guy had been in the Great Hall for the duration of the lectures, none had seen him leave, nor had any of them noticed him missing at any time. Checking the list for pupils they hadn't yet spoken to, Lawrence sighed. 'I think we're wasting our time.'

'Do you think Guy was telling the truth?'

'I don't know, but it certainly looks that way. I'm still inclined to wonder whether Curt was responsible.'

'I can't see it. From all I've gathered, he and Fray are very close. And I know plenty of homicides involve friends or family, but they're rarely so calculated.'

'I don't know,' Lawrence replied. 'What was it Sid said to you? He's not as sweet as he seems, wasn't it?'

'Something like that.'

'I should think it would depend on whether or not anything is going on between him and Guy, and, if it is, how deep his feelings for Guy are. As a teenager relationships can be very intense.'

'True,' Rebecca acknowledged.

'He had ample opportunity the night Scott died, too, didn't he? He was in a room, alone, at ground level in the san – he could easily have climbed out of the window,' he paused for thought. 'I wonder whether it's possible to fake an asthma attack?'

'Vivien said not.'

'Well perhaps we ought to get a second opinion on that from someone on our side of the fence. Do you want to try giving Leighton a call?'

Leighton's mobile rang for some time before he answered, and Rebecca was just expecting his voicemail to kick in when he picked up. 'Hello hun,' he greeted, cheerfully. 'Missing me already?'

'Desperately,' Rebecca joked. 'What are you up to?'

'Oh I'm hard at work.'

Rebecca glanced at her watch. It was quarter to eight. 'Of course you are,' she replied, sarcastically.

'Wait, is that not what you're calling about? Is this the *other* kind of call?' He tutted to himself. 'Sorry, let's start again. What are you wearing?'

'Is that how you open all non-work calls?'

'Absolutely not. What d'you think I am, easy?'

Rebecca giggled. Lawrence raised his eyebrows pointedly, and she got to the point. 'Right,' she said, in a different tone. 'So. We were wondering whether it would be possible to fake an asthma attack. Convincingly, I mean.'

'That would depend on all sorts of things. Who am I convincing?'

'Someone with medical training.'

'Ok. Well, to begin with, the way asthma presents varies from person to person, so it would depend in part on what you were trying to fake. Obviously you can make yourself cough, but you can't wheeze on demand. But if you were already experiencing low-grade symptoms you could probably exaggerate those fairly easily. And if people know you're asthmatic they're not likely to doubt you. Asthma kills three people a day in Britain, so the first response of a medic faced with a seemingly distressed asthmatic is unlikely ever to be to question the veracity of the situation.'

'How about if you wanted to convince someone who'd seen you have a number of attacks before?'

'From a baseline of zero symptoms I think you'd struggle to pull it off. But again, if your breathing wasn't great to start with you could easily play that up. Although in so doing you'd run the risk of actually triggering an attack. I managed to do that once trying to get out of a maths test.'

'So if you wanted to make a really convincing case it would be possible to induce a genuine attack.'

'Perfectly possible, but you wouldn't want to. It's a dangerous game, and you're going to feel like crap afterwards.'

'How bad would you feel? Bad enough that you'd be unable to commit murder?'

'That's like asking *how long is a piece of string*. Everybody's different, and all attacks are not equal. So in some cases yes, others no.'

'Ok. Thanks.'

'No problem. I'll send you my bill.'

'Enjoy your evening.'

'But of course.'

Rebecca rang off, looking to her superior. 'There seem to be a number of variables, but it sounds as though it wouldn't be impossible to fake an asthma attack or to engineer a real one.'

Lawrence nodded. 'Right. Well what we need to do now is ascertain whether anyone can account for Curt's whereabouts between nine and nine-thirty on Tuesday evening. And the first person we're going to have to ask is Curt himself.'

That question, it turned out, was one they would have to wait for an answer to. On their return to the sanatorium Curt was asleep, and Vivien made it quite clear she wasn't going to sanction waking him. Hoping Sid might be willing to give her more insight into whatever had or hadn't happened at the observatory, Rebecca headed back to Windsor House. When she arrived, Sid and Oli were engaged in a game of cards, and when Rebecca asked if she might have a few minutes of Sid's time, Oli obligingly offered to make himself scarce. As the door closed behind him, Rebecca perched on the less unmade of the room's two beds. Sid sat at his desk, looking distinctly uneasy.

'When I spoke to Curt, he denied ever having been to the observatory,' Rebecca began.

Sid shrugged. 'Like I said, he does sweet and innocent very well.'

'Given that you clearly know all about it, perhaps you could fill me in instead.'

Sid dropped his eyes to the floor.

'Who did Curt meet at the observatory?'

He shrugged again.

'That's not an answer.'

Sid didn't reply.

'If you're wasting my time just to make life difficult for Curt, I can make life very difficult for you,' Rebecca warned him.

Sid sighed heavily. 'I don't actually know who he met,' he admitted. 'Scott didn't say.'

'So everything you told me last night was based on something Scott told you?'

Sid nodded wordlessly.

Rebecca felt irritated. 'I see. Well, I think the least you can do is tell me exactly what he did say.'

'He didn't say a lot. Just the odd comment here and there.'

'What did he say?' Rebecca pressed.

Sid licked his lips nervously. 'He said *Curt gets away with murder*. I mean, I don't think he meant it literally, just –' he trailed off.

'What else?'

'I don't know really – stuff about him being good at lying and breaking the rules – he implied stuff more than anything.'

'And where did the observatory come into it?'

'Scott used stargazing as a euphemism for –' Sid broke off, clearly uncomfortable.

'For?' Rebecca prompted, impatiently.

Sid cast his eyes down, his cheeks colouring. 'Sex.'

'And you've concocted an assignation at the observatory on the strength of that?'

Sid looked put out. 'Not just that. He said other things too. He liked only giving you a bit of the story. I think he liked people to know he knew stuff they didn't.'

'Did he make any of those remarks in front of Curt?'

'No. And he didn't like it if I did, either.'

'Why do you suppose that was?'

'I dunno. I guess he didn't want to piss him off.'

Rebecca raised her eyebrows. 'On Monday you told me Scott wasn't one to talk behind people's backs. Would you like to tell me which part of this story that doesn't add up is wrong?'

'Mostly he didn't,' Sid responded. 'I don't know why Curt got special treatment. I never got why they were friends. Curt's the kind of guy Scott would usually –' he stopped himself.

'Pick on?' Rebecca completed the sentence.

Sid shrugged. Rebecca suspected that translated to *yes*.

'Do you know whether Scott ever used the observatory?'

'No.'

'No he didn't, or no you don't know?'

'I don't know.'

'And do you have any idea at all who Curt might have been meeting there? Even whether or not it was someone from the school?'

Sid shook his head.

'Have you ever been inside the observatory?'

'No.'

'Ever left the house at night?'

'Sure. That's pretty much a rite of passage.'

'When did you last do that?'

Sid seemed to have to think about this. 'Before Christmas,' he answered, at length.

'For what purpose?'

'We were playing a game.'

'And what were you doing after lights out last Friday night?'

'Nothing. I just went to sleep.'

'Are you sure about that?'

Sid nodded.

'So you wouldn't expect us to find your fingerprints on Scott's windowsill or the drainpipe outside, or in the observatory.'

Sid's brow furrowed. 'No,' he replied, warily.

Rebecca nodded, moving to stand. 'Ok, well I think that's all I need for now. Thank you. I'll pop back if it turns out we need a sample of everyone's fingerprints.'

'A sample?' Sid looked alarmed.

'Yes,' Rebecca confirmed, meeting his eyes and giving him a polite smile. 'Still, if you haven't done anything you won't need to worry about that, will you?'

Davide Awde didn't look pleased to find Lawrence outside his door, and given the hour Lawrence couldn't blame him.

'Yes?' He greeted, with a frown.

'Sorry to bother you so late,' Lawrence apologised. 'I won't take up much of your time.'

'I suppose you'd better come in,' Davide responded, turning from the door and moving back into his apartment. Reaching for a remote control, he flicked the television to standby before saying, 'Please – sit down.'

Making for an armchair, Lawrence surveyed the room. It was a pleasant, compact space, clean but not altogether tidy. There were magazines scattered about, dirty mugs and glasses on the coffee table, and the shelves were overloaded with books, so that some were stacked at right angles to others. Davide sat at one end of the sofa, directly in front of which half a pint of beer and an empty crisp packet lay on the table. Lawrence guessed he had intruded on a quiet evening in.

'I'm interested in the photography class that some of the sixth form attend on Wednesday afternoons,' Lawrence began. 'Do you run that?'

'Yes. We provide a number of activities for the sixth form on a Wednesday – it's to give them a bit of light relief from their studies.'

'Fray Bircham participates in photography, I understand.'

Davide frowned. 'Is he the kid who was in my lab the other night?'

'We aren't sure. Fray hasn't confirmed it.'

Davide looked irate. 'I'll murder him,' he muttered, darkly. Seeming to realise what he'd said, he grimaced. 'Excuse my choice of words.'

'Do you think Fray would be able to develop photographs unsupervised?'

'Certainly he would. All I do on Wednesdays is keep an eye on the boys, because for legal reasons we can't leave them alone in the labs.'

'Do you actually see much of what they're doing?'

'Not necessarily.'

'So it's possible they could develop pictures you might not – how shall we say – approve of during the workshop.'

The physics teacher's frown returned. 'I'm not sure what you're implying.'

Lawrence drew Nicky's photographs of Suzanne from their envelope. 'Pictures like these, for example.'

Davide took the photographs. 'Good God,' he said, after a shocked pause. He leafed through them. 'These weren't developed here were they? Where'd you get them?'

'Do you think they could have been developed on a Wednesday afternoon?' Lawrence persisted.

'I'd like to be able to say no, but I have to admit it's probably possible,' Davide acknowledged. 'I tend to just let the boys get on with things. Clearly I should be paying more attention to what they're up to.' He took another look at the topmost photograph before returning the bundle to Lawrence. 'Pretty girl,' he commented.

'She's going out with one of the pupils here.'

'You're kidding?' Davide exclaimed. 'I didn't think Fray was – well – I assume these are his pictures?'

'Apparently not – we're told he simply assisted in developing them. They belong to one of his friends.'

'Ah.'

'Why would you be so surprised if they were Fray's?'

'These pictures aren't much like the ones he usually takes. And I –' he stopped. 'I don't know.'

'Meaning what?'

'I suppose one tends to form ideas about the boys without really knowing them. I've sometimes wondered whether he and Curt –' Davide averted his eyes, shifting his position slightly. 'They're together so much of the time –'

'You think there's something more than friendship between them?'

'I don't know. I only wondered whether there might be. I'm probably wrong.'

'So it wouldn't surprise you if either of them was that way inclined?'

'Not really.'

'Ok,' Lawrence concluded. 'Well, thank you for your time,' he smiled, moving to stand. 'I'll leave you in peace.'

Davide nodded, stopping suddenly as if something had just occurred to him. 'Chief Inspector – I wonder – would you be able to let me know if you find out what did or didn't happen in my lab? It's just that safety in there is my responsibility, and if the boys are finding a way around the regulations, I need to know.'

Lawrence guessed he was also anxious to punish anybody who had been breaking the rules, and he couldn't really blame the man, thinking that he would have felt much the same in his position. As he turned to leave, he replied, 'We'll certainly keep the school informed.' Opening the door out into the corridor, he finished with, 'Sorry for interrupting you so late. Thank you for being so patient.'

Davide replied with a rather distracted, 'Goodnight,' reaching for the remote control and returning his attention to the television. Lawrence wondered what was on that was so riveting. He hadn't seen so much as the news all week.

Eight

Leighton was waiting in the front room when Rebecca descended the stairs on Friday morning, and glanced up from his iPhone as she appeared.

'Christ, you look shattered,' he said. 'Couldn't you sleep?'

'Not really,' Rebecca joined him on the sofa. 'Ian called me at one a.m. to tell me Elliot was in A and E, so after that I was pretty much wide awake.'

'Is he ok?'

'According to Ian his stomach is very inflamed and he's been told to quit drinking.'

Leighton frowned. 'How much *is* he drinking?'

'I don't know. I didn't think that much, but Ian says he was told the recommended intake is twenty-one units a week, not a day, so I guess more than I thought.'

Leighton raised his eyebrows, saying nothing.

'He's seemed ok recently. I mean, he hasn't been a hundred per cent, but he's been coping. I figured it was just a matter of time. Although he was pretty down on Tuesday night.'

'What's he on? Medication-wise, I mean.'

'Prozac.'

'How long's he been taking that?'

'About six months.'

'After six months Prozac should have well and truly kicked in. If he's still not right he needs to talk to his doctor about trying a different dose. Or a different drug.'

Rebecca sighed. 'Getting him to take anything at all was an uphill struggle. He stopped taking whatever he was on before because he said it was interfering with his creativity.'

Leighton hesitated before asking, 'Do you think he's actually taking anything?'

'I don't know. I thought so. But then I didn't think he was drinking a lot, either. How did I not notice that?'

'Some people are very good at controlling their drinking so that they're perpetually tipsy but not obviously drunk. Which may not have been particularly noticeable if he wasn't himself in the first place.'

'I don't understand what goes on in his head. He says he doesn't want to take medication because it makes him feel numb, but he uses alcohol to achieve the exact same effect!' She shook her head slightly. 'I know it's not his fault he's depressed, but getting him to do anything to help himself is such hard work!' She sighed. 'I need to talk to him. I'll see how he is later. I might get a train up to Newcastle tonight and head back in the morning.'

'Is that where he is now?'

'No, that's where the band is playing tonight.'

'Is he continuing with the tour?'

'Yes. Which is hardly going to help, because of course it's perfectly acceptable to drink in clubs.'

Leighton nodded. There was a pause before he said, 'Try not to be too hard on him. I know it's tough dealing with someone who has a drink problem, but if he's using alcohol to get through the day he's probably feeling pretty overwhelmed by life already.'

Rebecca felt inclined to point out that having a medical degree didn't confer any real understanding of what it was like living with a heavy drinker, but she knew her colleague meant well, so she simply nodded. Elliot's behaviour the previous summer had stretched her patience almost to breaking point, and she wasn't sure she could go through that again.

'You might find –' Leighton began, breaking off as Lawrence walked through the door. He stopped short, looking surprised.

'Oh – hello Leighton. I thought you were heading back to London?'

'I was. But then I had an idea about what the boys might really have been doing in the lab, so I ran a few more tests.'

'I'm all ears.'

'I think they were synthesising methamphetamine.'

Lawrence stared at him. '*Crystal meth?*'

'Yep.'

'*How?*'

'It's not difficult. It's dangerous, but it's not complicated.'

'Are you sure?'

'I tested a few bits and pieces of Nicky's that I picked up by mistake along with Scott's stuff. I found traces of meth on one of his jumpers.'

'What makes you so sure they were making it, as opposed to just taking it?'

'Where Nicky's concerned I can't be. But I'm pretty sure Fray was involved in its manufacture from the red phosphorus and iodine on his sheets. You can make crystal meth by reducing ephedrine with hydrogen iodide or iodine and water, and then removing the iodine with red phosphorus. I don't think there's any way of proving it, but it all adds up.'

'Bloody hell,' Lawrence remarked, with a lift of his eyebrows. 'Where on earth did they get an idea like that?'

'At a guess they've been watching *Breaking Bad*.'

'That rings a bell.'

'It's a US TV show about a chemistry teacher who sets up a meth lab when –'

'There was a DVD,' Lawrence interrupted. 'I think that's what it was called. It was hidden under the drawers in Scott's desk.'

Leighton grinned. 'Yeah, I don't imagine it's approved school viewing.'

'Do you really think school kids would be able to do something like that?'

'Easily, if they had a decent grasp of chemistry. In fact, for one or two pathways you wouldn't even need that. Some addicts use a one-pot reaction that's so simple they can do it whilst driving.'

'If it's that easy why risk using the lab?'

'I said simple, not safe. Meth synthesis involves hazardous chemicals and it's potentially explosive. You wouldn't want to do it outside a fume cupboard.'

'How much would they have been able to make in a school laboratory?'

'Hard to say for sure, but I don't imagine much. Certainly not enough to bring in big money, if that's what you're asking. But probably enough for their own little party.'

'Do you think that's what they might have been doing on Friday night?' Rebecca suggested. 'In the woods, I mean. Maybe they already had the drugs by then. And then had some sort of falling out. Meth can make people pretty nasty.'

'Maybe,' Lawrence agreed. 'Which would take us on to the question of how many of them were in on it. Fray and Nicky, clearly, and presumably Scott as well,' he looked to Leighton. 'Are we still waiting on a tox report?'

'Yep. Although even that will tell you nothing about what he might have been *planning* to do.'

'Curt told me Scott and Nicky used the woods to take drugs when I first talked to him,' Rebecca put in.

'And how did he know?' Lawrence asked.

'I don't know. At the time I believed him when he said he'd never participated on account of his being asthmatic.'

'And now?'

'John Richardson mentioned that Curt's health has deteriorated considerably during the past six months. Maybe that's because he's been smoking crystal meth. And why he's been so reluctant to go home.'

'Maybe he just doesn't much like home,' Leighton suggested. 'Sometimes the answers can be a lot simpler than we make them.'

'It would also explain why Fray was so wired when we spoke to him on Monday and Tuesday,' Lawrence noted.

'And why he's barely eaten in weeks,' Rebecca added.

Leighton frowned. 'What time did you talk to him on Tuesday?'

'About six.'

'Well that doesn't really add up. If he was high on meth at six it's pretty unlikely he was asleep by nine. Unless he took something else to bring him down. Meth users often stay awake for days.'

'Is there a chance he just doesn't remember what happened?'

'Unlikely. Meth can cause memory problems, but it doesn't cause the kind of blackouts you see with alcohol or benzo use.'

'In which case he's not telling us the full story,' Lawrence concluded, with a sigh. He raised a hand to rub his brow, then dropped it, looking to Rebecca. 'And he almost certainly knows full well who was responsible for what happened to him.'

The school receptionist looked up rather conspiratorially as Rebecca and Lawrence signed into the visitors' book. Nodding towards the row of chairs on the opposite side of the room, she said, quietly, 'There's someone waiting for you.'

Turning, Rebecca immediately identified the boy sitting just inside the double doors to the main corridor as Oli. He looked nervous. Taking the visitor's badge proferred by the receptionist, she headed over to join him.

'Hello,' she smiled, sitting in a chair at a right angle to his. 'I understand you wanted a word with us.'

He nodded, his eyes flickering up and then down again as Lawrence joined them. 'There was something I should have told you on Wednesday. You didn't ask, so –' he shrugged.

'Didn't ask about what?'

'After I finished my essay on Friday night I did go to sleep. But then –' he hesitated. 'I woke up a bit later, and –' he faltered again. 'Sid wasn't there.'

'What time was that?'

'About one forty-five.'

'Do you know how long he was gone?'

Oli shook his head. 'I didn't think anything of it at the time. I just assumed he was in the bathroom.'

'And how long were you awake?'

'I don't know.'

'Have you asked Sid about this?'

Oli nodded.

'And?'

'He said he went to the toilet.'

'Given that you're talking to us I'm guessing you don't believe him.'

'I don't know,' Oli admitted. 'I don't know what I believe, really. Sid's my mate, but so was Scott. I didn't really know what to do.'

'I can understand that,' Rebecca replied. 'Thank you for telling us.'

'Ok,' Oli gave her a nervous smile, moving to stand.

'Hold on,' Rebecca stopped him. 'When I spoke to you before, you mentioned being privy to an altercation between Sid and Fray on Tuesday evening. What can you tell me about that?'

'Why?'

'I'm just trying to fill in a few blanks. What exactly happened?'

'Um – well, not much, really – Sid called Fray queer, and when Fray came back with a smart remark Sid lost it with him. I pulled him off and –'

'So he actually went for Fray?'

'Kind of. He pinned him against the wall. Although Fray didn't do himself any favours, he seemed to be going out of his way to antagonise Sid.'

'And how were things left?'

'Sid said something about it not being over, and Fray replied along the lines of *you don't know what I'm capable of.*'

Rebecca raised her eyebrows. 'What do you suppose he meant by that?'

'I don't know.'

'Do you think he might have been referring to Scott's death?'

'I don't know,' Oli repeated. 'I just thought he was trying to spook Sid, but –' he shrugged. 'Scott said the other day he was just one loose screw away from unhinged, so who knows.'

'Sid and Scott both seem to have had a fair few unkind things to say about people,' Rebecca observed. 'Does that not bother you?'

Oli cast his eyes down. 'No, it does. But – I –' he sighed. 'I mean, it's all very well for Curt to stand up for Fray – he's his best mate – but if I did it –' he shrugged. 'They'd just take the pi–' he stopped himself. 'You know.'

Rebecca nodded, concluding Oli was of the personality type that Elliot and a few of his friends rather uncharitably referred to as *sheeple*: life's followers.

'Did Curt and Scott ever fall out over that?'

'Not that I know of. But then Scott tended to be pretty careful about what he said about Fray in front of Curt. It drove Sid mad.'

'Scott doesn't seem to have censored his opinions for anyone else,' Rebecca observed. 'Why do you suppose he did it for Curt?'

'I don't know. Curt's the only –' Oli broke off. '*Was* the only one of Scott's friends who didn't – wasn't – part of our group. I don't know him that well. I got the impression Scott admired him. Maybe because he could beat Scott in an argument.'

'I thought you said they didn't argue.'

'Not that kind of argument. A debate. Philosophical, usually. Most of it went right over my head, but Scott loved it.'

'And do you think they might have had a real argument had Curt learned Scott had done something to hurt Fray?'

'I don't know. Maybe. Curt's very protective of him.' Oli paused, then added, 'And vice versa. They have a very intense friendship. I've always found it a bit weird, to be honest.' He paused again. 'Although sometimes I kind of envy them as well. It must be nice having someone who's always on your side no matter what.'

* * * * *

Rebecca knocked on the door of the office sandwiched between the chemistry and physics laboratories, and within a matter of seconds it was opened by a stout white-haired man in a lab coat carrying a burette and a conical flask in his free hand. Rebecca introduced herself and the man did likewise, revealing himself to be Ted Latimer, the school's head of science.

'Am I interrupting a class?' Rebecca asked.

Ted shook his head. 'I'm preparing for chaos,' he said, raising his ample eyebrows expressively. 'Also known as my fourth-form group. How can I be of assistance?'

'I'm trying to get to the bottom of a rather unlikely tale one of the boys told us about what he was doing the night of Scott Ribet's death,' Rebecca explained. 'At present I'm really just looking to work out whether it would even have been possible. I understand the main corridor is alarmed out of hours; is there any other way of getting between the labs?'

'Certainly,' Ted confirmed, stepping back into his office and indicating the doors on either side. 'The labs and the offices are all interconnected, and there's no need to lock these doors when nobody can get in in the first place. Do come in.'

Rebecca did as bid, closing the door behind herself.

'So if someone was able to get into the physics lab, they'd also have access to the chemistry one?'

'Yes.'

'How about access to chemicals?'

'The chemical stockroom? We keep that locked most of the time.'

'And how many people have a key?'

'All members of science staff – including the technician – the caretaker, the –'

'All the science teachers? Not just chemistry?'

The look on Ted's face was a mix of exasperation and amusement as he said, 'The sciences are not discrete entities, Sergeant, they all overlap. Chemical elements, compounds and reagents also have their parts to play in physics and biology.' He paused momentarily before adding, drily, 'Although whether the same can be said for Davide Awde's potassium permanganate volcano experiment I'm not so sure. My laboratory ceiling could certainly have done without it.'

'What do you teach?'

'Chemistry.'

'Ah. Were you teaching the sixth form last Friday afternoon?'

'I was indeed.'

'And presumably that would include Curt Wilkinson and Francis Bircham?'

'Nominally, yes, although I don't think either of them heard a word I said.'

'Oh? Why not?'

'I don't think Curt was feeling well. He was white as a sheet.'

'And Francis?'

'Who knows. To be frank, Francis rarely pays much attention in class these days. I'm aware he has his problems, but it's very frustrating.'

'Did you ask either of them why they were distracted?'

'I suggested Curt go to the san. He didn't want to. He's a good student but I do think he's inclined to push himself harder than perhaps he ought to. He was shaking.'

'Do you think he might have been worried about something?'

Ted's expression indicated that he hadn't previously given this any thought. After a moment he said, 'Perhaps. He looked –' his eyebrows drew together as he considered his answer. 'Panic-stricken, actually. Frightened, even.'

'And Francis?'

'He didn't seem any more out of sorts than on any other day last week,' Ted replied. 'I'd love to know what goes on in his head. Although I don't suppose it's anywhere near as interesting as one might imagine.'

Rebecca smiled politely. She suspected that, at least on the preceding Friday afternoon, it might well have been considerably more so.

The sixth-form biology pupils were in the middle of a practical when Lawrence arrived in search of Sid, and were clad in a laboratory uniform of white coats and safety glasses. Sid removed his glasses as he joined Lawrence in the corridor, looking apprehensive. The left sleeve of his lab coat was peppered with holes, and Lawrence wondered whether they had resulted from the spillage of a corrosive chemical and – by extension – whether Sid also studied chemistry.

Stepping away from the classroom, he paused beside a window overlooking the quad's central courtyard and introduced himself before saying, 'Would you mind running through what you did after classes on Tuesday?'

'Tuesday? Um – well I went for dinner – then back to Windsor for – I don't know, I guess an hour or so. And after that I had to go to some lectures in the Great Hall. They started at eight.'

'And how long were you there for?'

''Til half ten.'

'Did you leave the hall at any time?'

Sid shook his head, then stopped and corrected himself. 'I went for a –' he broke off again. 'To the toilet. At nine. Between the lectures.'

'Can anyone confirm that you were there the whole time?'

Sid frowned. 'Why?'

'Yes or no?'

'I was sitting with a mate. Miles Anderson.'

Lawrence noted this down. 'Ok. Let's rewind by a couple of hours to dinner time. I gather you had a falling out with Fray on your way to the dining room.'

'Hardly a falling out.'

'What would you call it then?'

Sid shrugged. 'We had words. That's all.'

'In the version of events I heard, you pinned him against the wall. Is that not true?'

Sid squirmed. 'I might have pushed him towards the wall. But he started it.'

He started it. A line Lawrence often heard from Elise, the accusation levelled at Jimmy. He sincerely hoped she wouldn't still be trotting that one out at age eighteen.

'Would you have done more than push him if your room mate hadn't been there to stop you?'

'No,' Sid countered, defensively. 'I wasn't – I didn't –' he stopped. 'I never did him any harm. I was just trying to teach him some manners.'

'Trying to intimidate him, you mean.'

'If he can't handle comeback maybe he ought to watch his tongue.'

'Just so you know, that's not a defence that would hold up in court if you were charged with assault,' Lawrence observed. 'You might want to bear that in mind going forwards.'

'What did he say?' Sid asked, in some consternation.

'I'm sure you don't need a recap of the events from me. Let's rewind further, to Friday night. Or, rather, Saturday morning. I understand you had cause to leave your bedroom during that time.'

Sid's eyes darkened, and Lawrence guessed realisation had dawned that Francis hadn't been the one to spill the beans about Tuesday evening's fracas. 'I went to the toilet.'

Lawrence raised his eyebrows. 'That takes two minutes.' Oli might not have been willing to admit that Sid had been gone longer, but the implication was clear. 'What were you doing the rest of the time?'

'Nothing.'

'Nothing?' Lawrence echoed. 'Do you often get up and do nothing in the middle of the night?'

Sid fiddled with the arms of the safety glasses that he held. 'I was just messing about. In the bathroom.'

'Was there anyone with you who can corroborate that?'

Sid sighed. 'I was with Scott,' he admitted.

'Anyone else?'

'No.'

'Very cosy,' Lawrence remarked, with a slight lift of his eyebrows.

'It wasn't anything like *that*!' Sid flared, his disgust palpable. 'I'm not fucking queer!'

'Was Scott?'

'No!'

'So what were you doing in the bathroom in the middle of the night?'

'We were just having a laugh! Messing around. Writing on the mirror in toothpaste and moving things about to confuse people, stuff like that.'

'How very adult,' Lawrence observed, drily.

'I didn't say it was clever,' Sid retorted. 'But I never hurt him. I swear! He was *fine* when I last saw him.'

'And what time was that?'

'About two.'

'Did you leave the building at all?'

Sid shook his head.

'Did Scott say anything to indicate that he might do so?'

'No.'

'Do you have any idea who he might have been with in the woods?'

'*No.*'

'All right,' Lawrence nodded. 'I presume from the fact that he was at the lectures organised by your biology teacher that your friend Miles is also in class with you this morning?'

'Yes.'

'I'd like a word with him. Could you send him out here when you go back in?'

Sid nodded.

'Great. Thanks.'

'Is that it, then?'

'Yes,' Lawrence confirmed, waiting until Sid was at the laboratory door before adding, 'For now.'

When Rebecca arrived at the sanatorium, Curt was up and dressed in jeans and a warm jumper. He was sitting on the bed, leaning against the wall with a notebook resting in his lap, writing out chemical equations. He looked considerably better than he had done the previous afternoon, but was clearly still on edge, and jumped when Rebecca spoke his name.

'Feeling better?' She asked.

'Yes. Thanks.'

'I'm sorry to interrupt your work. Do you have five minutes?'

Curt nodded, setting the notebook aside.

'Yesterday you told me you were scared,' Rebecca said, as she sat down. 'Could you tell me why?'

Curt shrugged, lowering his eyes. 'I just keep expecting something else bad to happen.'

'Is that all you meant?'

He looked back up, his expression anxious. 'Isn't that enough?'

Rebecca didn't push the matter. Nodding, she moved on. 'Do you think you could tell me where you were and who you saw between nine and nine-thirty on Tuesday evening?'

Curt appeared to give this a moment's thought before beginning, 'After I left the Great Hall I went down to the quad. I felt really faint, so I sat there for a bit.' He coughed. 'About ten past nine Nicky came running out of the building – he asked if I was all right, and I said I was, because I felt a bit better by then. He said he had to get to Windsor and ran off in that direction.'

Curt paused. 'At quarter past I started the walk to come here – halfway I bumped into Chris and Sam who were on their way to the library – we exchanged a few words, but they were in a hurry too, because the library closes at half nine. I –'

'Could you give me their full names?'

'Oh – sorry, yes – Sam Ireland and Chris Flint. They're both in Bailey.'

'Ok. Then what?'

'I didn't come here in the end – by the time I made it as far as Windsor all I could think about was getting to somewhere I could lie down. When I entered the foyer Jesse Robertson, one of the fifth years, was there with someone – I'm not sure who – I was feeling really dizzy. I just remember hearing Jesse laugh. After that –' he shook his head slightly. 'I don't really remember much of what happened.'

'Do you remember what Fray was wearing? I'm sorry, I realise this must be difficult for you.'

'No. All I remember is the blood.' He looked pained. 'I still see it every time I close my eyes.'

Rebecca nodded, giving the boy a sympathetic smile and wondering whether the comment was heartfelt or just intended to stave off any further questions. There was no harm in letting him think the ploy – if that was what it was – had worked, and she suggested they talk about something else. This seemed to take Curt by surprise, but he made no objection.

'One of your teachers said that during lessons last Friday you were struggling to focus and looked –' Rebecca made a show of checking her notes. 'Panic-stricken. Can you tell me why that might have been?'

Curt coughed. 'I was feeling pretty rough on Friday. It's all a bit hazy.'

'Even so, there must have been something on your mind for you to look so anxious.'

'Not being able to breathe is pretty scary.'

'I don't doubt that, Curt, but if you were well enough to be in class your breathing can't have been that restricted.'

Curt didn't answer, his eyes in his lap.

'What was worrying you?'

At length, Curt opted for the easy answer. 'Fray.'

Rebecca sighed. 'And why were you so worried about him on Friday afternoon?'

'I was scared he might do something stupid. To himself, I mean. Because of the blackmail.'

'Again, why did that particularly concern you on Friday? It had been going on for months.'

Curt's eyes came up sharply, and he opened his mouth to reply before stopping himself. Rebecca guessed from his expression that he hadn't been aware of that. He swallowed hard, saying, 'He only told me on Wednesday evening.'

'What made him suddenly decide to share it with you?'

Curt shrugged.

'Did he ask you for help?'

'I would have given him money if he'd have taken it,' Curt said, with a cough.

'But that wasn't what he wanted, was it?' Rebecca replied. 'He wanted to get into the chemicals store, didn't he?'

What little colour there had been in Curt's face drained away.

'Did he ask you to help him with his little experiment?' She pushed.

'He didn't mention an experiment,' Curt responded, his voice unsteady. 'He just – he said – he didn't know what to do. I was scared he might –' he shrugged, wrapping his arms around himself protectively.

'Did he ask you to help him?' Rebecca repeated.

Curt didn't meet her eyes as he said, 'No.'

'You're lying.'

'I didn't do anything!' He protested, desperately, before starting to cough.

'Was it just the key he wanted from you? Or was it an accomplice?'

'I don't know what you're talking about!'

'I think you're quite clear what I'm talking about. Crystal clear, in fact.'

Curt gulped, reaching for the inhaler that lay on the bedside cabinet. Rebecca suspected the look of panic on his face wasn't dissimilar to that which his chemistry teacher had described half an hour previously.

'Although if you'd rather we could start with what happened in the woods on Friday night.'

'I didn't,' he shook his head, his respirations audible. '*I didn't!*'

'Didn't what?' Rebecca pressed. 'Didn't break the rules? Didn't take drugs? Didn't commit murder?'

'I think that's enough, don't you?'

Rebecca turned to see Vivien standing in the doorway.

'I might remind you that you're dealing with school children, not career criminals,' she observed, crisply, as she approached the bed.

'Curt's eighteen. That makes him an adult,' Rebecca replied, as Vivien perched beside Curt, who was coughing badly.

'Hush, my love,' she soothed, resting a hand on his shoulder before looking to Rebecca. 'That's as may be, but it doesn't give you the right to bully him. Going forwards, I'd appreciate it if you'd check with me before interrogating boys who are in my care.'

'I'm just doing my job.'

'Likewise,' Vivien replied, coldly. Curt raised a hand to his chest, wheezing, and as he used his inhaler she turned her attention back to him. 'It's all right, Curt, you're ok. Just relax.'

Curt used the inhaler again, and Vivien looked to Rebecca. 'I think it would be best if you went,' she said. 'He's quite clearly in no state to be answering questions.'

Much as she wanted to pursue the matter, Rebecca had to agree. 'Ok,' she nodded, getting to her feet. She walked as far as the door, then paused and looked back. 'But we're not done.' She caught Curt's eye. 'And sooner or later you're going to run out of ways to delay the inevitable.'

Lawrence and Rebecca split the job of verifying Curt's account of Tuesday evening between them, and having tracked down and interviewed the two fifth-form pupils he had seen in the foyer of Windsor house, Lawrence went in search of Rebecca. He found her sitting in reception, struggling to keep her eyes open.

'Any joy?' He asked, as he joined her.

'Both of the boys Curt saw on the walk back to Windsor confirmed what he told me,' she responded, rubbing her eyes. 'How did you get on with the fifth years?'

'It seems neither Guy nor Nicky even ventured so far as up the stairs of Windsor House between nine and nine-thirty. Curt they were less clear about. They couldn't tell me whether he was up there one minute or five. But if he was responsible for what happened to Fray he clearly couldn't go through with it.'

'Maybe he never actually intended to kill him,' Rebecca replied. 'Just make him look guilty.'

'Possibly, yes,' Lawrence agreed. 'What else did he have to say for himself?'

'From the look on his face when I alluded to the crystal meth I don't think there's much doubt he knows something about that. And when I spoke to Ted Latimer, the head of science, he mentioned that in class on Friday afternoon Curt looked frightened and panic-stricken. Curt initially claimed he was just worried about Fray, but when I pushed the matter he went to pieces, so there was obviously more to it. But just as I was hoping he might crack Vivien interrupted and chased me out.'

'Pity.'

'Ted also told me the labs are all interconnected by way of the staff offices, so it wouldn't have been difficult for Fray and whoever else might have been with him to get into the chemistry lab via the physics one. The chemicals are kept under lock and key, but it sounds as though there are a number of keys. For starters, all members of science staff have one. That would include Guy Markham.'

'Which could offer a whole new slant on why Curt might have been cosying up to him,' Lawrence observed.

'Quite.'

Lawrence nodded slowly. 'I have a feeling Sid was probably right on the money. Curt seems to have more to hide with each day that passes. And I suspect he is nowhere near as sweet as he seems.'

'Sid, on the other hand, is the antithesis of sweet.'

'Yes,' Lawrence agreed. 'He was clearly up to something on Friday night, and I don't buy his story that he was just messing about in the bathroom. But we're going to need more than Oli's vague account to pin anything on him.'

'Where was he on Tuesday evening?'

'Good question. He went to the same lectures as Curt, and he was certainly at both of them, but he popped to the toilet at half time and the boy he was sitting with said he returned after the start of the second lecture. He couldn't tell me how long Sid was actually gone. I don't think it would have taken him long to sprint to Windsor and back again.'

'Did either of the fifth-formers remember seeing him?'

'No. But I'm not sure how much attention they were paying to everybody who walked through the door. They spoke to Nicky, and they remembered Curt because of what happened immediately after his return, but I'm not sure everyone would have been as memorable.'

Rebecca sat forwards. 'He needn't have walked through the door at all,' she said, excitement in her voice. 'In fact, nobody needs to have done. The boys don't just get out of the building via the window, they get back in the same way. And when I mentioned checking the drainpipe for fingerprints last night, Sid looked less than thrilled.'

'That's a very good point. Although I doubt Leighton thought to dust the drainpipe.'

'I'm not sure that would prove much anyway. Plenty of the boys admit to having climbed in and out that way at some stage in the past few months.'

'True. Maybe the more pertinent question is how easy it might have been to get in that way. Nicky would be the obvious candidate, it's his bedroom that has access from the drainpipe.'

'That's not the only way in. One of the boys told me it's also possible to get in and out via Fray and Curt's room.'

'That doesn't help narrow things down much, then. Although presumably the bedroom windows are fitted with the same security bolts as the lab windows, so I imagine whether Fray's room was accessible would have depended on whether those were in place.'

'I think we're going to have to ask Fray for an answer to that.'

'Yes,' Lawrence nodded. 'I'm afraid we are. I need to talk to him about the chemistry lab, as well. You'd better come with me. Make sure *I* don't commit murder.'

Nine

Mr Bircham wasn't with Francis when Rebecca and Lawrence arrived at the hospital, and a plain but smartly dressed woman of fifty-odd was sitting with him, his hand in hers. Francis stiffened as they appeared in the doorway, and the woman turned towards them.

'Now what?' Francis snapped, irritably.

'Fray.' In just saying his name, the woman conferred mild admonition. Of Rebecca and Lawrence she asked, 'Are you the police?'

'Yes,' Lawrence confirmed.

'I'm Fray's mother.'

Lawrence had guessed this much already. 'I'm sorry to intrude. We just have a few questions for Fray.'

'Of course,' she nodded, with a polite smile.

'Fray, perhaps you might start by telling us what you know about methamphetamine.'

Francis didn't even blink. 'It's a synthetic derivative of phenylethylamine.'

'One that you've been synthesising, I understand.'

He lifted an eyebrow. 'That's an interesting story,' he said, levelly. 'Who told you that one?'

'Your bed sheets.'

A smirk pulled at the corner of the boy's lips. 'Like I'm the only person to sit on my bed.'

'And Curt.'

'If you'd said Nicky I might have believed you.'

'From what I gather, he knows all about it as well.'

Francis regarded Lawrence in silence, his face expressionless. Lawrence had had no real expectation that he might admit to his activities, and had asked primarily to gauge the boy's reaction. His impassive response was unnerving.

'We'll come back to that,' Lawrence continued. 'How about we move on to Tuesday evening?'

'I don't think Fray can tell you much about that,' Mrs Bircham answered for her son. 'He doesn't seem to remember what happened.'

'No, that doesn't entirely surprise me,' Lawrence replied. 'From what we've established, it seems likely someone else was responsible for what happened to him.'

The woman stared at him in shock. Several seconds passed before she managed a response. 'You – you're saying – you mean someone tried –'

Lawrence clarified the situation with, 'Currently we're treating what happened to Fray as attempted murder.'

Francis didn't move a muscle. His mother paled, turning to him. 'Oh Fray – love –' She took him in her arms. 'Fray,' she whispered, holding him close. Tears came to her eyes. 'Why?' She asked, looking rather desperately to Lawrence and Rebecca for some sort of explanation. 'Why would anyone want to hurt Fray?'

'That we don't know, I'm afraid.'

'Oh love –' Mrs Bircham kissed the top of her son's head, her arms still tight around him.

Francis himself appeared remarkably unconcerned by Lawrence's revelations. He looked neither shocked nor upset, and after a moment disentangled himself from his mother's embrace, muttering, 'Stop fussing.'

'Could you tell me what you remember about Tuesday evening, Fray?' Lawrence asked.

Francis shrugged. 'Not much.'

'I understand this is difficult for you, but I need you to be more specific.'

'You don't *understand* anything,' Francis returned, contemptuously.

'Fray!' His mother objected. Turning to Lawrence, she said, 'I'm sorry.'

'Don't apologise for me!' Francis bit back. 'I haven't lost my mind, and if I wanted to apologise I'd be quite capable of doing it myself!'

Mrs Bircham pursed her lips, raising a hand to her mouth. She looked shaken and upset. Given the circumstances, Lawrence wasn't surprised.

'What you do remember about Tuesday night?' He persisted.

Francis didn't immediately answer, and for a moment Lawrence thought he might refuse to do so at all. Eventually, he yielded. 'I went to band practice after class. Then I talked to your colleague. I was very tired, so after that I went back to my room and went to sleep. After that all I can remember is being in an ambulance.'

'Do you remember much about that?'

'No.'

'I think they sedated him,' Mrs Bircham offered.

Lawrence nodded. 'Was your window open on Tuesday evening, Fray?'

'It's February,' Fray answered shortly.

'I'm aware of that, I'd like a definitive yes or no.'

'No,' Fray replied, icily.

'Are you sure?'

'Quite sure. That place is cold enough as it is.'

Lawrence had never thought so at all, but supposed Francis might feel the cold more than most, since he was so thin. 'Does your window have security screws?' He continued.

'Yes.'

'Have they been removed at any point this term?'

'Not to my knowledge.'

'You and Curt don't ever climb out at night, then.'

'How exactly do you expect Curt to climb out of a window and down a drainpipe?' Francis asked, scornfully. 'Do you think he's pretending to be ill or something? The school hasn't made getting out of that place easy, you know!'

'Francis, *please*!' His mother exclaimed, clearly horrified by her son's insolence.

'No one asked you to stay and listen,' Francis returned, matter-of-factly. 'If it bothers you so much that I'm not perfect like your beloved Adam, then get out.'

Lawrence had grown fairly accustomed to Francis's behaviour over the previous few days, but even so, his blatant disregard for his mother's feelings came as a shock. Mrs Bircham didn't look shocked so much as upset, and since he had gathered the information he wanted, Lawrence decided to bring the interview to a close, thinking she probably had quite enough to contend with for the time being. Besides, he wanted to have a proper look at Francis's bedroom window. He wondered exactly how easy an exit it really was, for more reasons than one.

*****

Whether or not the security screws had been on the window on Tuesday night, they were there now. Having established that much, Lawrence had returned to ground level, leaving Rebecca in the room with instructions to wave to him from the window. Standing at the front of Windsor House, he looked up at the building. Rebecca was peering out of the third floor window where he had left her. The window directly to the right, he concluded, must be one of those belonging to Nicky's bedroom. In between the two, a thick metal drainpipe ran down the wall, firmly held in place by sturdy brackets. Between the first and second floor, it ran close enough to a part of the fire escape that Lawrence could see it would be possible to climb across. Shortly below this, the pipe disappeared into thick thorn bushes. Clearly the only way in was via the fire escape and pipe, and Lawrence wondered how difficult a climb it would be.

Ascending the first flight and a half of the fire escape, he paused on the landing. To get to the drainpipe would require him to climb over the narrow handrail and then lean across. It would have been a precarious feat, followed by a tough ten foot climb up the pipe and a risky transfer to the bedroom window. Lawrence understood what Francis had meant when he had asked how Lawrence expected Curt to be able to make the climb: it would require some considerable strength and energy. He wondered whether Francis really had that either. He started back down the fire escape, then paused and reached into his pocket for his phone to take some photos. Perhaps one of Francis's doctors could answer the question of whether the boy might be capable of scaling the side of the building.

Nicky's art teacher was clearly very displeased when Rebecca asked if she might have a word with the boy, and protested that the lesson had only just started. Nicky himself seemed unimpressed by the interruption, and followed her from the art room with a rather bad grace, kicking the rubbish bin on his way out.

'I thought you might welcome a break from your lessons,' Rebecca began, lightly.

'I like art,' Nicky replied, sullenly. 'Can't you come back in an hour? I don't mind missing English, because I haven't done my homework.'

'Is that your last lesson of the day?' Rebecca asked, conversationally, as she headed towards the door out into the quad.

'Yeah. After that I'm going to go and see Curt. It's weird being in Windsor by myself.' He opened the door and held it for Rebecca. She thanked him, surprised by the gesture, and headed for a wooden bench. Perching on it, she motioned for the boy to join her. Nicky sat, hunching his shoulders against the cold.

'Curt told us he saw you in the quad shortly after nine on Tuesday evening. You were apparently in something of a hurry to get back to Windsor. Why was that?'

'I had to call my girlfriend.'

'Why was that so urgent?'

'She was going out at nine-thirty, and I only realised the time at ten past nine, when I was in the art room sketching. I didn't have my mobile and the phone outside the Great Hall was in use, so I had to leg it back to Windsor.'

'I thought you couldn't remember any details about Tuesday night.'

'I couldn't. You just reminded me.'

'Why was it so imperative that you call her on Tuesday night?'

'I have a really bad memory. I forget to ring her quite a lot, and, as a rule, she's not very impressed when that happens.'

'So if you were back at Windsor before half-past nine, why were you not there when Curt found Fray?'

'The phone in Windsor was in use as well, so I ended up using the one in Pirie.'

'Why didn't you use your mobile?'

'I wasn't sure where it was and I didn't have a lot of time to look for it.'

'Can anybody confirm where you were?'

Nicky looked perplexed. 'I guess perhaps the phone company. I can give you Suzanne's number if you'd like it.'

'We'll come back to that. I understand from my colleague that you and Fray were in the lab on Friday night.'

Nicky nodded.

'Could you tell me how you left your boarding house?'

'We climbed out of Fray's window.'

'That must be quite a feat. It's a long way down from the third floor.'

Nicky shrugged. 'It isn't that hard.'

'So you can get in and out easily that way.'

'Oh yes. I go rock climbing in the holidays, and compared with that it's fairly tame.'

'How long would you say it takes you to get up or down from ground level to Fray's bedroom?'

Nicky paused only briefly to consider his answer before saying, 'Maybe a few minutes. Not long.'

'That's impressive.'

Nicky grinned. 'I won this competition we had last term to see who could get down, run around the building and then come back up in the shortest time.'

'So on Tuesday evening it wouldn't have been hard for you to gain access to Fray's room without anybody seeing you inside Windsor.'

The question took Nicky completely by surprise. He opened his mouth to answer, then his expression changed as he realised how easily he had been trapped. 'No –' he frowned, anxiously. 'I – I was on the phone –'

'I'm not asking what you were doing, I'm asking whether it would have been at all difficult or time-consuming for you to have entered and left Fray's room via the drainpipe and the window.'

'Well – I – I guess not – but –' Nicky stammered.

'Thank you,' Rebecca interrupted.

Nicky shook his head, looking dismayed. 'I was on the phone. To Suzanne.'

'Nobody can confirm that you were on the phone the whole time, can they?'

'Why would I hurt Fray?'

'I don't know, Nicky, I'm just concentrating on the facts. As it stands, you are unaccounted for at the time of both Scott's murder and the attack on Fray, and you say you're very good at getting in and out of Windsor House via the drainpipe. Which is interesting, considering that Scott was killed outdoors in the middle of the night, when access to Windsor House through the main door was denied.'

'But Scott was my friend! Why would I have wanted him dead?'

'I don't know, Nicky. Maybe it had something to do with the class A drugs you've been partaking of.'

Nicky's reaction to this accusation wasn't as acute as Curt's had been, but his consternation was palpable. There was a pause before he managed to respond. 'What?'

'You heard me.'

'I don't know anything about that.'

'Yes you do. We found traces of crystal meth on one of your jumpers.'

Nicky swallowed hard. He didn't respond.

'Is that what you and Fray were really doing in the lab on Friday night? Cooking up something for the weekend? Or were you not in the lab at all? Were you in the woods enjoying the product of that little experiment?'

'I've never taken meth.'

'Just helped to supply it,' Rebecca assumed.

He shook his head.

'We will get to the bottom of this, Nicky. Lying to me really isn't going to help you.'

'I'm not lying,' Nicky replied, his confidence seemingly returning. 'I've never taken meth, and I've never supplied it to anyone. And that's the truth.'

'I don't believe you.'

Nicky shrugged. 'No one ever does,' he responded unconcernedly, and Rebecca wondered how often he got away with his misdemeanours simply because nobody was able to separate fact from fiction. It was hard enough to make the pieces of a puzzle fit together without some of them continually changing shape, and, with a sigh, she dismissed the boy. As she watched him walk away, she felt her mobile phone vibrate.

So far that day, Elliot hadn't taken any of her calls, and she drew the phone from her bag, hoping he might finally be ready to talk about the events of the past twenty-four hours. The phone, however, wasn't ringing, the icon on the screen instead announcing the arrival of a text message. That wasn't from Elliot either, and she flicked through to see what her younger brother had to say before smiling to herself. What a terrifying thought: Nathan was now loose on the roads. He'd passed his driving test.

'I need to find a ladies before we do anything,' Rebecca informed Lawrence as he turned into the hospital car park.

'If you will live on coffee,' he teased.

'You can laugh at me later – right now just let me out of the car.'

'I'll meet you by the lifts in five minutes. I want a word with the doctor before we visit Fray.' Lawrence pulled the car into a tight space. 'Just don't go drinking caffeinated beverages while you wait.'

'Yes, yes, ok.' Rebecca opened the car door and squeezed out, avoiding hitting the adjacent car by about half an inch. Slamming the door behind herself, she hurried into the building before Lawrence had even turned off the ignition.

Lawrence had to wait several minutes to speak to a doctor, but was eventually approached by a slight man in his fifties who introduced himself as Dr Manser, the consultant. He had keen blue eyes and grey hair cut so short that it stood on end, a style that struck Lawrence as rather odd for someone of his age and standing. His manner was pleasant enough, and he smiled a polite greeting before asking, 'What can I do for you?'

'I'm here about Fray Bircham.'

'Is that just to talk to me about him, or did you want a word with Fray as well?'

'I wanted to speak to you before talking to him.'

'I can't let you do that this afternoon, I'm afraid. He tried to leave this morning and we had to physically restrain him – he got very worked up, and in the end we sedated him. He's not really compos mentis at the moment.'

'Where did he want to go?'

'I have no idea.' Dr Manser dug his hands into the pockets of his white coat before asking, 'How is it that I can help?'

'Physically, how strong do you think Fray is?'

'In what sense?'

'Do you think he'd be able to climb out of a third floor window and down a drainpipe, and then get back into a building in the same way?'

Dr Manser's expression indicated that he was unsure even before he said, 'I don't know. He's quite malnourished, but that doesn't mean he couldn't do it if he really wanted to. I've seen anorexic kids emaciated to almost nothing, and they somehow have the stamina to run five or ten miles a day. It's strength of mind, more than anything. Fray's not as fit as he might be, but I should think he's still capable of doing just about anything that he really set his mind to.'

'But he's ill enough that you're keeping him in?'

'Fray's life isn't in any immediate danger – not from starvation, anyway. I know he looks quite frail, but it would take another few months before his minimal diet would make him poorly enough to necessitate hospital admission. I'm more concerned about his mental health, although I suspect that fundamentally it's all part of the same problem.'

'You don't think he has an eating disorder of some sort, then.'

'I don't know. I suspect the starvation is about control, but I think there's a lot more going on than just an issue with food. It's very difficult to know what, though, because he's refusing to talk to any of us. This morning was the second time he's tried to leave, and if he does it again the psychiatrist may well have him sectioned and transferred to a secure facility.'

Lawrence raised his eyebrows. 'I see.' He paused. 'I don't know if this is relevant, but we're not sure Fray did attempt suicide – we're currently investigating it as attempted murder. Does that have any bearing on the situation?'

'Not really,' Dr Manser replied. 'However he came to be admitted, I'm fairly sure from what I've observed of his behaviour and what his parents have told me that there's something seriously wrong. I can only speculate about what might be going on inside his head, but I suspect his perception is quite distorted.'

'Is it possible it's drug-related?'

'That's always a possibility with mental-health disorders. Do you have reason to believe that might be the case?'

'We think he may have been using crystal meth.'

Dr Manser's eyebrows shot up. 'Goodness. That's not something we see much of. Thanks for the heads up.'

Not wanting to exclude any possibility, Lawrence asked, 'Do you think he's disturbed enough to commit murder?'

Dr Manser adjusted his tie while he considered his answer. At length he replied, 'To be truthful, I don't know. Right now, I don't think it's possible to say what Fray might or might not do, and that's precisely why we're keeping him here.'

Lawrence nodded. Thanking the man, he terminated the interview and made his way to meet Rebecca, reaching into his jacket pocket for his mobile. His next task was to telephone Cambridge University.

*****

'Excuse me?'

Rebecca turned from the washbasin, shaking the water from her hands, to find Mrs Bircham hovering behind her. 'Hello,' she smiled.

'I hope you're not here to speak to Fray again – he's been very upset today – the doctors had to sedate him.'

'We did want a quick word with him.'

'Oh,' Mrs Bircham nodded anxiously. 'I'm sorry he was so impertinent earlier – his behaviour recently has been appalling.'

'Do you have any idea why?'

'None at all. We didn't bring him up to have so little respect for people – until the past few weeks I wouldn't have thought he was even capable of saying half of what he came out with this morning. He's always been quiet and reserved, and he sometimes used to come across as a bit abrupt when he wanted time to himself – but he was generally polite and he always had respect for authority. I don't know what's happened to him. He's been insolent, offhand, at times downright rude – and there doesn't seem to be anything I can do about it.'

'Do you think it's a result of his depression?'

'Perhaps,' Mrs Bircham said, looking unconvinced. 'But that was diagnosed almost a year ago. He's been very withdrawn since then, but now –' she lifted her eyebrows. 'He seems so angry – and impatient – I barely recognised him over half term.' She sighed. 'He used to be such a lovely boy. I don't know what's the matter with him. What you must think –' she shook her head slightly. 'Anyway, I just wanted to apologise for his behaviour this morning. I hate to imagine how unacceptable it must have been on other occasions.'

'We realise this has been a difficult week for him,' Rebecca replied, hoping to ease Mrs Bircham's obvious distress.

'Yes, it has,' she agreed.

'Especially after what happened on Tuesday night. He must have been very frightened and confused.'

'Yes. I feel a little better knowing that he wasn't responsible for what happened. It was dreadful thinking he could have been so unhappy that he wanted to die.' She paused. 'I should get back to him. Thank you for being so understanding.'

'I'll see you shortly.'

'Oh – yes, of course.' Mrs Bircham turned for the door. 'Thank you,' she said, again, in parting.

Rebecca moved towards the mirror, regarding her reflection critically, and thinking she looked even more tired than she felt. She reached into her handbag for her make-up, thinking it must be possible to make some improvement. She could only hope she might get a better night's sleep in Newcastle.

Lawrence was on the phone when Rebecca arrived at their agreed meeting point. He finished the conversation as she approached and pushed the device into his pocket.

'Who was that?'

'One of Tuesday's guest speakers. He works at Cambridge University, but apparently he's off to Edinburgh this evening. He said he'd be more than happy to meet with one or both of us tomorrow morning. As you're off to Newcastle tonight I thought it might make sense for you to go, because you'll be halfway to Scotland already.'

'Yes, you're right, it does. What are you going to do while I'm there? Visit the other speaker?'

'I don't think he'll be able to tell us anything useful.'

'Why not?'

'I've been thinking about what we do know of the events of Tuesday evening. Guy must have been in the hall at nine, because he excused Curt after the first talk. Several of the boys remember that. So if he did have anything to do with what happened to Fray, he can't have done anything between – say – eight fifty and nine ten, because you've got to allow him time to get from one place to another. If he'd cut Fray's wrists during the first talk, Fray wouldn't be here now. You saw the state of his sheets – he must have been bleeding heavily – if he'd been there long before half-past nine he'd have bled to death. If Guy was involved, I'm convinced it was after nine, and it was Professor Yates who was talking between nine and ten.'

Rebecca nodded.

'Unfortunately we're not going to be able to talk to Fray this afternoon, the doctor tells me he's been sedated.' Lawrence turned for the exit.

'I just bumped into his mother – she said he was quite upset.'

'That may be an understatement. From what I just gathered, he's likely to be sectioned.'

'God. Poor kid.'

'I feel bad for being so firm with him. I didn't realise he was so ill,' Lawrence opened the door out onto the car park. 'Although that's not to say I'm ruling him out.'

'Do you really still think he might have been responsible?'

'His doctor thinks it's possible. He wasn't prepared to say what he thought Fray might or might not be capable of.' Lawrence drew his car keys from his pocket.

'Even if he were psychotic, it wouldn't explain Tuesday night,' Rebecca observed.

'Come on, Becky – why shouldn't Fray think of faking a suicide attempt? Someone did, and Fray could have thought of that as easily as anybody else,' Lawrence unlocked the car doors.

'I think he might have had trouble anaesthetising himself.'

'I had forgotten about the chloroethane,' Lawrence admitted. 'Mind you, we're assuming that isn't a red herring. Fray studies chemistry, and so does Curt. Perhaps it really was a simple suicide attempt.'

'But why would Fray deny knowing anything about it?' Rebecca countered, as she climbed into the car.

'Who knows what goes on in that boy's head,' Lawrence replied, settling himself in the driving seat. 'Besides, if I were seventeen and had just attempted suicide and failed, I don't know that I'd want to have to explain myself to my parents. With Scott's murder still unsolved, Fray has a perfect opportunity to wriggle out of that one.' He started the engine and glanced over his shoulder before beginning to reverse.

'Do you think chloroethane is something he's likely to have come across in everyday laboratory experiments?'

'I don't know. I'm not sure how available it is.' Lawrence pulled the car out of the parking space. 'First year university students are let loose on ether.'

'How do you know that?'

'My niece is studying biology, and when I saw her at Christmas she was telling me about some absurd experiment where they anaesthetised some flies, divided them into groups and then mated them to see what results they got. She thought it was hilarious, because the flies started coming round halfway through, meanwhile all the students were high on ether.' He turned left out of the car park. 'I'll have to ask the chemistry teacher what the sixth-form class have worked with this term. Although if the boys have been in the chemicals store after hours there's probably a limit to how much he can help us.'

'Or how much we can narrow down who might have had access to what.'

'Very true,' Lawrence agreed.

'We don't seem to be ruling many people out.'

'You're not the only one who's noticed that,' Lawrence replied. 'Between the myriad versions of events we've had from Nicky, Fray and Curt, I'm starting to wonder whether we're ever going to get to the bottom of it all. What I think we ought to do now is go back to the guest house, sit down with our notes and go through everything one page at a time. See if there's anything we've missed. If we still haven't come up with anything after that, then –' Lawrence shook his head. 'I don't know. We'll worry about that when we get there.'

Rebecca hadn't managed to get hold of Elliot on Friday afternoon, but he had clearly received her messages communicating her intention to attend the gig in Newcastle, as her name was down on the venue's guest list. When she arrived, shortly before nine, the band's set was yet to start and Elliot was crouching on the stage. He had his back to her, making it impossible for her to see at a distance what he was doing. She guessed he was probably tuning his guitar because, despite the fact the band had a technical crew, it was a job Elliot always insisted on doing himself. The powder blue Fender Stratocaster appeared to be his most prized possession, and he was very touchy about letting anybody else near it. Making her way though the crowds and nearing the stage, however, she saw that what he was actually doing was copying down one of the set lists taped to the floor of the stage. Leaning forwards, she tapped him on the shoulder.

Elliot looked irritated by the interruption as he glanced up, then, seeing who had disturbed him, his expression brightened and he hurriedly climbed down from the stage to embrace her.

'I didn't think you'd get in 'til later!' He exclaimed, pulling her close and kissing her. 'I'm so glad you're here!'

'So am I,' Rebecca replied, returning his embrace. It was a great relief to have him where she could see exactly what he was doing.

'Can I get you a drink?' He released her. 'We've some beers backstage –'

'I think I might get something smaller from the bar.'

'I'll get it. What would you like?'

'G and T. Thanks.'

Elliot linked his fingers through hers and led her towards the bar. Fishing into his pocket and bringing out a handful of loose change, he rested an elbow on the bar and leaned forwards to try to catch the attention of one of the bar staff. Having done so, he placed his order and deposited an impressive collection of pound coins on the counter in front of him.

'How are you feeling?' Rebecca asked.

'Lousy.'

'Have you had any dinner?' She enquired, well aware he often didn't eat much ahead of going on stage.

He shook his head. Rebecca wondered how much he'd had to drink.

The barman set two plastic glasses down in front of him, and Elliot retrieved them, turning to pass one to Rebecca and taking a sip of his own.

'Jack Daniel's?' She guessed aloud, estimating the volume of the amber liquid to be a treble.

'Becca, please, not now.'

'The doctor told you to –'

'I'm all right.'

'You weren't last night! I was awake for hours worrying about you, and all you can do in exchange is get drunk and make yourself sick!'

'I'm ok,' Elliot insisted, downing the contents of his glass. 'I have to check my guitar – I'll see you after the set.'

'But –' Rebecca stopped as Elliot kissed her quickly and turned to thread his way through the crowd, back towards the stage. She sighed. She hadn't really expected to have much chance to talk to him ahead of the gig: if he stood still for more than a matter of seconds within a venue a crowd would quickly begin to gather, and backstage the band, their support act and assorted crew members were usually falling over one another in a space barely big enough to swing a cat. On top of that, the last hour or so before the band went on stage tended to be quite fraught. Although he loved playing live, Elliot found the build-up ahead of a performance incredibly stressful, and Rebecca had more than once seen him have a panic attack as the band's stage time neared.

The fact that there was less than half an hour to go before the set was due to start perhaps explained why he was downing neat whiskey, but the problem clearly ran deeper than that: until this week it had been more than a month since he had played live. Moving towards the centre of the venue, where she would have a better view, she watched Elliot tweaking the guitar's machine heads and fiddling with the dials on the amplifier. He couldn't avoid the subject forever. She would have a proper talk to him later, when the performance was over and the bars were closed. When he had no excuse to run away.

Ten

Lawrence was about to put his book aside and turn out the light when his mobile rang. Given that it was after eleven, he assumed it would be Katie, or perhaps Elise. He was more than a little surprised to find Donald Chadwick on the line.

'I haven't woken you, have I?' The head asked, anxiously.

'No. Has something happened?'

'I've just had a call from the hospital – apparently Francis has something he wants to tell you. I don't know what it is, but the doctor I spoke to sounded very concerned, and he wondered whether you might be able to go up there now.'

'Certainly.'

'Oh good – thank you. I'm sorry to disturb you. I'll let you get on. Good night.'

Lawrence hung up, intrigued. Perhaps he might finally be on his way to getting some answers.

Francis wasn't in bed when Lawrence arrived at the hospital fifteen minutes later. In fact, he wasn't in his room. A member of hospital security showed Lawrence up to the fifth floor of the building and out onto an extensive balcony. Several hospital employees were clustered in the doorway; Francis perching on the wall at the edge of the balcony some ten feet away. He had, Lawrence was told, been sitting there for over half an hour, and had threatened to jump off every time anyone moved towards him. His only demand had been to speak to either Lawrence or Rebecca, and Lawrence could see the relief on the faces of the assembled staff when he arrived. Francis was now, at least in their eyes, his responsibility. Dressed only in thin pyjama trousers and a t-shirt, he was sitting with his knees drawn up into a right angle and his arms wrapped around his thighs, shivering violently. Lawrence wasn't surprised; it was a very cold night.

'Fray?'

He glanced around.

'I gather you wanted to speak to me. Now I'm here, do you think you might come inside?'

'No.'

'All right. Where would you like me to stand while we talk?'

'Right there is fine.'

Lawrence nodded, still a good eight feet from where Francis was balancing precariously above a seventy-foot drop. 'Ok, I can stay here. Is there anything else you want?'

'For everyone else to go away.'

Lawrence turned to the group behind him and indicated for them to leave. As they began to do so, he looked back to Francis. 'Anything else?'

'Just to be listened to.'

'I can listen for as long as you want.'

There was a long pause. Lawrence stood still, trying to appear calm, all too aware that one wrong move could endanger the boy's life. At length, Francis spoke.

'This isn't a confession,' he said. 'It's just a conversation about a hypothetical scenario.'

'Ok.'

Some seconds passed before he continued. 'A few weeks ago, Scott may have asked if I could synthesise methamphetamine.'

'And if he had, what would you have said?'

'No,' Francis answered, coldly. 'I watched smack steal my brother. I would never have any involvement in the supply of illegal drugs.'

Lawrence nodded. Clearly, however, that hadn't been the end of the matter. 'So what might have happened next?'

'If he had made some threats, I might have re-evaluated the situation,' Francis replied. 'And it might have occurred to me that possession of a class A drug was grounds for immediate expulsion.'

'You went to the trouble of synthesising crystal meth to get Scott expelled?' Lawrence exclaimed.

Francis shuddered violently and, for one horrible moment, Lawrence thought he might lose his balance. 'I only said I might have *thought* about it.'

'Right,' Lawrence acknowledged. 'So when might you have considered doing that?'

'Friday night.'

'With Nicky?'

'Curt.' Francis bit his tongue, his teeth chattering.

'Wasn't Curt in the san on Friday night?'

'I'm only telling you what I *considered* doing,' Francis reminded him, sharply. '*If* I had been going to ask someone to help, I would have asked Curt.'

'And what do you think Curt might have said?'

Francis shuddered again. 'I think he would have wanted to help, but I don't think he would have been able to go through with it.'

'So is that where Nicky might have come into it?'

'The synthesis I could've handled myself,' Francis replied. 'But I'm not sure I'd've been able to get in and out of the lab alone.'

'I'm not sure how you'd have done that at all.'

'The security screws on the windows come off, you know. All you need is an Allen key. I could easily have taken care of that on Friday lunch time.'

'When you were in the physics lab with Curt,' Lawrence observed, remembering what Davide Awde had told him.

'Don't interrupt,' Francis snapped. 'You can ask questions when I've finished.'

Lawrence raised his eyebrows, wondering whether this stunt was simply Francis's way of gaining attention and exacting control over people. If so, it was working.

'I'm sorry, I thought you had.'

'If the screws aren't in place, all you need is a thin blade to force the window catch aside.' Francis rubbed his upper arms with his hands, wobbling alarmingly before grabbing hold of the ledge to steady himself. 'And first thing Saturday we have chemistry, so I could easily have come in through the physics lab next door to replace the screws.'

When Francis said nothing further, Lawrence concluded that he had finished, and asked, 'Have you ever used meth?'

Francis met his eyes. 'No,' he replied, icily. 'Drugs have already ruined my life once. I'm not letting them do it again.'

'Ok,' Lawrence nodded. 'I think I get the picture. Now do you think you could come inside? You're going to get hypothermia out here.'

Francis didn't answer.

'Please.'

'I can't.'

'Yes you can. Nobody's going to be angry with you.'

'No, I mean I *can't*. I'm really dizzy. I think if I move I might fall.'

'Would you like me to help you?'

After a long, drawn-out pause Francis whispered, 'Yes please.'

'You're not going to jump if I come closer, are you?'

'No.'

'All right.' Lawrence walked slowly towards the boy, feeling rather shaky himself. Eight feet was a long way to travel when he didn't know what Francis might do. The feeling of relief on reaching the boy was enormous, and he carefully lifted him from the ledge. Francis felt stiff and cold in his arms, and Lawrence guessed he would be unable to stand, so carried him back inside the hospital, where two nurses took over. Lawrence glanced at his watch. Less than ten minutes had elapsed since his arrival. It felt like ten times that, and he leaned against the wall, watching as a nurse wrapped Francis in a blanket and helped him into a wheelchair.

Up until now, he had presumed the attack on Scott had been premeditated; the chances of anyone carrying a knife around the school grounds without malicious intent had seemed minimal. Francis's description of how a sash window might be forced open added another dimension to the picture, and he wondered what had become of the blade in question. And, if a search of Francis's and Nicky's bedrooms yielded nothing, what its absence might mean.

Rebecca stirred, only half awake, so that sounds took some time to filter into her consciousness, still longer to be recognised. Feeling uneasy, she forced herself to open her eyes. The room was light enough that she could see Elliot sitting up in bed beside her, leaning against the headboard with his head tipped back against the wall.

'Elliot?'

He didn't respond. Rebecca sat up and rested a hand on his arm. 'Elliot, come on, talk to me. Tell me what's wrong.'

'I don't want you to leave,' he answered, flatly.

'Hey, you'll see me again soon enough.' Rebecca glanced at her watch. It was ten past seven, and in a little over an hour she would have to head for the station.

'That's not what I meant.'

'Oh.' Rebecca understood. 'Elliot, if I was planning to leave you, do you think I'd have come all the way to Newcastle for one night just to see you?'

Elliot shrugged. 'I dunno.' He paused. 'One day maybe you'll see sense and realise you don't want me. I don't think I could cope without you.'

'Right now that isn't something you have to worry about.'

'I'm sorry,' he met her eyes for the first time.

Rebecca reached for his hand.

'Do you have to go?'

'I have a job to do. I'm meeting somebody in Edinburgh at eleven.'

'Can't you get some time off or something?'

'You know I can't.'

Elliot looked away. 'I don't know what to do,' he said at length, rather hopelessly.

'About what?'

'Anything. I can't cope with anything any more.'

'Are you still taking your medication?'

He hesitated, and Rebecca guessed the answer before he said, 'No.'

Rebecca tried to keep her tone reasonable as she asked, 'Why not?'

'Because I don't want to go through life numbed by tranquillizers and antidepressants.'

'But you're happy to spend it numbed by alcohol?'

Elliot closed his eyes momentarily. 'No,' he replied, at length, his voice unsteady. 'I don't want to spend it numb at all, but –' he drew a deep, shaky breath. 'I don't seem to be able to do that. I just –' he gave up with a shrug, pursing his lips.

Rebecca waited for him to regain control of his emotions before asking how much he had been drinking. Despite having anticipated that it was going to be fair amount, the answer came as a shock.

'About a litre.'

'Of what?'

'Vodka.'

'A litre of vodka a *day*?'

Elliot bowed his head, raising his hands to cover his face. 'I know,' he managed, his voice wavering. 'I'm sorry. I didn't – I mean –' he paused. 'To begin with it was just a couple of shots –

to get me out the front door – or so I could sleep – or – whatever – but –' he trailed off, shaking his head.

'But that wasn't enough,' Rebecca concluded for him.

'I just feel like – like I can't *breathe* – and I feel sick all day – and –'

'If you're drinking that much I'm not surprised you feel sick.'

Elliot turned his eyes on hers. 'I meant sober.'

Rebecca sighed. The previous summer the doctor had said something about anxiety, but Rebecca had thought it a minor issue relative to the depression. Clearly she had underestimated the scale of the problem. She slipped an arm around her fiance. 'Elliot, you have to talk to someone about this. You're making yourself ill.'

Elliot didn't reply.

'How about I see if I can rearrange my meeting for later on today so that I can come with you to see a doctor?'

Elliot rubbed his forehead. 'I don't want to see a doctor.'

'I know, but you can't go on like this.' Rebecca paused, then, hoping it might have more effect, added, 'And neither can I.'

Elliot looked around sharply, pulling away from her. He stared at her for several seconds before saying, 'So this is ultimatum time, is it? Sort your life out or you lose me, is that what you're saying?'

'No!' Rebecca exclaimed. 'I'm just telling you how *I* feel. I know you're not well, and I will do whatever I can to help, but you also have to help yourself. I can't do that for you. And I can't cope with this forever. That's not a threat, it's a simple fact.'

'Please,' he whispered. 'Don't leave me. *Please.*'

Rebecca reached to take his hand. 'I'm not going anywhere right now.'

Elliot didn't answer. He looked on the verge of tears.

'Are you going to let me call a doctor?'

There was a long pause before he shook his head.

Rebecca didn't immediately reply, trying to swallow her impatience. 'I'm going to take a shower,' she decided, at length, climbing out of bed and heading towards the bathroom. 'I won't be long.'

'Oh,' Elliot responded, rather vacantly.

Rebecca paused in the doorway before entering the bathroom and closing the door. A few minutes alone would do both of them some good. She was glad she'd had the opportunity to talk to

Elliot about how she felt whilst he was sober – or at least relatively so – because by the time they'd returned to the hotel the night before he had been fairly intoxicated, and there had been little point trying to make him listen to her when he wasn't likely to remember a word in the morning. Now she would just have to hope that what she had said might have a positive effect. If it didn't, she wasn't sure what else she could do.

Seth Adey was clearly very apprehensive at being called from his maths class, and chewed on a fingernail as Lawrence posed his first question.

'On Wednesday morning, you told me you'd seen one of the sixth formers outside at one-thirty on Saturday morning. Could you tell me where you saw him from?'

'The window.'

'Which window?'

'Bathroom.'

'What were you doing looking out of the bathroom window at that hour?'

Seth shrugged, swallowing hard.

'That's not an answer.'

'I went to the toilet.'

'I tell you what, we'll walk over to Windsor House, and you can show me this bathroom window. Then I'll have a clearer picture of exactly what you saw.'

Seth didn't move.

'Come on,' Lawrence started off down the corridor.

'But I've got maths –'

'It won't take long.'

The boy still looked very anxious, so Lawrence added, 'You're not in any trouble, Seth, I just need you to answer a few questions. You're helping me out. Do you understand that?'

Seth nodded, but didn't appear at all reassured. Lawrence used the five-minute walk to Windsor House to try to put the boy more at ease, but Seth volunteered little information without being asked for it, and on arrival at his boarding house seemed no less tense than he had to begin with.

'Where's your bedroom?'

'First floor.'

Lawrence climbed the first flight of stairs, turning off into an unfamiliar corridor. Aside from the precise positioning of the doors, it looked identical to the third floor.

'Right. Which one's your room?'

Seth pointed to a door near the end of the hallway.

'And where's the bathroom?'

He indicated a door on the opposite side of the corridor.

'Right, let's have a look at the view from the window,' Lawrence suggested, pushing the door open.

The room was divided into two, the air heavy with the combined aromas of stale urine and antiseptic, a smell that transported Lawrence straight back to his own school days. Funny how some things never changed. At one end of the room were three shower cubicles and a stall containing a rather antiquated bathtub, while at the other end a row of urinals was affixed to the wall and two toilets crouched between partitions. The only windows in the room were above the washbasins, and were of frosted glass, so Lawrence was forced to open one to see anything at all. To his surprise, this made little difference: the room had no view. Leaning out of the window, Lawrence could see that the building had been extended, so that where once it might have been possible to see out onto the grounds from where he stood, now all that was visible was a brick wall. Looking up, he noticed that the extension was only two storeys high. Mentally mapping what he had seen of the house and its surroundings, he turned back to Seth.

'We're on the wrong floor.'

Rebecca was running late by the time she arrived at Edinburgh Waverley Station, and, seeing the length of the queue for taxis, decided to make her way to Randolph Crescent on foot. From the map Lawrence had drawn for her it didn't look far, but having sprinted the length of Princes Street, she realised it wasn't anything like to scale. As she turned into Queensferry Street she was hot and breathless, and, approaching her destination, she slowed, hoping to get her breath back before arriving.

Professor Yates opened the front door to her himself, a copy of the *Saturday Telegraph* and a pair of spectacles in his left hand. He wasn't overly tall, solidly built, although not overweight, with wiry grey hair that looked as if it hadn't seen a brush that day.

Clad casually in beige corduroy trousers and a green sweater, he looked considerably more relaxed than Rebecca felt, and smiled as he said, 'Good morning.'

'Hello – I'm Detective Sergeant Palmer,' Rebecca fumbled for her warrant card.

'You'll be looking for me. I'm Warren Yates.' He offered a hand.

'I'm sorry I'm late,' Rebecca apologised, shaking the man's hand.

'Oh, don't worry about it,' the professor waved the hand holding the paper carelessly. 'I know what the trains are like – I have to use that line every fortnight. Come on in.' He turned from the door, leading her through the hallway and into the front room. The place was chaotic, with papers and journals piled everywhere, spilling from boxes and stacked haphazardly on shelves. A laptop computer sat on the coffee table, a blinking *New Mail* icon on the screen and, amidst it all, a miniature schnauzer was curled up asleep on the sofa. Warren sat beside the animal, reaching to stroke her as he did so. 'Please sit down,' he invited. 'I apologise for the mess – I'm trying to put together some lecture notes for my students – I've eight different groups, and it's a nightmare.'

Rebecca perched on the only chair not swamped by photocopied pages, wondering whether the room was always in such a state of disarray. She might have been thinking aloud; as he checked his email, Warren remarked, 'My wife's not been up here for a month or so – if she saw the place like this, she'd have me lynched.' He closed the computer, sitting back and resting his hand on the dog's head. 'What is it that I can do for you? Your colleague said something about my visit to Treelore last week.'

'Yes. One of the pupils was found unconscious after an apparent suicide attempt, but we're not satisfied it wasn't more than that, so we're making a few enquiries.'

'I suppose you have to after what happened last weekend. Guy was telling us about it on Tuesday evening.'

'Do you know him well?'

'I wouldn't say well – especially not now – I've barely seen him in eight – nine years. I knew him when he was one of my students, but that's all he was, and I've had a lot of students pass through my courses over the years. He's done very well, and I was more than happy to give a talk to his pupils about my work – it was nice to be asked.'

'I'm interested in his movements during your talk.'

Warren's eyebrows contracted in consternation. 'Do you think he was involved?'

'We have to follow up every avenue.'

'Of course. So what are you asking me?'

'Would you be able to say whether Guy was in the hall throughout your talk?'

Warren looked thoughtful. 'I don't know that I could answer that with any certainty,' he admitted, at length. 'I wasn't aware of anyone going anywhere, but that's not to say they didn't.'

'Would you not have noticed?'

'The hall was dark for the duration of my talk – I was showing a good many slides, and Guy moved to the back before I started to keep an eye on the projector.'

'So was he sitting behind everybody else in the hall?'

'I think so.'

'And you couldn't see him clearly from where you were?'

'I had a projector glaring almost into my eyes – the rest of the hall looked virtually pitch black from where I was standing.'

'So Guy could have left the hall at any time, unnoticed.'

'Most of the audience could have done, to be honest.'

'Where did Guy sit during the first talk?'

'In the second row, where I was.'

'Were you sitting beside him?'

'Yes.'

'And were you still there when one of the pupils asked if he might be excused at nine?'

'I was just about to stand up and make a start.'

'Do you remember where the boy said he was going?'

'I think he said something about the matron. He didn't look well. I was surprised Guy let him go by himself.'

'Oh?'

'He was very pale and he looked rather unsteady on his feet. He said he felt faint, and I half expected him to collapse there and then.'

Rebecca nodded. 'Did Guy know in advance that you would be using slides?'

'I mentioned that I'd need a projector. I always use as many visual aids as possible – I'm well aware people tend to absorb more information that way. Especially school kids and students.

I was one once myself.' He smiled ruefully as he added, 'Rather a long time ago, now.'

'So did you lecture in that way when Guy was one of your students?'

'I still do.'

'Guy probably guessed that's what you were likely to do, then.'

'I suppose he might have.'

'Did Guy's behaviour seem at all odd that evening?'

'Not that I noticed. He seemed very relaxed, but then, as I've said, I don't know him well.' He paused, glancing down as the dog beside him rearranged herself. 'I can't think of anything that struck me as odd. I felt quite at home there, to be honest. It was almost like being back at school.'

The third-floor bathroom bore a large sign stating that it was solely for sixth form use. The word *only* had been underlined three times. Lawrence opened the door and ushered Seth inside. The room was almost identical to the one they had left minutes earlier, and once again Lawrence went straight to open the window. Having done so, he was pleased to find that on this occasion he did have a view, and, as he had hoped, could see an area of the grounds that lay between the boarding houses and the main school building. Beckoning Seth towards him, Lawrence asked, 'If this bathroom is exclusively for sixth form use, what were you doing in here?'

'I wasn't –'

'But you wouldn't have been able to see anything from any of the other bathroom windows in this house.'

'Maybe I was in my bedroom,' Seth shrugged. 'I don't remember.'

'That's on the other side of the house. You mentioned the main school building to me when we first spoke, and there's no way you'd have been able to see that from any side other than this one.'

Seth dropped his gaze to the floor, saying nothing. Employing a gentler manner, Lawrence asked, 'Did you come in here of your own accord on Friday night?'

The boy didn't move.

'Seth, did someone bring you in here?'

There was a long pause. Eventually, Seth nodded.

'Who?'

'Watson.'

'Was anyone else here?'

'Ribet.'

'So you were in here with Sid and Scott at half-past one?'

Seth nodded again.

'And how could you recognise the boy you saw from here? You must have given him some close attention.'

'I was by the window.'

'I assume it must have been open, for you to have seen anything?'

Seth shrugged.

'Ok, come here,' Lawrence took the boy's shoulders and guided him towards the open window. 'Is this where you were standing?'

'About.'

'And what were you doing?'

'Nothing,' Seth whispered, beginning to cry.

'Why was the window open?'

'He opened it,' Seth managed, with a gulp.

'He? Do you mean Sid or Scott?'

Seth closed his eyes, nodding again. 'I thought they were going to drop me!'

'Did they have you out the window?'

'Yes!'

'Ok,' Lawrence reached to close the window, then led Seth away from it. 'What time did you get back to bed?'

'Bit before two.'

'Did Scott – or Sid – say anything about what they might have been going to do after that?'

'No.'

'Had they brought you in here before?'

Seth nodded. 'All the time. My dad said to tell my housemaster, but that just made things worse.'

'Did you tell your dad that?'

'Yuh. He said he was going to talk to Mr Chadwick.'

'Do you know whether he ever did?'

Seth shrugged.

'Did Sid or Scott ever take you anywhere else?'

'Not in the night.'

'But they did take you elsewhere.'

Seth sniffed. 'Scott did.'

'Where did he take you?'

'He used to – to –' he drew a sharp breath. 'He used to shut me in the dark!'

'Where?' Lawrence persisted.

'The observatory.'

'Was anyone else involved in that?'

'I don't know!'

Lawrence frowned. 'What does that mean?'

'One time someone else was there. I ran away while he was trying to get the light to work.'

'Do you know who it was?'

Seth nodded.

'Who?'

'Wilkinson.'

Lawrence raised his eyebrows. 'Was he involved in bullying you at other times?'

Seth shook his head. 'No. I thought it was Scott coming back, but –' he trailed off with a shrug.

'So if you were locked in, both of them must have had a key,' Lawrence concluded.

'I guess.'

'What did Curt say to you?'

'Nothing.'

'Did he know you were there?'

Seth shrugged again.

'Ok,' Lawrence nodded. 'You obviously know some of the sixth formers' names – do you know the names of all the boys in your house?'

'No. Mostly just the prefects. A lot of the seniors don't talk to us.'

'How about Francis Bircham?'

'I don't know who he is. I've heard about him.'

'What have you heard?'

'He tried to kill himself. On Tuesday.'

'Is that all you know?'

'Yes.'

'All right. How about this boy you saw from the window? Which direction was he going in?'

'Towards the quad.'

'Did you see his face?'

'No.'

'How did you recognise him as being from your house, then?'

'He's tall. And thin.'

'Your form prefect Nicky Greenwood's tall and thin. How can you be sure it wasn't him you saw?'

'I know how he walks.'

'Who? Nicky, or the boy you saw from the window?'

Seth swallowed hard. 'Both of them. I see them around every day.'

'Did you see exactly where he was heading? Which side of the quad?'

'No – I wasn't watching him all the time –' Seth cautiously raised his eyes. 'I was scared.'

'I can understand that,' Lawrence replied, sympathetically. 'Well, I think that's all I need to know. Thank you, Seth, you've been very helpful.'

Seth returned his eyes to the floor, not seeming to know what he ought to do next.

'You can go back to your class now.'

He turned and left the room, leaving Lawrence alone in the bathroom. Opening the window again, he watched three boys walking in the direction of Bailey House. His next stop would be the headmaster's office. Scott had clearly terrorised Seth, and he could only imagine how he might feel should someone do the same to Jimmy. He wanted to know just what Mr Adey might have had to say.

'Do you have any answers yet?' Donald asked, as Lawrence took a seat in his office.

Lawrence had already waited in reception for over half an hour, and felt rather irked by the question. It inferred that the man didn't have much faith in his abilities.

'Some,' he replied. 'And I'm hoping you'll be able to provide me with one or two more.'

'On Wednesday I thought –' Donald paused. 'What with that shirt – and –' he broke off again. 'What's going on?'

'Francis may not have attempted suicide at all. We think somebody else just made it look that way.'

Donald didn't answer immediately, clearly horrified. 'So – Scott *and* Francis –' he managed, at length.

'I've a few questions about one of your pupils' parents.'

'What? Who?'

'Seth Adey told me Scott was bullying him and that his father was planning to contact you about the situation. Did he do so?'

Donald nodded. 'I've had him in my office more than once.'

'When was that?'

'Most recently?' Donald gave the matter a moment's thought. 'Two or three weeks ago.'

'What can you tell me about the situation?'

'Seth reported Scott to Edward Quast last term. We did our best to find out exactly what was going on, but getting any other boys to point a finger at Scott was nigh on impossible. The younger boys are always frightened of getting involved in that sort of situation in case it ends with a similar treatment for them, and none of Scott's year were prepared to spill the beans. You don't tell tales, as they say – I expect you've found a lot of the boys holding back information during the course of your investigation for the same reason. Without some sort of proof there wasn't much I could do, and Mr Adey wouldn't accept that. He got extremely angry, but I couldn't exclude any boy solely on the basis of another's testimony.'

'Is it likely he would have made something like that up?'

'No, of course not, but it's always possible. Dominic Greenwood is proof enough of that. It was made more difficult because Seth had only been here two months when he reported Scott, so none of the staff knew him that well. If I acted in that sort of situation and it weren't true it could do a lot of damage to an innocent boy's future, and would also have serious implications for the school.'

'I realise that,' Lawrence acknowledged. 'How was it left with Mr Adey?'

'He wanted to have words with Scott himself – which obviously I couldn't allow – and he demanded to know –' Donald stopped short, his expression changing. 'You aren't suggesting –' he swallowed. 'Do you think he might have been responsible for the boy's death?'

'Why? Do you?'

Donald blinked. 'Uh – I – well, I thought – is that not what you were getting at?'

Lawrence chose to ignore the question. 'Do you think he might have gone that far to eliminate the problem?'

'Well I don't know – I've only met the man a couple of times – I suppose it's possible –' he trailed off, looking flustered.

'I'd like his home address.'

'Of course – my secretary can give you that information – his place of work, too,' Donald reached for the telephone receiver, presumably to ask her to do so, then looked up with a frown. 'But what would he have wanted with Francis?'

'I don't know. He may have had nothing to do with any of it, but I have to follow up any possibility.'

'Yes, of course,' Donald nodded, reaching for the telephone again. 'I'll ask Janice to look that out for you immediately.' He paused. 'I just hope for the boy's sake it's a wasted journey. By all accounts he's been through more than enough already.'

'Hello,' Dr Manser greeted Lawrence, bumping into him on his way through the hospital's main reception. Lawrence started, having not recognised the man immediately without his white coat.

'Oh – hello.'

'I hear you did us a big favour last night. Thanks for your help, and well done for getting Fray inside so quickly.'

'How is he today?'

'He's pretty agitated. The psychiatrist is trying to get some sense out of him.' He hooked his thumbs into his waistband. 'I guess you were wanting to speak to him again, were you?'

'Yes.'

'I'm sorry, but I really don't think he's in any state to answer questions at the moment.'

'If I leave you my contact details would you mind letting me know if that changes?'

'Not at all. I'll be keeping a very close eye on him, because there's no way I want a repeat of last night's performance during my shift.'

'He certainly knows how to get attention when he wants it,' Lawrence observed, reaching into his pocket for his card.

'Indeed,' Dr Manser agreed, with a lift of his eyebrows. 'Oh, by the way, I'm not sure whether it's of any interest, but we ran a urine test yesterday to check for meth and that came back negative.'

'How long does it stay in the system?'

'To a point it depends on dosage and frequency of use, but generally three to four days.'

Lawrence nodded. 'Thank you.' He held out his card. 'You should be able to contact me through either of these numbers.'

'Right,' the doctor pocketed the card. 'I'll keep you posted. I'm afraid I've a lot on, so you'll have to excuse me.' He turned to go. 'Thanks again for your help.'

'No problem.'

Dr Manser nodded, hurrying away. Lawrence turned for the exit with a sigh. He had already visited the san earlier in the day in the hope Curt might corroborate at least part of Francis's story, only to learn that Vivien had sent him home. He was running out of options. The only other way he could see to reinforcing Francis's version of events was through Nicky, who might well prove more of a hindrance than a help. In which case, Lawrence decided, he really would arrest the boy. Enough was enough.

Eleven

Rebecca observed the list of delays and cancellations on the departures list with a sigh. The next train to York now wasn't until two o'clock, and she had over an hour to kill in Edinburgh, which wasn't a pleasant prospect considering it was bitterly cold and had started to rain. Turning back the way she had come, she followed signs to the shopping centre, thinking that at least in there she would be warm and dry. Having climbed the steps by platform eleven, she made her way along the walkway above the train tracks, watching the crowds milling about on the platforms beneath her. Rounding the corner, a fierce gust of wind took her by surprise as she approached the Waverley steps, whipping her unbuttoned coat back against her arms. Pulling it closed, she hurried up the steps against the wind. It was a great relief to reach the entrance to the shopping centre, and she raised a hand to dry her face, looking around for a cafe, suddenly feeling very hungry.

Breakfast had been rather subdued. Elliot had been withdrawn and distant, speaking only in answer to questions. Her departure had been still more difficult, and Elliot had been rather abrupt, responding stiffly when she hugged him and gave him an awkward goodbye kiss. She hadn't wanted to leave things like that, but she wasn't about to apologise for speaking her mind, and when she had tried to bring the subject up again Elliot had snapped, 'I don't want to talk about it'. Now she would just have to wait and see what sort of mood he was in the next time they spoke.

Finding a cafe, Rebecca purchased a mug of coffee and a tuna sandwich, found a quiet corner and sat down, reaching into her bag for a magazine. Opening it to where she had left off earlier in the day, she read a couple of paragraphs before her mind wandered back to Elliot. She wished she could understand his ongoing reluctance to accept medical help: his complaint that medication made him feel numb seemed to pale in comparison to how desperately miserable he clearly felt without it. And he certainly hadn't seemed numb when they had met. Then a would-be musician with a day job as a sound engineer, he had been so vivacious and charismatic that Rebecca had been quite captivated by him. She had never dreamed that their relationship would become so involved; in fact, given his chosen career path and the amount of female attention he'd always received, it hadn't initially occurred to her that he would even want it to. For a long while she had felt quite insecure as girls fawned over him at gigs, often behaving as if she wasn't even there. Somewhere along the line, the tables had turned and he had become convinced that, sooner or later, she was going to leave. Ironically, these days it often seemed he was almost going out of his way to make it happen.

She wondered whether he had any idea how difficult he was making life for her; whether he was even capable of seeing things from her perspective in his current state of mind. More and more, she was keeping her own worries to herself because she didn't feel she could share them with Elliot when he was struggling to cope with his own. At times her job had the propensity to be upsetting, and the last thing she needed at the end of a difficult day was to feel uneasy at the thought of going home. Worse was the prospect of Elliot leaving for the US whilst so depressed, especially in light of the fact he was drinking so heavily. Rebecca didn't think she would be able to cope with six weeks similar to those she had endured the previous summer with Elliot the other side of the Atlantic. She suspected that whatever happened during that time was likely to be the deciding factor as to whether they really would have a future together. It was a decision she didn't want to have to make.

Nicky was playing his guitar when Lawrence looked into his room shortly after lunch. At least, that was what he appeared to be doing, although his strumming was barely audible.

'You don't seem to be making much noise there.'

'Oh, I'm not intending to,' Nicky replied, stopping what he was doing. 'We're not supposed to play musical instruments in our rooms, so I can only get away with doing it unplugged.'

'You're telling me those things only make a racket when they're plugged in?' Lawrence asked. For some reason the idea had never previously occurred to him.

'Yes,' Nicky confirmed, looking amused. 'Why? You want to learn?'

'No, my son does.'

'Oh,' Nicky smiled knowingly. 'Parents always freak out about volume. Just buy the kid some headphones.' As he spoke, his left hand fingered chords that he didn't play. His fingers moved incredibly quickly.

'I'd like to ask you a few more questions about your activities on Friday night.'

'Uh-huh?'

'Could you tell me what route you and Fray took when you left here?'

'Straight across the lawn to the poplars around the chapel. From there you're covered to walk up to the lab.'

'Did you make the journey together?'

'Uh – no. I went first, then Fray joined me a bit later.'

'How much later?'

'I don't know. Five – ten minutes? I didn't time him.'

'Why did you go separately?'

Nicky shrugged. 'No idea. That's how Fray wanted to do it.'

'Could you show me how you got into the lab?'

'Sure.' Nicky set his guitar down on the floor by the bed, reaching for a pair of shoes. 'I thought you'd never ask.'

The walk between Windsor House and the main school building was considerably more comfortable in Nicky's presence than it had been with Seth that morning; for all his faults Nicky was easy company and had plenty to say for himself. Leading Lawrence through the trees that surrounded the chapel, he stopped twenty metres from the corner of the main quad, looking up. Pointing to a drainpipe, he said, 'That's how we climbed in.' Moving his finger, he added, 'Through that window.'

Lawrence made a quick note of how many windows from the end of the building it was, so that he would later be able to check it really did lead onto the physics laboratory.

'And Fray climbed in with you, did he?'

'Yes.'

'I wouldn't have thought he'd be strong enough.'

'It's easier than it looks.' Nicky moved towards the pipe. 'See, you can just climb up these brackets.' He reached up, wrapped his hands around the pipe and stepped up onto the first bracket, deftly moving his hands up the pipe as he climbed onto the second one.

'All right, Nicky, I get the idea – could you come back down, please?'

Nicky let go of the pipe, jumping backwards and landing in the flowerbed. 'Oops,' he grinned, stepping back onto the grass.

'Surely it's more difficult getting in the window?'

'I guess,' Nicky shrugged. 'But I went in first, so I gave Fray a hand. It's best if you go up far enough that your feet are at the same level as the windowsill, because then you can just step across. The trickiest bit is holding the window open, because it doesn't stay up of its own accord.'

Lawrence noted this detail, thinking that if Nicky wasn't telling the truth he was going to some effort in embroidering this particular story.

'Ok,' Lawrence looked back up. 'How did you open the window in the first place? I understand Fray had removed the security screws, but presumably the catch was still on?'

'You just slide a knife between the two panels and pull the catch round.'

'Where did the knife come from?'

Nicky shrugged. 'I don't know. Fray brought it.'

'And let me guess, you don't know what became of it after the event either?' Lawrence asked, wearily.

'Fray had it,' Nicky replied, sounding unusually apologetic.

Lawrence sighed. 'And what's the betting he'll tell me the opposite?'

Nicky shrugged again.

'What can you tell me about the dark room? What does it look like in there, for example?'

Nicky hesitated. 'It's small. Poky.'

'And?' Lawrence prompted, when Nicky didn't continue.

'I don't remember.'

'That's very convenient, isn't it?' Lawrence observed. 'Although not entirely surprising, I'd guess you've never actually been in there.'

Nicky didn't respond.

'I'm quite prepared to believe Fray developed those pictures for you, although I think he probably did that on a Wednesday afternoon. And I have little doubt that at some stage you and he have been in the chemistry lab after hours, synthesising crystal meth. But I'm not convinced that's what you were doing on Friday night. In fact, I'm not convinced you were doing anything on Friday night; I suspect either you're trying to protect Fray, or you're just leading me a merry dance for your own amusement.' He glanced at his watch. 'I'm going to give you until midnight tonight to decide whether or not you'd like to tell me the truth about what happened that night. Otherwise, when I get to the bottom of this – and I have every intention of doing so – I will come after you for every single lie you have told us and I will charge you with obstruction, wasting police time and anything else that applies. Do you understand me?'

Nicky swallowed hard.

'Are we clear?' Lawrence demanded.

The boy nodded.

'Right. I'll leave you to think that over. You might also want to bear in mind that if you've provided someone with a false alibi, that may make you an accessory to murder,' he paused. 'And that prison rules will be considerably less flexible than school ones.'

'How were the two Es?' Lawrence asked, as Rebecca climbed into his car at Harrogate station shortly after four-thirty.

'Sorry?'

'Elliot and Edinburgh.'

'Oh – Elliot was much as I expected. Edinburgh turned up nothing very concrete other than that Guy moved to the back during the second talk – supposedly to keep an eye on the slide projector – and that, because the slides were showing, the hall was dark for most of the hour. Proves nothing, but makes it possible Guy could have left undetected, Professor Yates couldn't say with any certainty whether he was there throughout.'

'Pity, I was hoping for a more definitive answer.'

'Oh, there was one other thing – the professor remembers Curt asking to be excused, and said he thought Curt looked as if he were about to pass out, which suggests it wasn't just a ruse to get back to Windsor to murder his room mate.'

'Who knows,' Lawrence replied. 'He may not have done anybody any harm, but I'm pretty sure he's involved somewhere along the line. I suspect that's what's making him ill. I dropped in to talk to him earlier and the matron told me he was in such a bad way last night that she sent him home. His father drove up to collect him this morning.'

Rebecca didn't reply, feeling guilty for having put so much pressure on the boy on Friday morning.

'Although if he thinks he can get out of talking to us that easily he can think again,' Lawrence continued. 'I have his home address, and unless we get some answers by close of play today we'll be paying him a visit tomorrow.'

'Where is his home?'

'Grantham.'

'Where's that?'

'Lincolnshire.'

Rebecca grunted in acknowledgement, still not much the wiser. She had a handle on the basic whereabouts of the counties in the south east of the country – and a few, like Cornwall and Devon, in the south west – but otherwise her knowledge of British geography was largely limited to the vague location of the major cities.

Her mobile chirped, and she retrieved it from her handbag. Hoping for an opportunity to talk about the situation with Elliot, she had sent Leighton a text message asking whether he still fancied visiting the pub he had mentioned on Monday evening. Underneath all the jokes and frivolity, there was a gentleness and a kindness that made him a very easy confidant. He never seemed to judge people, and he never made fun of people's feelings. She kept meaning to ask at what stage during his medical training he'd decided to become a pathologist; given how much he clearly cared for people she couldn't help thinking it was a shame he had opted to work with the dead.

Reading his reply, she sighed: he was already out with friends. She knew she shouldn't be surprised, it was rare for him to have no plans on a weekday evening, never mind at the weekend. Lawrence had once remarked that he'd never met anybody who needed so little down time. She keyed in a quick reply.

'Did you make it to Newcastle in time for the gig?' Lawrence asked, as Rebecca hit send.

'Yes, thanks. How about you? Nice quiet evening?'

'Quite the opposite. At quarter to midnight I had a call asking me to go up to the hospital – I then had to talk Fray down off the edge of a fifth-floor balcony. Longest ten minutes of my life.'

'Is he all right?'

'Well he's safe, but I think he's a fair way from all right.'

'What was it all about?'

'Attention, in part, I think. He wanted to talk to me about what he was really doing on Friday night, but why he thought he had to risk his life, I don't know – if he'd asked someone to call me I'd happily have gone in to talk to him in his room.'

'He may not know either.'

'No,' Lawrence sighed. 'He probably doesn't.'

'So what was he doing on Friday?'

'He didn't actually admit to doing anything, he couched the whole thing from a hypothetical angle. But the essence of it seemed to be that Scott asked him to synthesise meth, and he agreed to do so with the intention of later engineering Scott's expulsion for possession.'

'Well that's an interesting twist.'

'I was hoping to get a clearer picture of exactly what might have happened today, but when I visited the hospital the doctor didn't think he was well enough to see me, and I've obviously not been able to talk to Curt either. I did have a chat with Nicky, who showed me how he and Fray supposedly got in and out of the lab. Whether or not that's what they were doing on Friday night is anybody's guess, but I've little doubt they've been making meth in there at some stage. The big question, in light of what Fray said last night, is for what purpose.'

'If he was intending to get Scott expelled he wouldn't have had any reason to kill him,' Rebecca observed. 'But then I imagine he's as aware of that as we are.'

'Quite,' Lawrence agreed. 'I'd certainly like his answer to the question of why he's taken so long to tell us. And, given the delay, why he told me at all. Perhaps he's frightened. Or perhaps he's just playing games with us. Anything seems possible with that kid.' He paused. 'What I do have a fairly clear picture of is what Sid was up to in the early hours last weekend. It seems he and Scott were tormenting one of the third-year boys. Kid called Seth Adey. He reported Scott for bullying last term, and I'd like to have a chat with his father. He's been in to see Donald Chadwick more than once, and it sounds as though he was nearing the end of his tether over the situation.'

'Understandably,' Rebecca replied. 'Although murder seems a pretty extreme response when he could just have withdrawn the kid from school.'

'True enough,' Lawrence acknowledged. 'But there's a difference between resolution and retribution. Some people still incline towards *an eye for an eye*,' he paused. 'And if what Seth told me is true – and I suspect it is – Scott would have had quite a penalty to pay.'

Nobody appeared to be in at Mr Adey's home address, so Lawrence and Rebecca headed on to his place of work on the off-chance he might be there late on a Saturday afternoon. It turned out to be a small and exclusive boutique in central Manchester, and Rebecca hung back to flick through a rack of skirts as Lawrence presented his warrant card to one of the assistants and asked if he might speak to Mr Adey. He was, she informed him, the owner of the store, and, promising to fetch him, the assistant hurried through a door at the back of the shop. Lawrence turned to look for Rebecca, who glanced up from what she was doing and mouthed, 'How much?' Lawrence referred to a nearby price tag, raised his eyebrows and nodded, not surprised the merchandise cost a small fortune, considering the proprietor's son was a pupil at Treelore Grammar.

Several minutes after their arrival, the shop assistant returned, accompanied by an obese man of forty-something dressed in a voluminous grey suit and ice green shirt, with a very busy tie. He removed his glasses as he approached, offering Lawrence a hand. 'Russel Adey,' he greeted, with a smile.

Lawrence introduced himself and Rebecca, displaying his identification once again, and Russel asked, 'How can I help?'

'Do you have somewhere private where we might have a chat?'

'Private?' The man queried, suspiciously. 'What's this about?'

'It's standard procedure,' Lawrence replied, affably.

'Oh, ok, fair enough.' Russel nodded, seemingly satisfied with this explanation. 'Uh – why don't you come through to my office? Would you like a drink?'

'No, thank you.'

'It's just this way.'

Lawrence and Rebecca followed him through the door beyond which the assistant had disappeared minutes earlier. At the end of a short corridor, Russel showed them into a small room cluttered with boxes and rails of clothing: it seemed his office doubled as a store room. Amidst the clutter was a substantial desk, and Russel squeezed himself behind it, motioning for them to take a seat on the near side.

Rebecca and Lawrence obliged, Rebecca pulling her notebook from her handbag as she did so.

'We'd like an account of what you were doing on Friday night a week ago, please,' Lawrence began.

Russel looked affronted. 'You aren't suggesting that *I* –' he trailed off.

'Suggesting what?'

'Well – I mean – what happened at the school – I assume that's why you're here?'

'What makes you assume that?'

'Am I right?'

'Yes, but I'd like to know why you assumed that so readily.'

'It was the only explanation I could think of. It's not as if I have CID calling regularly.'

'Well, now we've established what we're doing here, perhaps you could give us some idea of your activities on Friday night. Between midnight and six in the morning.'

'I was at home. I spent the evening going over the books, because there was an anomaly in our accounts which I was keen to straighten out. I think I finally had everything in order by two, and I went to bed soon after.'

'Were you alone?'

'Yes. My wife is in Barbados.'

The man seemed to answer a little too readily, as if he were already prepared for the question. With this in mind, Lawrence observed, 'You answered that very quickly, considering the night we're talking about was over a week ago.'

'What do you mean by that? You think I'm lying?'

'Perhaps we could speed this up if I ask the questions,' Lawrence suggested. 'Is there anybody who can account for your movements between midnight Friday and six on Saturday morning?'

'No,' Russel replied, through clenched teeth.

'How about Tuesday evening between eight and nine-thirty?'

'Tuesday? What is this? What happened on Tuesday?'

'Answer the question, please.'

'Tuesday – uh –' Russel hesitated, looking ruffled. 'Oh – yes – Tuesday I met with my partner, over in York. We have another store there.'

'What time did you meet?'

'Six-thirty. We met early because she was dining with clients at eight-thirty.'

'So what did you do then?'

'I went home. If it's any help, I popped in on my neighbour when I arrived back.'

'What time was that?'

'About half ten.'

'Why did it take you so long to get back?'

'The traffic was appalling.'

'Ten-thirty seems rather late to visit a neighbour.'

'The lights were on,' Russel replied. 'She's in her seventies, and she lives alone. Her son asked if I might keep an eye on her because she had a stroke shortly before Christmas. I'm happy to do so.'

Lawrence nodded, then paused for a moment before asking, 'Does the name Francis Bircham mean anything to you?'

Russel didn't appear in the least fazed by the question. There was a momentary pause before he said, 'No, I'm afraid it doesn't. Should it?'

'Not necessarily. When were you last at Treelore Grammar?'

'Um – I couldn't give a date – a couple of weeks ago. It was a Wednesday.'

'And that was to speak to the head about Scott Ribet?'

'Yes. He'd been bullying Seth, and the school had done nothing to improve the situation.'

'Did you ever meet Scott?'

'No. I would have liked to.' Russel sounded grim.

'What for?'

'To give him a taste of his own medicine.'

'You're obviously aware of what happened to Scott last weekend, when did you hear about that?'

'Sunday afternoon. I had a call from Seth's housemaster.'

'Have you spoken to him again since?'

'No, I haven't. Why? What else has happened?'

'Another boy from your son's house narrowly escaped an attempt on his life.'

Russel's shock at this piece of information appeared authentic enough. 'What?' He exclaimed. 'Why wasn't I informed? I don't want my son in school if his life's in danger!' He shook his head. 'I thought a boarding school like that would be safe. It seems I was wrong.'

'This is something of an isolated incident,' Lawrence observed.

'What that boy did to my son was not isolated. It was repeated and vicious. If the school can't control that, I'm not surprised if the pupils are running about killing one another. God only knows what they're going to do next, but I'm not going to wait to find out. Seth is coming home. *Tonight*.'

Twelve

Andrew Wilkinson awoke shortly before five a.m. to find himself alone. Noticing as he sat up that the top sheet was still tucked neatly beneath the other side of the mattress, he guessed his wife had never turned in. With a sigh, he climbed out of bed and drew the bedroom door open, reaching for the dressing gown that hung on the back of it as he did so. Pulling it on, he ambled down the hallway towards his son's bedroom.

Curt was lying on his back, staring blankly at the curtains. In the dim glow cast by the bedside light he looked ghastly, and Andrew could well understand why Nicola hadn't wanted to leave him. When she had informed him early on Saturday morning that the school matron had recommended Curt come home for a few days, he had assumed the cause was another chest infection, and hadn't been at all prepared for the state in which he found his son. He had grown accustomed – as far as he supposed one ever did – to Curt's health being chaotic, but seeing Curt himself all over the place was an entirely new experience. The boy had always been stoic and self-possessed, and until the past 24 hours the last time Andrew remembered seeing him cry was at the age of eleven, when he had broken his arm coming off his bike. On Saturday evening he had been quite clearly distraught, and if his reddened eyes were anything to go by, nothing had changed. Despite the hour, he looked wide awake, and Andrew wondered how long it had been since he had slept.

Conversely, Nicola looked as if she was almost asleep where she sat. She jumped as Andrew rested a gentle hand on her shoulder.

'Oh – Drew – what time is it?'

'Ten to five. Go and get some sleep. I'll sit with Curt.'

Nicola hesitated before nodding. 'Ok,' she agreed, sitting forwards and turning towards Curt. 'If you need me I'll be just at the end of the hall, love, all right?'

Curt nodded so slightly that the movement was almost imperceptible. Nicola reached for his hand and squeezed his fingers before getting to her feet. She gave Andrew a quick kiss, then made for the door. He took her place by the bed, sitting back and crossing his legs. Curt didn't move. Andrew wondered what to say. Over the course of Saturday evening he'd asked the boy several times what was worrying him, but each time Curt had dissolved into fresh tears, and on the third occasion Nicola had given him a look that said *just leave it.*

'What are you thinking about?' He asked, in the end.

Curt still didn't move – even his eyes remained fixed on the curtains – and Andrew wondered whether he had even heard the question. Almost a minute later, he finally spoke.

'Would you still love someone if –' he drew a deep breath. 'If – if they – if they –' he pursed his lips, tears filling his eyes.

'Killed someone?' Andrew guessed.

Curt nodded.

'Love isn't logical, kid. If it was, the world would be a very different place.'

'But would you?' Curt asked, rather desperately, meeting Andrew's eyes for the first time.

Andrew frowned. 'Are you asking whether I would still love you?' He asked. 'Curt, Nic and I will always love you – and Avril – very, very much.'

'But – what if –' he gulped. 'If we weren't – your children. Then what?'

Andrew's frown deepened. 'I'm not sure I understand the question. You and Avril *are* my children.'

'Do you think it would be wrong?'

'I'm afraid you've lost me, kid.'

Curt raised a hand to wipe away his tears. 'I just –' he closed his eyes. 'I don't know what to do.'

'About what?'

There was a long pause before Curt replied. 'If you knew – about what happened – would you – could you – keep it – to – to yourself?'

Andrew wasn't sure what Curt was asking. Whether that was the question he himself was trying to answer, or whether he was posing it as a prelude to a far more serious revelation. Either way, Andrew wasn't at all sure he knew the answer. In the ordinary run of things, he liked to think he did. He liked to think he'd bear in mind the words that had hung above his desk – for many years misattributed to Abraham Lincoln – since before Curt was even old enough to read. On a visit to the office, when he was eight or nine, Curt had asked what the quote meant. He had been quite taken with it, and a few years later had had it engraved on a silver pen for Andrew's birthday. *To sin by silence, when we should protest, makes cowards out of men.*

Andrew liked to think he wasn't a coward, but when it came down to it, he'd never truly been tested on the matter. Perhaps, he thought, when dealing with a hypothetical question, the best one could hope to provide was a hypothetical answer. In the current context, he sincerely hoped he wouldn't find himself facing the question for real.

'I think you know the answer to that, Curt.'

He nodded slightly.

'Do you want to tell me what's been going on at school?'

'I can't,' Curt whispered. 'I *can't*.'

Andrew sighed. 'Is there anyone you can talk to?'

Curt didn't answer.

'Kid, there's sinning by silence and there's suffering in silence. You can't keep this up indefinitely. Whatever's happened, and whatever happens, we will be there for you. I promise.'

Curt still made no reply.

'This isn't going to go away, Curt. You're going to have to tell the truth sooner or later, so you might as well just get it over with.' Andrew paused. 'Besides, I honestly don't think there's much that can be worse than the torture you're putting yourself through right now.' He met his son's eyes. 'Do you?'

Awaking early on Sunday to a dry – if misty – morning, Lawrence had decided to go for a run before breakfast. The Leeds Liverpool Canal ran within a mile of the guest house, and by seven-thirty he was jogging down a frosty towpath, catching the occasional whiff of woodsmoke from the narrowboats scattered along the waterway. The smell took him back to his years at university; he and Katie had often run from their halls in Bloomsbury up around the back of Kings Cross station and along the canal to Regent's Park. In those days, Katie had often talked about attempting the Grand Union Canal Race from Birmingham to London. Lawrence hadn't been sorry when that plan never came to fruition; to him the idea of running 145 miles in under 48 hours had seemed little more than a test of endurance for the sake of it. Marathons had presented enough of a challenge, not least in terms of finding the time and motivation to train, and after accompanying Katie on the first few on her list – London, New York and Paris – he had stopped competing and switched to supporting her from the sidelines. Some twenty years later, she was still adding cities to the list: clearly she got a kick out of running for hours at a time. Lawrence just got bored.

Narrowboats had also featured in their student conversations: on their jaunts along the Regent's Canal they had several times discussed the possibility of holidaying aboard one, something else that had never come to pass. Not that they couldn't still realise that particular daydream, although Lawrence guessed the idea was considerably more romantic than the reality. As impressive as features like Pontcysyllte Aqueduct and the staircase locks of Bingley and Banavie might be, he suspected navigating them was considerably harder work than many people anticipated. And, much as they might look picturesque in good weather, he didn't imagine being confined to a barge with two children in tow would be much fun on a rainy day. To all intents and purposes, the vessels were little more than floating caravans.

The idea turned his mind to the approaching Easter holidays. Katie had booked a week at a forest cabin in Cornwall on a resort that offered activities from cycling to archery to kayaking. In light of recent events, Lawrence couldn't help thinking Jimmy didn't really deserve that opportunity; then again, perhaps a week away from his friends and computer games would do him good. It might also give Lawrence the chance to explore what lay beneath the recent deterioration in his son's behaviour. Over the course of his eighteen months at secondary school he had grown increasingly discourteous and combative at home, and having originally put that down to the onset of adolescence, Lawrence was fast coming to the uncomfortable realisation it probably wasn't that simple. He had tried to draw some sort of explanation from Jimmy on Wednesday evening, but his son had refused to play ball; questions had been met with one-word answers and non-questions with silence. It was difficult to lay down the law over the telephone, and in the end Lawrence had decided to defer any further action until his return home, hoping that by the time he got there he might have more idea of how to tackle the situation.

His phone ringtone filtered through his thoughts and he slowed to a walking pace as he unclipped the device from his waistband. He glanced at the display before answering, hoping fervently that nothing further was amiss at Treelore or at home. Neither the number nor the area code was familiar, and he wondered who – besides Katie or Rebecca – might have reason to call him at 8 a.m. on a Sunday morning.

'Hello?'

'Good morning. Is that DCI Forrester?'

'Yes.'

'My name's Andrew Wilkinson. I believe you've met my son, Curt.'

Lawrence confirmed that he had, feeling intrigued.

'I wonder – would you perhaps have time to come and talk to him later today? He obviously knows something about what's been going on at the school – I've never seen him so upset – and I don't have a clue what to do with him. I've not been able to get any sense out of him at all.'

'I'd be happy to.'

'Thank you,' Andrew replied, relief evident in his voice. 'We're in Grantham, I –'

'Yes, I know, I already have your address.'

'Oh,' he sounded taken aback. 'Right. Ok.'

'I'll be with you later this morning,' Lawrence promised, guessing the drive to Grantham would take the best part of two hours. He hoped it wouldn't turn out to be a wasted trip.

Lawrence had expected the Wilkinsons' home to be of a similar ilk to the Ribets' mansion, and was surprised when it turned out to be an attractive but perfectly ordinary detached house in a quiet suburban street. Inside, the building was equally unremarkable – although exceptionally tidy – and he guessed Curt's years at Treelore had not come without sacrifice.

Andrew Wilkinson showed Lawrence up to the first floor and into a cosy room at the rear of the building. The low window afforded a view of a long, tiered garden; the room itself was sparsely furnished with a three-piece suite, a couple of side tables and a vast wide-screen television. Lawrence supposed it was the modern equivalent of the TV room he and his sister had shared as teenagers; their version had involved beanbags on the floor and a fifteen-inch screen, the channels and volume controlled by knobs rather than a remote control. In an earlier incarnation, the machine had served as the monitor for an Acorn Electron computer.

Curt was sitting at the far end of the sofa, dressed in jeans and an England rugby shirt, his hands clasped tightly in his lap and his long fringe obscuring half his face. Lawrence closed the door behind himself before perching a couple of feet further along the sofa.

'Hello Curt.'

The boy didn't respond.

'Your father tells me you've been very upset since you've been home. He's quite concerned about you. Do you think you might tell me what's worrying you?'

Curt closed his eyes. Some seconds passed before he spoke. 'Nicky – Nicky said –' he began, before falling silent again.

'What did Nicky say?'

Curt met Lawrence's eyes. His were bloodshot. When after a moment he spoke, it was haltingly, his voice strained. 'Do you really think – that – that Fray – didn't –' he stopped. 'Did someone else – do that – to – to Fray?'

'It looks that way.'

The expression on Curt's face indicated that he had been desperately hoping Lawrence would answer differently, and his blue eyes filled with tears.

'Curt, do you have any idea who it might have been?'

Curt didn't answer. He blinked and tears ran down his cheeks.

'If you know anything about who might have been responsible you must tell me.'

'I can't!' He whispered.

'Yes you can.'

Curt shook his head, his breathing audible.

'Keeping it to yourself isn't going to help anyone, least of all you.'

There was a long pause. Curt coughed and raised his right hand to rub his chest.

'Do you know who killed Scott?'

Curt didn't reply. After a tortured silence, he slowly uncurled the fingers of his left hand and held out a balled up piece of paper. Lawrence took it and flattened it out.

£500 at the observatory by midnight Friday or Donny Boy hears all about your extracurricular stargazing club.

Lawrence identified the handwriting immediately as Scott's. He presumed *Donny Boy* was Donald Chadwick. He looked back to Curt. His head was bowed, a hand clasped over his eyes.

'Was this addressed to you?'

Curt shook his head. 'I found it,' he managed, his voice sounding strangled.

'Do you know what it relates to?'

'Yuh,' he managed, roughly drying his tears with the heel of his hand. They were immediately replaced.

'And do you know who it was intended for?'

He nodded.

'Do you think this had something to do with Scott's death?'

Curt squeezed his eyes shut, raising a hand to cover his face again. His thin shoulders shook as he sobbed.

'I'm guessing that's a yes.'

'It's all my fault!' Curt managed, before starting to cough.

'Do you mean you were responsible?'

Curt couldn't answer, his breaths coming in ragged gasps.

'Calm down,' Lawrence counselled.

'I didn't – I didn't know – I –'

'Did you kill Scott?'

'No!'

'Do you know who did?'

'I don't know – I think – I –' he trailed off with a shrug.

'If you have any idea who might have been responsible you have to tell me. If someone's capable of killing one person, they could easily kill another, and I'm sure you don't want that to happen.'

Curt drew several rapid, unsteady breaths before he whispered something through the tears.

'What did you say?'

'Guy,' Curt repeated, his voice barely audible.

'Guy Markham?'

He nodded.

'And what makes you think he might have killed Scott?'

'Because of me.' Curt hiccupped, which set him off coughing again.

'What about you?'

'He's – he's – not –' Curt stopped, breathless. 'He's not – not – just – my teacher!'

'You mean you're having a relationship?'

'Yuh!'

'And was that blackmail note sent to Guy?'

'Yuh. I didn't think –' Curt gulped. 'I knew Scott knew but –' he shrugged weakly.

'Do you think Guy was also responsible for what happened to Fray?'

'I dunno! I never even thought about it – until Nicky said –' he gulped. 'He was in the Great Hall – until nine. When I left – I said I – I – he thought – I was – going – to – to –'

'Slow down. Where did Guy think you were going?'

'The san! But I – I didn't – I sat in the quad – then I went to my room – and Fray –' he swallowed hard.

'Did Fray know about the relationship?'

Curt nodded. He took a slow, careful breath before saying, 'Everything. He knows everything.'

'Including your suspicions about Guy's involvement in Scott's death?'

There was a long pause before Curt whispered, 'I didn't have to tell him that.' He drew another deep breath and shuddered. 'Fray had that figured out before I did.'

Leighton had spent Saturday afternoon at the Fire and Police Museum with Millie and Dylan. The trip had been followed by pizza and a DVD at their flat and – as had most of their meetings in recent months – culminated in a night in Millie's bed. Leighton was aware that the hybrid of friendship and casual relationship they'd stumbled into was a car crash waiting to happen, but had come to the half-conscious decision to deal with the problem as and when it became one. When Millie reached to take his hand on the walk to the park on Sunday morning, he had the uncomfortable feeling that moment wasn't far off, and wished he hadn't treated the situation so carelessly. The return to London suddenly couldn't come soon enough.

Dylan had been desperate to show off his new skateboard, so Leighton had agreed to make the trip to the skate park prior to his journey home. Having kitted her son out in knee pads, wrist guards and a helmet, Millie had headed off in search of a coffee shop, leaving Leighton to watch Dylan whizzing fearlessly up and down ramps, executing moves Leighton had once been adept at himself. After about ten minutes, the boy came skidding to a stop in front of him.

'D'you want a go?'

Leighton smiled. 'No, you're all right, mate. Thanks.'

'Can you show me how to do an Ollie?'

Leighton very much doubted he would be capable of pulling off the trick some fifteen years after he had last been on a board, and suspected any attempt would probably culminate in his spending the afternoon on the wrong side of the doctor–patient divide. The best he was likely to be able to achieve was a description of how to create the move. 'You need to start by learning to jump up and down while you're rolling,' he suggested. 'You want to crouch down like this,' he bent his knees. 'Then jump,' he demonstrated, 'And try to keep your balance when you land. Ok?'

Dylan nodded and scurried off. On his first attempt at the jump he landed on the board, wobbled and stepped off it. The second time he touched down on the tarmac. The third, he made it back down onto the board, then fell over.

'Well I can see that's going to end in tears,' Millie observed, joining Leighton as Dylan picked himself up and prepared to try again. Handing him a cardboard coffee cup, she glanced up from beneath her thick black fringe and even thicker black eyeliner, her hazel eyes reproachful. He drew breath to apologise for encouraging the boy, but Millie beat him to it, and he realised the change in her mood had nothing to do with Dylan or his skateboard.

'Why didn't you tell me?'

'Tell you what?' He replied, guessing the answer. He had been hoping to avoid this conversation – or, more likely, argument – since Friday evening, when his mother had informed him that a date had finally been set for Tom's appeal. Amber, Tom's ex-wife, was a long-time friend of Millie's, and Leighton suspected Millie felt some misplaced sense of responsibility for having introduced the two of them in the first place.

'You know what.'

'Actually I haven't been on the Met psychic training course.'

'You're not funny,' Millie snapped. 'Tom's appeal, as if you didn't know.'

'I wasn't aware I needed to notify everyone. It's hardly a surprise. He made the application months ago.'

'Do you think they should let him off?'

'It's not a question of letting him off. The issue is whether the conviction was the right one. And that comes down to the matter of intent.'

'*I didn't mean it* is no excuse.'

'That's not what I said. Don't put words in my mouth.'

'But you support his decision to appeal.'

'If evidence was omitted from the original trial he's within his rights to ask that it be considered.'

'Why does everyone always espouse the criminals' rights? What about the victims' rights?'

'Not providing any way for people to challenge the court's decision runs the risk of creating more victims. Twelve years is a long time.'

'And you don't think he deserves that? He could have killed her!'

'Mills, you know I don't condone that. That isn't the point. I'm trying to explain how the legal process works.'

'I didn't ask how the legal process works, I asked what you think!'

'What I think doesn't matter! What matters is whether he has a case!'

'What you think does matter to me!'

Leighton sighed. 'I don't know what I think,' he replied, after a moment. 'I wasn't there.'

'Oh don't be pathetic.'

Leighton looked around at her in surprise. 'Excuse me?'

'You must *have* an opinion! What is it you don't have the guts to do? Tell me something you think I won't want to hear, or stand up to Tom?' She shook her head. 'God knows why I'm surprised, you've never had the guts to stand up to your dad, either!'

'Well who do you suppose he'd take it out on if I did?'

'Your mother doesn't deserve half of what you do for her! Your dad scarred you for life, and she stood by and did *nothing*! Never mind social services, if someone did that to Dylan I'd call the fucking police! How the hell are you not angry with them?'

'Is that really what you want?' Leighton demanded. 'You've seen where anger got Tom, you've just slammed his behaviour, and now – what – you're complaining I'm not more like him? What should I be doing, running around taking it out on other people? Giving everybody else second-degree burns?' He rubbed his eyes with the thumb and middle finger of his right hand. 'Christ. I can't bloody win.' His mobile started to ring and he pulled it from his pocket, glancing at the display before answering. 'Hiya Becks.'

'Hi. I didn't wake you, did I?'

'No, you're all right.'

'You sound strange. Are you ok?'

'I'm fine. What do you need?'

'Are you still in Sheffield?'

'For my sins.'

'We're on our way to make an arrest. Forrester was hoping you could go over an apartment for us.' She hesitated before adding, 'This afternoon.'

'Yeah, no problem,' Leighton replied. 'If you'd like to send a helicopter I can be there inside an hour. Otherwise it's going to be more like two.'

'Thanks. I'll see you then.'

'One day someone's going to send me a helicopter.'

'Yeah, probably an air ambulance when your inability to work to his schedule finally drives Roddy over the edge.'

'Any day, then,' Leighton joked, as he hung up. He returned the phone to his pocket.

'Work,' he said, shortly, without meeting Millie's eyes. 'I have to go.'

'Lee –'

'Don't presume to tell me how I ought to feel or what my mother does or doesn't deserve,' he pre-empted. 'I'm the one who has to live with what happened, not you.' He turned to call Dylan over to say goodbye. Millie grabbed his arm and pulled him back.

'I'm sorry, I didn't mean to –' she faltered. 'I just worry about what living with it is doing to you! Nobody should be put in a situation where –'

'We're not having this conversation,' Leighton interrupted, before calling Dylan's name and giving him a wave. The boy swung his skateboard around and headed in their direction. 'I'll be back up in a fortnight,' he added, as Dylan neared. 'I'll maybe see you then.'

Even as he said it, he suspected that doing so would be unavoidable: he'd already promised to take Dylan to the cinema on the Saturday afternoon. Although given that the following day was Mother's Day and Lorna already had a visiting order waiting on the kitchen windowsill, it might not be a bad time to reconnect with Millie. At least he would have a legitimate excuse not to stay the night.

Guy seemed to take the news that he was being arrested surprisingly calmly, and Lawrence wondered whether he was relieved to no longer have the prospect of its happening hanging over him. Then, as he swung the car out of the school gates onto the main road and Guy's attitude turned with it, he realised the man had just been keen to avoid making a scene on school grounds. On arrival at the local station, Lawrence gave him half an hour to calm down before commencing the interview.

Rebecca cautioned Guy and asked – for the second time – whether he wanted to contact a solicitor. Guy replied that he didn't require legal assistance when he'd not committed a crime. Lawrence sat back in his chair, asking, conversationally, whether Guy had been in touch with Curt that weekend.

'Curt Wilkinson?' Guy frowned. 'No. Why?'

'You're not aware of the state you've left him in, then.'

'I'm sorry?'

'The events of the last week have made him quite ill. I assume that's a result of knowing all the details. I'm surprised you can watch him go through that, considering how much you apparently care for him.'

'I'm afraid I have no idea what you're talking about.'

'Schools don't generally tolerate relationships between staff and pupils, especially not schools like Treelore. You must be quite attached to Curt to have paid out such large sums of money to keep Scott quiet. In fact, Curt must be very special to you given that –'

'What's Curt been saying?' Guy asked, his eyebrows contracting into a frown.

'I should think you have a pretty good idea. You're the one who's been sleeping with him, after all.'

'I've been *what*?' Guy exclaimed. He shook his head. 'I've been doing nothing of the sort! I guessed the kid had a crush on me, but I didn't encourage him! I thought it was all pretty harmless.'

'So you deny having a relationship with him?'

'Damn right I do!'

'Why do you suppose Curt told us otherwise?'

'How the hell should I know? Maybe he's as deranged as his room mate!'

'Maybe,' Lawrence mused, nodding slightly. 'And do you think the other pupils who've mentioned your affair to us are deranged as well?'

Guy went to answer, then stopped himself. After a moment he said, 'Well I wouldn't put too much store in anything the likes of Fray and Nicky have to say.'

'No, I'm inclined to agree with you there,' Lawrence responded. 'But they aren't the only ones in the know. Perhaps you should have been a little more discrete.'

Guy didn't reply, his eyes on the table.

'And I imagine we'll find a key to the observatory in your possession. Although that's academic, really, we already have evidence of your little trysts from inside the building.'

Guy sighed heavily. 'All right,' he conceded. 'Yes. I didn't want to love him, but it happened. He's eighteen. That's not illegal.'

'No, you're right, it isn't. But murder is a different matter.'

'What, I've been having a fling with one of my pupils so you think I must be capable of killing another?' Guy demanded. 'That's a pretty gargantuan leap!'

'Scott knew all about your relationship with Curt. He was blackmailing you. To start with I imagine you thought you could keep him quiet, but you underestimated quite how greedy he was going to get. He wanted more than you could give him, didn't he?'

'No.'

'We're well aware of Scott's predilection for blackmail. Are you telling me he didn't try to make money out of your situation? I find that very hard to believe.'

'No, that's not what I meant. Scott was blackmailing me, but he never asked for more than I could give him. I figured I could keep paying him until the end of the year, then he'd leave and I'd not have to worry about it.'

'I doubt he'd have let it lie just because the school year was over. You offered a very easy source of income. He could have gone to Donald Chadwick any time he wanted. And I hardly think Donald would have viewed your activities in a favourable light. It probably would have marked the end of your career. So you thought you'd eliminate the problem.'

'No,' Guy shook his head. 'I never laid a finger on the boy.'

'Considering what he's been through in the past week, Curt's feelings for you must really be very strong. So if you're innocent, why do you suppose he told me that you were responsible for what happened to Scott?'

Guy held his hands out. 'I don't know. The past week has been very upsetting for him. Perhaps he's trying to make sense of everything and has added two and two to make five.'

'I suspect he knows enough to do the maths rather better than that. Although I think he could have kept quiet about what happened to Scott. Your mistake was in going one step further and trying to implicate someone else. He couldn't cope with what you did to Fray. That was too much.'

'Fray?' The look of confusion on Guy's face appeared so genuine that Lawrence felt a grudging admiration for the man's acting abilities. 'What does Fray have to do with it?'

'Fray made a perfect scapegoat, didn't he? He'd had a row with Scott two days before his death, threatened to kill him. I presume Curt told you all about that, since he seems to have told you everything else. Fray also had a shirt covered in blood. His own blood, admittedly, but perhaps you hoped we wouldn't check that. As Curt told us, Fray leaves things lying about. Shirts, poetry books – and with the amount of time I imagine you've spent in that room, you had enough information to make his suicide look authentic. If –'

'You think I had something to do with *that?*' Guy exclaimed, incredulously. 'Jesus!' He shook his head. 'Look, I don't know what Curt's been saying – or Fray for that matter – but I was nowhere *near* Windsor House that night! I was in the hall all evening! With over fifteen other boys!'

'Ah, but you were sitting at the back, keeping an eye on the slide projector. The hall was dark for most of the evening, and I don't think it would have been impossible for you to slip out unnoticed. Difficult, perhaps, but not impossible. You could easily have made it to Windsor and back within half an hour.'

'I didn't leave that hall for so much as one second!'

'There doesn't appear to be anyone who can confidently confirm that.'

'Is there anyone who can confirm otherwise?'

'We're still checking a few details of a couple of the boys' accounts.'

'You mean no,' Guy surmised. 'I know nobody can confirm it, because I know I didn't go anywhere! And anyone who says otherwise is lying!'

'So,' Lawrence began, returning to his seat after leaving the room to take a phone call. 'Apparently there are traces of blood on the livingroom carpet and bathroom tiles in your apartment,' he rested his forearms on the table. 'At this stage we don't know whose blood it is, but my colleague tells me it shouldn't be difficult to find out using a technique called PCR. Of course, you've studied genetics, so I expect you understand how that works.'

Guy didn't reply.

'Did you arrange to meet Scott to hand the money over, or did you drop it off at the observatory and then lie in wait?'

'Neither. I didn't have any arrangement with Scott for Friday night.'

Lawrence placed a plastic wallet containing the blackmail note Curt had given him that morning on the table. 'This seems to indicate otherwise.'

Guy took it in at a glance before raising his eyebrows. 'I don't see my name anywhere on there, do you?'

'Curt found this in your apartment.'

'No he didn't.'

'Are you saying he's lying?'

'No. Someone's lying, but I don't know that it's Curt.'

'He was beside himself. His father said he'd never seen him in such a state. Mind you, he doesn't know all the details yet. I imagine he'll be less than delighted to hear about his son's seduction at the hands of one of the teachers entrusted with looking after him.'

'Seduction?' Guy echoed. 'Is that what he told you?' He shook his head. 'It was nothing of the sort! He was more than bloody willing!'

'I should hope he was, otherwise you'd be guilty of abusing more than just your position,' Lawrence replied. 'He seems a very nice boy. I can only hope your actions haven't done him too much damage.'

'*Damage*?' Guy looked incensed. 'What the hell has he been saying? I've done nothing to damage him!'

'Besides kill one of his closest friends.'

'I didn't touch Scott!'

'So why do you suppose Curt says differently?'

'I don't know! Maybe he's trying to protect himself!'

'Are you implying that Curt murdered Scott?'

'Curt didn't want our relationship to come to light any more than I did! I'm sure to you his father came across as the epitome of care and concern, but the picture Curt paints is rather different!'

'Mr Markham, I'm not daft. On the night Scott died, Curt was in the san after a bad asthma attack. Do you really think I'm going to believe he could have attacked someone bigger, stronger and fitter than him and actually succeeded in murdering them? He hasn't even been well enough play sport this term!'

'He's nowhere near as frail as he likes to make out,' Guy returned. 'He's not incapable of playing rugby, he just doesn't *want* to!'

'Right.'

Guy shook his head. 'I don't know why I'm surprised that he's succeeded in manipulating you, he does it to everyone. He's very bright, and he knows how to play people. He comes across as so gentle and unassuming, but he can twist words and arguments like you wouldn't believe. How do you think he won the regional debating championships?'

Lawrence frowned. 'I thought that was Scott?'

'They compete in pairs.'

This revelation came as a surprise. Lawrence couldn't imagine Curt having either the confidence or the drive for debating. Clearly he'd kept that side of his personality well under wraps during the previous week.

'You have no idea what goes on behind those big blue eyes,' Guy added. 'I used to think Fray was the twisted one.'

'Which is presumably why you tried to implicate him.'

'I did nothing to Fray! Or Scott! And if Curt thinks I'm going to take the fall for him he's going to be sorely disappointed!'

'Is he. Well perhaps you could fill me in on whatever you think Curt might have missed.'

Guy sighed. He sat in silence for some time, and Lawrence was on the point of prompting him when he said, 'I don't know what happened between them. I woke up to Curt knocking on my window at quarter past three. He was crying and he had blood on his jumper. He said he'd been in a fight – I didn't realise –' he stopped. 'I really had no idea of the seriousness of the situation.'

'Despite the fact he had blood all over his jumper?'

'There wasn't that much of it – Curt said something about a nosebleed – I just assumed –' he held his hands out. 'Like you said, Curt seems like a very nice kid. It didn't even occur to me that he might have done anyone serious harm! He's not exactly one to go around starting fights. My immediate assumption was that someone had been picking on him and he'd hit back in self-defence.'

'Did you not ask him what had happened?'

'Of course I asked! But that upset him even more, and I was worried he might have an asthma attack, so I let it lie.'

'So what did you do?'

'I did my best to calm him down. I sat him down, got him a drink, lent him a clean jumper –'

'What did you do with his jumper?'

'Um –' Guy frowned. 'I'm not actually sure what happened to that, thinking about it. I was really more concerned about him.'

'About him, or keeping him quiet?'

Guy hesitated before saying, 'Both, if I'm honest.'

'Did he stay long?'

'About half an hour. After he calmed down he was keen to get back to the san in case he was missed.'

'Given that's where he was spending the night, did you not think it odd he'd managed to get into a fight?'

'I didn't really think much about the specifics at the time. I know that probably sounds strange, but the whole thing was a bit surreal. It wasn't until the following evening, when I heard the news about Scott, that I realised the enormity of what had happened. Even then I couldn't really believe Curt would have –' he held his hands out.

'No?' Lawrence raised his eyebrows. 'A minute ago you described him as twisted, now you're saying you couldn't imagine he'd have done anyone serious harm. I have to admit to feeling more than a bit confused.'

'I've been struggling to make sense of it myself,' Guy replied. 'In the past week I've seen a very different side to Curt. I should have listened to Fray. He did warn me.'

'Fray?' Lawrence frowned. 'What did he say?'

'That I was playing with fire. I assumed he meant the teacher–pupil aspect of the relationship, but when I replied in that vein he smirked and said that should be the least of my concerns,' he paused. 'I didn't think much of it, at the time. I just put it down to Fray being odd.' He shook his head. 'I had no idea I might end up being framed for murder.'

Lawrence had left a message for Donald Chadwick when he and Rebecca had first taken Guy in for questioning, but to his surprise didn't hear back until shortly after six, and he wondered what the man could possibly have been doing that justified switching his phone off for so long in the circumstances. Donald answered the question within seconds of opening his front door, saying, 'Apologies for not getting back to you sooner,' as he led Lawrence into a living room lined with mahogany bookcases. 'My mother had a fall this morning. I'm only just back.'

'I'm sorry to hear that. I hope she's all right?'

'Rather shaken, but nothing broken,' Donald replied. 'Do have a seat,' he gestured towards the rose beige suite. 'Can I get you a drink? Tea? Coffee?'

'No, thank you.'

Donald nodded, heading towards the fireplace and bending to switch the gas fire on as Lawrence sat on the sofa. 'Have you reached a conclusion yet?' He asked, as he turned towards an armchair.

'Not quite,' Lawrence replied. 'But I'll tell you what I can so far. First of all, it seems one of your staff members has been having a sexual relationship with one of your pupils.'

Donald froze halfway between standing and sitting. 'What?' He exclaimed, aghast. 'You mean that – I mean –' he sank down into the chair. 'No. *No*.' He shook his head. 'Not *here*.'

'How would you deal with a situation like that?'

'Uh – I don't know – I've never had to – obviously that sort of behaviour is completely unacceptable. Clearly the staff member involved would have to go. Whatever the circumstances.'

'And the pupil?'

'That would depend. Why? What's going on?'

'Guy Markham appears to be rather deeply involved with Curt Wilkinson.'

Donald stared at Lawrence, his mouth half open. 'Guy?' He managed, at length. 'Guy's been –' he stopped, awkwardly. 'With *Curt*?'

'Yes.'

'Oh good God –' Donald raised the fingers of his left hand to his forehead and drew them slowly down over his face. 'Uh – I – wh –' he stopped, taking a deep breath. Swallowing hard, he tried again. 'Thank you. For bringing that to my attention.' He ran a nervous hand through his hair. 'I'll see that the situation is suitably dealt with.'

'I'm not sure you'll have to,' Lawrence replied. 'We've arrested Guy.'

Donald's features registered total incredulity. Some moments passed before he spoke. 'No,' he breathed, shaking his head. 'Not a member of *staff* –' he raised his right thumb and forefinger to pull at his moustache. 'What could he have had against Scott? He never even taught the boy – there must be some mistake – *surely* –'

'Scott knew all about Guy's relationship with Curt. He was blackmailing Guy. For a considerable sum, if the recent increase in his bank balance is anything to go by.'

'Has Guy admitted to any of this?'

'He doesn't deny the relationship and he admits Scott was blackmailing him. We're not sure at this stage whether he was responsible for what happened to Scott.'

Donald sat shaking his head from side to side. It was a small movement, his expression almost dazed. He looked shell shocked. 'How awful,' he managed, at length.

'At the moment we're waiting on forensics. Hopefully we'll have a clearer picture of exactly what happened to Scott in the next day or two.'

'What about Francis?' Donald asked, suddenly seeming to remember other recent events. 'Where does he fit into this?'

'We aren't sure. I suspect whoever murdered Scott thought he would make a perfect scapegoat. Several people overheard Fray threaten to kill Scott during an argument last week, and he had no reliable alibi for Friday night. Doubtless the idea was to make him look guilty.'

Donald shook his head again. 'I don't know what to say,' he admitted, at length. 'Ten days ago nothing seemed amiss – now I've one boy dead, another seriously ill in hospital – a staff member under arrest –' he paused. 'It makes me wonder what else is going on that I don't yet know about.'

All sorts, Lawrence suspected, from what he had learned during his week at the school, although he doubted there was anything that could top Francis's crystal meth project. That was a conversation for another day. He was just wondering what had become of the product of that experiment when he felt his mobile vibrate. Drawing it from his pocket, he checked the name on the screen before excusing himself and heading to the hallway to take the call.

'Leighton. What have you got?'

'One six-inch knife and a grey uniform jumper nicely spattered with blood. Although obviously I can't tell you whose blood it is yet.'

'Any clue to its ownership?'

'Yeah, a name tag. Curt Wilkinson.'

Lawrence raised his eyebrows. 'That is interesting. Where did you find it?'

'In a locker at the sports pavillion.'

'Was it his locker?'

'Yep. They all have one, apparently. Complete with a combination lock. The caretaker opened it for me.'

'Right, we'll bring him in. Let me know if you find anything else.'

'Sure.'

'Oh – actually, hold on – would you mind coming with me to collect Curt, and sitting in on the interview? His health isn't good and I don't want to risk him coming to any harm at our hands.'

'Yeah, no problem.'

'I'll meet you in the turning circle in five minutes. With any luck, we can put this thing to bed tonight.'

Thirteen

'Have you ever been scared of the dark?'

Leighton raised his eyes from his mobile. He had been sitting in an interview room with Curt for the best part of forty-five minutes, and after twenty minutes of watching Curt stare at the table had turned his mind to crafting a reply to the text message Millie had sent that afternoon. Almost half an hour later, he still had no idea how to respond to the words *I'm sorry. I love you x*. Curt's question gave him an excuse to put the task off a while longer.

The boy had seemed stunned when Lawrence first asked him to accompany them to the police station to answer questions under caution; shocked silence had then given way to fervent protests followed by panic. They had waited for him to calm down before putting him in the car, and he had been silent for most of the journey and the time that had elapsed since their arrival at the station. His father had left the room to take a phone call and Rebecca and Lawrence were waiting elsewhere – at Andrew's insistance – until a solicitor arrived. Now Curt was looking at Leighton expectantly, his blue eyes bloodshot. Leighton set his phone down on the table.

'No, not really.'

'Me either,' Curt replied. 'I used to tease my sister. I wish I hadn't.'

'I'm sure she'll forgive you.'

'We moved house. When she was eight. She used to sleepwalk, and she woke up in the utility room. It was pitch dark and she couldn't find a light switch. She screamed the place down.' There was a long pause. 'I kind of know how she felt now. I don't know how I got here, and I don't know how to get out. But screaming isn't going to help me.'

Leighton absorbed this before responding. 'You must have some idea of how you got here.'

Curt thought this over. 'Yuh,' he acknowledged, eventually. 'I listened to my dad.'

Leighton raised his eyebrows. 'What did he say?'

'Tell the truth.'

'Well that's better advice than my dad ever gave me.'

'What does your dad do?'

'Gets drunk, mostly. Yours?'

'He's an actuary.'

Leighton nodded.

'Do you have any brothers or sisters?'

'A brother.'

'What does he do?'

Leighton sighed. He never actually lied to people about Tom's whereabouts; usually he simply deflected attention with jokes or flippant remarks. In the circumstances, that seemed inappropriate. 'He's in prison.'

'What for?' Curt asked, at length.

'Attempted murder.'

Curt swallowed. There was another long pause before he said, 'Do you believe he did it?'

'I know he was responsible for causing serious injury. But I don't know whether he intended to kill her.'

'Who did he –' Curt trailed off.

'His wife.'

'Do you know why he did it?'

'I'm not sure he does. They were fighting and it got out of control.'

Curt nodded slightly. 'So if you don't know whether he meant it, how did the court decide?'

'I don't know. I wasn't on the jury.'

'How often do you think they get it wrong?'

Leighton didn't suppose anyone could answer that accurately. 'I've no idea.'

'I wonder how they really have any chance at all,' Curt reflected. 'You can know someone for months and still get them totally wrong.' He coughed. 'I can't believe –' he shook his head. 'I thought –' tears came to his eyes and he bowed his head. Seconds ticked by. Then he raised his eyes to meet Leighton's. 'Can they convict me on what they have?'

'That's a question for your lawyer.'

Curt nodded. Several seconds passed before he said, 'What do I do now?'

'I'd take your dad's advice if I were you.'

'That's what got me here in the first place.'

'No it's not. Whether or not what happened to Scott was your doing, your dad isn't to blame for any of this. And he's here, and he's on your side. You should be thankful for that.'

Tears pooled in Curt's eyes again. 'I know,' he whispered. 'I am. Really. It's just –' he drew a slow, careful breath. 'I'm scared. And I'm so tired.'

'It's ok, I won't let them keep you up all night.'

'I can't sleep,' he replied, hopelessly. 'I'm scared of dreaming. Although I'm not sure it can be any worse than this.' He cast his eyes down. 'I never thought I'd understand how Fray feels,' he added, his voice shaking. 'I've thought I was going to die so many times. But I've never actually thought I might want it to happen.'

It was coming up to ten by the time Lawrence and Rebecca commenced their interview with Curt. Despite the circumstances, Rebecca couldn't help but feel sorry for him; his face was ashen and he was shaking. She half hoped Leighton might call a halt to the proceedings, and felt glad she wasn't leading the questioning. She wasn't sure she wanted her friend to see her in that guise – at least, not when they were dealing with a fragile and clearly terrified teenager.

Lawrence switched the tape recorder on and completed the formalities before suggesting Curt give them his account of recent events. There was a long pause before he drew breath and said, 'Fray and Scott had a fight. On Wednesday afternoon.' He coughed. 'Fray told me Scott was blackmailing him but that he didn't want money. He'd asked before if Fray could make crystal meth, and that's what he wanted him to do.' Curt pulled at a loose thread in the cuff of his jumper. 'Fray asked if I'd help him. In the lab. On Friday night.'

'And what did you say?'

'Yes. I wanted to. Help him, I mean. But I couldn't stop thinking about if – if it went wrong – or we got caught – and I –' he shook his head slightly. 'I couldn't do it. I wanted to, but I couldn't.' He paused. 'I thought he'd be upset when I told him, but he took it really well. He said he'd sort something out. I never imagined he might still go ahead with it.' There was another pause before he added, 'And I had no idea how badly I'd let him down.'

Lawrence frowned. 'What do you mean by that?'

Curt swallowed. 'Scott was never blackmailing him,' he revealed, his voice unsteady. 'Fray agreed to the whole thing for *me*. He said – he – Scott was –' Curt drew a sharp breath before beginning to cough. He seemed to have trouble stopping, and when he did he was out of breath.

'What did Fray agree to do for you?' Lawrence asked, once Curt was breathing more evenly.

'He found out Scott was blackmailing Guy. Over me. That's what the fight was about,' Curt coughed again. 'He came up with the idea of making the meth so he could report Scott for possession. He figured nobody would believe anything he said after that. He was willing to do that for me and –' Curt gulped. 'I couldn't even help him!'

'Run me through what happened on Friday evening.'

'I went to dinner. I wasn't really hungry, but I thought if I didn't go people might ask questions. Scott joined me. I didn't know what to say to him. Fray made me promise not to challenge him and –' he broke off. 'I was so angry – with Scott – and myself, for letting Fray down – and I couldn't –' he shrugged. 'So I started on Sid. I half wanted him to hit me. Just to prove the point, really. But he knows better than to do that in a room full of people.'

'And what did you do after dinner?'

'I went to the library. I tried to work but I couldn't concentrate. I just kept going over and over everything. I didn't register how bad my chest was getting because I felt so tense already. When I realised I probably should have stayed where I was and asked someone to get Vivien, but I panicked and decided to walk over there, which just made things worse.'

'Vivien said you arrived at the san at ten past nine.'

'I don't remember.'

'Well what do you remember?'

'Feeling scared. Trying to breathe. Vivien talking to me,' he swallowed. 'Afterwards she made me a cup of tea. She asked if I wanted to go home.' He looked down. 'I wish I'd said yes, now.'

'What next?'

'I had to lie down. Too much Ventolin makes me feel shaky and sick. Vivien sat with me for a bit. And then Guy came to see me. I'm not sure how he knew where I was. I told him about Fray and Scott. Not about the meth – I didn't know whether he'd condone that – just the blackmail. I wasn't expecting him to be able to do anything, but I felt a bit better after I'd talked it through. And then I fell asleep.'

'When did you wake up again?'

'I'm not sure. Sometime in the night. I had a really bad headache. It felt like I was awake for ages. In the end I went to ask Vivien for some painkillers. Then I went back to sleep. And then it was morning.'

Lawrence regarded Curt in silence for several seconds before saying, 'We seem to have missed the bit where your jumper ended up spattered with Scott's blood.'

'I don't know how that happened. I didn't hurt him.'

'So how did your jumper find its way into the mix?'

'I don't know,' Curt repeated, weakly.

'You must have some idea of when you last had it.'

The boy thought for a moment. 'What does it look like?'

'It's a grey uniform jumper.'

'I have four of those. I have no idea when or where I last had each of them.'

'Unlike Fray's shirt. I'm sure you remember when you last had that.'

'What?'

'What happened on Tuesday? Couldn't go through with it? Lose your nerve? Or did you never plan to kill Fray? Just make him look guilty?'

'I didn't –'

'He made a perfect scapegoat, didn't he? He'd had a fight with Scott two days before his death, threatened to kill him. Plenty of people overheard that. Plus Fray wasn't about to admit to where he was on Friday night. And even if he had done, his partner in crime made for a less than reliable alibi.'

'No –'

'Meanwhile you planned things out very carefully. I'm not sure whether you faked or induced the asthma attack, either way I don't imagine you thought anyone would question it. And then you cemented your alibi by waking Vivien on your return to the san so she'd confirm seeing you during the night!'

Curt shook his head, tears in his eyes. 'No! I never –'

'I can understand why you wanted Scott out of the way. Besides the obvious consequences for Guy, I'm fairly sure sexual intercourse isn't on the list of approved extracurricular activities, so I should think if Donald Chadwick had learned of your affair you'd have been hauled over the coals as well. Hardly the conduct I imagine the school expects of a deputy head boy. Maybe you'd even have faced expulsion. I don't suppose your parents would have been too impressed. They're paying ten thousand pounds a term for your education, and although you've apparently not been well enough to attend half your classes this year, you've been perfectly capable of carrying on a relationship!'

This tipped Curt over the edge and he began to sob. He bowed his head, raising his hands to cover his face.

'Was your visit to Guy's apartment after you killed Scott a part of the plan? Make sure there'd be traces of Scott's blood there for us to find? Or did you just panic in the aftermath and go to him for help? He wasn't likely to turn you in, was he? Doing so would have spelt the end of his career.'

Curt shook his head, his breathing growing convulsive. Leighton sat forwards.

'Ok, mate, come on, calm down.'

'I didn't!' Curt gasped. 'I *didn't!*'

'Well I very much doubt that –'

'Can you lay off him for a minute, please?' Leighton cut in.

Lawrence sighed, leaning back in his chair. Leighton turned to Curt.

'It's all right. Try to breathe slowly or you're going to make yourself dizzy.'

Curt didn't respond, coughing and raising a hand to his chest.

'You're panicking and it's making you feel worse. Just calm down.'

Curt closed his eyes, his expression an odd mix of fear and concentration, and as the seconds ticked by his breathing slowed slightly. He opened his eyes, dropping his hand into his lap.

'Just take it easy.'

Curt coughed, raising a hand to dry his eyes with his fingers.

'Right,' Lawrence continued. 'How about we run through what happened after –'

'No,' Leighton interrupted, firmly. 'We're not running through anything right now.'

Lawrence looked taken aback. After a moment he said, 'Might I have a word? Outside?'

'You can have a word when I'm done here.'

Lawrence's eyebrows rose. 'I'm sorry, remind me, who's in charge again?'

'Why don't you wait outside?' Leighton suggested, his tone considerably more reasonable than his expression. 'I will be with you as soon as I can.'

Lawrence held his gaze for a moment before standing and turning to go without another word. Rebecca felt surprised. Leighton looked to her and indicated the door with a shift of his eyes. With a sigh, Rebecca got to her feet and followed her superior from the room. There was an empty interview room across the corridor, and Lawrence walked into it and leaned forwards, resting his hands on the desk as Rebecca closed the door to the room they had just left. He looked furious, and Rebecca felt uneasy. She suspected she was about to find herself caught in the middle.

'You had no right to do that!' Lawrence exploded the moment Leighton appeared in the doorway. 'I asked you to sit in in case of an emergency, not to give him an excuse to stop every time the questions get too intense for his liking! It is not in your remit to tell me what to do!'

'My remit is governed by medical ethics, not criminal law,' Leighton returned, evenly. 'I'm sorry if that's inconvenient.'

'His life was in absolutely no danger!'

'That's beside the point.'

'No, Leighton, that is exactly the point! That is why you are here! He isn't going to get out of this by playing on his asthma!'

'That wasn't asthma, that was anxiety. But if you're not careful, one is likely to follow the other. If you want to browbeat a petrified kid with no regard for the consequences, please don't ask me to be a party to it.'

'Fine! Go, then!'

'I can't very well do that. You told Curt and his parents I'd stay with him during the interview. You can't renege on that just because I'm not doing it the way you want.'

'It is not your place to tell me what I can or can't do!'

Leighton sighed. 'Ok,' he replied, calmly. '*I* am not going to renege on that. Better?'

'Not a lot,' Lawrence snapped.

'Maybe we should discuss where we want to go from here so we're all on the same page,' Rebecca suggested. Leighton lifted one eyebrow and she guessed what he was thinking. She could almost hear him say it. *We'd have to be working from the same book first.*

'And lay down a few ground rules,' Lawrence added. 'Number one, *I* am in charge of this investigation.'

Leighton made no reply.

'Clear?' Lawrence demanded.

'Yes, I heard you,' Leighton returned, coolly. 'I'm not deaf.'

'Don't be so bloody impertinent!' Lawrence shot back, stepping forwards and reaching for a chair. Leighton instinctively backed away, and Lawrence stopped in his tracks. There was a moment's uncomfortable suspended animation.

'Sorry,' Lawrence offered, holding his hands up and stepping back.

Leighton didn't move.

'I'm sorry. I didn't mean to alarm you.'

Leighton nodded in acknowledgement.

'Are you all right?'

'I'm fine,' he flashed a smile, seeming to snap back to normal. 'I might see if I can find some coffee before we sit down. Do you guys want?'

'Yes please.'

Leighton looked to Rebecca and she nodded. He turned and disappeared out into the corridor. Lawrence reached for the nearest chair and sat down. 'What happened there?' He asked. 'Am I that intimidating? Or was that an overreaction?'

Rebecca sat sideways on a chair the other side of the table, leaning back against the adjacent wall. 'I don't know,' she admitted.

'I don't think anyone's ever looked at me like that before. I think he really thought I was going to –' Lawrence stopped. 'I'm not sure whether that says more about me or him.' He looked shaken, and Rebecca tried to think of a reassuring response.

'Well, he's spent most of the last week on what you said is a pretty rough estate. Maybe that's made him jittery.'

Lawrence nodded. 'Maybe.' He frowned. 'Do you suppose that's what happened to his face?'

Rebecca shrugged.

'I really didn't intend him any harm.'

'I know.'

'Well he clearly didn't.'

'Do you want me to go and talk to him?'

Lawrence shook his head. 'No. That's for me to do. I'll have a chat with him tomorrow.' He sighed. 'Hopefully we can get through the rest of this evening without further incident. Although I'm not optimistic about our chances of squeezing a confession out of either Curt or Guy before bed time.' He sat back in his chair. 'Perhaps a night in the cells will have more effect.'

Fourteen

By Monday morning Curt looked more dazed than upset, and when Lawrence asked him to run through his activities on the night of Scott's death again, his delivery was rather vacant. None of what he had to say deviated noticeably from the account he'd given the night before, and Lawrence asked him to repeat the process backwards. Curt seemed thrown by the idea, but he did as bid without tripping up, and Lawrence moved on to Tuesday evening.

'Take me through what happened when you got back to Windsor House after the lectures on Tuesday. In detail.'

'I – um –' Curt's eyes flickered towards the wall on his right. 'I got in about half nine. When I walked into the foyer, Jesse and one of his mates were in there. I went up the stairs – I had to stop for a minute on each floor to get my breath back – then I –'

'You didn't mention that before,' Rebecca put in.

'What?'

'We've been through your movements on Tuesday evening twice before, and on neither occasion did you mention stopping on your way up the stairs.'

'It didn't seem important.'

'So you're not just trying to think of ways to fill the time Jesse and his friend might remember you taking between going up and coming back down the stairs?'

'No.'

There was a pause.

'Carry on,' Lawrence urged.

Curt rubbed the eczema blanketing the back of his right hand with the fingers of his left. 'I got back to the room – flicked the light on – saw the blood –'

Rebecca stopped him again. 'You told me on Wednesday that before you left for the Great Hall Fray had said he was going to bed early. So why did you turn on the light?'

'I wasn't thinking,' Curt replied, his voice wavering. 'I was feeling really dizzy.'

'Perhaps that was a side effect of the chemical you used to knock your room mate out before you slit his wrists,' Lawrence observed.

Curt closed his eyes momentarily. 'I didn't,' he countered, weakly.

'Well someone did.'

'I just – I thought – he's talked about it so many times –' Curt faltered.

'Which is presumably what gave you the idea,' Lawrence replied. 'Like the asthma attack on Friday night, you probably didn't think anyone would even question it. You could focus suspicion on someone else while at the same time removing the one person who knew enough to finger you for Scott's murder. I suspect it's unlikely Fray would ever have talked, but with someone that unpredictable you probably didn't want to take the chance. So what went wrong? Fit of conscience? Someone disturb you?'

'No, I –'

'When did you steal the ether from the chemicals stockroom?'

Curt hesitated, the change in direction clearly taking him by surprise. 'I've never been in there,' he responded, not falling into the trap of correcting Lawrence on his choice of chemical. Then, as Lawrence opened his mouth to continue, he added, 'Although I did steal Guy's key.'

'When did you do that?'

'Friday morning break. I stayed behind after my biology lesson. We were in his office. I said I felt faint and asked if he could get me some water so he'd have to leave the room.'

'What did you do with the key?'

'Gave it to Fray.'

'Did you ever return it?'

Curt nodded. 'On Saturday morning.'

Lawrence raised his eyebrows. 'So you planned ahead for Tuesday evening?'

'I didn't do anything on Tuesday evening!'

'So who did? Yesterday you implied that Guy was responsible, but he was in a room full of people at the time, so it can't have been his doing, can it? You also accused Guy of Scott's murder, but the evidence we have so far all seems to point in your direction! Why do you think that might be?'

'I don't know,' Curt replied, blinking rapidly.

'You don't know how a knife and your jumper came to be stained with Scott's blood and hidden in a locker only you have the code to?'

Curt frowned. 'What? Where was it?'

'In your locker at the sports pavillion. I suppose that was the last place you expected us to look, given that you don't play sport. Does anyone else know the combination?'

'They wouldn't need to. The lockers aren't particularly secure. Most of them can be opened just by yanking on the handle. Then you can slam them shut again.'

'I see.'

'I've not even been in there this term.'

'Just like you've not been in the observatory, I suppose? Funny that. We have a witness who not only saw you in there, but saw you let yourself in with a key. There's a common theme here, isn't there? Where did you steal that one from?'

'I didn't. Guy gave it to me.'

'So that you could meet up in there.'

'It seemed a pretty safe option, after dark. Nobody goes that way after they're done at the fields.'

'Except you weren't the only ones who thought so, were you? Scott had a key too.'

Curt nodded.

'Is that how he found out about the two of you?'

Curt nodded again. 'He promised he wouldn't say anything.'

'He didn't keep that promise, though, did he? Nicky and Sid both know more than a little bit about it. And I don't suppose they're the only ones. Did that make you angry?'

There was a pause before Curt nodded for a third time.

'And then you found out he was blackmailing Guy as well as blabbing about it, and you decided enough was enough. I can understand that, I –'

'I *didn't*!' Curt protested, with considerably more force than on previous occasions. 'I didn't do a thing to Scott! I don't know what happened! I have told you everything I can, and I can't tell you any more because I don't *know* any more!' He drew a deep breath before adding, his tone more measured, 'We can go round and round in circles all day, but I can't give you the answer you want. I'm not going to admit to something I didn't do.'

*****

Forty minutes into the interview, a young police constable interrupted to inform Lawrence that he not only had a visitor, but one who was insisting on talking to him immediately. His curiosity getting the better of him, Lawrence left Rebecca and Curt where they were and headed for the foyer. Hovering at the front desk, clad in a rather incongruous ensemble of old jeans, a uniform school jumper and tartan slippers, was Francis. He appeared to be alone. Lawrence wondered how he had made his way to the police station, and whether the hospital – or indeed his parents – had any idea where he was.

'I need to talk to you,' he said, the moment he saw Lawrence. 'It's important.'

'Ok,' Lawrence nodded. 'Shall we sit down?'

'In private.'

Lawrence sighed, turning to the duty sergeant at the front desk. 'Sorry, do you have another interview room I might use?'

The man checked the computer in front of him. 'Sure. Room three's free.'

Lawrence thanked the man before indicating for Francis to follow him and heading back down the corridor he had walked along moments earlier. Ushering Francis into room three, he took a seat without closing the door. Francis moved to shut it before sitting the other side of the table and regarding Lawrence expectantly.

'What was it you wanted to say?' Lawrence asked, when Francis didn't volunteer anything.

'Don't you have to record it?'

'No. This isn't an official interview. It's just a conversation.'

'Can you make it one?'

Lawrence frowned. 'This isn't a game.'

'I'm not here to play games.'

That would make for a refreshing change, Lawrence thought, although he wasn't optimistic.

'Well perhaps you could tell me why you are here, and we can take things from there.'

'I was in the woods. On Friday night. With Scott.'

'I see,' Lawrence responded, disbelievingly. 'And what were you doing in the woods?'

'We were going to the observatory. We wanted to conduct a séance.'

'Just the two of you?'

'It was going to be four of us, but Curt got freaked out about the whole thing, so it ended up being just me, Nicky and Scott.'

'So Nicky was with you as well.'

'He was behind us. He forgot something so he went back to Windsor.'

'What did he forget?'

'Cigarettes.'

'And what happened after he went back for those?'

'Scott had been on about making crystal meth. He asked Nick if he could get the chemicals through his dad's business. There isn't exactly a big stock in the chemistry lab. I said no. If someone else had said no, maybe Simon would still be here.'

'A bit late for that, don't you think?' Lawrence remarked. 'Given that you'd already been making it. And don't waste my time denying it, the chemical evidence speaks for itself.'

'I told you why I might have done that.'

'You also told me it was with the intention of having Scott expelled. What happened to that part of the plan?'

'I had second thoughts.'

'Right. So, you were in the woods, waiting for Nicky and debating the merits of setting up a meth factory. Then what?'

Francis cast his eyes down, linking his fingers together. 'When I kept saying no, he got nasty.' He dug his fingernails into his skin. 'About Simon. He said addiction was an affliction of the weak and that if people couldn't use drugs sensibly then they deserved to die.' He swallowed. 'I – I –' he looked up. 'I didn't really think – I just reacted and –' he shrugged, returning his gaze to his hands.

Lawrence waited ten seconds to see whether Francis had anything to add before saying, 'I can't just assume the rest. You're going to have to be explicit.'

Francis squeezed his fingers together. 'He was walking ahead of me so he didn't see the knife coming. He didn't even scream straight away.'

'Do you usually carry a knife?'

'No. But the window catches are on a spring. If the window slips down you can get shut out.'

'How long was the blade?'

'I don't know, I didn't measure it. Maybe about this?' He held his hands some five inches apart.

'And where is it now?'

'I got rid of everything on Saturday afternoon. In town.'

'Where in town?'

'A big bin behind the Coach and Horses pub.'

Lawrence sat forwards, resting his elbows on the table in front of him. 'So how do you suppose the knife found its way back to the school sports pavillion?'

Francis hesitated, his dark eyes flickering slightly.

'I thought you said you weren't here to play games.'

'This isn't a game.'

'Well I'm glad you recognise that. Perhaps now you might like to fill me in on why you've been wasting my time?'

Francis dropped his eyes to the table.

'You've led us up and down just about every garden path in town over the past week. Did Curt ask you to do that, or did you do it off your own bat?'

'Curt had nothing to do with it.'

'Now I know that's not true. Did he tell you he'd killed Scott or did you work that out for yourself?'

Francis's eyebrows contracted into an anxious frown. 'What?' He breathed. 'Curt didn't do anything to Scott!'

'We have rather a lot of evidence to suggest otherwise.'

Francis shook his head. 'You can't have! You *can't*!'

'And the fact you've just confessed to a murder you clearly didn't commit is very interesting. I can't imagine you'd do that for anyone else.'

'But I –' Francis stopped. 'That's not why –' he shook his head again. 'Curt didn't kill Scott! He *can't* have!'

'I'm afraid he can. And that's not all, is it? Who do you suppose was responsible for what happened to you on Tuesday evening?'

Francis blinked. 'That wasn't Curt! That was me!'

Lawrence sighed wearily. 'Fray, I really don't have time for this. Do you –'

'I dripped chloroethane on my pillow so you'd think someone else had tried to kill me and make it look like suicide. I left the bottle in one of the toilet cisterns in the first-floor bathroom.'

'And what earthly reason would you have had to do a thing like that?'

'I was trying to distract you.'

'I suspect that's more like what you're trying to do now. Where did you get the chloroethane?'

'The chemicals stockroom.'

'When?'

'Tuesday afternoon.'

'And how did you come by a key to the stockroom?'

'We borrowed one on Friday.'

'You mean Curt stole one.'

Francis shrugged.

'He told me he returned that on Saturday morning. So how did you manage to use it on Tuesday? Time travel?'

'I had a copy cut. After lessons on Friday afternoon. In town.'

'How very convenient,' Lawrence responded, drily.

Francis looked perplexed for a moment before saying, 'The receipt is probably still in my coat pocket. And the bus tickets.'

'Well that tells me someone got a copy cut, but it doesn't tell me who.'

'Everyone else was at dinner when I got the bus back. The time should be stamped on the bus ticket.' He paused. 'Oh, and Dr Latimer will remember me being in the lab after hours on Tuesday. He came in just as I was leaving and asked what I was doing in there.'

'And what did you say?'

'I told him I was trying to focus fog.'

'What?'

'Yeah, that's more or less how he looked at me. Then he shook his head and told me to scram.' The boy broke into a strange half smile. 'It's amazing what you can get away with when people think you're crazy.'

Lawrence looked to Rebecca as he paused the videotape of the first interview they'd conducted that day. 'What do you think?'

'I don't know,' she admitted. 'If he is lying he's very good at it. But then more than one person has suggested as much.'

Lawrence nodded. 'And you don't win awards for debating without being able to think on your feet, however vulnerable you might come across.' He sighed. 'He's certainly very bright, there's no doubt about that. And I'm sure his solicitor has made him aware that we're unlikely to secure a conviction solely on the basis of the evidence we have so far.'

'I wouldn't want to. I'm not at all sure he's guilty. Are you?'

'No,' Lawrence conceded. 'But if he's not I'd love to know what Fray was playing at offering up a confession.'

'Do you think he and Curt could be in it together?'

'I doubt it. Given how tight they managed to keep their stories last week I can't believe they'd not have discussed something as crucial as the location of that knife.' He paused. 'Although I am prepared to believe Tuesday evening's stunt was Fray's doing. But again, I don't see him going to those sorts of lengths to distract us on Guy's behalf.'

'Perhaps he doesn't actually know who was responsible and he's hedging his bets,' Rebecca suggested.

'It's possible, but I doubt it.'

Rebecca shook her head. 'I don't know. I'm not sure what I think any more. Do you mind if I go for a quick walk around the block?'

'Not at all.'

'Can I get you anything while I'm out?'

'No. Thanks.'

Rebecca gathered up her handbag and coat before standing and heading out. Lawrence reached for the sandwich he'd abandoned earlier in the interests of focusing on the video. He'd barely eaten two mouthfuls when a knock came at the door. As he glanced up, the door opened and Leighton looked in.

'What's this?' He greeted Lawrence, with a grin. 'Slacking off?'

'Late lunch.'

'A likely story. I bet you've been sitting around drinking coffee all morning whilst I've been hard at work.' He dropped into the chair Rebecca had recently vacated. 'How's it going?'

'Rather frustratingly. We've been going around in circles, and the only confession we have had today was a false one.'

'Who was that from?'

'Fray.'

'Your crystal meth chemist.'

'That's right. He also claims it was his idea to make a suicide attempt look like attempted murder, and crazy though it sounds I suspect that much might be true.'

'Presumably he's been assessed by the hospital psych team since then?'

'Last I heard they were having trouble pinning down a diagnosis because he wouldn't talk to them. Why, what do you think the problem is?'

'Without talking to him it's impossible for me to say, but from the bits and pieces I've heard from you and Becks my money would be on a hypomanic episode. Or maybe a mixed episode.

Either way, he probably has no real comprehension of the consequences of carrying out a dangerous chemical synthesis or confessing to a serious crime. If you haven't already, you should fill whoever's treating him in on what he's been getting up to.'

'I'll do that.'

'And you should probably discount any plans to charge him with wasting your time, because chances are he's not going to be found to have been of sound mind.'

'I'd already reached that conclusion,' Lawrence replied. 'Besides, if he's genuinely not well I don't want to add to his troubles.'

Leighton nodded.

Lawrence set his sandwich down on the table top. 'Leighton, look, I'm sorry about what happened last night. I didn't mean to alarm you.'

'Oh, don't worry about it, my fault. I shouldn't drink Red Bull. It makes me jumpy.'

'I really didn't intend you any harm. I know we have our differences, but I wouldn't ever want you to feel you weren't safe to voice your opinion freely.'

'You might come to regret saying that.'

'Please, this isn't a joke. The fact you obviously felt threatened concerns me.'

Leighton sighed. 'It's really not you. Ok?'

Lawrence regarded him carefully for a moment. 'Is everything all right?'

'Yes. Good, actually, I have something for you.'

Lawrence gave up. Leighton was clearly determined to change the subject, and if neither jokes nor work succeeded in doing so Lawrence imagined he would find some other means. 'Go on.'

'First up, the dimensions of the knife and the blood spatter on the jumper are consistent with the injuries inflicted on Scott, so the jumper was almost certainly at the scene. Although I'm still waiting on DNA results to confirm it.'

'Well that's good to know, but it's not really taking us anywhere unexpected. Did you find anything else?'

'I did. There were quantities of cornstarch around the cuffs. It's used on laboratory gloves to make it easier to pull them on and off.'

'So whoever did the deed may have worn gloves.'

'More specifically, latex gloves.'

'How can you tell?'

'DIY testing,' Leighton responded, displaying a rash running across the back of his left hand. 'Latex proteins give me contact dermatitis. I checked to see whether they use latex gloves in the labs at the school in case it was an artefact, but they don't. Which brings me on to this.' He reached into his pocket. 'Now don't get too excited,' he said, with a mischievous smile. 'This isn't a proposition.' He placed a wrapped condom in front of himself and slid it into the centre of the table with his index finger. 'But it is the point at which somebody's story starts to fall apart.'

'Sorry to have kept you waiting so long,' Lawrence began, on joining Guy in the interview room. 'I hadn't factored a trip to the hospital into the day.'

Concern swept across Guy's face. 'Is Curt ok?'

'No, not really,' Lawrence replied, shortly, leaving the man's imagination to spin something more dramatic than the return of Francis to the psychiatric ward. 'I know you said yesterday that he'd be quite capable of playing rugby if he wanted to, but I'm really not convinced. It must be terrifying being unable to breathe.'

Guy looked down. 'That was probably a bit unfair,' he acknowledged.

'As, I suspect, were a few other things you had to say. You risked your career for the relationship, so you must have been pretty taken with him. Or do you make a habit of sleeping with your pupils?'

'Of course not.'

Lawrence nodded thoughtfully. 'Were you his first?'

'I didn't push him into it, if that's what he's told you,' Guy replied, guardedly.

'He's told us nothing of the sort. In fact, he's barely had a bad word to say about you, which frankly I find extraordinary, given everything we've put him through and the fact he must by now be well aware of who it is that's trying to frame him for murder.'

'I'm not trying to –'

'Oh, sorry, no, of course not,' Lawrence interrupted. 'You weren't there. Let's go back to your relationship. Were you his first?'

'Is this really necessary?'

'Yes or no?'

Guy sighed. 'Yes. At least, so he told me.'

Lawrence nodded, pulling the condom Leighton had matched to the foil fragment he'd found in the observatory from his pocket and laying it on the table. 'Do you recognise this?'

'Oh for God's sake, what sort of a question is that? Are you wanting to know whether we had safe sex now?'

'Do you recognise the brand?'

'Yes,' Guy confirmed, looking suspicious. 'Why?'

'I'm guessing this was Curt's choice.'

'So what if it was?'

'Did you not think it strange that he had a preference if he'd never slept with anyone before?'

'Not really. He said they needed to be hypoallergenic.'

'Did he say why?'

'I didn't feel the need ask. He suffers from severe eczema and he can't even use liquid hand soap without coming out in a rash, so I can understand why he'd want to be careful about –' Guy tipped his head towards the condom.

Lawrence nodded. Placing the evidence bag containing Curt's bloodstained jumper on the table, he asked, 'And do you recognise this?'

Guy shrugged. 'It looks like a school jumper.'

'Curt's jumper, to be precise. My colleague looked this over and, in addition to confirming that this jumper was worn by the same person who attacked Scott, found traces of cornstarch on the cuffs. He tells me that's used to lubricate latex gloves. Do you know whether that's something Curt might have come into contact with in the lab at school?'

'I've no idea.'

'Well, we checked with Ted Latimer, and he says not. Apparently the school stopped using them a few years ago after a pupil almost died of anaphylactic shock.' Lawrence paused. 'A pupil called Curt Wilkinson.'

Guy didn't reply.

'I imagine as a biologist you know more about this kind of thing than I do, but I understand from my colleague that if people are that sensitive to latex the contaminated cornstarch alone is enough to trigger a potentially fatal reaction. Which makes it rather hard to believe that Curt might have turned up in this jumper, alive, outside your window the night Scott died.'

Guy swallowed.

'You, on the other hand, are presumably not allergic to latex. So there's no reason why you couldn't have been wearing it, or, indeed, have handled it after the event when you placed it in Curt's locker.' He paused. 'What I don't understand is why you decided to implicate him. Yesterday you told us you loved him, and the feeling seems to have been mutual. So why, when you could easily have slipped into a bedroom or changing room and appropriated any boy's jumper, did you opt to pin the blame on Curt? That just seems cruel.'

'I didn't –' Guy stopped.

'Didn't what? Didn't mean to shatter an innocent teenager's trust in people? Didn't expect us to put him through hell? Didn't consider that the stress of the ordeal might land him in hospital?' Lawrence paused, eyebrows raised. 'I could understand if you'd pointed the finger at him in a moment of panic, but you planned to pin it on him from the start! What possible reason could you have had to destroy his life as well as Scott's?'

'That wasn't what I –' Guy stopped short. There was a long pause before he said, 'I didn't *plan* anything. I didn't have the time.'

'Spur of the moment, was it?' Lawrence asked. 'What, you just happened to be walking through the woods in the middle of the night, wearing Curt's jumper and carrying a kitchen knife? That sounds very plausible.'

'No, but –' Guy sighed. 'I really didn't give it as much thought as –' he swallowed. 'I didn't have much time. It was already gone ten when –' he broke off again. 'Curt was talking about going to John. When I saw him on Friday night.'

'John?'

'John Richardson. His form tutor. Fray had told Curt that Scott was blackmailing him, and Curt was terrified Fray would do something reckless. He said he was going to go and find John after classes on Saturday.'

'And you guessed what might come of John's intervention.'

'Scott would have been only too happy to distract from his own misdeeds by airing mine, and I knew Curt wouldn't lie to John. I tried to talk him out of it, suggested he give it a little more time – even offered to talk to Scott myself. But Curt was adamant. He said he'd already been silent for too long and that someone had to stand up to Scott.'

'So you decided to act.'

Guy nodded. 'But I wasn't thinking about implicating anyone. Truly. I wore the jumper so that if anyone saw me from a distance they'd assume I was one of the boys. Not least because I knew the porter wouldn't set his bloody great Alsatian on one of them. And the only jumper I had access to at that time of night was Curt's, because he'd left it in my apartment earlier in the week.'

'Be that as it may, at some stage you clearly decided to pin the blame on Curt, otherwise you wouldn't have planted the jumper and the knife in his locker.'

'I put them in there because it was close to hand after –' Guy left Lawrence to assume the rest of the sentence. 'Nine times out of ten, the pavillion's left unlocked, and I knew Curt wasn't using his locker. I did go back a few times to try to retrieve them, but during the day there was always someone about, and out of hours the porter's been all over everything in the past week.' He ran a hand through his hair. 'Then when you said he'd accused me of seducing him I felt so angry – it was bad enough that he'd turned me in, without lying to try to cover his own back.'

'Actually, I was the one who accused you of seducing him,' Lawrence observed. 'Curt didn't say that. But I hardly think you're in any position to judge his actions! He was in pieces by the time he finally opened up to us! And you did that to him!'

'I know,' Guy acknowledged. 'I know. But I risked everything for him. And he knew that. He promised me he wouldn't breathe a word.'

'Well I don't suppose he anticipated you'd be prepared to kill to maintain that silence, do you? Or that you'd willingly sacrifice him to save your own skin! He spent last night in a police cell, and you have the gall to imply that was somehow *his* fault? I feel bad enough for my part in the proceedings, and I was acting in good faith!'

'I didn't say it was his fault,' Guy objected. 'But I didn't set out to hurt him. It wasn't that premeditated. None of it was. It was –' he hesitated. 'It was a mistake.'

'A mistake?' Lawrence echoed. 'That's something of an understatement, don't you think?'

'You weren't there!' Guy flared. 'Scott wouldn't leave me alone! Every time I turned around he was taunting me, or threatening me with something! And I was far from the only person he was tormenting! Christ knows what Curt ever saw in him! The younger lads were terrified of him and he made Fray's life miserable! He was a nasty piece of work, and I can't say I'm sorry that –' he stopped abruptly, his eyes flickering in the direction of the tape recorder. There was a long pause before he continued, 'But I am sorry for what I put Curt through. The last thing I intended to do was hurt him. I wish I could –' he trailed off with a shrug. 'You're not going to charge him with anything, are you? Perverting the course of justice, or something?'

'As far as I'm aware, Curt's not actually guilty of that. Although having falsely accused him, *you* are. Given the amount of distress that has caused – not to mention the possible consequences it could have had – I really have no option but to charge you.' Lawrence paused. 'And if you've any decency, you'll plead guilty and spare Curt a trip to court.'

Guy didn't reply, his eyes on the table.

'If you ask me, it's the least you can do.'

Fifteen

Elliot seemed in good spirits on the last night of Astatine's tour, and the band delivered a blistering performance. Rebecca watched from the rear of the venue, where she wouldn't be crushed by enthusiastic fans pogoing and crowd surfing, and when the set came to a close it took her several minutes to make her way through the crowds surging in the opposite direction to reach the backstage door. Showing her pass to security as she entered, she ran into Squidsy, a member of Astatine's road crew. He seemed on edge, and after a brief exchange of pleasantries hurried off muttering something about a club night, leaving Rebecca wishing, not for the first time, that she could be more a part of Elliot's world. His friends were almost invariably wary of what they said to her, and were reluctant to include her in their social activities because her presence might curb their use of illegal substances. She was well aware that Ian and Damian disliked Elliot taking her backstage for that very reason, and guessed Elliot probably did his fair share of recreational drug-taking when she wasn't around. She sometimes felt he put her in a rather compromising position, and wondered how it might affect her career were Astatine ever successful enough for their activities to come under scrutiny from the mainstream media.

By the time she reached the claustrophobic, heavily graffitied space that served as a dressing room, Ian and Damian had already bounded off to the aftershow party, and Elliot was sitting alone with a bottle of lager, wearing a long-sleeved t-shirt emblazoned with the words *I'm not an alcoholic I'm a drunk. Alcoholics go to meetings*. It might have been funny had it not been so close to the truth. He smiled as she entered the room.

'Hey,' he sat forwards, holding out a hand for hers.

'That was great,' she said, sincerely, giving him a kiss as she joined him on the bench that ran the length of the rear wall.

'You think?'

'Absolutely.'

He smiled again. 'I love playing in London.'

'It's good to see you smile like that.'

Elliot nodded slowly, a more serious expression taking over. 'I'm sorry. The last couple of months I've been a complete mess. I'm going to sort myself out before we head to the States.'

Rebecca wondered whether he would still feel the same the next day. She had heard similar statements before. 'I'm glad. I've been very worried about you.'

'I know. I'm sorry. I'm going to do something about it. I promise.'

'Good,' Rebecca squeezed his fingers, feeling reassured.

'Oh, I told Damian we'd be at the party in five minutes. I just wanted to see you alone first.'

'I thought you didn't want to go to the party.'

'That was before I went out on stage,' he said, rather dreamily. 'It was electric up there, Becca.' There was a momentary pause before he seemed to come back down to Earth. 'Why? Do you not want to go?'

'I don't mind,' Rebecca lied, really wanting to go home and have Elliot to herself. 'If you want to go, we can go.'

Elliot nodded.

'Come on, then,' Rebecca chivvied, getting to her feet. As Elliot did the same, the dressing room door opened. Rebecca turned, expecting to see one of the other band or crew members, hearing Elliot draw a sharp breath as she did so. Standing in the doorway was a young man who looked vaguely familiar. Tall and slender, he had short dark hair and equally dark eyes, which looked out from behind delicate glasses. Dressed in a white shirt and grey trousers, with a jacket hanging over his arm, Rebecca guessed he had come to the venue straight from work. He was clearly nervous.

'Hi,' he said, warily.

'Get out!' Elliot responded, his voice sounding strangled.

'I just wanted to –'

'Get *out*!'

The newcomer stood his ground. 'You were really good,' he said. 'I like the band.'

'What the fuck are you doing here?'

'I didn't know where else to find you.'

'How'd you find me at all?'

'I saw your picture in the NME.'

'Fuck,' Elliot muttered. Rebecca turned back towards him. His face was white, his expression caught somewhere between horrified and furious.

'Look, I –'

'What do you want?'

'I wanted to see you.'

'Well you've seen me now, so how about you fuck off back to wherever you came from and leave me alone?'

'Elliot, what's this about?' Rebecca asked.

'None of your business!' He responded, hotly.

'Who is this?'

'Nobody you need to know about!'

'I'm his brother,' the young man in the doorway offered, quietly.

Rebecca stared at him. The possibility that someone from Elliot's past might one day show up had often occurred to her, but, despite this, the reality of it actually happening gave her quite a jolt.

'Not now, you aren't!' Elliot spat. 'You haven't been my *brother* for twelve years! Now get the hell out of here and leave me alone!'

'Can't we – I don't know – talk maybe, try to –'

'After what you *did*?' Elliot exclaimed. 'What, you think I can just write that off, like it never happened? You never even said you were fucking sorry! Now get out!'

'But –'

'Out!' Elliot moved towards him.

'Ok, I'm going. If you change your mind, that's my number,' he proffered a business card. Elliot snatched it from him and ripped it to pieces, throwing them in the air.

'I won't change my mind.'

'I'm sorry about that. I thought you might have grown up by now. Evidently not.' He turned and walked away.

'Go to hell!' Elliot yelled after him, slamming the door and holding it shut with his right hand, raising the left one to shield his eyes and bending his head to meet it. He was shaking, his respirations audible.

'Elliot?' Rebecca rested a gentle hand on his arm.

He shook his head, refusing to look at her.

'Are you ok?'

Elliot shook his head again, dropping his hand to his mouth. His dark eyes were wet with tears. He blinked, drawing a long, unsteady breath.

'Come and sit down,' Rebecca suggested, slipping an arm around him and leading him back to where they had been sitting prior to the arrival of Elliot's brother. Elliot dropped down on the bench, biting his lip and pulling at the collar of his t-shirt. Rebecca moved to hold him, but he pulled away.

'What happened, sweetheart?'

'I can't!' He gasped. 'I *can't*!'

'Why can't you tell me?'

Elliot just shook his head. Rebecca sighed, trying again to give him a hug. This time he didn't resist, and clung to her, his slender body shuddering. Rebecca kissed the top of his head, wondering why he couldn't trust her with the details to his past. Clearly something dramatic had happened involving his brother, and probably, Rebecca guessed, the rest of his family. Having seen how losing his brother had devastated Francis's life, Rebecca couldn't help thinking how intensely sad it was that whilst Elliot *had* a brother, he couldn't even hold a civilised conversation with him. Elliot wasn't one to bear grudges, and Rebecca suspected that whatever lay at the root of the animosity, it hadn't been something as simple as a family row. She was beginning to doubt she would ever get to the bottom of whatever had happened to him, and wondered whether she could live with that long term. He was excluding her from a large part of his life, and she felt very aware of the fact. *Locked Away Forever* wasn't just a song title. It was most of Elliot's life.

A note from Sadie

Thank you for choosing to read my second book. If you have enjoyed *Sins of Silence,* I would be very grateful if you would consider rating it, or even writing a review – just a few words can make a difference in helping to persuade others to give my books a try!

Printed in Great Britain
by Amazon

63581408R00161